"A YOUNG MAN LOOKED at me, tears in his eyes. I knew his name once. An officer of mine. For the past few days, we lived off the meat of our dead brothers with no game present to hunt. Our vile ways turned us into a cannibalistic clan of hopeless vagabonds, loyal only to survival, with no honor left among us. The horses would not last with nothing to forage on in this sinister landscape of rock, ice, and snow. Their heads hung low and their hooves dragged, scraping across the bitter, cold ground."

- from Chapter 10, *The Road*

DARKNESS OF THE NORTHERN SKY

by

A. E. ENGLE

Speed Limit Anarchy, LLC

Dedicated first and foremost to my everything:
my wife and my children, for without whom I would cease to exist.

Special Thanks to Mr. Moorcock
for setting the stage for this dream to play on.

Many thanks to Neil, Alex, and Geddy, for providing the theme music in
the beginning from which to drive.

Thank you Ms. Rand for writing the best book ever written.

Up the Irons!

Hey Lasley! I finally did it!

Part One

ALL THAT IS SACRED

Chapter One

Resignation

"Saka'Ali."

That is what he called me before I ran him through with his own sword. His hands went to the blade protruding from his chest as he dropped to his knees. His tan uniform turned copper as the blood came. He scowled at me, partly from the pain, mostly from hate and anger. Then his eyes changed and became despair. As if some veil of shadow was suddenly lifted from his vision, and he did not know what happened.

The look was unsettling.

He no longer gazed upon me as his enemy, but gazed beyond me at a great loss, at some part of him he could no longer hold. Some apparition known only to him. He frowned as the glimmer, the hate, the hope, the fight, all faded from his eyes, then looked down at the sword piercing his heart, and a tear dropped to the dry, dusty ground beneath him, and he slumped.

Dead.

The high sun broke from behind a wisp of cloud setting everything alight in a blaze. Sweat dripped from my face. I let go of his sword and the body of this Rogues Army soldier, crumpled to the desert earth, next to the bodies of his associates. He was the last to fall. Another manifestation of death.

I stepped back from the body, horrified at what I witnessed in his eyes.

In my ages as a soldier in the Northern Army, all I have known is death. Death of my fellow soldiers. Death of my enemy. Death of—

Enemy.

The word given to us to describe the brigands along the Eastern border known as the Rogues Army. The militants. The hostiles. The combatants.

Soldiers.

They were fighting for some new Herra in the Eastern Lands, their reasons behind the attacks still unknown. Despite the name, they were not the Rogues Army Guard, under Herra Jalali, ruler of the Eastern Lands. The elite soldiers who serve where honor and dignity are expected. The rise of this faction of the Rogues Army only served chaos and destruction, darkness and shadow, attempting to upset the balance with their constant attacks on our border villages.

It was not enough for me anymore to continue. They were not a threat. They were not invading. They were not any different than the desert bandits and reavers from long ago who raided and pillaged the same villages and towns.

But, in that moment, when the glimmer faded from his eyes I realized it could be me at the end of my sword. Understanding I would never hold or cherish my wife and daughter again. Never to experience joy, or love. Only the cost of my actions, and the rage that had propelled them.

I turned away from the corpse of my *enemy* and left to return home.

I sat upon my horse, Outo, on the banks of the Black River. It is not a wide river, and at this point, crossing is easy. As the water eased by, its calls and whispers calmed the torrent of thoughts that plagued me the last few days of my journey.

I nudged Outo into the quiet rush and he relished the cool water across his legs. I dismounted and guided him across to a small grove of trees on the other side. I stood near the water's edge.

The sunlight flickered through the trees as it waned from its high point. By evening I would be home with my wife and daughter. When I last saw them the chill of winter was ending and branches were full with the buds of a new season. Now, as I returned, the rains had passed, the trees were full of leaves, and the heat of the day would soon rise compelling the people of the city to look for relief in the waters of the fountains, or here in the Black River.

I bent over and pulled some of the fresh water to my lips. Outo did the same. I scooped the water over my head and the trickles of the cool liquid refreshed me. Outo watched, then splashed his nose in the water.

"You are a strange one."

I patted the side of his black neck. He nickered and turned to graze on the fresh grasses.

I walked for a bit on the banks, then reached into some tall reeds and pulled two purple lotuses from the water. They grew plenty in the Black River. Their deep purple leaves with red streaks were a symbol of my homeland. I held them close to my face, took in their sweet fragrance, then walked to Outo and placed them in a pouch hanging from my saddle.

"Come, we are almost there."

In the far distance stood the walls of the city. From the walls emerged the tall Tower of the Fallen, and the domed top and spires of the Great Hall, where my sickly Lord sat.

"We have one more stop, Outo."

I climbed up on his broad back and slipped into the saddle. He grunted. I slid my black gloves on and saw a streak across the back of one.

Blood.

Not my own.

"It is time to speak with Cousin Airik." Outo grunted and stomped a foot. "Yes, I know. But this means no more long journeys and riding into battles, my friend. It means, for you, grazing on pleasant green hillsides with the others." He swayed his head back and forth and neighed. "A battle horse to the end. Sorry, my friend, to cheat you from an honorable death."

He brought his head high and whinnied.

"Come, let's go."

We trod along the road toward the North Gate of the Great City. Its broad-arched opening welcomed us like the mouth of a dragon welcoming its prey. The stone bridge, which lay across the stream that runs around the city, protrudes from the gate like a tongue. Still, the walls of the city are a welcome site.

Sentinels walked along the ramparts. The gates stood open for residents of the city to trade in the Grand Bazaar just outside it. The swathe of land, usually occupied by hundreds of caravans and shops of the Eastern Roama people, now sat empty, save for a few wagons and carts.

I stopped Outo and allowed a stream of carriages and carts to travel past me, heading away from the city to the Black Road. I watched them, they watched me. There was fear painted on their faces.

I rode across the stone bridge and to the gate.

A guard snapped straight as I approached.

"Tell me, where are they going?" I gestured to the caravans and the empty bazaar.

"We know not Commander Soltari. Our inquiries go unanswered. They have been departing for the last five days."

I looked at the empty land. Only one band of merchants remained. They were finishing packing their wares, and hitching their horses. The Grand Bazaar has never been empty in my lifetime. Even as a boy, memories run deep of hundreds of caravans set up to sell or trade. My family sold many a horse to the Roama.

"Strange." I nudged Outo, then halted him. I glanced one more time at the empty bazaar. A feeling of dread washed over me. "Close the gates and secure them. Nobody enters unless they are from the city."

The sentry nodded and saluted with his sword.

I continued along the wide cobbled road toward the Great Hall. We passed three city squares and approached the central square. We stopped in the shadow of the Tower of the Fallen, a tall pillar of white stone, a symbol of the blood shed for our lands. A memorial to the dead. It stands amid a large fountain made from slate pulled from the Black River. Children run around the fountain, splashing in the water, unaware of the sacrifice the tower represents.

I dismounted and handed Outo to a groomsman outside the Great Hall, the central building of our city, and home to our Lord. It has had many names, but to us, it is the Great Hall of Fallen Empires, or simply the Great Hall. It is a massive structure with long, wide stairs leading to the vast hallways of marble floors. Its crown a dome of crystal and glass. Tall, thin spires accent its four corners atop which stand statues of our former Lords, battle ready warriors, their swords raised high.

No such Lord walks like that within its halls these days.

I climbed the stairs to the entrance and entered the breezeway to the grand hallway leading to Lord Airik's chambers.

Two guards stood at the entrance, their long pikes crossed the open doorway. They raised the pikes, and I entered. The floor was made of black-and-white marble. Tall pillars of white lined each side of the room with an armed guard holding a long pike posted at each one. Long flags of blue and white hung from the sides. Sunlight filtered in on the center of the hall from the high glass and crystal dome and bathed the inlay of a sword cut from onyx in the center of the floor.

More light filtered through small casements set high around the top edge of the chambers and glistened off the clear water in the two decorative pools on each side of the hall. The smell of freshly lit braziers filled the air. What was once a throne room for emperors, was now home to the sickly Lord of the Northern Lands, and his counsel. Lord Airik sat at the end of the hall on a dais of aged and worn black marble.

He wore a long blue and white robe, allowing him to move freely and hide the true nature of the body underneath. Beside him sat an older woman in a white gown. She had a narrow, gaunt face and long shimmering blonde hair being tended to by two chambermaids. He struggled to sit up as I entered the room. The lady beside him put her motherly hand on his wrist, as if to stabilize him.

I walked to the center of the room and stood at the tip of the sword. I drew my long sword, holding it before me as I kneeled and bowed.

"Lord Strome, I have returned from the Eastern Borders and request counsel."

"Cousin Soltari, rise. As an officer in my service, there is no need for the formality. It bores me. Counsel granted." I stood and sheathed my sword. He has aged worse, mostly skin and bones now, plagued by some sickness since our childhood. His mother dismissed the two chambermaids and rose, placing a hand on her son's shoulder. His great protector... always. She glowered at me. I bowed my head to her.

"Lady Hellenia."

"What is your counsel, Commander General Soltari?" she said.

"My counsel is with Lord Airik, Lady Hellenia."

Lord Airik was sitting up and leaning slightly forward. A slight grin rose on his haggard face.

"Lord Airik," I reached to my left collar and pulled the silver clasp from my uniform. "I am here to resign my commission in the Lord's army, effective immediately."

He stood, wavered, then sat back down.

"Commander Soltari. Rini, you—"

"I am - I am weary of battle. You would not understand. The gore of battle does not surround you. You are not a man of war, as am I."

Airik struggled to stand again on broken legs. His mother grabbed him by the arm and helped him up.

"I fight a different sort of battle, Commander."

He straightened and stood tall, his lanky frame wobbling as he did so, and then he was still. Regal. He held his head up, showing his personal victory over himself, if only for the moment.

"Declined, Commander. You are too valuable an asset to us on the Eastern borders."

His legs shook again, then he sat back down on the cushioned throne from a bygone era, where the last Emperor of the Eastern Empire died before being overthrown by his own army from the South.

I set the silver clasp on the floor at the tip of the sword inlay, straightened, bowed my head, then turned.

"Did you not hear me, Rini? Did you not hear the words of your Lord, your..." his voice trailed off under the sound of my footfalls echoing in the chamber as I walked to the door and into the long hallway. I paused at one of the marble pillars, and leaned against it to catch my breath.

I exhaled.

I glanced over my shoulder at the guards posted by the doorway. From within, Airik was yelling something at me. I left the Great Hall and retrieved Outo from the groomsman.

I followed the westward streets, which would take me out of the Great City and into the village outside the West Gate. I led Outo down the flagstone road, past the shops and barracks of the city. The fragrant blooms from the flowers and vines hanging from the garden bridges over the streets permeated the air and went to war with the sweet smells from the baker's shop. We walked down the slight hill to the village, and the further I removed myself from the Great Hall, the greater the burden lifted from my shoulders. Soon the burden would be peeled off my body and burned, never to torment me again.

CHAPTER TWO

The Coming Storm

Soldiers snapped to their posts as I passed by the West Gate. The gate stood tall and wide, and its decorative archway hung over me like a storm cloud, ready to strike out in anger. I mounted Outo.

"Alright then. Let's go home."

I heeled him down the stone streets, past more shops and homes, past the candle shop my wife's mother and father owned, and out to the edge of the village.

I reached the dirt road at the end of the street, and I nudged Outo into a run, ready to be home and rid myself of this uniform. I turned onto the path leading to my ancestor's home in the country, where they bred war horses for the Northern Army. My home appeared behind a copse of trees on the hillside, and I could see a red flame dancing around in the grass. My daughter ran, waving and skipping through the spring blooms. I turned on the trail that led up the hill to the house. My daughter ran toward me. She seemed to have grown since I last saw her.

"Daddy!" she yelled as she scampered down the road. I reached out, grasped her by the arm, and lifted her onto my lap.

"You have grown, my dear. I have the right daughter, yes?" She giggled. "Let's see, flaming red hair, brilliant green eyes. And her name is—"

"Stop it, Daddy. You know it's me."

"Then who is this?"

I pointed to a doll she was holding. It had red string for hair and green button eyes.

"Present from Daddy," she said, then leaned forward and hugged Outo. "Hello Sal'ama, welcome home. Thank you for bringing my daddy home to me."

Outo nickered and stomped.

"Easy Outo, don't get a big head on your shoulders."

She sat up. "Sal'Ama Daddy. His name is Sal'Ama."

"Yes, it is. But I call him Outo." She frowned and wiggled a finger at me.

"No, no, no."

Then I saw her.

She stood on the front porch of our home, dressed in a flowing gown of light blue. Her auburn hair flitted as it was caressed by the breeze. She came to us barefoot and smiling. She took my daughter from my lap and set her down.

"Run along," she said in a voice as smooth as the silk she wore, a blessing on the wind, and I took a deep breath.

I slipped from the saddle and fell into her arms. There we stood, embraced, lost in time. Lost in the moment. The longing for each other's touch fulfilled. Never again will battle separate us. I let go, held her face in my hands, stared into her eyes, and kissed her. My daughter came out of the house.

"Eww!"

We giggled, the spell broken by our wicked child.

She pulled away and looked me over, then put her hand where the silver clasp should be. She looked up at me, questions circling in her eyes. I smiled. She put her hand to her mouth, and tears welled up.

"Now, I live. Now, we live," I whispered. "Here."

I reached into the pouch hanging from Outo's saddle and removed the two purple lotuses. I handed one to her, kneeled, and gave one to my daughter.

"Here. This is for you, my darling spirit. Come, let's put them in water."

We walked into the house. I kissed my wife on the cheek and went to our room while they picked a container for the lotuses. I stared at an old chest. Its dark brown wood from the Karvas forest nearby glimmered in the lantern light. I opened it. Inside were linens and family things. Soon it would hold the burden I've carried for over half my life.

I unclasped my swords and laid them on the bed. I unbuckled the leather armor from my body and my legs and slipped it all onto the floor. I stripped off my uniform. The stained and worn black fabric lay in a heap at my feet. The sweat-stained underclothes, gone. I stood naked, a man reborn from a black cocoon. I folded the heap, placed it into the chest, and closed it. I placed my short sword behind the chest.

I dressed in clothes of my own, picked up my long sword, and walked to the front door, where I hung it above the frame as a grim reminder of my past and a life I no longer willingly chose. I looked at my wife and smiled.

It was done.

We sat near a small fire in the cool evening air, looking out over the valley to the western village and the Great City.

"We must travel," she said.

"Travel? I am weary of traveling." She took my hand.

"We will go west to see your brother." I leaned back in my chair and exhaled. My daughter ran out of our home.

"Travel? Can we see the mountains, Mommy?" She ran around the fire and us with wild exclamations.

"Rini, it will be good. I know you've only just arrived home, but it will be good to go somewhere of your own choice. And you have said yourself the eastern borders are not safe. As much as I would like to travel east to Ca'Bri and see the desert, and meet this strange woman you talk about, I think west is better."

"Iliana?" I smiled. "Iliana is old enough to be my mother. No. There is a strange darkness in the East now. Something has changed it." I put my hand on hers. "You are right. Neither of you have met Tass." I looked at her. "West is good. Forget Ca'Bri, the desert, or even Laiho Lakes. We travel west."

She smiled, then a strange look fell across her winsome face, and a hint of sorrow showed in her eyes. No, not sorrow... serenity.

"You know, maybe while we are out west, we could see about locating—"

I chuckled. "My uncle? My love, if that man had any care for the Northern Lands or his family, he would have visited many ages ago, especially after my father's murder."

"I am sorry." She grasped my hand and patted it. "We are all we have. It would be nice to know your family."

"All we have?" I let go of her hands and stood. "You have your family. You are fortunate to have your mother and father and to know them both."

"I—I am sorry." Her face now became a mask of sorrow.

My Uncle. Why had she mentioned him? I knelt before her and took her in my arms.

"No. No. You are right."

Her warm embrace fired many emotions, and my body became confused by the maelstrom. I released my embrace and stood.

"I've never met the man," I said. "And my father only spoke of him during my training. He had much respect for his brother, always claiming he was the greatest swordsman he knew."

I wiped away a tear on her face, and she smiled.

"We travel west. We will leave tomorrow."

She wrapped her arms around me and pulled me close again.

"Daddy?" my daughter said, with a hint of fear. A distant rumbling told me why.

"Thank you," she whispered. "It will be a special birthday for our daughter."

Another rumble, this time not so distant.

"Daddy!"

I let go of my wife. My daughter was staring at the Great City. I followed her gaze, then stood. From the north, a storm was brewing. Lightning streaked across the sky, followed by a deafening call of thunder. My daughter winced and covered her ears.

"A storm from the North?" my wife said as she stood.

"Aye."

My daughter turned and ran into the house as a bolt of lightning shot from the darkened sky and hit what looked to be the North Gate. My wife screamed at the suddenness of the flash.

"Best to get inside."

Just then, the darkened sky turned an ominous green, and forming in the sky looked to be...

"Eyes?" my wife said.

"That's not possible, it's some—"

More lightning at the North Gate and a loud crack of thunder.

"Come."

We stood under the front covering of our home and watched the storm. Its violence was contained around the Great City. Lightning flashed across the sky and lit up the city and surrounding land.

"Is that... smoke?" she said.

"Possible. But, unlikely to be caused by the storm. It is just a storm."

"But the green in the sky... it looked like eyes, Rini."

I agreed with her, but it was not possible. I turned her to me.

"My love, it is only a storm. It will pass, like all things."

I looked away and cocked my ear to the wind.

"What is it?"

An all too familiar sound. My heart raced, and a certain dread filled me as the sound became louder.

I hung my head.

"No, no, no."

"What is it?" she said.

I looked toward the road that led to our house. I stepped inside, pulled my long sword from the doorway, and stepped back out.

I pulled my wife behind me.

"Riders."

Chapter Three

The Attack

T HE RIDERS FAST APPROACHED, and I held out my sword. They slowed, then stopped.

"Ho, Commander Soltari sir." I lowered my sword as a Captain broke from the other two, dismounted, and stepped into the firelight.

"Palo Astonzi, what brings you here?" Captain Astonzi was a former pupil I swore I would look after when his father, a good friend of mine, died on the Eastern borders under my command.

"The Great City is under siege, Commander. Lord Strome has requested all available to help defend. Your presence, sir, was... specifically requested." My daughter stood behind me, her arms wrapped around my wife. She peered out between us. At seven ages, she cowered, trembling at the soldier in the darkness.

"Under siege?"

"It is the Rogues Army, sir. Along with—"

"Rogues Army? Unlikely. They would never... I have resigned my commission, Captain. I no longer serve the Lord's army nor command his forces. I serve only my family now. You tell Lord Strome he'll have to do without my service." I looked at my wife. "Bar the windows. We will shelter here." The worried look in her eyes was foreign to me. It was fear, and desperation. "I was born here, my love. And like my mother, I will die here." She stood straight, and a great resolve washed over her.

"No. This is your homeland, and as a citizen and Northerner, it is your duty and your birthright to protect her." Tears welled up in her eyes. "We... we will be fine here. We are far enough away from the city that we will be fine."

"I... I can't." My whole being shook, trembling, and I nearly dropped my sword. "I cannot be without you, and her, another day. I have been gone too long, too often. We will stand our ground here." She reached up and caressed my cheek.

"I love you. But you must do what is right, and I know in your heart, as much as you won't admit it, you have already gone to the battle." I nodded without considering what I agreed to. I did not want to leave, but weary of battle as I was, she was right. The city was our home, and her family was there. She feared for them. It screamed in her eyes.

"Aye." I cleared my throat and then kissed her full on the lips. I hugged them both. I let go and stood tall before Captain Astonzi. "Fine, you have your servant of death one last time." I whistled, and Outo came out of the darkness. I led him to the side of the house, saddled, and bridled him. I sheathed my long sword in the saddle scabbard, mounted him, and rode to the front of the house.

"Fear not, little one, Outo will keep me safe." She smiled a half-smile.

"Sal'ama Daddy. His name is Sal'ama. Not Outo." Then, the tears flowed down her sweet face.

"Yes, my dear. Sal'Ama." Outo nickered and stomped his front leg. My wife stood before me, proud and strong. My daughter stood in front of her, in her mother's protective grasp. "Go inside now, shut the windows and doors. Take shelter." I paused, trying to hide the cracking in my voice. "I love you. Both of you."

She blew me a kiss, then did something odd... she clutched her stomach and pulled my daughter closer. They turned and ran into the home. I snapped the reins and reared up Outo. I rode off into the night, one hand grasping the reins and the other wiping tears from my face.

We entered the western village outside the gate. Two riders approached us.

"Commander, they are in the west village. They have spread out through most of the city and are at the Great Hall." Fear struck the young soldier's face. It was hard to tell if the fear was for his life, or someone else's, or both. Or was it something else? "Lord Strome and the Lady are safe, for now."

"Aye. Gather some horsemen. We will not push the rogues from our city."

"Sir?"

"We will slay them all where they stand. Understood?"

The soldiers smiled, and a new rage filled their eyes. They turned their horses and galloped into the fray. I and the others followed.

The Rogues Army soldiers I encountered fought but appeared confused, lost. They were not the master swordsmen and horsemen engaged on the border. Some ran as we came through the West Gate. I watched one throw a cobblestone through a window and run. Another rode to me with a sword raised. I knocked him from his saddle. He had no fight, and the horse kept on without him. He rolled on the ground, staggered to his feet, and ran down a side street. I heard a scream that was cut short.

From the same side street, a creature emerged that was wholly unsettling. Not a man, nor any creature I knew of, but a tall, hunched, black creature whose skin was like that of a beetle, hard and black, with a ridge of spikes down its back. It had large black eyes, like polished onyx, on the sides of its skull. The arms were too long for the body and stretched out to grasp, pull, and drag me from my horse with its long and silver clawed fingers, like claws of steel. They dripped with fresh blood. It charged at me. I swung with my sword, severing the head from its body. The creature made no sound in its death beyond a guttural hiss. Black blood oozed from its gaping neck. It crumbled to the ground like a black husk. An empty shell.

"Commander?" Astonzi muttered.

A cold shiver ran through me. More came at us from my right. Unarmed, the creatures relied on their grasp and claws to kill or maim. They fell easily under our swords.

"Come, make haste to the Great Hall," I said.

Another of the black husks came at us, and Outo reared up and kicked the creature, smashing its face. It flew back and crumpled without a sound.

Buildings burned, and the streets lay in ruin. The arched gardens were broken, and chunks of the stonework lay in the street. This attacking force was not here to lay siege to or claim anything. Their only purpose was to wreak havoc and damage our spirit.

We reached the western gate, where a small band of soldiers were engaged with the black husks. Beyond them, riders from the Rogues Army approached.

"Come, we will put an end to them all!" I spurred Outo through the melee, followed by Astonzi, and we met the Rogues Army soldiers head-on. One rode to my left and across my blade, severing his neck. He wasn't carrying a sword or any weapon, nor did he attempt to avoid the sword. Blood spurted from the open wound, and the rider collapsed, but the horse carried on into the fight behind us, trampling black husks and soldiers. A Rogues Army soldier unhorsed Astonzi, and the two were in a battle on the streets as their blades flashed in the torchlight.

This fighter appeared to be genuine.

I leaped from Outo, grabbed a rider from his horse, and pulled him to the street. He rolled over, a grin on his face, and I smashed it with the hilt of my sword, knocking him unconscious. I stood and ran to Astonzi, who was fighting fervently against his foe. The fighter had his back to me, and I grappled him to the ground. He landed hard against a small wall, and his sword tumbled from his hands. He coughed and started muttering something in his language. I dealt a blow to the back of his head, sending him into the abyss.

"Bind and take these two to the Great Hall."

I stood, ran to Outo, and leaped on just as another Rogues Army fighter rounded a corner. He saw me, then reared his horse back.

"Saka'Ali!" he yelled and turned his steed. I gave chase, and Outo, my spirited horse, drew upon him hard and fast. I slashed across the rider's back, reeling him off his horse. He fell hard to the ground and tumbled onto the remnants of dead husks. I pulled Outo back and dismounted. The soldier was moaning. I pulled off his head covering and bound his hands. Blood oozed from a gash on his head. I called out to a nearby horseman.

"Take this filth to the Great Hall and present him to Lord Strome in my name. Do it now!" The horseman jumped from his steed and lashed a rope to the prisoner, then remounted and dragged the man through the streets to the Great Hall.

The battle persisted through the night. We routed the Rogues Army and captured a few more. We lost few men, but the black husks left a mark on our minds.

The Captain and I sat on our horses under the Tower of the Fallen, covered in the ire of battle. We watched as the battle moved toward the North Gate.

"They have no fight left," he said.

"They had no fight to begin with, Captain. They only had one purpose here."

"Agreed. There is one thing I do not understand."

"What is that?" I said.

"Why the Roama didn't say anything. Clearly, someone warned them."

He was right, it was strange. Our relations with the Roama go back ages.

"Aye. It still seems..." Astonzi said.

"Too easy?"

He turned to me.

"Yes."

A horseman approached us.

"Commander, we have pushed the rabble to the North gate. But the battle has moved towards the West Gate again. The... those creatures, sir, they came in a swarm and drove past our forces."

I caught the glimmer of dawn over his shoulder. I looked to the west.

"Palo, gather your men and clear the west village."

I pulled on Outo's reins and spurred him down the road to the West Gate. Black things leaped from the road at me and landed, severed in two, their black shells scattering on the cobblestones. They hung from the bridge gardens over the street. They climbed on buildings and leaped to me, impaling themselves on the end of my sword. Soldiers fought them. Horses trampled them. The stench of them permeated the air. One latched on to Outo, and he halted and reared back, nearly loosing me from the saddle. I swung and sent the husk's head tumbling down a side street. The rest of it fell from my horse, its claws dragging through Outo's hide under the weight. Outo screamed and turned toward the pain, and I reeled him steady. Blood flowed, but the wound was superficial.

"Easy there. You've had worse." He shook his mane and nickered at the movement ahead.

There, in the torchlight of the street lanterns, one of the black husks dragged a body, a small body. I turned Outo and rode down on the thing hard and fast and slashed it up its back, severing its spine. It collapsed on the wet street.

I jumped from Outo and knelt next to the body. I stared at it for a moment. It was a little girl. She was as silent as a still night. Her hair was a caked mass upon her young face from blood and tears. Tears which no longer fell. I parted the hair and saw the most solemn and porcelain face I ever laid eyes upon. And then the fog of war cleared from my mind, and tears welled in my eyes and forced themselves out and to the ground.

The face was of my own.

Everything around me went silent as if nothing existed in the space except the two of us. Dark, empty silence, broken by a scream, a broken scream from a man, a man slipping into an abyss of despair, and then all went silent again.

No air moved. Nothing existed.

Empty.

Emptiness.

The tears dried, the flow dammed. I stood and hacked the hand that bound my daughter and peeled it off. I bent down and scooped her limp body into my arms, then placed her on my horse. I mounted behind her and continued down the side road and around the next corner. The smell hit me all at once. The smell of death and decay. A pile of bodies blocked my way westward. The husks were dragging the dead to this place, and I knew something more sinister and dark existed beyond understanding, beyond reasoning. I retched at the smell and the sight, turned Outo away from the mess, and rode back to the main road.

I urged him on as hard and as fast as he had ever run. I rode out of the city under the West Gate, through the village, and into the darkness of the night to my home.

A flock of thoughts flew through my head.

I caressed the broken body before me as the well of sorrow opened again, and tears streamed down my face.

Fear, like that I've never known, tore at my soul and heart.

Chapter Four

Vengeance

I SLOWED OUTO TO a trot. The front door of the house was broken, and there were what appeared to be claw marks around the edge.

"No."

I jumped from my horse, carried my daughter to the open doorway... and stopped. Blood covered the floor and walls. I made a vain attempt to call my wife's name. Only air escaped my throat as I tried to overcome the lock that forced it shut. My parched lips useless to utter her name. My throat constricted like a viper wrapped around its prey and refused the passage of words. I entered my home and saw my daughter's doll, torn and stained with blood. I stepped to the doorway of the bedroom, petrified.

The massive amount of rusty red liquid on the floor reflected my horrified face. The color of the blood faded to black, the walls white, and everything else gray. I looked upon my daughter's face, her hair no longer a fiery red but now a matted sorrel. I dropped to my knees, holding her limp body as the grief took hold, defeating me with its swift and sudden attack. I shrouded her with my body. Protecting her from the evil in the world.

But it was too late.

I sat up and placed her body on a cushion next to me. I brushed her hair from her face. She was so quiet, so solemn. Nothing in this world would ever harm her frail body again.

I stood. My legs trembled, and I steadied myself against the wall. I entered the bedroom, preparing myself for the sight I was about to behold. Her feet appeared from behind our bed across the room. The normally white fur rug was stained copper and red.

I went to her. She lay on the floor between the bed and the wall, partially leaning against a cabinet. My mind tried to make sense of what it saw.

Her eyes, her crystal blue eyes, stared vacantly at the blood-smeared wall. I knelt and took her bloodstained hand. Black and dark red streaked her auburn hair. There was a gash across her abdomen and her chest. Partially torn clothes hung from her body. I stemmed the urge to vomit. For all the death I have seen at the end of my blades, this is the most dire, the most unspeakable horror. I stood and looked around the room, and there, on the floor behind the door, was a black husk. Its head was nearly severed from its body. The sight and smell caught me, and I vomited into the corner. I wiped my face and looked at my wife. She was clutching a small dagger. She fought hard. And paid dearly for it. She was probably trying to save…

I went to the front room and gathered my daughter. I was numb. The tears had stopped, the fear now replaced with the embers of rage. I took her into my bedroom and lay her on the bed. I picked up my wife's limp body and laid her next to our daughter. I closed her eyes. They both looked calm.

Peaceful.

Still.

I went to the chest and opened it. I pushed my uniform and leathers aside, pulled some white linens, and closed the lid. I wrapped both my wife and daughter in shrouds. Their grim and obscene death, now masked in the dressing.

They became nameless, faceless, lifeless.

Two white figures on the bed made as still-life memorials for all that I lived for. All that I cared for. All that I was.

I grasped the black husk by a foot and dragged the shell from my home, out the door, and down to the gates at the end of my road. I finished removing the head with the dagger my wife used to kill it. I placed the head on top of the post, rammed the dagger through the top of the skull, and into the wood.

"Let all who dare come to the home of Soltari see this gruesome visage and know that wrath now lives here."

I walked away and left the body on the road for the carrion, if they'll have it.

I entered my broken home. On the table sat a pot filled with water, and resting in the water, were the two purple lotuses. And my heart cried. I lifted them from the water and took them into the bedroom. I placed one on my wife and one on my daughter and knelt at the bedside. The rage turned to torment, which yielded more tears. Hard tears like a hard rain.

Relentless.

I clutched the bed covers, trying to find some stable ground, but found none and collapsed to the floor. There was no life without them. Here, I shall die next to them.

I failed to do the one thing I promised.

I opened my eyes. A leather-bound journal my wife would write in from time to time laid under the bed. Her words, her notes of things while I was away at the eastern border. I grasped the journal, and pulled it to me. I sat against the wall and opened the journal to her last written words. I wiped the tears from my eyes.

"On the eve of the birthday of our daughter, a strange thing occurred. A storm outside the northern gates, at first, but then they came for Rini and said we were under attack. I had to tell him to go. He can be stubborn. Very stubborn. Earlier tonight, we decided to travel West to see his brother. It will be nice to travel and finally meet Tass. I hope Rini will return in the morn, and then I will tell him of the news or our second child. I hope it is a boy. If it is, we shall name him Taivas, after Rini's father."

I re-read her entry, then clutched the book in my arms, clinging to it as if my life depended on it, and held it close to my heart.

A child.

I gripped the book hard in my rage, and pages fell across my lap. I went to scream, but only air came out. Again and again I wheezed until finally, all the rage within me unleashed itself like hounds of death, and in my rage I tore the book scattering the pages across the floor and bed. Some fell into the blood, drinking it up. One fell atop her body. The last page. Her final words. It lay there like a feather upon a rock. The blood from her shroud began to soak through the page, staining it. I picked up the other pages and placed them on the bed beside her. I unleashed another scream, a scream that silenced all things around me. A scream of tortuous rage and threnody.

Then, silence in the void. I gently picked up the page with her last words.

I stood tall and straight. I knew there was only one course of action.

I was the harbinger of vengeance.

I became wrath.

I am death.

I faced the chest, knowing the ruination I would bring upon myself if I opened it. I looked at the page and then walked to the chest. I stared at its stained wood top. Old, dry, used. I kicked open the top, and it splintered into fragments. There, sitting on top next to my leather armor, was a pouch. A leather pouch she made with her loving hands. I folded the page, grasped the pouch, and moved to the bed. I placed the page inside, collected the purple lotuses, and carefully placed them in the pouch. I laid it on the bed. I retrieved my uniform, armor, and gauntlets from the chest and laid them on the bed beside the pouch. I retrieved my battered short sword and scabbard from behind the chest and laid it on the bed, completing the mosaic of misery.

I undressed and once again pulled the burden of my life upon my body. The black armor, the black uniform, the black gloves. I became a shadow of myself.

A husk.

I latched the scabbard to my belt, then unsheathed my sword. A sword forged for my father before I was born. The blood of old enemies and rain tarnished the steel. But the sword was strong. I slid the sword into the sheath across my back. I picked up the pouch, gently caressing the soft hide, then lashed it to my belt.

There were no more tears. No more pain. I was stone, a solid rock, with only one purpose now...

Vengeance.

I walked outside to Outo. He grumbled at my cruel and twisted visage. I led him to his stall and prepared him for battle. I attached the long sword and scabbard to the saddle, then led him to the house.

I pulled the sword from its sheath and its cry rang out and sang of the coming doom across the lands. I returned to the house and into the bedroom. The blood was glistening red mess, but a calm, dry copper. I raised my long sword, pointed it at the floor, and knelt before it. I bowed to my wife and daughter.

"I swear to you my loves that I will unleash my wrath upon your murderers. I am woe. I am sorrow. I am vengeance. Vengeance is all they will see until I mount the head of the one responsible at the top of the North Gate. Or I am slain. For it matters not if I die, I am already dead without you. Either way, I will find peace."

I knelt in the silence, then rose and walked outside. Outo backed up a few steps as I approached him. I sheathed my sword, and he pawed at the ground. I reached into the fire pit and pulled a log from the night's fire, still glowing with embers. I blew on it until it became fire once again.

"Fear not Outo. Soon you will see the glory of battle again."

I looked at the house, exhaled a deep breath, and went inside. I set the log to the bloodstained covers of the bed. The linens caught quickly and became a funeral pyre for all that I loved in this world.

I walked to the front room, tossed the log on a chair, and walked outside. I mounted Outo and patted his side. I watched as the flames took hold, and soon, my house was an inferno consuming all that I was, am, or will be. The fire raged with a vengeance like the fire inside me. Soon, the passage of time and the winds of storms will scatter the ash across the land, leaving nothing but a spot of what was and could have been.

A tear escaped but was quickly dried by the heat. I pulled on Outo's reins and turned him toward the road. I stopped.

Three riders approached. Soldiers of the Northern Army. They slowed, seeing me battle-ready upon my horse. One turned and looked at a Lieutenant near him, questioning if they should continue. They stopped. The Lieutenant, a young man named Estarenza, approached me, keeping his horse in a slow, guarded trot.

"Commander Soltari," he said, trying to look at me, but his attention was pulled by the raging blaze behind me. He cleared his throat. "The battle is won, sir. We have cleared the city and the village of Rogues Army, and um... the black—"

"Husks."

"Yes sir. We were sent, uh," he said, still staring at the fire. "Um..."

"Come Lieutenant Estarenza, what is it?"

He looked at me.

"Lord Strome requests your immediate counsel in the Great Hall."

"Gather your men and meet me at the Tower of the Fallen."

Lieutenant Estarenza glanced questioningly at the fire, then back at me, before he turned and spurred his horse down the road. The other two soldiers followed as the sun crested the horizon, spreading a red fire across the gloom-covered sky.

CHAPTER FIVE

The Promise

I RODE THROUGH THE streets of the western village. The air was thick with smoke and the distant screams of the injured. Shops lay sacked and burned. A glaze of copper and a black oil-like substance covered the black cobblestone as the remnants of the husks lay scattered about the street. Women wailed, and men sobbed, reduced to nothing at the loss of family and livelihood. I passed the short road where I ran down the husk. Its body still lay there, surrounded by a few men. One turned and vomited. Another was covering his face with a cloth and pointing down the street to where the bodies were piled.

I considered stopping by the candle shop my wife's family owned, but rode past instead. I knew not what to say. The shop was dark, but intact. I made my way under the West Gate and into the city. The smell of death and charred wood permeated the air. Smoke wafted from rooftops. People wandered vacantly among the destroyed residences and shops. The remaining bridge gardens, which spanned across the tops of the streets, still hung with spring blooms, adding a dissonant canvas to the city. I reined in Outo at the Tower of the Fallen in the central city square.

The area was littered with bodies. The grand fountain in the center sat silent. The Tower loomed over the death and cast a grim shadow. Blood spattered the pillars, now scarred by battle. Soldiers and citizens wandered around in disbelief. The battle was vicious, but not the end of the city.

I dismounted and tied Outo to a post. I pulled my long sword from the saddle scabbard and sheathed it on my side, then climbed the many steps that led to the entrance of the Great Hall. I looked back toward the North Gate. It sat intact in the hazy distance. The damage was contained to the main streets from the North Gate to where I stood, and from here to the

West Gate. The steps to the Great Hall were spattered with blood and black muck.

Two guards approached me.

"Commander," a guard said and saluted. "Lord Strome awaits."

They escorted me into the grand hallway and to the Lord's chambers. He sat on his dais surrounded by soldiers. Lady Hellenia, his mother, stood near. They were in a heated discussion. I paused. On the floor before Lord Strome were three Rogues Army soldiers on their knees, their hands and feet bound, and faces blindfolded. He saw me enter.

"Soltari."

He moved to stand, but a hand on his shoulder from his protective and watchful mother kept him in his seat. The others turned to me and greeted me with a contemptuous gaze. One of the Rogues Army soldiers raised his head upon hearing my name. I walked to the dais and kneeled.

"My Lord," I said. I stood and glanced at the prisoners.

"Yes, Major Hildebrand, please tell our beloved Commander General what—"

I walked over to the soldier who perked up upon hearing my name and kicked him in the face, sending him reeling backward onto the floor. Blood streamed from his nose and into his mouth. He gagged and coughed.

"Soltari!" someone said, a female voice. I gave it no heed. I stood over the prisoner and picked him up by his shirt, and smashed him in the face again with my gauntleted hand. He dropped to the floor. I drew my short sword and pushed the tip to his throat. He bled and sobbed, and I grinned, unsatisfied.

"Soltari! Stand down," Lord Strome said.

A hand on my sword arm interrupted my rage. I spun to the person who dared touch me. Standing over me was Major Hildebrand, one of my cadre from the Eastern borders. I shrugged off his grasp and stood tall, still in the shadow of this formidable man of unnatural height. His face was blackened from battle, and his blue eyes glared at me.

"Mind your manner, Major," I said and brushed off my uniform. He backed away.

"Commander Soltari," Lord Strome said. "Our prisoners here tell us of another impending attack. One they say will be far worse than this one." His voice echoed through the hall and was unusually imposing and unfitting for a man in his condition. "It appears our Great City has been promised to the reaver General A'avé El Friz of the Rogues Army."

Two of the prisoners spoke something in the eastern tongue at the mention of General A'avé, probably praise or blessing. The other lay motionless on the floor, blood trickling from his nose and mouth.

"And who has promised this to the reaver, A'avé?"

"Some self-proclaimed Queen they're calling the Queen of Shadows out of the Syn Ka region of their lands," Major Hildebrand said.

"Yes, and so I want you Commander to set up a defense around the city and send scouts to the north, specifically Farwic Outpost."

"No," I said.

Lord Strome sat up on the overly large marble throne and made to stand. This time, Lady Hellenia helped him to his feet.

"No? Do you dare question the orders of your Lord?" I smiled a grim smile.

"Lord Strome, I resigned my commission. I am no longer in your service, however—"

"I accepted no such resignation, Commander General Soltari. I would be foolish to do so. Despite our family history, you have served the Northern Lands with honor and distinction, far surpassing even your expectations, I'm sure."

He motioned to his right, and a guard stepped forward and walked toward me. He held out his hand, and in it was the silver clasp signifying my rank in the Northern Army.

I sighed. I knew what taking the clasp meant and the burden it carried. I've borne it for so long. But now it was a gift. A gift that would empower me to guide my vengeance with a force unequaled in the lands.

I took the clasp and attached it to my uniform. I looked to the Lord, who had a solemn smile like he had just won some glorious battle.

I bowed. "My Lord." Then, I raised my head high. "I will take the army and lead the expedition to this Queen's doorstep."

"We will wait for help to arrive Commander. While I appreciate your... fervor... to lay waste to these invaders, now is the time to prepare and defend. I have sent word to Commander Versol. In four days, his force will return from Feren Ta. The combined force will be enough to fend off any attack."

"Who was sent?"

"One of your cadre," Major Hildebrand said. "Captain Astonzi. I sent him and five others."

"Who gave you the right to send one of my men on some errand?"

"You did, Commander, when you resigned your commission."

"Commander. Rini. I know of your relationship with Captain Astonzi," Lord Airik said. "His father was a great warrior."

"And a friend, as you'll remember."

Lord Airik nodded.

"Yes. His death was a significant loss, and you have done your best to train his son. I have no doubt he—"

One prisoner hailed General A'avé again. This time it was Major Hildebrand who kicked the prisoner in the face, knocking him unconscious. The other whimpered. I looked at the Major, and he looked at me. This was an odd and unbecoming manner for any Rogues Army soldier, even a foot soldier, young and untrained. He continued mumbling.

"Musta kuori, musta kuori... musta kuolema," then he laughed. "The Queen of Shadows will come for you... Cannot fight the musta kuori." Again, more laughter.

I grabbed him by his shirt and stood him up.

"What is this... musta kuori you speak of?"

"Black. Black husks. Black blades. Cannot survive..."

He laughed, then cried. I ripped off his blindfold so I could look him in the eyes. They were crossed and half-witted. Empty.

"He is an idiot. Not a soldier. This is a ploy." I tossed the man to the floor and turned to face Lord Strome.

After a brief silence, he cleared his throat and spoke. "Is he saying those foul black things are the musta kuori?"

"Yes. But they were unarmed. They carried no sword... no 'black blade' as he said. Pay him no heed, my Lord. This attack—"

"A'avé," the man screamed, and Hildebrand ordered 2 guards to carry the man from the chambers.

"Hang him from the gates, with the others," Lord Strome said. They bowed and took the man, who was screaming and laughing, then crying.

"He is fraught with madness, my Lord. He knows not what he says," I said.

"And who is this General A'avé El Friz he praises? Do you know?"

"He is the top general and the son of Herra A'Avikon Ha'amu Al Friz, self-proclaimed Lord of this reaver band of the Rogues Army," Hildebrand said.

"I see."

"My Lord, as I said—"

A hoarse mumble came from behind me.

"He speaks... the truth..." The man whose face I smashed was speaking. "Against A'avé El Friz and the Queen of Shadows... you cannot win."

I waved my hand, and two guards came over.

"Stand him up."

They complied, and a large amount of blood fell from the prisoner's mouth down the front of his tan uniform, covering the two blue strips of cloth, indicating he was an *El Friz*, a master swordsman.

"Her sorcery... too strong."

"Sorcery is a thing of myth and legend."

The man grinned. "So say you, Soltari."

"Silence this animal," Hildebrand said, but I held up my hand and approached the bleeding man.

"You know me?"

"Aye. You are the murderer from the North. You... kill my two brothers. You kill... many, Saka'Ali." He spat at me.

"If your brothers died by my sword in defense of my land, I have no remorse. Or sympathy for you, or your blood."

"Your... land?" He grinned. "So you say." He coughed, and this time, a stream of blood came from his nose. "You remember me. You remember... my name, Commander. Soltari. Murderer." He went limp in the guard's grasp, then came too. He shook his head a bit.

"I care not for your name."

I turned to Lord Strome, who, by some miracle, was still standing.

"Take him to the pits," he said.

The guard's footsteps echoed across the chamber and they grabbed the soldier under his arms and dragged him away.

"I am..." the man screamed. "Hauk'atu Uli El Friz!" He laughed. "You remember me... Saka'Ali... You—" He struggled in their arms as they led him to the door and out of the chambers.

I looked at the last prisoner lying on the floor, then turned fully to Lord Strome and bowed my head.

I sheathed my sword and straightened.

"Lord Strome, I will take our force to the Northern outpost at Farwic. There, I will assemble the army from the Eastern borders and attack this Queen of Shadows. I suspect she is in the old fortress in Ro Isto Pass."

"Soltari, we can ill afford to leave our city defenseless. Commander Versol—"

"Can set up a defense on his return. I must oblige my Lord. This is not a request." He sat. Every part of his rail-thin body snapped and creaked as he did.

"I see. Tell me Rini, why this change of heart? Yesterday you were here to give up your life as a soldier, and today—"

"To defend my home," I said.

"Then defend her now."

"And to avenge my family." Lord Airik squirmed a bit in his oversized throne.

"I do not understand."

I cleared my throat. "They are..." The flurry of images from the events of this morning fluttered through my head and landed on two bodies wrapped in bloody shrouds. "They are dead." A gasp came from Lady Hellenia, and she covered her mouth. "My wife, my daughter. Killed by... black husks."

"Musta kuori."

"Aye."

"Commander Soltari, you may rally the forces. But whether it be for the defense of the Great City, or... more to your liking, to seek revenge for your family and those lost here in the Great City, I will contemplate and counsel, then decide. In the meantime, consider this. If you take our force and attack the fortress in the Eastern lands, they will consider it an invasion by the Northern Lands upon sovereign soil."

"Forgive me, my Lord, but they have already invaded us, as they have been doing on our Eastern border for ages."

"Those who invaded are the reaver band of the Rogues Army. They are not recognized by the one true Lord of the Eastern Lands, Herra Ennu Staya Jalali."

"As I am aware."

"His guard, the true Rogues Army, escort the merchant caravans..." I grumbled. He was wasting time with words. "This invasion by a faction of the Rogues Army is not a cause for war with the Eastern Lands. We must maintain that. And whomever this Queen of Shadows is—"

"I promise the response will be swift, and bloody."

He clenched the edge of the marble throne. His mother fumed, squeezing her son's shoulder. He winced.

"Soltari, you are mad with anger, and I will not stand—" she said.

"Then I will let my anger, and my madness, rain down upon this Queen from the north and will stop at nothing until her head is mounted above the North Gate as a grim reminder to any who dare attack our city!"

Airik looked up to his mother, whose expression changed to a blank, stunned facade. He looked at me.

"You could seek help from your brother in the West."

"Seek help? I am not an envoy like my father. I am a warrior. Talk amongst counsels and bartering is for those with forked tongues. I will do this, my Lord, if I have to do it on my own." I drew my long sword and held it before me as a salute. "This is my battle to win."

I sheathed my sword, turned, and walked from the chambers. The echoes from my boots, hard and furious upon the black-and-white marble floor, once again, drowned out any protest from my cousin, the sickly Lord Airik Strome.

CHAPTER SIX

Farwic Outpost

I EXITED THE CHAMBERS and entered the hallway, where a small cadre of my officers waited. The smell of smoke from burning buildings and the reek of death hung in the open air. Bright sunlight filtered in from the outside.

"Mobilize your forces, for we leave on the morn from the Tower of the Fallen," I said as I walked past them. They bowed, and dispersed.

I walked out of the chill stone structure and stood atop the steps in the warm rays of sunlight. The city stood scarred by the attack. Townsfolk and soldiers were making quick reparations and cleaning up the remnants of battle. In a distant square sat wagons filled with husk remains. In the square before me to the east of the Tower of the Fallen, bodies of soldiers and city folk lay lined in rows. Those who tread among the dead wept or stood in stunned silence.

I stepped down the long stairs to Outo. He nickered at my approach. I stroked the side of his black neck, then climbed into the saddle. I sighed and closed my eyes. I saw their faces from the night before. Smiling, laughing. Outo grumbled, the weight of me becoming unbearable. I exhaled, long and hard, and opened my eyes, wiping away a tear that escaped.

"Come boy, we have work to do."

I rode to the Tower of the Fallen, where Estarenza waited.

"Lieutenant, assemble your forces and post them at both gates, along the ramparts, and outside the city. Prepare to ride at dawn."

"Aye, Commander. I fear, however, I may not have the men to fulfill your request." His head hung slightly.

"Is that what you fear the most, Lieutenant?" He lifted his eyes to me, then sat tall in his saddle.

"No, Commander Soltari. I—"

"Then find the men. This order comes from Lord Strome."

I turned Outo, and we rode down the western street to the village, though I knew not why. I was driven by some other force, some reasoning unknown to me. I had no home to go to. The thought of that twisted my gut, and my heart ached. They were gone. Forever. I tried to find solace in something, anything I could put my eyes to, but everything was out of focus.

Destroyed.

Diminished. Like the haze of a dream lost after wakening.

Unreal.

Now all I needed was packed on my horse and across my back.

I passed under the Western Gate and entered the village. Outo stopped a moment later and stomped, raising his head up and down. We were in front of the shop owned by my wife's family. I saw her mother inside. She saw me and came out. And I felt the weight of the world upon my shoulders, and could not avoid it.

I sighed and patted Outo.

"Bastard horse."

A dark blue line took shape along the Eastern horizon as the night turned blackest and dawn announced its coming. I sat on the top step of the Great Hall and watched the movements of the people and soldiers. Torches moved about like flittering nightflys. Flaming braziers burned around the Tower of the Fallen, and the nickers and grunts of horses and men filled the air, mixing with the songs of early birds. The creak of leather, the jangle of harnesses, and the hammers of smiths announced the preparations of war. They all took shape and became the new sound of the Great City. Yesterday morning, this city was in the grasp of death. Today, it breathed new life, restored.

The scent of fresh bread and smoked meats drying replaced the malodorous stench of death. The smell crept across the obscene daybreak as bakers and shopkeepers had worked through the night to supply the vast army I intended to take North with provisions.

I sent word to Lord Strome that the force would be assembled by first light to await his blessing of the Order. I stood, stretched, and walked down the many steps to my horse. I stopped and stroked Outo's face, then slipped into the saddle. I was prepared to make the long march to Farwic Outpost, though there was no joy in it. Only the profound and confusing sensation of leaving this empty place behind me, after only just returning.

Shortly after, as the dark blue sky of dawn changed to orange, the force was assembled and ready. In lines, the mounted soldiers and their horses stretched down the Western road under what remained of the hanging gardens of the village. And on the eastern side of the tower, supply wagons lined up. Wagons filled with foot soldiers, archers, and pikemen stretched down the southern road past the Great Hall.

I sat atop Outo at the head of my cadre of officers, ready to lead this force of over 1,500 soldiers hungry for battle, hungry for vengeance. I leaned over and whispered in my horse's ear.

"Soon we ride, Sal'ama." He nickered and shook his black mane. From the mounted force came more nickering and grunts, the jangle of tack, and restless footfalls upon the dark streets of the Great City.

The first rays of sunlight pierced the sky with blood-red streaks. Moments later, the city was alight from its radiance, and upon the top of the steps, Lord Strome appeared, assisted by his mother and a nursemaid. It was a rare occurrence for our sickly Lord. It would likely be his last. I drew my long sword and held it in front of my face.

"We stand ready and await your blessing, my Lord," I said. The Blessing of the Order, a custom from so long ago, we no longer knew its history.

"What is your intent, Commander General Soltari?"

"To take this force my Lord and march to Farwic Outpost, assemble with the Eastern Forces, then lay siege to the Fortress of Ro Isto Pass."

He frowned. "That is your intent, even beyond my wishes?"

"It is. We will be at Farwic Outpost by the time Commander Versol arrives, my Lord, and ready to march. A small force remains, as you requested, to guard the gates."

"I see."

He looked at his mother. Her empty gaze hung on the destruction of the city, seeing it for the first time. Lord Strome noticed nothing beyond his own intentions. Then he followed her gaze and saw what his mother was looking at. The city in ruin. The burned buildings, the destruction, the wisp of death still on the air, and he knew somewhere stacks of the dead lay in repose awaiting their final rites as warriors, and as citizens of the Great City.

And then he saw me. Sword raised. A statue, unwavering. He knew no amount of talk would sway me. This he knew well. Growing up together after my father's murder, he knew I was a man of action and little talk. He looked at his mother again, and for a moment, he seemed like a lost babe in her arms, cradled, suckling, as she stood petrified with fear. He found no comfort in her then.

He turned to me.

"So be it, Commander General Soltari. You have the Blessing of the Order."

I raised my sword high, and the city filled with a roar, and hearty cheers burst forth from the massed force and citizens of the city. A chant soon formed as the soldiers reveled in the words of our Lord.

And the city smiled.

I bowed my head and lowered my sword to a salute. I turned Outo around to face the North Gate and reared him up on his hind legs. I whirled my sword in the air to rally the force, then sheathed it across my back. Outo dropped into a canter, and I led my cadre around the Tower of the Fallen. We rode past the central square and the hopeful faces of the people of the Great City. We continued to the North Gate, then onto the road toward the Black Road. We rode from the city, a thundering hellion force powered by the fresh memory of those we lost and the destruction of our home.

On the morning of the fourth day of our march, we were almost in sight of Farwic Outpost, a small village with shops, stables, and quarters for some, mostly the officers. Most of the force would be outside the village in tents, the village itself not large enough to house 1,500 bodies and stable the large number of horses supporting them.

I held my head high in the chill air of the northern wastes. The valley between the two mountain ranges was barren. The Shope'Ta Lakes to the west glistened in the daylight. The ominous Syn'Ka mountains to the distant east rose into the air, silhouetted in black by the rising sun.

We crested a ridge and saw the pillars of smoke. Lt. Estarenza was riding near me and gasped at the sight.

"Commander?"

"Fires. Fires that should not be." I halted my horse, and the force behind me slowed and stopped. "Lieutenant, gather fifty men. We ride hard to Farwic."

I looked at the officer on my right, Captain Solodore, a fat, bearded man whom I shared no respect for, and who had even less respect for himself.

"Captain, you will wait here with the remaining force until we return, or I send for you."

"Aye Commander. My arse can use the break, anyway."

I stared at the man drowning in his own complacency. Still, with Major Hildebrand rallying the eastern force, and the remaining cadre amongst the group behind us, I had little choice.

"Yes. Of course."

The lieutenant approached, followed by fifty horsemen. We spurred our steeds across the cold, unforgiving plain toward the outpost. The closer we were, the more damage we could see. The outpost was burning. We slowed at the sight of bodies lying outside the gate. One slashed across the midsection, another across the throat. One torn by heavy claws.

I turned to Lt. Estarenza. His head hung from his shoulders, and he was sobbing.

"Head up Uri Estarenza. Take a long breath of the chill air." He looked up and wiped the tears from his face. "Come, let us learn what has prevailed."

We entered under the arched gate into the small village outside of Farwic Outpost. Bodies lay about frozen in the snow. Village folk and soldiers both.

And black husks.

Three of the buildings still burned. One was a stable. Horses stood in the village like statues of brown and black. They glanced at us, uncaring. We reached the central square, then rode around the station, surveying the destruction. A short-lived battle was fought here. The area was painted red with frozen blood. We found more dead near the mess hall. More husks. A few Rogues Army bodies among them.

Some looked as if they had been torn apart at the throat.

"Commander?" Estarenza said, a notable hitch in his voice. The scene was horrific, beyond comprehension. "What—"

A scream came from a stable.

"That was no horse," I said.

We rode to the stable and dismounted. I crashed through the door. A soldier lay in a stall, shaking. I went to him and picked him up by his furs.

"What is your name?"

Drool leaked from his bloody maw, and he leached out something in-comprehensible.

"Your name. What is it?"

"Galnin," he said.

"Galnin. What happened here? Who did this?"

He laughed.

"The black things..." His face switched to fear, but he was still laughing. Then he stopped as fast as he started. He shivered, staring at nothing. A strange calm came over him, then all at once he screamed and covered himself with his arms as if some apparition came at him. I grabbed him and stood him up against the wall. He smelled of urine and excrement.

"How long?"

His tormented eyes turned to me, vacant, and he looked through me from some abyss. Then confusion set in.

"Who... are you?" And his eyes rolled back into his head and he went limp.

"He is useless to us."

"Is he dead?"

"No, he lives, but only in his nightmares now." I stepped back. "Get the others, bring in the force. We start cleanup immediately. Number the dead, see if there are any others left..." I looked at the man called Galnin. "... alive."

The air was fresh, clean, and bitterly cold. We spent the previous day stemming the fires and surveying the damage. We were fortunate it was not more significant, but were unfortunate, for all but two of the forty or so residents of Farwic Outpost were dead, and the two who still drew breath were mad.

Most of my cadre sat around the fire, laughing, joking, and eating, engorging themselves on hot tea and liquor to fend off the early chill. I could find no humor here. A small man was cooking bacon alongside fish pulled from the Shope'Ta Lakes.

Behind me, the sky became inflamed with the rising sun, and the dark-ness passed to a darker blue from the black.

Captain Solodore sat across from me, his beard littered with food and wet with drink and slobber. I stood, and took two steps before my stomach boiled and its contents expelled onto the ice. Captain Solodore laughed heavily. His furs did nothing to hide his fat belly.

"Bad fish Commander?"

He laughed more.

"Mind your tongue. Captain."

He stuffed a piece of bread into his mouth before he could say another word.

Lieutenant Estarenza came to me. "Are you alright Commander?"

"Aye." I stood. "Excuse me."

I wiped the spatter from my mouth and walked toward the command quarters. I stopped halfway to the hitch and looked around the encampment. Four horsemen rode by me. One saluted by raising his sword in front of him. Grooms led horses from stables to tethers to saddle and armor them for patrols.

I reached the command quarters.

"Commander!"

The voice was behind me. I turned, and a tall young man ran toward me, at first unrecognizable. I staggered a bit from the suddenness of my turn. His hair was golden, and his brown cloak flowed behind him. He wore minimal furs. His ignorance annoyed me.

"Commander!"

"What is it Major?"

He stopped, out of breath.

"Commander. The eastern forces travel from Tasa-Arvo and will be here in the morning. They number almost 500, Commander."

He stood tall, and when he did, he towered over me. This gave me a queer feeling of submission. He looked down at me like he did in the Lord's chambers.

"That is unfortunate Major Hildebrand. The plan is to ride for Ro Ista Pass at first light."

"Will we not wait for the force to arrive, Commander?"

"We can ill afford to wait long here, Major. Little food remains because of the attack before our arrival, nor sufficient quarters to house everyone for days while we sit idle. We have already lost several horses to the cold."

"Commander, is our force strong enough without the Eastern Guard? I suggest we wait for them to arrive. Surely it will help—"

"We leave at first light. If you want your Eastern Guard to partake in the glory of battle, then ride fast, Major, and tell them to make haste."

He stared over me now towards the south and took a deep breath.

"Aye Commander. As you wish."

He turned and walked toward the stables. He whistled for a groom to bring him his horse.

I looked at the northern sky, toward Ro Ista Pass, and a chill rolled through me. Black clouds, ominous and foul, grew up into the sky. The clouds appeared to emerge from the pass. I knew this outpost was susceptible to storms, but the season was past us. This... seemed irregular. It would reach camp by midday. We needed to take shelter now, and not waste another moment.

My stomach churned.

I returned to the fire. The officers were engaged in a heated and unnecessary debate.

"Captain!"

Captain Solodore stood and straightened in one well-trained move. His fat belly pushed through his furs.

"Yes, Commander General!"

"Get all the men and the horses you can into the stables and hard shelters and secure them with extra lines. Nobody is to stay in the tents. Hard shelters only."

"Commander?"

"Do it now Captain, we have little time. A storm is upon us." I pointed to the North.

Captain Solodore turned and saw the ominous battle of dark clouds forming and his eyes went wide. He bowed his head to me and began dispatching orders to the other men around the fire. They left in an organized rush, leaving the fire and all the food in their stead. The small man cooking fish offered me a plate and smiled. I stared at the food, and accepted it, bowing my head in thanks.

"Go now, kind sir. Take cover."

He bowed and left me in solitude at the fire. I sat down, poured a cup of tea, and ate what I could before the inevitable storm.

The sun disappeared mid-morning, left to fend for itself in the gathering gloom. The outpost was a desert of snow. Not a soul moved. The troops and horses were all sheltered in place. If the storm reached them, Major

Hildebrand would have to seek cover in the Syn'Ka mountains somewhere in Zhalé Pass.

I stood alone amid the oncoming storm, alone in the northern wastes. The wind picked up and bit into me. An unnatural sound came from it, like hissing, moaning, and laughter mixed together. The dark gray and black clouds swirled, and in their midst... two greenish orbs appeared, like... eyes. Like the eyes in the storm before...

I took shelter in the stable next to me and secured the door.

Outside, the wind laughed.

Outside... the inevitable came.

CHAPTER SEVEN

The Blizzard

THE STORM CAME WITH a manner and fury foreign to us. We huddled in the stone stable amongst the horses, curled around a small fire we managed to start in a steel trough. The wind outside sang and laughed and whistled through the stable. The metal roofing shuddered in the rage. We could not hear ourselves speak over the din of the wind and sat motionless and silent, waiting.

Waiting.

Waiting...

Waiting for the end of a storm that dragged on, thrashing the outpost and our refuge. There was no sleep to be had, or discussions to be heard, over the tumult of the wind and ice beating against the clapboards.

Lt. Estarenza looked at me, shivering, trying to warm himself near the small fire.

Soldiers lay in fetal positions, hands on their ears, some screamed from madness as the storm raged on. Eventually, the intensity of the wind quieted and ceased to blow through the cracks, and the stable warmed. The horses calmed, and we fed them. A couple of them lay down in the hay. A few soldiers lay next to them for the warmth from the large body and buried themselves in the hay.

The reprieve was short-lived.

The wind whistled and howled, finding entrance through any available hole it could find. The fire shuddered and twisted in the breeze coming through. A rumble came from outside as something crashed, thunderously. A gust of wind outside screamed deafeningly and sheared the roofing of the stable off, where it disappeared into the fray above. Ice swirled in the air, battering us, tearing at flesh. Horses at once shot up and crushed the soldiers lying next to them. Outo and the others found an escape and ripped their way from the stable and into the white death. A metal sheet of roofing crashed against two posts near us, nearly severing us in half.

Soldiers screamed silently into the gale and ran. The icy wind shredded their flesh, ripped from their bones, and their eviscerated blood blew into the white horror as they disappeared.

I ran the length of the stable, rallying the men into positions, and was nearly trampled. I escaped through a side door and fell into a deep drift of snow. I dug in and buried myself alive, shielding myself from the screaming sky and the icy death. I survived in my cocoon of snow as the wind outside shrieked in from the north and the storm progressed on and on...

When the wind calmed I emerged from my shell and stood. It was night. I went into the stable and found ten soldiers alive. To their good fortune, the part of the roof that nearly killed us shielded them. We foraged through the remnants of the outpost and acquired a significant staple of dried meat and grain from the underground food stores, where we found several more bodies, frozen. The hatch covering the shelter was gone, and with no way to build a fire, they died, huddled together, as the storm raged over them.

We gathered some wood from the remains of carts and tents and built a small shelter by using the piece of metal and fashioning it across a stall. We dug into the ground and made like living souls in a mass grave. We moved the trough with the fire into our makeshift shelter, drank water from the melted snow, and rationed the dried meat and grain.

The night was short.

The daybreak on the third day was brief as the white fury came again, and two of the men went mad and clawed at their faces, screaming as they did. They now laid frozen against the wall, eyes as white as the snow outside. The wind howled and swirled and we heard cracks and screams upon it as it lay siege once again to Farwic Outpost. Our shelter was good. We had water and food. Our body heat, along with the fire, kept us warm and alive. The storm raged throughout the day.

And, as swiftly as it began, the storm died. The swirls of snow and ice disappeared. As did the sun.

Thirty-five of us were in the stable when the storm began. Eight of us emerged. The sky above was black but clear. Stars crossed the sky. The air was chilled, frosted, an void of any breeze. Still, like the frozen bodies of my soldiers. Our footsteps crunched atop the snow and ice. The snow was deep and covered our knees in some areas.

The winds had ripped the tents up by the stakes, and destroyed all the stables. The quarters were blown out and crumbling. We found a few soldiers near a dead fire, huddled together, frozen into one giant tortuous statue of red ice. We found a few others alive, blinded or disfigured, wearing masks of blood and sinew. Nobody knew who was who. They later died. I found Outo, torn by the shards of ice, suffocated as his lungs froze. A handful of soldiers survived in the rubble of one building, still coherent but dazed by the maelstrom of events.

The only member of my cadre alive was Lt. Estarenza.

Apart from the stone stables and the tower of Farwic, not one thing remained standing. Not one thing showed the presence of a large army. Like a slate wiped clean. The storm had wiped out our entire camp, and our force of nearly 1,500 soldiers and horses. Gone. Like the day we arrived, there were no signs of life save for me and the gaggle of twenty soldiers who now stood with me.

A vast plain of bluish snow lay in every direction. The moon cast not one shadow save our own. The ground was as smooth as a frozen mirror. We stood before its omniscience, fearing one step would send us tumbling through to the nether worlds waiting below. We did not speak for a very long time. The night was chilled in silence and the ground was encased in glass. We stared into a black moonlit abyss at a land frozen.

I shuddered.

Not from the cold, but from myself.

I failed.

I failed my family, my homeland, and its people. And my army, my dead, or dying force. I hung my head and sighed. The path to redemption lay ahead, across the frozen waste, to an empty land, to nowhere. Pulled by an unknown force, I stepped forward and my boot cracked into the snow and ice, sending the sounds of my movement across the desolate plains. My foot sank up to my knee in the deep snow. We were doomed to die a slow, frozen death. To reach the far side, where the snow and ice would end, will take four days on a horse with no snow. Assuming there was an end. Fear settled in, unwelcome, and unforgiving. It coiled itself around my spine like a hungry serpent. Around me, nothing but bluish moonlit hell.

"Commander?" One of the men said. The sound of the voice was startling.

I was not alone. I had twenty men left alive. No words came to describe how I felt or what orders to give. Their frozen faces stared back at me, looking for an answer I did not have. I turned away, disgusted. Would I fail them, too?

"We will have to wait until morning," I said under my breath. Weariness, hunger, and thirst all set in, and now the fear. Not the fear of death. Death was soon to come across our borders with the siege from an army of whose origin and name we knew not. But not tonight. And if we were fortunate, which we were anything but, the invading army we expected also received the thrashing of this storm and was decimated. My thoughts ran rampant, and my guard dropped after heaving one last weak sigh of breath. And a panic gripped me.

"I cannot get my bearing," I said.

"Commander?" the voice said again.

I summoned the last remaining strength of will and turned to face the haggard lot. I was still their leader, but this went beyond rank and file. This was survival.

"We shall wait for dawn before we move out. In the meantime, we will stoke the fire in our shelter and look for more provisions." I looked at the Lieutenant, known only by the rank on his tattered uniform, his name and face fading to a lost memory, so distant, like our homeland. Like my home. "Make it so, Lieutenant." He bowed his head and left.

The soldiers scrounged pieces of wood, a bit of horse meat, and some dried meat from a buried source, but not much else, save for a single pinch of tea.

Salvation comes in the slightest and purest forms.

We cooked the meat and brewed enough tea to share one cup. Our spirits lifted and soon we engaged in conversation, almost excited about our return home. Our retreat. Not wanting to cast a dim light on their exultation, I excused myself and wandered off into the moonlight.

I walked along an area of the plain so frozen from the ice and wind my weight was not enough to break through. The ease of walking returned, and I covered a great distance. If our trip were under these conditions, we may have a chance. But I now knew I was walking West, for the snow had disappeared, and nothing but ice was under my feet. I stood on the frozen Shope'Ta Lakes just to the north of Farwic Outpost.

For three days we survived absolute chaos and destruction, drinking melted snow, hunkered underground like starving rats. Three days. Versol would be at or near the Great City by now. And with that thought, there came some sense of relief.

I stared at my reflection in the frozen pool below me. The moonlight cast an eerie shadow of my face in the ice. I aged many seasons in a matter of days. My bones ached, and my skin felt like leather wrapped tightly around a frail shell. If we survived this trip, my wife and daughter would not recognize the withered man I had become.

The mere thought of them and something inside me ached. Some unknown wraith tugged at my core, though I knew not why. A longing, an emptiness... grief.

I dropped to my knees and stared at the moon until my eyes ached, blinded by the brilliance. Tears froze on my face. My wife and daughter were gone, and yet, I spoke of them as if they were alive. Madness crept into my core, eerie and light, like a mist under a door.

There would be many specters on this journey.

I stood. Knowing which direction we faced, I knew the course of our path.

I returned to the shelter and sat with the surviving soldiers.

"We must press on to Ro Ista Pass," I said.

The Lieutenant was gnawing on some dried meat and stopped, then looked to the sizable soldier on his right, then back to me.

"Commander?" he said.

"Aye. We are a fortunate few who still draw breath. But a journey south would surely kill us. Starvation and the cold would take us one by one. We are closer to the fortress and the shelter of the Pass."

"Commander, may I speak honestly sir?," the Lieutenant said.

"Proceed."

"Any patrol we encounter would roll over us without even stopping. A journey to the fortress is futile. And death is inevitable. And certain."

His eyes hung, worried. He was young and inexperienced. But he had heart and was smart. Like his father.

"Noted. The snow here goes to our knees. We have no horses. In a day or two, we can be in Ro Ista Pass where the snow should taper. The fortress is another two days beyond that."

"Aye Commander, on a horse."

He was right and was beginning to make me look like a fool. He set down his food. He looked at me, then around at the rest, and hung his head.

"Forgive me, Commander, I have spoken in disrespect." He looked at me again, his blue eyes serious. "We will follow you where you lead us, Commander. There's no doubt. In normal conditions."

"Explain."

"Sir... We have been... I apologize. You are right. We are too close not to go to the Fortress." Again he hung his head, breaking the eye contact.

"And you were doing so well," I said. Estarenza looked up at me, confused. "You are right. These are not normal conditions. They attacked our Great City, and we are now decimated by this unexpected blizzard from the North, and yet, here we sit. I appreciate your candor, Lieutenant. But you gave up too early. Next time, do not concede defeat so soon. We may be past the concept of rank and file, but still need to maintain order, or we will dissolve into decay." I looked around at the men before me. "Anyone else here believe it's a fool's errand to journey to the fortress of Ro Ista Pass?"

They sat in silence. Some hung their heads, fearing to speak with candor. Save one.

"I agree with Lt. Estarenza, Commander," said the large man beside the Lieutenant.

The name floated over the fire to me. Estarenza. His name. And the man, Liber. I frowned, then looked over the remnants of men. They were unknown to me. Phantoms in memory. I collected my thoughts.

"Thank you, Liber... for having the courage to speak up." Again, I looked at Lt. Estarenza. "When others would not." I stood. "Lieutenant, we prepare to journey to the south, keeping the Syn Ka Mountains to our east. We will make our way to the village outpost of Tasa-Arvo."

Heads lifted, and eyes went wide. The Lieutenant stood.

"Tasa-Arvo. Aye, Commander."

A grin emerged from the weather-beaten face. I left the small group to find solitude in a land of nothing but solitude.

Chapter Eight

The Journey

A N ICY AND BITTER wind blew in from the North, piercing us to the bone. We spent the rest of the night preparing for the journey, making torches, packing water skins with snow, and creating drags to carry supplies. We huddled near the fires we set around the area we worked from.

The first light of the day crept over the Syn'Ka mountains in the East, lighting a cold gray sky. Before us lay a frozen, barren, and white forbidding landscape with no discernible direction, save for the mountains to the West and East of us. The sun stayed hidden behind the gray blanket. We set out South toward our home. By midday, the gray gave way to the sun, blinding us.

We high-stepped through the deep snow, shielding our eyes from the glare, unable to mark waypoints on the flat, barren horizon. We only knew we trekked southward. Our march continued into the night with one sole purpose directing each step.

Survival.

The depth of the snow slowed our journey, and we gained little distance while the moon trekked the lonely sky, keeping a watchful eye and laughing at the same time. Nobody spoke. Only the crunch of snow under our boots and the scraping of our drags disturbed the silence and echoed across the frozen waste. Our shadows under the dying torchlight danced upon the frozen ground. I caught glimpses of my soldiers turning their heads backward, expecting the inevitable.

But the inevitable lay before us.

We traveled for two days and nights before making a proper camp. The flat, barren horizon before us, never waning. Four soldiers succumbed to the cold during that time, collapsing into the deep snow. We had no choice but to scavenge what we could from them in the way of furs, coins, and food. My thoughts became grim when I considered the possibility of needing the body, too... but the thought quickly left. Now, I sat in silence at the fire and wondered who would be the next to fall. Would we need their flesh to sustain us one more day, their clothing for fire? Would it be me? Would I ever see home again? Or be consumed by the snow, the ice, the wind, or those seated next to me around the fire?

We broke camp.

We were fortunate for the moon lighting our way. We traveled half of the night when the depth of the snow tapered off. Our pace quickened. We made haste as best we could, driven by this new hope.

I shivered, my teeth chattered, and my sweat froze to my skin. I was a shambling inferno of ice, ready to collapse at any moment, as my foundation shook under my frame.

"Commander, look!" the Lieutenant said.

The sudden voice startled me. He was pointing south. I could make out the faint glimmer of firelight along the horizon of the flat plains. Surely, madness was taking over.

The men, my walking dead, all looked. Their eyes lit up at this new glimmer of unreality. I stopped them from going any further. An act that just moments before our discovery would have gotten me killed. Along the horizon, several fires loomed—enough for a small military force, or a caravan of travelers.

"Lieutenant, you and the men stay here. Liber and I will move in for a closer look," I said.

"Yes, Commander."

I noted a hint of anticipation, followed by regret in his tone.

We made our way closer to the fires. The moon sat at the top of the twisted peaks of the Syn Ka mountains, and would soon disappear behind them, concealing us in darkness. A light snow fell.

We continued toward the fires, low and hunched over. We took each step as carefully as possible, ensuring the sound of the snow beneath our feet would alarm no one to our presence. Shadow was the only cover we had here, and archers could surely pick us off if this were a hostile force.

As we moved in closer, the fire lights grew brighter. We crested a small ridge. The fires were more significant than first thought. Large flames burst into the night, reflecting on the snow and ice with a sick orangish hell. The snow laughed back as it melted, quenching the thirst of the fire with a hiss.

Shapes reflected the dances of the fire. Tall shapes. Square shapes. A still life of destruction. Our journey had come to its own end.

"Tasa-Arvo," Liber said.

"Aye. Come."

The village of Tasa was marked by a tall tower in the center which held the warning bells. Arvo had a watchtower of equal height. The outpost, and its small force, were gone. The village burned. Both an abandoned graveyard and only the fires that emaciated and scorched the buildings lived.

I rushed the scene, plodding through the snow, until I stood at the edge of what used to be the small village of Tasa.

"Commander, this—?" I hung my head. "But sir, what could have—" his words cut short as he collapsed to the ground on his knees and sobbed. Tears streamed from his eyes and froze to his leathery cheeks. Not even the warmth of the fires from the wreckage of the barracks, the towers, or the stables could warm his icebound soul.

"This is impossible," I said. "It cannot be," A vision of some uncanny and mystical conjuring fluttered through my thoughts.

Liber looked at me with questioning eyes washed by an internal rain.

"The blizzard?" he said. He looked at the remains of the outpost and stood.

"The blizzard did not do this. No, this is the work of some strange and powerful force."

"But we passed no such force, Commander."

The truth was undeniable. Farwic burned, the citizens and soldiers killed, it's buildings destroyed. As Tasa-Arvo was now. The madman in Farwic spoke of strange creatures.

"No. This makes no sense to me."

"They must have traveled within the blizzard," Liber said, echoing my earlier thought. I shuddered and tried to understand how... but it was beyond my scope of reasoning.

"Only one truth exists - their hunger for waste and destruction is undeniable. And the sorcery, unimaginable."

"And they will reach the Great City as we flounder through the snow," he said in a half breath, then dropped to his knees again and sobbed.

"Sorcery like this does not exist," I muttered to myself, only half-believing my own words.

I grabbed Liber by the shoulder of his coat and brought him to his feet.

"Come. Let us return. Soon, we will warm ourselves by these fires of destruction and light the torches of revenge in all of us. We will forage through the devastation and scrounge what we can."

We reached the others just before daybreak. They had sheltered themselves from the cold and were asleep. The Lieutenant was standing over them, alerted to our approach. His sword was drawn.

"Lieutenant! Wake the men, we move out!" I yelled.

He sheathed his sword and roused the survivors. All rose, save two, frozen in an eternal slumber. My stomach twisted, and I grimaced at their restful bodies.

"Bring them," I told the lieutenant. He looked at me, questioning why, then understood.

"Yes, Commander. Of course." The lieutenant's reply had saved me from explaining our grim reality.

The blue of the early morning was building behind the mountains. Soon, the sun will rise, and its glare again blind us.

"Today, we search the ruins and forage for food, water, weapons, and horses," I said to the Lieutenant.

A glimmer of life crept back into everyone's eyes as we neared the fires.

We reached the burning outpost and laid the two corpses on the ground in the snow outside the village, away from the fires.

Everyone stood near a gutted, burning building and warmed their bodies, melting away the melancholy of a long journey. The grief of the travel was replaced by a new grief, a grief my men were becoming too familiar with.

Cleansed by fire, they took refuge in the warmth and slept. I wandered the outpost. Not a single structure was left intact. Everything was burned or burning. No single body, or horse, lived amongst the burned-out structures or in the streets.

I returned to the sleeping men, and drew my blanket around me. I lay down, covered my eyes from the sun, and fell fast asleep.

A scuffle awakened me, accompanied by the strange sound of jubilant voices. An eerie alternative to the mood of days passed. Night had fallen while I slept. I sat up, frozen, next to a fire that still burned, but without the glorious intent it had earlier in the day.

I rose to my feet and peered into the darkness. Four soldiers were next to one of the other building fires trying to corral a horse! No — horses! There were two of them, their reins entangled. The lieutenant was with them, watching from the wayside with the rest of the men.

I ran toward them.

"Lieutenant! What is this?"

"Commander! Horses! Can you believe it? Our salvation is at hand!"

"I don't understand. Where could they have come from?"

"They were standing near a fire, foraging in the snow. It is a blessing."

"This is most odd, Lieutenant."

The horses looked healthy, unscathed from battle.

He looked at me, his head tilted to one side.

"When I surveyed the area before I slept, there was nothing to be found. No bodies. No horses. No food. And certainly no shelter. While the return of these horses certainly brings new life, I fear we are no better off than when we arrived."

He looked over at the horses, then back at me.

"Commander, forgive my rudeness, but I do not believe we are as damned as we were before. We have quicker transport now, or we can send for help."

"Help?" I laughed at him. "Lieutenant, you are naïve. From where do you think help will come?"

His gaze wandered back to the horses and the men.

"I have to believe, Commander. These horses represent a new strength to me. A strength and advantage that, until this day, we haven't had since the blizzard. These two spirits are a gift with which to drive out the enemy."

My joy at seeing two strong-spirited steeds before me was subdued by the chill, and the naivety of one young lieutenant.

"Forgive me, Commander Soltari." He faced me again. He was becoming bold and arrogant. "The sight of these two stallions does not vanquish the enemy which caused this destruction, but the enemies who have taunted us since we emerged from our shelter at Farwic Outpost. Nevermore will the thought of defeat, despair, and so many other enemies we can not lay a sword to, conquer my determination or my will. Look in their eyes, Commander," he pointed to the four soldiers, now with the steeds under control, reined in. They stroked and patted their battle brothers, the grins of madness replaced by smiles of joy.

He was right. I had no argument left within me.

"No, forgive me, Lieutenant. Naïve was too strong a word. You are wise and see things clearly. We do not have to worry ourselves about this supposed army. They do not hunt us here. That battle is lost. They have without question laid siege on most of the inner villages by now, and even our Great City. We fight a much stronger enemy here. An enemy so strong not even this Queen's army could withstand its wrath."

He was pale, and his eyes had sunken. He averted his gaze away from mine.

"Look at me, Lieutenant."

He looked down at the ground, hesitated, then looked up at me. He was younger than I thought. Wisdom loomed in his dark eyes. Wisdom beyond his years. I hadn't seen it until now.

"Your father would be proud."

Chapter Nine

The Earth Below

W E TRAVELED THROUGH THE night and found three more horses wandering in a knotted grove of trees near a frozen stream. They were saddled. One was dragging a broken harness. A black one, which reminded me of Outo, walked to me and snorted, then shook his long black mane. A prideful black male. He stood with two buckskins. Miraculous was their survival. Their presence warmed our hearts, and gave us a glimmer of hope. We found the riders face down in the snow a short while later. I rolled one body over.

A thin strip of cloth covered the eyes like a veil.

"Is it a woman?" Estarenza said.

I knelt next to the corpse and removed the veil.

The face was eastern, male. "Rogues Army," I said. I brushed snow from the chest, revealing two blue stripes.

"An El Friz. Odd. Maybe the veil was used as protection from the wind."

I stood. "I care not. Strip them of their clothing, armor, weapons, anything we can use to keep torches and fire lit or protect ourselves. Leave the bodies where they lay."

Lt. Estarenza reached down and pulled a black dagger from the belt of the dead man.

"Black as night, like a shadow," he said.

Estarenza pushed the dagger into his belt and stood.

The snow became deep again, taking its toll on the soldiers on foot. We were weary and hungry. We rotated men on the horses and hitched the drags to two of them.

The sky brightened behind the Syn Ka mountains, announcing the coming day. We crested a small hill, and before us lay another grove of trees which ran in a line across our path.

The Lieutenant and I stopped. The men continued, their pace quickening in high tromps through the snow, working to get to the grove and the river on the other side. I followed the line of trees along the horizon to the west, where they disappeared into a gray mist.

The snow lightened and thinned at the edge of the grove, the trees having blocked its path to the ground. Trees had fallen throughout the grove, broken under the weight of the ice and snow, or snapped by the relentless wind. Relieved to walk unburdened, the men ran through the grove and stopped in a clearing. I watched as they cut limbs, dragged broken trees, and built a large, all-consuming fire.

The sun rose above the horizon and sparkled off the frozen White River in the distance. The shelter from the wind and the warmth of the fire filled our souls with renewed vibrance. We collapsed from exhaustion, warm near the large fire.

The sun crossed over the sky as we slept and had set behind the trees when I woke. The rays sparkled through the high treetops as they whispered in the wind. The fire burned well. The Lieutenant sat next to it, a grim look on his face. He saw me, stood, and walked to me. I sat up.

"We've lost another one. An older foot soldier. He collapsed retrieving wood."

The wind blew, slightly jostling the firelight. The sound of the wind became like laughter, distant. Or grief, a moaning, whimpering sound as branches creaked in the cold.

Most around camp were still asleep. Two rose at the sound of the wind, all around us now, sighing, moaning, like the last breaths of the dying. The sun died behind the trees, shrouding us in a gray dark in its final moments in the sky. Shapes moved in the darkened forest, and a mist rolled in from the White River. The mist filled the grove and even darker shadows moved about.

The moans continued.

The whispers continued.

The creaks grew louder.

All were awake and on their feet now, eyes wide, looking at the mist in the grove around us and the slow-moving dark shadows within it.

"Commander?" Estarenza said.

The horses whinnied and pawed at the ground. One rose and whinnied and kicked out, catching a soldier in the head and knocking him into the fire. Two others ran over, pulled him from the flames, and rolled him on the ground. He was lifeless, his charred clothes smoking, his face caved in. The horse bolted, and another followed. My horse also rose and bolted. All three ran along the edge of the clearing and into the forest.

A soldier screamed and clawed at his face and ears. He ran headlong into the forest, into the mist, and we watched as the shadows darted around him, surrounding him, his muffled screams beckoning for mercy, before they were silenced.

"They live in the forest, in the mist," I said.

One horse stood in the clearing, unmoved by the sounds of the misty shadows. It looked at me, then eastward. He sauntered out of the clearing after his brothers.

"He cannot hear," Lt. Estarenza said.

"Aye. We follow him. He will lead us to the others. Come, grab our gear. There will be no rest here tonight."

We lit torches from the fire and hurried through the grove. The mist parted around the flames, the shadows whined. We stepped onto the open plain. The wind was stronger without the forest cover. We found the horses at the edge of the river. Across the river on the other bank was an endless forest filled with mist and shadow. To the west, the forest stretched out of sight. We would not be crossing the river.

"We could follow the grove west, along the edge," the lieutenant said.

"The forest ends in the mountains at cliff-sides and steep climbs. And we cannot approach from the North," I said.

He turned to me.

"Then we wait until daybreak when the shadows and mist die."

"Lieutenant, we are at the edge of Zhalé Pass. That is the White River, which comes from the mountains west of here. With the depth of the forest here, we cannot make it in a day, and without a suitable clearing, we shall all die of madness running into the mist like our comrade." There was an odd glimmer in his eyes. "We must go through Zhalé Pass."

"Commander—"

"It is the only way. We will continue southeast, which will take us to the Black Road. From there, we can make our way to the Great City."

"The Great City?" He looked at me. He looked older now, but none wiser.

"Aye. We must return to the city."

"Commander, you know as well as I that the force from Ro Ista Pass has already laid siege to the Great City. We are, but what, fourteen men with three tired horses? What can we possibly—"

"Your outlook is based on an assumption, Lieutenant." I gripped the hilt of my sword. "While they surely have laid siege, Commander Versol would have returned in time to counter them."

He shook his head. "No. I don't believe that, Commander. I don't feel—"

"That is all, Lieutenant."

He stared at me, lost, then turned and walked into the darkness.

We dug a hole in the snow to build a fire. When we reached the earth below, we saw familiar stocks of a once great crop. Bent and broken from the harvest, it was a welcome site, and building a fire became an easier and more grateful task.

"We rest here until dawn," I said. I looked to the east.

Zhalé Pass headed into the heart of the Eastern Lands. The mountains around it appeared like upturned claws protruding from the earth, as if some slain colossal beast lay buried and all that remained were its fearsome hands. Our small party would be defenseless against any reaver band of Rogues Army, or bandits lurking within the range, or in the foothills beyond at the edge of the desert.

My group huddled around the fire, others lay fallen in the snow in restless sleep, the rest a tired and haggard, defeated group of the half-living.

A brisk wind blew and turned the fire, then dissipated. A gray gloom hung over the land, the moon hid behind a swathe of clouds. I laid with my back to the wind and fell into a fitful sleep.

I dreamed of my daughter with her flaming red hair running from me, laughing playfully. She turned and looked at me. Her smile slowly faded, and her eyes widened with horror. My wife screamed behind me, and I turned away.

I woke.

Some men stood over me where I lay, staring. They looked at me with suspicion. Maybe the thought of insanity filled their hungry minds. I stood and ordered them to stoke the fire to warm our bones and wake the others. They complied without haste.

Everyone soon had their fill of tasteless meat and melted snow. They craved spice and sweet things. They craved soft women with a warm touch, luxurious rooms, and wine. They craved the joyful company of others and not the grim, tired trek of the doomed.

They craved all the things that made us complacent.

We would be thankful for the feel of metal in our hands, to stand as warriors again.

But we were none of that. The honor of a pitched battle coming our way and dying gloriously while the blood of our enemies caked our boots, now, was only a dream.

We changed from warriors to wanderers with no strength to lift a foot to take one more step through the deep snow. Driven by the desire to return home, to return to the lie of contentment, should it still exist. The belief we could avenge this land and our families while upon a great black steed descending from dark gray clouds above, landing on the necks of our enemy, was a shimmer of madness. But this shimmer, this faint glimmer of hope, was all we could cling onto while the recesses of our minds became poisoned by the thought of knowing we would die out here in this never-ending sweep of snow and ice, without a drop of blood being spilled for our homeland. The pitched battle was now against the one enemy we could not kill.

Time.

We stood against forces we could not reckon with. The land, the wind, and the snow. The demoted veterans of a once dominant force, reduced to mere rubble in a thick snow, before the moon even changed its face.

And so we entered the mouth of Zhalé Pass.

We continued, only able to see a small distance, as the wind blew through the pass stirring the light snow into a fury. The clouds descended upon us. In the range, I could make out sharp crags sticking up from the ground. Then, an unexpected sound broke the cold silence. A sound I had not heard for some time—the sound of a voice.

"Where...?" the voice said. It was raspy and dry. It was my own.

Ridges with tall, sharp peaks jutted out of the ground like spears and arrowheads. I was confused at the sight of the reddish-gray cliffs. They jutted out in every direction, ominous, spear-like, striking into the darkened clouds. We trekked through walls of stone with a ceiling of cloud, enclosed, constricting, trapping...

I wiped the cold sweat from my brow and sighed. Footsteps crunched in the snow around me as men and horses passed me, uncaring, or oblivious to the direction we traveled. I nudged my horse on headlong into the biting wind.

We were able to increase our speed, for the snow could not penetrate the steep crags and canyon. We were in the grasp of a giant clawed hand, and nothing made sense. The sharp cliffs began to take shape, blend in with each other, separate, crack...

A horseman next to me spoke into the wind.

"Commander?"

A tower... the top was carved to two points to resemble the terrain of the pass. A gap cut into the tower's body to light the way... like the Tower of the Guardian in Soldier's Pass. But no beacon came from this tower. It's light, extinguished, non-existent, a figment of... hope.

Diminished.

We trudged toward the tower, then the shape of the tower split into two distinct pinnacles. As we rounded a short bend, they separated. This was not the Tower of the Guardian, nor were we in Soldier's Pass. What I saw and knew ripped the last remnants of my spirit out and left it frozen in the cold waste.

I stopped and looked around.

"There, we make camp there," I said. "It... it is not a good day to travel."

We camped in a crevice in the cliffside, sheltered from the wind and snow, and built a fire. The flames reflected on the walls and soon heated the small space. There were 14 of us now, and six horses. One by one we would be picked off, collapsing into the waiting hands of the white death. A jumble of mangled corpses, too tired to move.

And there in the crypt of Zhalé Pass, we slept, as the fire burned to embers, and the last of our torches flamed out into wisps of smoke.

Chapter Ten

The Road

EVERYTHING WAS WHITE, ABSENT of all color and dimension. The glare was bright as the day. The hideous peaks of Zhalé Pass hovered over us like stone carrion, waiting for the last wisp of death. A bitter wind blew through the pass. A voice interrupted the hiss of the wind. No. Several voices. Calling me.

From dimensions beyond the infinite, a single deep voice broke through the white void.

"Commander! Commander!"

I was shaking. No. I was being shaken.

Someone I knew once appeared over me, blocking the glare and the vision of the vile peaks. He was shaking me. It was near dawn.

"Commander?"

I sat upright and shook my head, trying to clear the thoughts of the damned from my mind.

"Yes. Yes, I am fine." I glared at the man. He was an officer... a Lieutenant. I sat up. "Was I?"

"You screamed, sir."

The fire was smoldering smoke. I stood.

"We have no fire?"

"No," he said.

The word dribbled from his shaking mouth and echoed across the vast expanse as I stood, and it transformed into a scream, so great, so profound, that when it died, I followed it, and collapsed into the snow as it escaped my grasp.

Black. Void. A glimmer of light. Shadows. Voices. Cold.

I opened my eyes.

I was lying on the cold earth. It was night. I lay next to the dim remnants of the fire. I sat up, stoked it, and added some kindling and clothing from fallen soldiers — anything. I pushed on the last of the wood and the fire came alive. I looked at the flames and sighed. Lying around the fire were the last of my men. One of them, naked and frozen. His clothes in a heap next to him.

The Lieutenant rose and saw me. He sat up and came next to me.

"Commander Soltari," he said.

The world spun out of control and the moon shot across the sky. I rolled to my hands and knees and retched into the snow. My head throbbed. My body became like crumpled paper. I heaved.

I leaned back onto my feet and looked at the Lieutenant.

"What... what did you just say?" I said, with a voice like ash. I was rust. His eyes bled, confused.

"Commander?"

A war hammer to the skull.

"Yes. Soltari," I whispered. "That... is my name." I stood. "Commander General Soltari."

The lieutenant shuffled a maniacal laugh across the fire. I stared up at the sharp peaks of a mountain pass and the walls of our prison from the white death. Alas, the winds of madness blew through the canyon and carried away our souls. Someone screamed. Something. Screamed.

Soltari

I heaved over, but nothing escaped my gullet save for a wisp of dry air.

Laughter, sinister, beguiling.

There's nothing there.

I am alone in the darkness. And in a flash, my mind snapped, separating from my body, and disappeared in a flicker.

The fresh air of the icy wasteland burned my throat. I counted twelve men. Two frantically worked to stoke some semblance of fire with the meager kindling from one of our drags. We had started with twenty men. Escaping alive from this frozen hell became less of a possibility with each passing sun. We were meandering in a joyless cavern of gloom, dejected and lifeless. We were sojourners on a quest to nowhere. Hope abandoned us as swiftly as life. Melancholy, desperate, tired, hungry.

A young man looked at me, tears in his eyes. I knew his name once—an officer of mine. For the past few days, we lived off the meat of our dead brothers with no game present to hunt. Our vile ways turned us into a cannibalistic clan of hopeless vagabonds, loyal only to survival, with no honor left among us. The horses would not last with nothing to forage on in this sinister landscape of rock, ice, and snow. Their heads hung low and their hooves scraped across the bitter, cold ground.

My own will collapsed beneath me, swallowed bit by bit by the snow and ice, freezing it for all eternity. Prisoners of the ice, and defenseless against it. In time, we would all die here, consumed by this pass. Time weighed against us, waiting, watching. It would strike at its desirable moment. Its laughter echoing off the stone walls as it consumed another relieved soul.

I regained my covers and shielded myself from the world, collapsing into the cold embrace below me, waiting for death. My will to continue this futile journey was no longer driven by vengeance. My eyes rolled, and I was soon asleep. My dreams, encased in ice, congealed in the chill frost.

Several days passed, and the sun broke on the eastern horizon and shone through Zhalé Pass, its rays unhindered by the morbid peaks. We were in the Eastern Lands now.

It was getting more difficult to distinguish between the pained snarls etched on the faces from the grins of madness. Their color a agonized bluish-white. Eyes as pallid as the moon, extinguished. Bodies transformed into phantoms. We no longer carried the dead. We brought the half-living. Sanity was freezing or frozen, and nobody slept with their back to another, if they truly slept at all.

Then we found the road.

The sun peered over the horizon, and a streak of road lay before us, stretching out beyond the hills. There were no tracks to observe apart from those we left behind, echoing our presence in this icy void. The snow surrounded us, save for this stretch of road out of the abyss.

I dismounted and my horse sighed with relief, free from the heavy burden of grief it carried. The others followed. We stood before the red dawn as it covered us with its glow and warmed us with its fiery eyes.

The frail grips of sanity loosened momentarily as we were brought to our knees before the rising sun.

We all wept. All at once we were drawn into a pool of despair mixed with a stream of happiness as we thought of families and the green plains and rolling hills of our homeland.

I did not have the will to move as I kneeled before the sun and cherished each memory that passed before me. It did not matter if the memories were horrifying or joyful; they were all that remained.

And a vision of my loved ones appeared before me, my wife and daughter, staring back at me with wondering amazement as if I was some unrecognizable beast. My beard was long, my eyes sagged from the tugs of insanity, and my skin was dry, coarse, and broken. My heart belonged to nobody, yet inside my heaving chest, a light of warmth burned as I looked upon their faces and said two of the most precious words to me. Words I had not spoken in ages. Words, which were the life and the reason I lived, and continued on this perilous journey to a home made of nightmares and ash.

Their names.

The words passed through my mind and down to my lips and my lips moved and no sound emanated. I could no longer hear or speak their names, and then, as quickly as the vision appeared, it was gone.

And along with it, their names.

I leaned back onto the heels of my snow-covered boots and looked toward the sky. I lowered my head and drew in a deep contorted breath, tilted my head backward and all the pain and all the anguish and all the despair from eons deep burst from my body and from my torn soul like a vortex of sorrow.

And I screamed.

The sound echoed northward through the pass and across the icy plains of death, westward to the far-off mountains that separated our land from everything else, eastward toward the desert wastes, southward to the forest and seas, and homeward to the Great City and all the death which lay in a shadowed hulk.

My men covered their ears and winced as gallops of streaming tears flooded their eyes and drew virtual blood, unable to block the horrific sound cursing their lives and wishing them dead. Their mouths contorted in a seemingly endless twist. They collapsed and rolled in the ice and snow, beckoning for the relief death would bring to silence my agony. The fine line of sanity and insanity vibrated in their heads like a highly tuned string on a musician's instrument, suffering the stress, threatening to break, disharmonized and discordant.

My horse reeled and whinnied as it tugged at the reins secured in my tightly clenched hands.

Upward toward the sky, the stars fell. The sun cried out as it shut its eyes of flame, fearing to peer out upon the tortuous visage of one so deep in the threshold of pain that it would burn its own eyes out.

The breath faded and stopped, yet I still screamed, the wretched laments echoing inside. Fearing my flesh would burst, covering this land with my irascible torment, I stopped.

The mute wisp of air ended, and all around was dark and silent.

I leaned forward, drew in another deep breath, and let out a cold beckoning sigh, a cry for help in this endless world of nothingness as my senses sank beneath the mire and all went black, black as the void beyond death.

Beyond reason.

Beyond sanity.

Beyond...

Part Two

TENDER RAGE

CHAPTER ELEVEN

Found

A LINE OF HORSE-DRAWN carriages, riders, and carts traveled along the East/West road in the Northern Lands, known as the Black Road. The road was a key passage across the northern region of the Northern Lands for the traveling merchants of the East, reaching from the largest city of the Eastern Lands, Bin El Omen, to Kirves and Ahjo in the mountains of the Western Lands through Soldier's Pass. In the Southern Lands, they traveled the Kinelot Road past the City of the Southern Moon, the gated capital of the Southern Lands, and on to the Gal Abed, the fortress city built into the white Croft Vale Cliffs, in the mountainous Western Lands.

The merchants, roamers from a time before the last great empire which covered all the lands in the east, north, and south, to the mountains in the west, now traveled these long distances selling their finely crafted silks, bone and gem jewelry, woodcrafts, and highly sought after boneware (for the ones who can afford it), and some say, enchanted items. Craftsmen, mystics, and revered and feared swordsmen, the Eastern Land's new empire is one of enterprise, and mystery.

The caravan rolled along the edge of the foothills, toward the desert corridor to the gateway of their homeland, Kaksoset Canyon. On the other side of the canyon, the road continues to the prosperous city of Bin El Omen, the epicenter of the trade routes. The caravan was one of the longest and most famous of caravans, for in one carriage, a gilded masterpiece of arcane art, traveled the Priestess Kristava, a descendent of mysticism, advisors to the former emperors of the Empire of the Eastern Star.

Four master swordsmen on proud horses lead the massive caravan from the west to the east. Without warning, the long line of carriages, horsemen, carts, and beasts of burden loaded with packs filled with the wares bartered in the Western Lands, stop at the edge of the foothills.

High overhead the sun hung, and cast long rays across the desert and the red foothills of the nameless range. The four horsemen glanced at each other, unsure how to approach what they saw.

A man in worn black leather armor and a tattered blue cloak sat leaning against a dead black horse. Carrion birds were feasting on the horse's eyes, as the man sat hunched over, dead or close to it, head hung, hair draped across his bearded face. He clasped a bloodied long sword in his hand, and a dagger, the color of shadow, protruded from his side.

A merchant on a gray stallion rode up from the side of the caravan.

"What is it?" he said.

"A dead man," a swordsman said. The merchant nudged his horse closer to the body. The horse nickered anxiously.

"Easy, Sumu," the man said, then dismounted. He looked at the man, then back at the swordsman whose eyes were stricken with wonder and confusion. "A northern soldier?"

The merchant heard something on the wind, then the dead man twitched and the merchant jumped back.

"He lives!"

A swordsman dressed in a tan uniform with a blue sash around the waist approached and stood beside the merchant. He cast a long shadow over the dying man. His head and face were covered, and a long, thin sword hung on his side.

"He will be dead soon enough, Igvar, leave him."

Igvar turned a bitter stare at the swordsman, then tilted his head, as if listening to the wind. He looked upon the foothills, then to the desert.

"The priestess," he said. "She has spoken to me, Var'Tiya El Friz. Go, now, get one of the empty carts here. We will take him with us."

The swordsman, not one to question the Priestess's will, turned and called back to the others. They spurred their horses to the rear and returned with a merchant and his horse and cart not so weighted down with goods.

"The black dagger," Var'Tiya El Friz said. "That is a foul omen Igvar."

"Help me pick him up," Igvar said.

They grabbed the man by his arms. He screamed out in a tortuous threnody as if trying to wake from a nightmare, over and over. They let go and covered their ears, wincing at the sound of the man's torment.

The horses whinnied and one reared up, tossing its rider to the golden silt. The man stopped screaming, then mumbled, and stirred in fits, jerking the hand holding the blood-stained sword. It rang out an eerie screech as it scraped across the sand and rock.

The man collapsed to his side in a heap.

"Now!"

They disarmed the dying man, picked him up, and placed him in the cart. Another horseman approached with a woman sitting behind him. She leaped and ran to the cart. Her feet slipped on the silky sand. She climbed in next to the dying man, and the horseman handed her a bag. She touched the dying man's forehead and cheek, then looked at Igvar, shaking her head.

"Do what you can. It is the will of the Priestess."

She sighed, nodded, and touched the man's lips with a moistened rag.

CHAPTER TWELVE
The Void

I WOKE UNDER A diminishing sun. The heat of the day penetrated me. My body swayed back and forth, cracking stalks of straw beneath me. I was in a moving cart. A shadow moved across my vision and a woman with dark, olive skin, wiped my brow, then saw my open eyes. She gasped and showed a small smile. She touched my lips with a moistened cloth, the water somehow cool, hinted at a spice I could not place. The woman's face was calm, older, but not aged, partially obscured by scarves or a cloak. I winced. The light of the sky hit my eyes when she moved away, and her shadow fell from my face. She cast me in shade again and looked into my eyes. Her pungent, spiced perfume filled my senses, and my eyes watered under the weight of the aroma. Maybe. Not perfume. Her clothes smelled of eastern sage, and jasmine. Eastern. Merchants. The Roama. Travelers of the Black Road. I moved to sit up and screamed and collapsed. The woman put a hand on my shoulder and shook her head.

She waved a small, smoking bundle of dried leaves bound with twine around my face, up to the sky, then down the length of my body in patterned motions, and my eyes grew heavy. The smoke drifted up in circles, caught in a dead wind, and hovered over me like a bird of prey. As she waved the smoldering leaves, she muttered a quiet song. A ritual. A ritual for the dead. Or dying. Her black hair swayed as she moved, and her hooped earrings clinked rhythmically with each pass over me.

She waved the incense across my face and disappeared into a flourish of smoke, and I slipped into a void.

I was in a dark well of sorrow. The black stone walls surrounded me. I tried to scream, but a muted hollow nothing fell upon the dead air. My head burst. My eyes bled. I could not stand, for there was no ground below me. My arms were limp and my legs would not move. I breathed. I stared up at the empty blackness above. Frozen. Trapped in my flesh. Not dying. Just... breathing.

"Commander?"

The voice echoed within me. It was light, female, and strong.

"Yes? Yes? Who is there?"

"Follow..." the voice echoed. "Follow me."

"I, I cannot move."

"Come. Follow me — Shaviska."

"Shaviska?" I said.

"Yes." I closed my eyes. "Yes. That is the way *Shavisssskaaaaa*." Echoes of...

The moon, in its full grace and beauty, appeared. It hovered over a flat landscape. A cold landscape. Winter. The Northern lands. My death march across...

The moon.

Focus.

"Yes, Shaviska! Come to me!"

The voice was closer.

Focus.

My lips curled back. Every nerve in my body, every sense in my soul, every rupture in my flesh, tore through from the inside, escaping the cell of myself and lifting my spirit beyond it.

A scream silenced by a broken sword. Final words drowned in blood.

Movement. Mine.

I screamed. Insufferable pain. Poisoned blood poured onto the wet stone floor before me. Crimson. Jeweled. Moon. Voice. Myself.

Free.

The pain subsided, and a dawning light appeared, along with a vision of a landscape and a shadow.

I opened my eyes, and before me were the faces of two feral children.

We had stopped. The children blocked the black clouds. A boy and a girl. They said nothing. Their startled looks said enough. Their eyes filled with the onset of tears.

Had I screamed?

I rolled over and coughed, and the sensation of a thick, salty liquid coated my throat. I wiped my face and saw blood on my hand glistening black in the twilight.

The boy looked at his sister, then back at me. They turned and scurried behind me to the front of the cart.

The blue light of twilight hung in the east while the last fires of daylight settled in the west. The chatter of several hushed voices drifted around me, muttering, some language distant to me but not entirely foreign. Quiet, whispers. Leather snapped from behind the cart. I sat up and grimaced as pain shot through me. Bloodied bandages lay next to me. I collapsed into the straw from the pain.

I awoke with the tilting of the cart, as a heavy man stepped into the seat at the front. He made a clicking sound and snapped the reins. The cart jerked into motion. I pushed myself up, then turned and leaned against the side, careful not to strain my injury. I wore some form of Eastern garb. A long beige and black robe covered my body. My swords, my leather armor, my uniform... all gone. My heart raced as I looked around the cart. And where were the others? Am I alone? We found a road... yes. But...

Their names... a face... screaming at me. And blood...

I turned away from my savage thoughts and found no escape.

A grunt came from the front of the cart. I looked at the two men guiding the team and noted the two children I had seen sitting between them. I wanted to speak, but knew the effort would be wasted. I was with the Roama, and my words would be lost to them. I exhaled and leaned back, falling in rhythm with the movement of the cart. The men kept watchful eyes on the desert. Another pointed to fires in the distance and said something to the other. No lantern hung from our cart. No lanterns hung from any cart.

The shadow of another cart or wagon moved about in the darkness in front of us. Behind us, a carriage drawn by two horses, steered by two drivers who also kept a watch on the distant fires. Clouds covered the stars and the hope of any light from a watchful moon to aid us was only a whisper of desire. Our journey across would be a dark and lonely venture in shadow. The only light came from the distant fires glimmering off the cloud cover like rainbows of flame from a long-ago nightmare.

We were being watched.

My eyes grew heavy with the lull and sway of the cart and I laid down and drifted off. The slumber caved in all around me.

The icy blackness enveloped me.

I stood before a wall of nothing, unable to see my hand before me, in a room devoid of light. All around me, I sensed the carnage and the blood running down the walls. There was warmth. The heat of a fresh battle. The smell of death. Whispers all around me. Screaming whispers. Painful spikes of sound drilled into my mind.

My eyes opened. The nightmare passed. I heaved a sigh of relief.

I glanced next to me, at my wife in a sound slumber, her back to me, her red hair caressing the pillows. Quiet. I rolled over, put my hand on her shoulder, and pulled her to me. Her body rolled listlessly, collapsing. Her eyes stared at the ceiling, black, complete as night. Her mouth a gaping hole, twisted and empty. Her face, a snarl of grief. She was as cold as winter. I turned to scream and only shadows spilled from my mouth and swarmed around me, covering me, shrouding me in their black embrace, and then everything stopped. All motion... all...

My eyes opened. The lull and sway of the cart were gone. We had stopped. The night hung above me. I pushed myself up and sat on my heels, trying to get a bearing, clearing the fog of the dream. The clouds in the distance still danced in fire. The cart behind us sat like an ominous black shadow, the horses as still as the night. A breeze crossed me, and my mind fell at ease.

A horse nickered nearby, startled me. I leaped into a defensive stance and nearly fell out of the cart as I struggled for balance, then screamed and dropped to my knees, holding my side.

"You fall, stranger, you open wound," said the man on the horse in a broken, although recognizable language.

I had not spoken to another person for so long that the sound was strange, foreign.

"You... speak..."

The horse turned its head to me and snorted.

"Yes, soldier, I speak your tongue." The man stroked the side of his horse's neck. "Easy, Sumu," he said.

So many questions.

"I don't—" But only one mattered. "My clothes. My... weapons." He interrupted me with a finger to his lips and pointed to the carriage behind us.

"The priestess. She will speak to you once we cross the desert. Answer questions."

The two children said something to each other, then looked at me with suspicion.

Priestess. There was only one Roama priestess I knew of, and only from my days as a boy traveling with my father.

My father...

The air exited my body as if pursued by death. I laid down and let out a deep sigh. The pain from my arm and side disappeared into the night, and I soon succumbed to the darkness once more, home again in the void.

CHAPTER THIRTEEN

Shaviska

A NUDGE IN MY side from a pointed boot woke me. The man who had spoken to me in the night was hovering over my aching shell. He had knocked me out of slumber, and like a lost child, I lay there staring up at him, blinded by the bright day. I rolled over and sat up. I winced at the pain in my arm and side.

"We have crossed the desert," he said.

I looked around. The sun sat behind the hills to the east.

"Dawn," I muttered.

"Aye. We call it *defs shavorik*. It means new day."

"You are Roama."

He laughed and slapped my good shoulder.

"Yes. Of course." The humor was a welcome relief from myself.

The forty or so carriages of the caravan were parked in squares within squares, and in the center sat an immense lodge and fire. What I assumed was the Priestess's caravan, protected from any would-be attackers, sat inside the innermost square, with the supply carts, like the one I was in. Some horses were tethered and fed from the carts. Another cart carried water. The caravan had converted to a small village on the edge of the desert.

Wafts of smoked meat and spiced tobacco drifted here and there and children ran around, chasing each other near the fire. A few of the women prepared breakfast, while an old man played some sort of instrument which lay across his lap. He smoked from a long metal pipe that extended from his mouth and lay on top of the instrument's body. His puffs synchronized with the notes.

A bead of sweat fell from my face.

"We get you fresh clothes, eh? Without blood." He smirked and nodded toward my injury. I looked down at the blood-soaked robe.

"My uniform and armor—"

"Ah, you may not be so welcome wearing that where we go, uh? Not good for travel in east." He smiled a cracked and worn smile. "Do not worry, soldier of the North, we will return your belongings. We are Roama, not desert thieves."

"Of course."

"But you have, uh, many questions, yes?"

"Many, yes."

He smiled. Something hid behind his jeweled eyes. There was a mark across the top of his left eye. And a bit of weariness lurked behind a mask of calmness.

"What is your name, traveler?" I said.

"I am Igvar," he said. "I am Councilman to the Priestess."

"Priestess," I muttered.

"And you stranger?"

My name.

I had not heard my name in so long that it was as foreign to me as my homeland. Thinking of my homeland, I thought of my wife and my daughter. Their faces. Their smiles. Their... shrouds. Then I remembered the road and... I could not remember either of their names.

A hand rested on my shoulder. Whose hand?

I could picture both of them so clearly. Much has happened since I saw their red locks and the green grass of my homeland or spoke their names.

"Are you alright, stranger?"

His question caught me off guard, whirling me back into this world.

"Yes, yes. I'm fine," I lied. I could not remember my name.

The man frowned.

I looked at my companion with hard eyes. "You... may call me by whatever name you would like to give me, for who I was no longer exists."

He smiled. "Well, my friend, you are known as *Shaviska* here." He chuckled.

"Shaviska?"

"Yes, Shaviska, eh, as you say, the Risen Dead!"

He started laughing and climbed out of the cart. He turned and wandered toward the food. Not feeling welcome suddenly, I stood in the cart and watched the fray of the gathering before me, brooding over their mysterious ways and odd sense of humor.

He stopped and turned back to me.

"Come," he said.

I slipped from the cart and landed awkwardly, collapsing to the ground as my knee surrendered under me, and I screamed at the sudden pain in my side. The laughter from a few children near me convinced me death and war may not be the most treacherous things I can face.

I struggled and stood with the aid of the cart as leverage. Igvar was back by my side, helping me.

"You should be more, um..."

"Careful."

"Yes, careful."

His motherly advice trailed off into thin air as I turned to walk out of the realm of coaches. Igvar grabbed my shoulder. I spun, instinct winning over logic, and I reached for a sword that was not there. He stared down at my empty hands. His look broke my wandering gaze. He was calm, and I lowered my hands.

"I have to leave."

"Leave?" He laughed. "We cross desert. Where will you go?"

I considered this. He placed a hand on my shoulder.

"Besides, my friend, Priestess Kristava wishes to speak with you. Will you oblige her?"

All air exited from me and I leaned against the cart. My head spun like a swarm of bats taking flight. Priestess Kristava, the mystic. Beliefs in sorcery did not exist in my land, but she was well-known and respected across all lands. Deep inside I felt compelled for the Priestess's counsel, though I knew not why.

"You do not understand?"

"I understand fine, Igvar." I wiped the sweat from my brow.

My stomach rumbled, reminding me of my mortal self.

"I must eat."

He smiled. "Yes, yes, of course. Come, eat with us this morning."

He threw his arm around me and walked me to an area near the fire, and we sat. A beautiful girl with strong green eyes approached carrying a tray. Her face was adorned with charms and strange drawings, and the sweet smell of incense on her clothing drifted on the still hot air. She pulled a plate with potatoes, eggs, and some form of spiced meat from the tray and placed it before me. She smiled, then disappeared into the throng of people. I found the Roama hospitable, and had known no different with them in my lands. But my distrust still lingered. I may be dead after my second bite. I have not trusted a soul, including my own, for much time. But trust had to be earned, so I ate. And ate. After my third plate, I resigned with the impression that I was amongst some of the most genuine people I may have the luxury of being around for a long time.

"Igvar, can you tell me something?" He stared at me as he took a bite. "You are traveling the Black road, so you have passed through the Northern Lands. Tell me, did you stop at the Great City?"

His eyes widened, and he put the food back on his plate.

"No. There is great darkness in the Northern Lands."

"Aye. We were attacked by... Just before the attack, all the Roama left. What do you know of that?"

"I know nothing, my friend. I apologize. We return from Gal Abed."

"Gal Abed?" I frowned. "But Gal Abed is on the Kinelot Road through the Southern Lands, how—"

"The priestess say we return through S'Ruh and Feren Ta in your lands, and take the Black Road. She, well, she is Priestess Kristava. She very persuasive."

He winked and smiled.

"Yes." More sorcery. My land reeked with it now. "Tell me about the darkness you speak of."

"The forests speak and move in shadow. The Great City..." He stared at his plate.

"Yes?"

"The Great City is... a dark shadow hangs over it. I cannot say more. I do not know words."

It was true. All that I had seen or lived through from Farwic Outpost and beyond was the work of sorcery. Work of this Queen of Shadows.

He then set his plate down, wiped his hands on the side of his pants, and sighed. He looked at me with his brown eyes set like stone.

"My friend, we travel Black Road through foothills below Zhalé Pass." His shoulders tightened and raised slightly. "We seen much there we cannot explain."

I set my plate down. I cleared my throat. Zhalé Pass... The haze of a memory hung in my mind like a phantom itch I did not understand. A memory shrouded in fog and ice.

"People question your sanity. Think you try to take life with dagger."

"Dagger?"

"Yes. We found you with dagger, in your side." He pointed to the wound.

I sighed. "A black dagger..." I whispered. Another wisp of a memory floated by and disappeared. My hand was shaking from the thought.

I looked at the mass of merchants before me around the fire and caught a few worried glimpses toward me, turning away, avoiding eye contact with the madman.

"The priestess," he said and laid a hand on my arm. "She will help."

Feeling unwelcome again, I stood. "It is not something I wish to discuss. I sense the memory is too dark."

I turned to walk back to the cart and found myself face to face with four soldiers from the Rogues Army.

So this was it. That sense of something not right. I stepped back and again reached to my side for the phantom sword. They also stepped back, then one held his hands up in front of him and spoke in his native tongue. Igvar came in a rush to my side.

"Please, my friend. They are hired to escort caravan."

His nervous laugh was not so reassuring. The soldier kept rambling at Igvar, waving his hands, eyebrows furrowed. Igvar returned with an onslaught of his own words and the soldier straightened himself, then walked away. The others followed. I heard a name, Var'Tiya El Friz. I breathed in quick breaths, my head spun. Igvar wiped the sweat from his brow, relieved. He turned to me.

"I, I have no words."

"Rogues Army."

"Aye. We pay them, escort caravan. They part of caravan, not enemy here."

Enemy. My eyes stung with sweat and I wiped them clear.

"Yes, of course. I know my friend."

Friend... A word as foreign to me as... home.

"I must lie down."

I stumbled to the cart, sat on the ground, and leaned back against the wheel of the cart. I rested my head, my soul, my thoughts, and my distrust.

Soon, the slumber took me hostage, and my head filled with a rage of disbelief and screams of colors. Colors of war. Flashes of images blinded me, first of my wife, then my daughter, the land, destroyed, fires. And of streets running with blood.

My wife turned to me and mouthed: "who are you?"

Then she screamed in horror and stopped as something silenced her and her blue eyes rolled back into her head and her copper hair turned into flowing locks of blood red and she vanished into dust. All around became dark and empty.

I fell into a black void...

I awoke with a start and winced.

A group of travelers surrounded me in a half circle. Confusion and despair wrote letters of suspicion across their faces. A tall one growled with disgust and left. Igvar was kneeling before me. I was sprawled in a heap, shadowed by the wagon. Half the day had passed during my restless slumber and the sun now cast long shadows.

I could not remember the last time I truly slept with a clear head.

Remembering them was only a nightmare. My emotions knotted. I should be fortunate I can still see their faces... if only I could remember the names. My name. Her name. My daughter. Faces without names, and me, the wretched *Shaviska,* a stranger even to myself.

I eased into a sitting position against the wheel of the cart, let out a deep breath, and wiped the sweat from my face. I stood and gathered my belongings. Igvar put his hand on my shoulder.

"She wishes to see you now," he said.

Chapter Fourteen

Kristava

IGVAR LED ME TO the carriage at the center. Its exterior was a grand display of intricate artwork, graceful decoration, and masterful skill. The craftsmanship was beyond anything conceivable in the Great City. From a distance, the beauty lay hidden, distracted by the other simple wooden carriages and carts. The illusion was spectacular. How much care and devotion went into the interior and how much worship and love they gave to the Priestess? The greatest power of this clan. And now I stood before that power. Their most cherished possession. Their... queen?

The word hung in the air before me, and a darkness covered my eyes like a veil. I blinked and everything cleared.

I stopped. Igvar looked at me questioningly. The thought of being in the presence of such a powerful entity froze every muscle.

Shaviska...

A voice. Her voice. I looked around and saw only Igvar. The rest of the clan seemed to have disappeared somewhere, somehow, and we were alone.

You may enter in peace, warrior. You need not fear...

"I fear no one," I lied. Igvar gripped my shoulder and hung his head as if in prayer.

You are welcome here.

A tear trickled from my eye and mingled with the sweat on my face. Igvar stepped up the few stairs to the door. I paused.

"Will I get my belongings after?"

He nodded and opened the carriage door.

I stepped the stairs and entered the carriage. Darkness greeted me and wrapped its black arms around me as the door closed behind me. The inside of the caravan was cool as the outside baked in the heat of the desert.

A small, faint light emerged before me, growing brighter every moment. A pale glow appeared behind a thin curtain. I pushed the curtain aside, and the candlelight flashed into several flames. Candles of various colors were lined up on a low table before the Priestess, where she sat cross-legged on an oversized purple pillow. The smell of the desert disappeared, replaced with the sweet smell of jasmine and sage. I sat before her on silk cushions.

The Priestess lifted her head, and bright yellow gold eyes, like the most precious of gems, reflected in the candlelight, and stabbed my weakened flesh like small darts.

"I know you..." I said.

A new world enveloped me.

A bright world. A white world. A blizzard of thought.

I remembered her...

I remember her red hair as it bounces playfully on her neck. She runs across the meadow and green fields. Her laughs echo through the valley of the dream. I chase her and she runs faster. I call after her and only a wisp of air escapes and disappears into the mist of a fading memory. I catch her and we tumble in the field, laughing and rolling like two children in a storybook world from a long, lost reverie. She is beautiful, my daughter. My wife looks on from a small knoll where she sits. Her auburn hair flits up in a warm breeze, and her green eyes cut through the vision, and through me, as a streak of blackness severs the dream and the terror bleeds through.

The flash and clash of steel, the setting of torches, the crackling of fires. The village ablaze. Laughter morphs into screams. Dying screams. Torment. The black turns to orange as the fires swell and the color filters into an intense white hot, and then becomes cold as ice.

A blizzard.

The dead heaped in a pile. A distant place with no flame and no heat. We freeze to death while others burn, and I watch the countryside melt before my eyes as the swarm of a nameless, unforgiving force takes hold, and a face appears... a woman's face... with dark green eyes... like emeralds...

A cold white light flashed across the horizon and turned the day black, and the smell of candles and incense filled my senses, and the chittering of light charms echoed in front of me.

A vision took shape, tilted, awkward. I was lying on soft pillows, and dancing lights and sparkles drifted across the room. I sat up.

Five faint glimmers came into focus before me. I remembered where I was. The Priestess stared at me through the wall of green silk as it touched my bare flesh, and she smiled.

She wore clothes of gossamer and silk of greens and blues. Beads dangled over her golden eyes and half covered her darkened flesh. Her blondish hair was braided and wrapped into a snake's coil. Large round earrings dangled from her right ear, and diamonds studded the left all along the edge. She was mummified in jewelry. Her long and aged fingers bore the weight of many large rings topped with an array of colored gems.

She outstretched her arms to me and turned her palms up. Tattooed on the palms were symbols of an ancient mystic origin. Her left arm appeared to shake uncontrollably, causing wristlets to jangle with a transcendent and hypnotic rhythm. Her eyes rolled and her head tilted back. She drew in a long, deep breath and exhaled slowly. She swayed her head back and forth. Her breathing became rhythmic with the motion, and she emitted a song.

The song danced in the air and hooked me with its pleasant barbs, pulling me in. My heartbeat slowed and my shoulders relaxed.

I succumbed to her bidding.

Blurred. Motion. Moving back and forth. Song. Wind chimes. Snake...

Shaviska krote con del trenzka sulara bel zen'tcha.

The sweet, rhythmic voice echoed in my head and loosened my spirit from my body.

Shaviska krote con del trenzka sulara bel zen'tcha sondalla!

Silver symbols etched in the air then rolled listlessly along before me, behind me, and all around, and I followed the trail of symbols with clear vision into a dark chamber of stone...

And there she was. Glorious in all her beauty. Faultless in her smile. Brilliant in her gaze. She was my torch to shatter the darkness. Her red hair flamed wildly in the wind atop a lush green hillside, the mountains her backdrop, the land her canvas, and she was the subject for all to look upon in wonderment. She wore a thin white dress that streamed out over the hillside, extending its arms to all who would embrace her with a smile. My wife. My beloved. My loss.

She looked at me and beckoned me closer to her. A fleeting moment passed for seasons, like falling leaves on the wind. I returned the smile, thankful, blessed to be within her presence, one who was in control of all that surrounded her. She was my dream. She was my everything. She gave me her heart, mind, and soul.

And I failed her.

I gave her only death.

She was my death. My solitude. My failure. My prison. Her smile turned to a frown as if recognizing my wispy thoughts. I walked toward her embrace, her arms wide open before me, ever beckoning one she could not hold. I reached her and her warm body radiated in the cool wind. I stepped into her open arms and fell through her, down into darkness, down through valleys of green, through cities, through wars, through snow and ice, through blood and vengeance, and into the black abyss. Only death could embrace her now.

My breathing slowed to a funeral march. The echo of one final teardrop rang out as it hit the floor of a stone chamber.

I crumbled beneath the weight of my sorrow and fell to the floor in a heap of desolation.

I became fetal. An infant of regret. A child of damnation. A wretched, hopeless man who failed his wife, his daughter, and his country. Names ripped from my memory, tearing through flesh and bone to escape into the eternal space that lies without.

What was her name?

I sobbed. I shook. I fragmented. I was a prisoner of myself. With death before me, I welcomed it with open arms and quiet solitude at the escape it would provide me from this mortal world.

And then she appeared again, her face next to mine, and she whispered in my ear.

"Rini."

I leaned back and her face and eyes melted, transformed, and a soldier, a northern soldier, kneeled before me with a broken sword protruding from his neck. His sword, held by my hand. He shouted, and nothing came out save for the blood from his wound. He pointed at me and again shouted. Blood gurgled and spattered from his throat. I knew him. I watched in horror as he fell to pieces and reshaped into another man, a sickly thin, frail man who walked to me in a strange discordant way as if escorted, assisted, by an invisible force, and he looked into my eyes and said "Soltari" and disappeared as vapor does on the wind and in the darkness five lights emerged and flickered and flashed.

I opened my eyes.

I was again lying on the floor of the Priestess' carriage. My face burned, and my head throbbed, beckoning for a release. A trickle of blood escaped my nose.

"Soltari... my name."

"A gift for you, Rini Soltari." I stared at her.

"Rini."

Her gaze dropped to her candles. The flames had died down and only three remained burning.

"Your mind is a mangled torrent ever crashing on unyielding rocks. You live in a web of despair, my child, waiting to be eaten by the spider who would so gladly take your life so that it may live."

I laid there, dormant. My arms wrapped around my aching legs. Thoughtless. Emotionless. A slab of meat waiting for a butcher.

"You would welcome the spider, I see. You wait for the spider to sink her fangs into your flesh and release her poison. But, I am afraid, my Shaviska, this will not release you from your world into the one you believe you will enter."

I uncurled my legs and sat up. I cleared my throat.

"You speak in riddles, Priestess, but I do not see your lips move. You say much, but your eyes say little. You proclaim me to be self-served and sorrowful, a drought in need of rain, a crop in need of culture. I would welcome death, Priestess. I would welcome the blissful smiting of my flesh so my soul may be freed and return to my loved ones, head bowed for forgiveness. What use does anyone have for a wretched soul such as I?"

A smile dawned on her lips, and the sun rose in her eyes. And once again she spoke, doll-like, whispering her words to me along the wind.

"You are a great warrior who now thrives on the nourishment self-pity and doubt provide. This is the food for the starving only to leave you still hungry. But you are still a great warrior."

A shell of a warrior, I thought.

"I knew your father, Commander Soltari." My breath hitched, then relaxed.

"Of course. My father traveled much as an envoy."

"We have also met, with your father." The well of sorrow once again took hold, and a tear escaped, then another. "I was sorry to hear of his death."

"Murder." The sorrow gave way to anger. "At the hands of the Rogues Army."

"Yes. The reavers. Tell me, young Soltari, did you think it odd the hands of the Rogues Army would commit a heinous act so far from the Eastern Lands?"

I thought of this often. He was murdered on the Kinelot Road at the western edge of the Southern Lands, far away from the Eastern Lands.

"It is not so odd when the Roama hire Rogues Army to escort caravans, and those same caravans travel the Kinelot road."

She nodded, then reached out and put her hand above the three candles, circling over them like a bird of prey. The flames grew more intense and brighter until they glowed with a white flame so brilliant that I shielded my eyes from their infernal fury.

"I wish," I said, "to continue my travels to the next town. Alone."

Her eyes met mine in the dim glow of candlelight. "Such as it is Shaviska. You are not my prisoner. Only your own. Nor do you belong to us. You are a nomad now, in search of reason and purpose, and an answer you may never have. You wish, Shaviska, for the impossible. You wish for the return of your wife and daughter." She rested her hands in her lap. "You are not yet aware of your destiny and the things which give you purpose. I have hope for you, great warrior, despite your recent... dark past."

I shuddered as a cold chill wind passed through my body.

"You may travel to the edge of this world, and may never find that which you seek. Death is not your answer, Shaviska."

"I do not fear death."

"Of course. You are the risen dead! For it has now been proclaimed, death cannot free your soul, or you would be dead. Now sit before me, my child. Let me embrace you with thought. Let me warm your flesh with food and wine, and ease your pain, if only for a fleeting moment."

I knew if I stayed, my body would succumb to more nightmares. How many times did I have to see their dead bodies before the eternal torment from the afterworld was satisfied?

"I will —"

"My Shaviska, I only offer my help so you may reconcile your guilt."

She motioned with her hands, and the door of her silk domain opened. A tauntingly beautiful young maiden walked between the curtains with a tray of meat, cheese, and wine. A curtain of black hair shrouded her face, and she wore a smock of green and blue silk. Her bare feet floated across the handmade rugs and carried her across the room.

She placed the tray on the table next to the candles, bowed before the Priestess, and left, stepping backward, foot to foot, to complete her brief journey. Graceful and courteous, never looking at her sovereign leader. Only here to serve, and serve well she did. As she left, she looked at me from behind her long dark hair and I felt a tug at my soul for a brief instant, and then she was gone like a shadow in the darkness and my soul righted itself.

"Our blood runs dark and quiet, always moving from one place, but with a purpose. Not unlike yourself, Shaviska. Your blood is a restless child seeking nourishment, and despair darkens the color."

She reached for wine, meat and cheese, and ate with me. She seemed to welcome the nourishment the food brought and almost reveled in its elegant trance. She sipped the wine slow and delicate. She appeared younger than she was when I first saw her. How playful she was, hiding behind a curtain of beads and braided hair.

"Can you help me remember—"

"Their names? No. Only time will reveal them. And their purpose."

She set her wine cup down. She closed her eyes and raised her arms. Then with her left arm shaking, jingling, she drew symbols in the air, and they appeared before me as symbols of orange light and purple. I knew not what the symbols were. She finished, then swiped across them with her right hand, and they disappeared. She rested her hands on her lap and opened her eyes. I sat dumbfounded.

She raised her wine cup.

"Your journey is long, Shaviska, and has only yet begun."

She sipped from the cup, then set it down carefully.

"There is a tender rage that lives within you. It is not my place to tell you how your journey will end. You will know when you find that which you seek. What it is you seek, Commander, that is the question." Her voice trailed into the silence.

The candles dimmed as she finished, and the room fell silent and dark.

The door to the caravan opened.

CHAPTER FIFTEEN

Night Bird

I ROSE AND MADE my way to the door. I walked down the wooden steps and into the moonlight. Outside, Igvar waited for me. He handed me my pack.

"Inside is clothing, belongings. Keep in pack for now, yes?"

I looked inside. I pulled out the pouch, opened it, and saw the lotus petals and the piece of parchment. I drew the strings closed and put it in my pack.

He handed me a new robe. "Change into this. We will toss other in fire."

I changed. The new robe felt good, refreshing. He smirked, then handed me my long sword in its sheath and belt. I took it, strapped the belt around me, and felt a bit at home with the sword at my side.

"Thank you."

He acknowledged with tilt of his head, then held out a black dagger, black as a shadow. I stared at it for a moment. Voices echoed and swirled in my mind. A man screamed, "You have failed us..." as blood spilled from him. "Murderer!" he shrieked. A Lieutenant's clasp lay in a pool of blood. I shut my eyes.

"You may keep the dagger, Igvar. It is not mine."

He smiled, relieved, then his face turned grim.

"And this? Is it yours?"

He reached over to the side of the Priestess's carriage and pulled out a short sword. My breath caught in a hitch, a gasp. My sword, with its gilded black hilt and my family crest. The circle of black onyx still mounted in the base of the pommel.

"It is mine. Was it not—?"

"No," he said. His face was grim. "It was found in foothills."

"Foothills..." A vague and horrifying memory tore at my. mind but was shrouded in darkness save for the face of the screaming soldier. I cleared my throat. "Thank you, Igvar. If it was lost, it is probably best if it had stayed lost. For now, I carry it as a burden, a grim reminder of myself. My... true self."

"Fear not, my friend. I am not here to judge your pain." I sighed and took the sword from him, then swiped a tear away.

I slid the sword into the belt and picked up my pack.

He reached out and put a reassuring hand on my shoulder.

"The Priestess requests your company until we reach Bin El Omen. Come. Join us at the fire."

Bin El Omen. The capital city of the Eastern Lands. The trip would take me even further from my home. My return to the Great City was becoming more distant. I lacked the energy to argue or begin a long journey at night to a destination now unknown to me, and without a horse.

Seated around the small blaze were the men of the clan. They conversed joyfully. Some held pipes whose smoke smelled like clove, others drank jasmine tea. An older man offered me a cup of the steaming liquid. I accepted it and seated my bones next to the warmth of the fire.

Their conversation was spirited. Words rolled off their tongues with a rhythmic speed and a cadence that mimicked heartbeats and music. Although I was welcome in their company, I sat as a spirit, a ghost of a man and country. I felt at rest, complete, and at peace with my surroundings. But accepting the joy and laughter and camaraderie grated at my being while my homeland burned and sat cast in shadow. The memory of my family ached in my heart and compelled me to run, into the darkness, into the desert, and succumb to the land, swallowed by the abyss. Laughter crumbled around me, and I smiled while tears leaked down my beaten face.

The cool night breeze danced around us. Wafts of aromatic tea and scented tobacco and wood fire penetrated my senses. I feared the night's slumber and the nightmares it would bring. For now, with my inside screaming, I sat in cadence with the people. Like them, I was now a wandering entity of this world. For now, I was part of something. In the deep recesses of my mortal mind sat the inevitable thought of soon being alone again, wandering these lands, searching for repentance, or death, as I sat on the cusp of eternity.

I drank another cup of the sweet tea. They offered a long pipe wrapped with colored leather strands and beads. The bowl was smoldering with clove tobacco. I welcomed both. And for a moment, I no longer feared the night. But night slowly crawled into my being and cast its long shadow in my heart.

I had to leave.

I excused myself and took refuge outside the camp to wait for the first light of dawn. I found an alcove of rock outside the confines of the camp and nestled my aching body inside the shelter, but found little comfort. Then the shrill of singing surrounded me. Chirping. Sing-song. I stepped from the alcove, and there, perched on top of the rock, was a yellow and brown bird, a desert night bird.

It glanced at me, blinked, and chirped. I smiled. It blinked again, then took flight and disappeared into the blackness of the night. I sighed, my heart heavy but touched by the birdsong. I returned to the alcove and sat against the rock wall staring out into the desert night. My head lulled, and the night claimed me as I fell into the world of sleep. Flashes of light, red and menacing, swelled through my mind, brighter and brighter the light became, changing from red to a white almost unimaginable, so bright, so intense, forcing me to shield my eyes lest I go blind.

Then a crack echoed in the light. The sound of a sword breaking. I stood over a man, a northern soldier somewhere in the foothills.

A name screamed at me. *Estarenza*!

I stood over him. His broken sword lay in front of him. Blood and entrails leaked from a gash across his stomach and he was on his knees, clutching himself with both hands over the gaping wound.

He screamed at me.

"You are a madman! Look what you have done! You," he coughed and choked and offal oozed between his blood-soaked hands. "You have failed... us..." he said. He wept. "My father... trusted you. Saved..." He coughed and a bloody froth filled his mouth. "your father—"

I picked up the broken sword, put the jagged point of it to his neck, and lifted his chin.

He smiled and his flesh paled.

"You cannot hurt me now. You, you are the damned, for all time—"

A sharp pain shot from my side as I thrust the tip of the sword into his neck, choking out his last words. He sputtered, then collapsed in a heap upon the dusty earth. His eyes were wide, staring back at my cruel visage. His Lieutenant clasp lay next to him in a pool of his blood. I looked down at my side and saw a black dagger protruding from it. Death surrounded me. I was the last. I was the harvester of death.

I killed them all...

A white-hot flash came, and I covered my eyes to no avail. A deafening roar filled the air like metal scraped across stone, continuous, unending. A scream penetrated the nightmare. Then with a loud crack—my eyes opened.

I was shaking, frozen by the crisp, early dawn air as a hard rain fell outside the alcove. A rumble of thunder rolled across the darkened sky.

The grove of rock sheltered me from the rain, but not from myself.

"Estarenza?" I sat up, shivering. I looked at my hands, my scarred hands. "I... why?"

It went beyond madness. And fear. And the merchants knew. All of them. I glanced at my short sword leaning against the rock, and I knew where it was found, and my heart sank into grief. I could see it now, the blood, the bodies of my men, the foothills...

The static of the rain set my mood. It came down in droves, soaking the dry land. The clouds were dispiriting and melancholy, floating amongst themselves, crying their pain upon the land and leaving.

All were prisoners of the sky now.

I sat for half of the day reflecting on my time with the Priestess, and Estarenza's death, his murder by my hands, before a glimmer of movement among the caravan caught my eye.

An older man appeared from behind a carriage. He stood in the rain, sheltering himself with a large piece of cloth over his head. He looked through the rain and the mist that had formed and saw me.

He dropped low and ran toward my rocky home. Halfway along, he slipped on a muddy slope and slid down the hillside. Regaining himself, he clutched and crawled up the slick side, clinging to each rock and plant for stability. He made his way to me and took refuge in my sanctuary.

He sat next to me and shook the water from himself. He laughed, looked at me nervously, and tried to catch his breath. After struggling with this for several moments, he finally regained his composure and looked at me.

"Shaviska, kelta hosh winto?" he asked in his foreign tongue. He could see that I did not understand and searched for the words. "Shaviska, uh, eat? Yes?"

I shook my head.

He tugged at my sleeve, motioning me from my dry quarters. The rain continued its deluge. I pulled away from him, and again, shook my head. It was pointless to attempt any relevant conversation with him. My words would fall upon silent ears.

He sighed. "Shaviska, you, uh, like, uh, food to eat? I make." He smiled. My stomach tightened from hunger, and I did not want to insult him by turning down his offer again.

I patted him on his chest and motioned for him to sit. I had no desire to go into the rain, nor did I have the desire to rise from my shelter, regardless of the hunger.

The man sat back against the wall and relaxed. He drifted off to sleep, caught himself, and looked over at me with a grin. His gray beard took a shape of its own on his worn and entrenched face. His eyes reflected an elderly wisdom.

The man moved to the edge of the opening. He folded his legs under him and stared at me for a moment. I wondered what he was thinking, what he was considering. I forced another grin with the hopes of putting him at ease.

The rain thinned, and the man stood outside and motioned me to follow. We made a mad dash across the road and up the slope toward the carriages. The sides of the lodge were dropped, creating a large tent around the fire circle. Smoke billowed out the top. The smell of cooked meat was in the air.

The man dragged me toward the tent and opened a flap so I could enter unhindered. Seated around the fire, eating, cooking fresh meat, and parting bread, was nearly the entire clan. All, save for the Priestess.

The smells were exciting. So many smells, from spice to perfume to incense. It sent my senses reeling for cover as they tried in vain to part each smell out for recognition. Igvar sat on the opposite side of the fire. Next to him was a spot where I could sit and enjoy his company.

I skirted around the others to the pillow next to Igvar and sat.

"Igvar, my friend," I said. He put his hand on my shoulder.

"Good to see you. I feared you had left us on some fool's errand back to your homeland." I nodded.

"The thought entered my mind."

"I am sorry for you, my friend. I cannot imagine your pain. When we traveled past the Great City, it was unbearable. We did not camp for two days. Some here still quiver in their sleep from it."

I stared at the dry, desert floor of the lodge, listening to his words, and wondered what he was not telling me. What he thought he was saving me from.

"The forest was... alive. The mists—"

"Spoke."

"Yes. You know?"

"Aye."

I told him about our experience along the White River.

"We too lost a few to the madness."

I could no longer remember their faces, only the twisted remnants of the men they once were. Still... there was more to his words.

"You are safe here, Commander." Safe. The word was unrecognizable.

"I fear none of us are truly safe with what lingers over my home." I pushed the conversation, hoping for some insight. He sipped his tea.

"She knows, doesn't she?" He appeared shocked, then regretful. "She knows more about what is behind the shadow over my land."

He looked at me, his dark eyes solemn, and nodded.

A woman passed a plate of food around to me. A cup of wine faithfully followed. I stared at the food, then took a bite of the meat. The senses in my mouth overloaded. The flavor of the cooked meat became a riot of bliss as I savored every bite. I followed it with bread and sweet wine and paused. The old man stood on the other side of the fire. He laughed, seeing the joy on my face, then touched his fingers to his lips, telling me to eat more. I nodded.

"But you cannot tell me, Igvar?"

He hung his head.

"I cannot bear to tell you, my friend. There is difference." He lifted his head, and the wet streak of a lost tear marked his dusty, dark face.

The fire snapped the bones of the kindling and threw up sparks of joy as it consumed the wood. Its orangish shadow danced a line between red and yellow, and white hot blues.

"Will she tell me, Igvar? Can she?"

"I, I do not know."

The tent drew in around me, closer and closer.

"Igvar, I am grateful for all the Roama have done for me. I would surely be dead had you not found me. But understand, I am doubtful I would have accepted your help if I—"

"I understand Shaviska."

"I wish to stay in the alcove again this night."

Igvar nodded and smiled a bit.

"It is for the best." He rested a hand on my shoulder. "We leave in the morning."

I left the warm shelter of the Roama lodge and walked to the alcove. Familiar chirps and singsongs of the yellow night bird danced around me. It stood on a pillar of rock outside my shelter, chirped at my presence, then fluttered away. I entered my small home with a full belly and quickly fell into the embrace of sleep.

Chapter Sixteen

Kaksoset Canyon

I WOKE TO THE distant sound of chattering, shouts, and jangles of horse tack. The Roama were breaking camp. The pack horses were eager to get moving, pawing at the ground. I strapped my swords to my side, gathered my belongings, and joined the caravan. Igvar saw me approach and raised his hand in greeting. He was standing near the Priestess's caravan.

"You will join us then?"

"Aye," I said. "I will stay until we reach Bin El Omen, where I can get provisions and a horse." I looked around. "And my bearing."

"We are fortunate you travel with us, warrior."

I noted a touch of worry behind his smile. He turned and disappeared behind the Priestess's carriage.

I assisted around the encampment the best I could with the injury to my arm. The Roama draped the horses with leather across their backs and sides, as if preparing for battle. I have never seen this upon the horses of the Roama. The leather was smooth and well crafted, with intricate details and eastern lettering. The lead horses wore face coverings made from metal.

Were we heading into hostile lands?

When the caravan was ready, I returned to the empty cart as the caravan rolled out. Igvar rode next to it. His stallion was dark gray with black spots on the hindquarters, and a white star emblazoned its forehead.

"That is a fine horse, Igvar."

"Aye. Sumu is a fine horse. A stallion of royal blood."

The horse, seemingly understanding our words, raised its head slightly, as if proud of his ancestry. Its eyes glanced at me a moment, then back. The horse reminded me of Outo.

The sky above was blank and blue. My body swayed and rocked with the movement of the cart. The caravan moved through rugged foothills on the dirt road as it wound through the shrubs and rock. We crested a hill, and in the distance stood two tall pillars of rock at the edge of a canyon in the foothills. They stood like natural towers on each side of the canyon entrance.

"This is Kaksoset Canyon," said Igvar.

The two men driving the cart muttered and looked around. One reached down and the familiar sound of steel pulled from a scabbard came forth. A dull metal shield hung from his arm. I looked at the cart behind me and one of the two drivers was also bearing a sword and shield.

The sight was unsettling. I kneeled, held to the cart's side, and drew my short sword. The driver turned to me, remembered I was in his cart, and nodded.

"Tell me, Igvar, is there something I need to know?"

"Kaksoset Canyon, my friend. It is full of bandits now. The canyon walls, give good um, blessing, for bows."

"I see. And the Priestess?"

"They care not. They are desert dwellers. They do not live by any rules or customs of the lands, or people. Scavengers."

"Does every caravan pass through the canyon?" He shook his head.

"No, only those from the Black Road."

We passed between the towers and entered the canyon. All sound stopped save for the crunch of rocks under the burdened carts, the squeaks and moans from the carriages echoing along the walls, and the trickle of a stream that ran through.

The red rock on both sides of the caravan stood like earthen book ends. The sunlight drifted across the walls of the canyon. We rode in shadows. The man next to the driver looked up and around, on careful watch. He was nervous. I had not seen this sort of fear in the Roama's eyes.

"I remember this canyon, but I don't remember fearing bandits."

"Aye." He looked at me. "Do you remember desert fires?"

"I do." He shrugged.

"They watch us cross. They scavenge, and are hungry. Caravan full of food. Fight for food and gold. Thieves, yes."

Our cart was near the rear of the caravan carrying supplies. The Rogues Army soldiers carefully guarded the Priestess's carriage, which rode in the center of the caravan, but was just as exposed as the rest.

A scream.

The scream came from the front of the caravan, and a rain of arrows started pelting the sides and roofs of the wagons around us. Igvar spurred his gray horse ahead to the front. We did not stop. The caravan quickened as a series of calls and a tang of whip cracks echoed through the chambers of the red rock. The arrows stuck into the leather draped on the horses.

I hunched down in the cart behind burlap sacks of grain and sheathed my sword to grasp the side of the cart. We lurched like we hit a large rock. Soon, the rain of arrows stopped, and I looked up. Our pace had quickened more. The driver sat hunched over the footrest, strangled by the reins when he fell dead, his body decorated with arrows. The man next to him was gone.

I rose to my feet, climbed into the seat, cut loose the driver, and grabbed the reins. His body fell and disappeared into the dust behind me. The dust kicked up by the carriage in front of me clouded my vision, but I could make out the gold and silver decorations, and the clanging of lanterns banging against the side gave me some sense of direction and proximity.

Then the dust cleared.

The horses screamed and tried to turn. We crashed into the back of the carriage, which had fallen to its side, sending my cart and all the supplies into a slide and a roll. The impact threw me from the cart, and I landed just below a cliffside. The cart snapped apart, and the horses broke free, disappearing into the chaos ahead.

I stood, wobbled, gained my balance, and ran to the toppled carriage for cover. I checked the ridge, then ran toward the front of the caravan, dodging panicked horses, bodies, and more arrows. All the carriages were stopped, and most had suffered the same fate as mine.

I ran to the Priestess's carriage. I was behind a group of makeshift swordsmen ready for battle. Before them stood a band of masked brigands, swords drawn. They charged us. We held our ground.

Swords clashed, and the ringing sound of steel echoed through the canyon. Men were slashed and hacked. Bodies fell to the ground. I dodged a crushing blow by a bandit who towered over me. I pulled my sword back for a death blow as two horses emerged from the dust in a scared panic and trampled the man to the ground.

I stepped back.

I saw a bandit climb onto the Priestess' caravan and open the door. I charged him, slashing two down in my path, loosing an arm, and slicing a throat. The chaos energized me. The bandit disappeared inside. I ran up the stairs after him and into the blinding darkness. I shut the door. I stepped against the side of the caravan. At the far end, a candle lit and cast a faint glow behind the silk, and an outline appeared as the light reflected on the robes of the bandit.

Estarenza's face appeared out of the darkness, his screaming dead face. A chill burst through me. I caught a glint of steel and I thrust my sword, finding flesh. There was a groan, and the darkness consumed the horrific vision of Estarenza. I pushed the body with my foot, and my sword lightened, and the bandit fell to the floor.

The door burst open, bathing us in sunlight. The man lay on the floor holding his side, his hands soaked in blood. His eyes were wide with fear as he stared at the dark shadow which appeared in the doorway. I stepped aside. The man on the floor grimaced under the pain. The shadow knelt before him, muttered something, then slid a dagger into the man's throat. I turned away toward the candle, now extinguished, then stepped out of the caravan.

Roama swordsmen stood on top of carriages, cheering and yelling at the bandits who made a feeble escape to the rear. I sheathed my sword.

To my left stood Var'Tiya El Friz. He looked me over and nodded. He turned and walked to the line of caravans. Standing in the doorway of the Priestess's caravan was a Rogues Army soldier holding a bloody dagger. He wiped the blood-soaked silver blade with a cloth, then stuck the dagger in his belt. He called over some Roama men, then stepped down. The two men bided their eyes as they entered. A moment later, they dragged the body from the caravan and laid it next to the other dead. A thin red line of blood traced the path in the dry dirt. The Rogues Army soldier looked at me and left. There was no expression of contempt on his face. I heaved a heavy sigh and contemplated all that had happened as the fog of the battle took hold.

My hands were shaking. The last I drew my blade was in the foothills, and my taste for bloodlust waned and was now poisoned by visions of a madman's undoing.

The fight was quick, furious, and bloody. The ragged swordsman let out a hearty battle cry and sang a chant, a prayer for the fallen comrades as the dust soaked up the remains of the life spilled.

I walked along the dismantled line of the caravans. A group of Roama hovered over a man lying face down on the ground. They cleared as I approached and I gasped. Lying there was Igvar with four arrows protruding from his neck and chest. I knelt beside him and took his hand and touched it to my forehead.

"Thank you, Igvar, for being my... friend." I let his hand drop and stood. Death followed me like a hawk on its prey. It surrounded me. It was all I knew and all I would ever know.

I walked toward the one place I would find comfort amongst the traveling merchants: the broken cart.

When I approached the Priestess's caravan, she was standing beside it. She wore a silken veil of green. A small gaggle of women surrounded her, all veiled behind masks of blue silk. The charms from her jeweled headdress blinked in the sunlight.

"You have fought bravely," she said with whispers that caressed the air. "For this, we are in your debt, and you, Shaviska, Commander Soltari, and he who remains nameless, you shall know life and purpose again."

Var'Tiya El Friz approached and handed me a blue sash. He bowed his head slightly to me.

"I saw you. You were grinning. You enjoy the fight. And you fight honorably. You are no Saka'Ali. Fare thee well, Shaviska."

Only the militants who fought in the border skirmishes called me or knew me as Saka'Ali. Or so I thought. I bowed my head slightly.

"The honor is mine, Var'Tiya El Friz."

A Roama woman approached and took the Priestess by the hand. She turned and walked away with the Priestess, and her escorts.

Var'Tiya El Friz smiled, turned, and followed.

Chapter Seventeen
Bin El Omen

THE SUN CARESSED THE sky as we pieced the caravan back together, lined up, and moved out of the canyon toward Bin El Omen for repairs and supplies. I was officially a vagabond, a man without a home. A rogue. A northerner in the Eastern lands, fighting alongside the Rogues Army, now welcomed with smiles by the people of Bin El Omen as we passed under the massive golden city gates.

Tall sandstone towers stood on each side and housed guards. From the top, long flags of yellow and white drifted in the breeze. The gates were wide and welcoming.

It was just before nightfall. I rode in the cart that was my home for the last four or five days with Igvar, who lay wrapped, along with five others, one a child. The mother sat next to her child's body, weeping. And I thought of my daughter. Her limp, frail body in my arms as I carried her into her home. My heart filled with grief. A lifetime ago.

The caravan entered a massive, bustling bazaar full of Roama caravans and shops. People bowed or kneeled as the Priestess's caravan passed them. The night sky was lit by many torches around the market and throughout the city.

The cart stopped. I stared at Igvar's body. He was home now. The cacophony of banter, caravans, people, horses, and other animals carried a rhythm and life of its own. Worn from despair, the woman slept next to me, her head resting on the body of her child. I gathered my things and climbed from the cart.

The old man who sat with me in the alcove and another man approached me. The old man spoke.

"He says that he is sorry to hear of Igvar's death," the younger man said. "He would like to pay his respects."

"Certainly he does not need my permission for that."

"No, but it is a private matter. He will pay his respects to all the dead here, which includes his granddaughter."

"Tell him, I understand. Completely." I put my hand on the old man's shoulder and bowed.

"I am sorry for your loss." The younger man mumbled some words that I assumed were what I said. The old man nodded, then climbed into the cart unaided.

"He has asked me to show you around Bin El Omen in the morn, as a guest, and to help you find your way."

"I look forward to it."

The caravans were parked and the main fire was aglow. I spent my last evening with the merchants, listening to somber music and dim chatter. I found a spot to rest.

"Sir?"

The young man stood over me. The sun hid behind the merchant wagons. It was early. I stood, then brushed myself off and collected my pack.

"What is your name?"

"Sayid."

"Then Sayid, please, show me the way."

"Aye, first, the Priestess has asked to speak with you."

An unnerving feeling washed over me. I followed the young man to the front of the caravan where a circle of twelve wagons sat parked around the Priestess's. He led me to the door and rapped once.

Shaviska...

The voice caressed me like a soft breeze. The young man bowed and turned his head from the caravan. I stepped up and entered.

She sat behind the veil, five candles in front of her. Sunlight streamed in behind her from a small hatch in the ceiling. Pinpoints of sunlight glinted through from holes in the sides of the caravan, presumably from our fight in Kaksoset Canyon.

"Commander, please, sit." She motioned to a large pillow. "This is where we part, yes?"

"Aye. I must make my way back to the Great City."

"What do you expect to find there?" I felt a loss for words for a moment, then breathed in.

"I'm not sure. I—"

"Returning to the Great City is not part of your journey, Commander. Not yet."

"I feel you know more than you are telling me, Priestess."

"Do you trust your instincts?"

"You know who this Queen of Shadows is?"

"I only know of her," she said with a voice smooth, but stern, as if the very thought of this Queen of Shadows violated some principle she bound to. "The answers will reveal themselves in time and are unimportant now."

She waved her hand across the candles, and the two on each end went out, lighting her face in a grim shadow.

"To be successful in your journey, fair warrior, you must reconcile what is inside you, inside your heart." The middle candle flickered brighter than the others, then went out. "Seek a man named Betir, for he alone holds the answer to a question long carried in your heart."

"Betir? An easterner." A candle flickered. "And where will I find this... Betir?"

"You will find him where the yellow night bird sings." Riddles. More riddles. I no longer had the stomach for it.

"And what is the question he will answer, Priestess?"

She sat up straight and clapped her hands twice. The candles died, and the door opened. From the darkness, her voice whispered. "Your bravery will not go unrewarded fair wanderer."

"Thank you, Priestess Kristava." I stood and exited the caravan. The young man shut the door behind me.

"Come, I will show you the great capital of the Eastern Lands." I slung my pack on my shoulder, lost in thought. Betir. Yellow bird. The young man handed me a small purse and my thoughts disappeared.

"What is this?" He shrugged. I opened the purse, and inside was a fair amount of coin. I looked at the young man. "I cannot accept this."

"It is not mine to take back." He motioned with his head at the Priestess' caravan.

"Of course." Rewarded, like a paid mercenary. Like the Rogues Army escorts. I closed the purse and put it in my pack. "Well then, friend Sayid, now you may show me the way."

We walked along sandstone cobble roads until they widened at the city center into an open area crowded with people. In the center was a large golden fountain made from marble and some other unrecognizable materials. Surrounding it was a garden full of flowers in full bloom, flowers of red, yellows, and blues. The water from the fountain flowed through the gardens and along small aqueducts to smaller fountains where children played. Beyond this large city center was the domed palace, the home of their Lord, or Herra. It was at least four times larger than our domed building in the Great City. From each of the four corners sprouted tall, thin spires. The architecture was identical to our Great Hall, and I wept inside for home.

"This is the palace of Herra Ennu Staya Al Jalali," he said, following it with a phrase in his tongue, a solemn bow, and a motion of his hand.

"What was that you said at the end?"

"Rau Hantu Oya means 'bringer of peace'. Some say Herra Al Jalali will be the one to announce the bringer of peace. He is a... how you say... hmm... maybe the word is..."

He turned unexpectedly to an old man on the street who wore traditional eastern garb of a long white robe and head wraps. They entered into an animated conversation. The Eastern man nodded, and I heard a familiar word, but the man's accent was heavy and the word indiscernible.

"He says the word is, um, prophet?" Sayid said.

"I have only heard this word in stories of fantasy."

"His father was Herra Rau Halak Sossa Al Jalali." Again, he mumbled a phrase and made a motion. "He is a direct descendent of the bringers of the dawn, or um, dawn breakers, something, don't know word. The line of the Eastern Star."

Religion. I've heard of such things, and know the Eastern lands are rife with it, as the Western lands are with their patron, Yoomala. I smiled. He seemed satisfied. As a traveling merchant, a Roama, the religion of the Eastern Lands would not interest him as they immersed themselves in their own brand of mysticism.

"You are religion?" He said. I didn't understand what he was asking at first, then I realized.

"No, we do not have religion as you know it. The way of the Northern Lands is the way of the sword."

He smiled. "Yes, of course." It wasn't a pleasant smile. He was placating me.

We moved on to the city center. There was a small crowd of men in a heated discussion. I recognized something of fear in their eyes.

"Those men, what are they saying?" The young man cleared his throat.

"They talk of the darkness." I stopped.

"The darkness?" The young man nodded and listened some more.

"They talk of lost time. They call it shadow time. The darkness that came from the south... um... a few ages ago." He wiped his brow. "What they talk about is old. I don't understand."

"They speak of the darkness of the northern sky, the darkness in the northern lands?" Sayid shrugged.

"There was a time when a darkness came through. There was split, in um, Rogues Army? A man, he claims to be Lord of the Rogues Army. He calls himself Herra A'avikon Ha'amu Al Friz."

"I know the name," I growled. "His son is A'avé El Friz and was promised something he has no claim to. These are the militant ones we battle against on our eastern border. They were the ones who attacked my city and homeland."

I spat on the ground and the young man's eyes went wide. I frowned, looked at the spittle, then at the young man.

"I apologize. I meant no disrespect."

"Meaning or no, that could get you arrested, my friend."

"Or course. Again, my apologies."

"This Rogues Army, you fight, yes? The faction... um... not sure of word."

"There is no name for them. Please." I gestured to the city center. I had no desire to discuss the dealings of the Rogues Army, or the faction from Ro Ista Pass. A new Lord. Any of it. It only kindled my desire to return and spill the blood of those responsible.

The aroma of sweet, spiced food from vendors filled the air in the city center. The young man led me to one, and he purchased two small plates of food full of savory meat, stained yellow and red from the spices, wrapped in a thin piece of bread. I remembered something similar in the bazaar outside the city gates, but not quite like this. The food filled my belly, raised my spirits, and touched my soul. And the previous, uncomfortable conversation from moments ago vanished in the day's haze.

We wandered from the city center and down a few side streets. We stopped at a crossroad, and he held out another pouch for me.

"This is for your stay here in Bin El Omen," he said.

He took my hand and placed the pouch in it. I could feel the weight of it. Gold coin. He pointed to a building across the street. It sat atop a hill and overlooked the city center of Bin El Omen.

"That is the Il Tatahti Inn. Priestess say journey begins there." He smiled, hiding behind the riddle. He pointed down the street. "Stable, yes. Priestess say there you will find horse and tack. Fare thee on your journey, Shaviska." He bowed, then mumbled something in his language. He looked at me. "Peace be with you."

"Of course. And with you," I said.

Sayid turned and left. I watched him walk down the street toward the stables, then he turned and disappeared from view. I suddenly felt an emptiness in my heart. A loneliness I had not experienced since I left my wife and daughter for the eastern borders.

I turned to the Inn. It was two stories, built from carved stone. Flags of the Eastern Lands, a yellow multi-faceted star on a white background, draped its front entrance. I crossed the street to the inn and entered.

Shadows cut the room as sunlight from the west filtered in through the high windows. Tables were arranged disproportionately, almost at random, and a few patrons sat amongst them. I found a table in a corner at the back of the room. The tavern was fair with the occasional banter and laughter. A small band played music in a far corner while two women dressed in silk and gold chains lined with charms danced near them.

A lady dressed in pleasant clothing, exposing her midriff, like the dancers, came to me. Her long, dark hair was pulled back and wrapped with blue and yellow beads and some sort of shimmering band. A small charm hung from her pierced navel. She spoke to me and pulled me from my trance, reminding me I was an outcast, a drifter.

"I'm sorry," I said in a hushed voice. "I do not understand."

Her green eyes lit and a small smile appeared. She turned slightly, and I could see strange dark markings on her neck, some sort of writing.

"You are traveler?"

"In a sense, yes." She frowned, and then her olive face went flush.

"I see. Well, traveler, how may I serve you?"

Her Eastern accent hung on every syllable, adding a rhythmic tone to the words. I told her I needed lodging for the night, and that food and wine would be fine.

"Welcome then, sir, to Bin El Omen, star of the Eastern Lands." Then she winked and turned away. I smirked and watched as she walked to the counter at the far end. Her hips swayed like a breeze under her dark green skirt. I noted the markings extended across her upper back. And on her lower back was a lotus with vines extending to the left and right.

My heart pounding in my chest. I reached into my pack. I removed the leather pouch and opened it. The fragrant petals lay at the bottom, atop the journal page. The smell took me back to a time of joy and a time of great sorrow. I drew the strings tight, closing off the memories, the smell, the vision, and sighed. I put the pouch in my pack.

A man at a table near me spoke, his tone on the verge of anger. I hadn't noticed the three men at the table before, as it was in shadow, but now, with the shifting sun, their appearance was unmistakable. Rogues Army. One was trying to explain something to the other in a heated discussion. The one in the middle put up his hand to silence his comrade, then shook his head, and the discussion became more heated. I considered moving but knew that would only draw attention to myself.

One soldier laughed at the other and said something I could only assume was an insult. The soldier was not smiling. Anger filled his partially bearded face. He slammed his fists on the table, jostling his drink over the edge of the cup.

The third one turned my way and caught my eye. He frowned. I looked around the room instead, breaking the glare. Their banter stopped and shifted to a whisper. A chair scooted on the wooden floor and all fell silent at their table.

A shadow appeared on my right. Then a female voice rang out. I glanced over. The lady stood between me and the man with a plate of food and a cup of wine.

"Sit down, Sooda," she said in the more common language. The man frowned, then smirked.

"I see. Bring a stranger food and drink before me?" I assumed he replied as he did, for my benefit, so that I understood every word and insult.

"Sooda," one man from the table called. He looked to be the leader of the other two. Sooda turned but kept his eyes on the lady, then glanced at me and grunted. He looked me over, and then something about me caught his eye, which gave him pause. He returned to his table. When he sat, he pointed my way and the other two glanced over. The man in the middle leaned back in his chair, shrugged, and they returned to their conversation.

The lady placed the food and drink on the table.

"Don't mind them," she said. "They're drunken fools."

"And Rogues Army," I said. She was a little surprised by the manner I spoke.

"Yes." She stood straight and brushed off her skirt. Gold wristlets clinked together as she did. "What is your name, traveler?"

Names.

"Igvar," I said. She frowned a bit, then smiled.

"Of course. Igvar. My name is Mia, and this is my Inn." She winked again and left. She was caught by one of the Rogues Army soldiers. He held her, and she resisted. He grinned, and the other two laughed. He said something, and she pushed him away, and he growled at her. He glanced my way and stopped. Mia turned too and gasped.

I realized I was standing, my hand on the hilt of my short sword. The man stepped back and faced me so I could see him clearly. His uniform bore the two blue swipes. An El Friz, a master swordsman. He grinned.

Then Mia began berating him in their language. She was in a full tirade now. The other two were laughing at this, and I sat down to my food. She stood her ground, and the man bowed to her, then offered what sounded like an apology, and sat.

She turned to me, then relaxed and left.

Tomorrow I would be out of this city and on the Black Road home.

I finished my food and wine and excused myself to my warm bed, awaiting me in the rooms above the tavern.

The quarters were small. A bed sat next to a window. In the corner sat a desk and a chair. I released my weapons and laid them on the floor beside the bed, my short sword beside my pillow. The sun had set and the cool desert air filled the room.

I undressed and, for the first time in what seemed like ages, laid my weary and worn body upon a soft mattress and covered myself with the stacks of blankets provided. Sleep came swiftly, like an ambush on my senses. And I dreamed of her.

A dream soon broken by shouts outside my window.

Chapter Eighteen

Tender Rage

I SAT UP AND peered out to the street below. A woman was being attacked by the Rogues Army soldiers I encountered earlier. One of them was on his knees, crying out. Her mouth was opened as if to scream, yet no sound came out. She was blindfolded and struggling in another's arms. The other man stood before her. He was wearing a veil to hide his face, like those of the dead we found near the grove of trees on our trek from Farwic Outpost.

I jumped from my bed and pulled on my robe. I grabbed my swords from their sheathes and ran down the stairs of the Inn and out to the alley. I set upon the back of the attacker holding the girl and with a clean stroke down his spine rendered him helpless. He fell to the ground, dead and twisted. The girl fell to the side of the road. The one who was crying out stopped, and struggled to his knees, then fell over, dead. Blood leaked from his eyes.

The third, the El Friz, stood there, towering over me. He tore off the veil and snarled, then drew his sword from an ornamented scabbard. He mumbled something like a curse, wiped spittle from his face, then raised his sword and held it in front and across his body. I stepped back and raised my long sword. I kept the other at my side.

He spoke to me.

I stared at him, then he looked at me oddly, and said something again. He saw the confusion on my face and grinned.

"Etta. Of course," he said. "I know you. Have seen you, earlier. You northerner who wear blue sash." He frowned then looked at his dead men, then back at me. "No matter," he said and spat at me.

He pounced, and I blocked his attack, then twisted his sword, and him, around. The smell of rank wine from his intoxicated breath filled the air around him, and he stumbled a bit. He wiped his face, then came at me again. I knocked his sword away, then ran him through with my short sword, piercing his heart. He looked down at the blood oozing from the wound, then at me as if emerging from his drunken stupor into a moment of clarity, realizing his fate.

"You... must... kill her," he said, motioning to the girl, his eyes wide as death came for him. "Shen al-kuryaaaa—"

He fell forward onto my blade, running himself through to the hilt. I caught him, then tilted my hand, and he slid off the sword to the ground.

Silence.

Silence broken by the low breaths coming from the blindfolded woman crouched in the street behind me. The bodies lay in three dead heaps. The words of the El Friz echoed in my thoughts.

"Kill her."

She cowered from fear and shock. Her black hair was in a tangle around her face and the blindfold. I reached down and grasped her arm. Her half-naked body shivered beneath her torn clothes as she stood. I removed the blindfold and bindings and stared into the prism of two dark emerald eyes, like emeralds on fire, and fell into a trance. She looked at the death around her, then grasped me and clung to me, helpless in her oblivion. I carried her to my room, weakened from the rush of events, and collapsed.

The sun sagged through the window. I awoke to the boy coming into the room with water and food. It was midday. She lay next to me still as stone. I went to rise and fell back to the bed lacking the energy to sit up. I managed to roll from the bed, crawl to the table, and drink a cup of water.

"Mia?" I whispered.

"Mia gone. Come back, um..." he held up two fingers.

"Two... days?"

The boy nodded. I slumped against the table. I managed to wave the boy off and he left. I blinked, trying to focus on my bloody sword lying on the floor across the room. I crawled back to the bed. She lay there, motionless, unaroused, save for a slight twitching in her legs. I fell to the floor and everything went black.

I opened my eyes to the pattering of bare feet on the floor. It was night or a dream. Two candles illuminated the room. She was dancing around, whirling, vibrant. A silhouetted shadow twirling in my mind. My thoughts ran astray as I tried to concentrate and find my bearings. My dreams were empty but even as I could not remember them, I lived in a darkened nightmare. She saw me watching her as I lay on the floor and I felt a slight tug at my senses. I coughed and sputtered. Something warm crawled from my nose and I raised my hand and touched it. I smear of blood was on my fingers. I rolled to my hands and knees and blood dripped to the floor. I found the strength to grab the bedside and pull myself in before collapsing, eyes open, unable to sleep...

I watched the sun rise and peer at me through the window. With each moment through the night, my body became weaker and my vision in my right eye waned to a dark haze. During the night I watched as she walked in sleepless dreams and screamed silently into the darkness. It was a gruesome thing to bear witness to in my sleepless slumber. When she came to bed, her sleep was fitful as if she were chased by some unknown force.

Maybe she is truly wicked.

Maybe I should have let her die.

Kill her...

But my sword was covered with his blood, and the err of my actions haunted me.

She whimpered with gasps of air as the sun streamed in and she rustled and climbed from the bed. I pushed myself up managing to slide to the floor and sit against the bed frame. My strength was gone, my energy only a memory. I raised my head to look at her. The loathsome sunlight from the window sparkled in her black hair and blinded me. She turned to me, then reached out and caressed my face, and my eyes drooped, my body slumped, my remaining energy disappeared. I collapsed to the floor.

I lay there, my body pale and aching. I rolled to my back and stared emotionlessly at the ceiling.

I would be dead by nightfall.

I rolled and crawled to the table. The boy must have already come in with fresh water and bread. I managed to pour some water down my throat and collapsed by the table. My body no longer functioned. No muscle twitched. I was a prisoner within myself. What wickedness has been put upon me? Is this my reconciliation for all the death I have wrought?

The bread will sit uneaten, rotting in the heat of the day. Everything, everyone, was a wisp, forgotten. Nothing, not even the blackness of the abyss existed. Just a barren empty void, gray and lifeless.

And death came for me.

I stirred throughout the night. The moon hung full outside the window and draped its brilliance across my broken body which lay in a heap on the floor near the table. I slept, but I am not sure how long. Finding a bit of energy I sat up and looked around. She was gone. I laid back on the floor and breathed out. I am certain if she stayed another moment, I would be dead.

The darkness of my visions did not shroud the dreams and apparitions I saw while I slept. Dreams of dark beings with enormous eyes and long fingers that reached out toward me with jeweled hands. I awoke from the dreams, but the creatures continued to reach out to me through the darkness. Their guttural screams echoed within my soul and my thoughts. The moonlight faded and quivered. I crawled to the bed and pulled myself into it, wrapping my body in the heavy blanket, yet blanket or fire could not calm the chills as my body quaked and a fever came as the moon died in the dark shadows of the night.

I woke with the sun bearing down on me in my bed as it set. I lay in a pool of sweat, drenched through. My body was sore, and it hurt to move. I pushed myself up. The boy entered the room with food and water. He saw me sitting up and turned away, then set the tray on the table.

"How long?"

He held up two fingers again.

"Two days," I muttered.

I looked around. My vision had returned in my right eye and I could see clearly. I saved her life, and she repaid me by stealing mine, my energy, nearly killing me, but yet I live. Things of sorcery in the land of mysticism. Maybe... she has spared me. I wondered who she was. The El Friz called her something. The word slipped my mind.

Mia entered my room. She said something to the boy and he left. She looked at me, and tears welled up and she came to me, and sat next to the bed. We managed to talk with our limited knowledge of our languages. I found comfort in her presence. The sense of danger disappeared with her near. She left and returned with fresh soup, which I ate and it warmed my soul.

She had the boy bring fresh clothes and linen and as the sun settled my body gave in and I laid down. I longed for sleep and knew I must rest until the morning dew drips from the sage and I left for what remained of my home. Mia pulled the covers over me and left.

I found it hard to rest or sleep. The nightmares of the blizzard, the attack on my homeland, and the deaths of my family, all lingered in the dream world behind my closed eyes.

In Mia, I had found refuge, or solitude.

Peace.

Serenity.

And yet, I had to leave. I had to make my way back to see if anyone... survived.

I remembered a name.

"Betir," I said in my drowsiness.

The Priestess's words echoed through my mind. *"Seek him where the yellow bird sings."* I must return to the alcove of rock where the night bird sang.

A presence came to me in the night. A woman. Her flesh, soft and inviting. Her warm breath upon my neck, moist lips upon mine.

Comfort. Solitude.

A dream.

The morning sun grazed across me and my eyes fluttered open. My body felt refreshed, recovered, and ready to make the journey to the alcove, then on to the edge of the desert and across to the border village of Ca'Bri. From there, I will get my bearings.

Mia was lying next to me in a soft naked slumber. A slight pang of absence and emptiness crept through my heart at the thought of leaving her. I took a deep breath and moved the thought of being without her aside. I traced the lines of the tattoo on her back, and she moaned and woke. She turned to me and smiled, and the smile faded to knowing. She nodded, caressing my cheek as she did.

I climbed from the comfort of the bed.

"I must prepare," I said. I grabbed my pack and checked its contents. I looked at Mia.

"They are being cleaned, and mended."

"You knew?"

"I have feeling. You do not look like traveling merchant, and I know Igvar, counselor to Priestess."

She winked. Again. Far too intelligent to be with the likes of me, I thought. She stood and slipped a gown over her olive skin. I didn't have the heart to tell her Igvar was dead, but then she looked at me oddly.

"You know Igvar, yes?"

"I do."

There was a knock at the door, and the boy entered. He had a plate of bread on top of a stack of clothing. My clothing. He laid them down on the desk. Mia said something to him I didn't understand, and he bowed and left, shutting the door behind him.

"Your son?" She laughed.

"No. Brother son." She sat on the edge of the bed. "Something happen while you sleep."

I picked up my folded leathers and uniform, and put them in my pack, then turned to her.

"Those three, um soldiers. Killed," she pointed outside the window. "Down there. Someone saw man fight them. Man with two swords." She looked up at me. "Tell me, why?"

"The girl. I saved her from them. They were going to kill her."

She gasped.

"One of them called her, um, kor ya, I think. He told me to kill her." I set the pack on the desk. "Now I know why."

"Kur'Ya?"

"Yes."

"Strange word, Kur'Ya. Means something like mistake, or..." She rubbed the side of her head. "No, I do not know your word. Mistake not right." She stood and placed her hands on my shoulders. "One man killed is Ruoska El Friz." She pronounced the word like 'freeze', el 'freeze'. It was not how the young man who showed me around pronounced it. It was more like 'fraise', the way we learned it.

"He was a, um, say, Captain, a leader."

"I knew he was an El Friz. He was also drunk," I said.

"He is from here. Much respect."

"Is he part of the faction under the new Herra, the Al Friz?" She shook her head.

"No. But you would give life to save poor girl. Who was she?"

"I know not," I said. "But I believe she is part of the darkness people speak of."

"How do you know this?" I grinned.

"I have feeling," I said, mocking her speech. She shook her head. I picked up my pack. "I must return to my lands after I find a man."

"A man?"

"Yes. Riddles and mysticism from the Priestess Kristava." Her eyes went wide.

"You speak to Priestess?"

"Aye." She sat in wonder for a moment.

"And this man, what is his name?" I sat next to her on the bed.

"All she said was Betir."

She gasped, then pointed a finger into my chest and tapped on it.

"You seek Betir El Friz," she giggled. "The Priestess Kristava, oh how I miss stories of her. This is blessing. A gift to you, um, Igvar," she said. Hearing the name, my heart filled with sorrow and I couldn't hide it this time.

"Rini. People call me Rini."

She smiled. "Rini. Much better name. But your face is filled with sadness now." I looked into her green eyes.

"I'm sorry. Igvar was my friend. He helped me—long story. Bandits attacked us in Kaksoset Canyon. They killed him."

Her hands went to her mouth as she gasped. Then, slowly, the acceptance showed. She lowered her hands and embraced me.

"I am sorry. Rini." She held me for a moment longer, then drew back.

"The Priestess, she wants me to seek a member of the Rogues Army?" She shook her head.

"No. He is wanderer, like you. Um, nomad yes. But he, he is master swordsman. He train El Friz soldiers. Or did. He is different. I know not why Priestess send you to find him. But if it her will, I do not question."

"Thank you, Mia. For... everything."

I dressed in the Roama garb. The sun was high overhead, and the daylight was thinning. I wanted to be at the alcove before sunset tomorrow and did not envy crossing through the canyon at night.

"Will you stay, one more night?"

"I..." I looked into her green eyes and disappeared. My heart screamed stay, my body screamed go.

"I will stay. But I must prepare to leave today so I can depart without delay in the morning."

She nodded, then slipped off her gown.

Chapter Nineteen

Sumu

I WALKED TO THE stables to purchase a horse, and an overly happy ostler greeted me. He was an older man who kept bowing and rambling in the sharp eastern tongue. He took me to a large steed. It was dark gray with hindquarters of black spots. A white star emblazoned its forehead. I looked over the horse—an ominous and majestic beast.

"A stallion of royal blood," I heard the voice say as we rode to Kaksoset Canyon.

"Sumu", I said. Igvar's horse.

I stroked his flank and felt a fresh wound from an arrow. The man seemed concerned. I closed my eyes and put my head on the horse. Igvar's smiling face appeared in my thoughts, then trailed away to a bloody shroud in a damaged cart.

The man lifted my hand to caress the snout, and the horse nuzzled into it. A bond was instantly made. He laughed an over joyous laugh then said something I understood.

"Priestess. She give." And he pointed to me and tapped on my chest. With the horse was all the tack and a few supplies. Items of Igvar's.

"Of course." I rubbed the side of the horse's head and looked into its eyes. "Sumu. Our journey will be long and hard, but I am thankful you are with me, friend."

I purchased additional supplies and made the horse ready. I told the old ostler I would return in the morning and gave him some money. He seemed more than thankful and bowed to me.

"Ke eto al Shaviska," he said, catching me off guard. He stared at me with dark eyes filled with joy. I feigned a smile and left the stables.

That night, Mia stayed with me, wrapped around me in a tight embrace. I welcomed the warmth of her body and the caress of her hands. But in my thoughts, I screamed to be alone. Visions of my wife faded to my daughter. And laying there with Mia, my thoughts churned in turmoil. I rolled over and put my back to hers, and wept for my family. She turned and pulled me closer, attempting to comfort me, but I was too far gone in my despair.

My wife appeared before me. Her red hair flowed in a phantom breeze. She smiled.

"I will never forget... my promise...," I said before I trailed off to sleep.

The new morning sun caressed us both. Mia rolled over and sat up. She looked at me and smiled. The smile was genuine, but it was a mask for the sorrow she felt inside.

"It is time," I said. She wiped a stray tear. She slipped her clothes on and pushed her dark hair behind her.

I dressed in the eastern clothing and held the blue sash in my hand.

"A blue sash," Mia said. "How did you get?"

"It was given to me by a Rogues Army escort."

"Ah. A gift. It is honor."

"I have never seen and Rogues Army soldier with a blue sash until then."

"Blue sash is royal escort. It brings um... respect? Only given to soldier of honor."

"I see." My emotions were mixed. I wrapped it around my waste. "Then I will wear it honorably until I reach Ca'Bri."

She leaned over and kissed me on my forehead. "I bring some food for you."

I washed my face from the clay bowl of water near the bed. I stared out my window at the capital of Bin El Omen. I was ready to leave this place. I glanced at the street below and saw two Rogues Army soldiers standing where I rescued that woman. I stepped back from the window, but still watched. A third joined them. A wash of distrust came over me.

"Mia," I muttered. It was doubtful, but my will to trust anyone was frail. The door opened, and I whirled, hand on the hilt of my short sword. She stood there with a tray of food. She came in and set it on the desk.

"What is it?" she said. I nodded toward the window. She set the tray down and walked over to me, then looked out and gasped.

"Yes, they are here to know what happen to Ruoska El Friz."

She called out to them in the Eastern tongue. They replied, and she became animated in her response, waving her arms like she was shooing them away like one would a dog. They looked at each other. One called out to her.

"Hmm," she said. She shook her head and pointed at them, then up the street away from the Inn. One called back, and they turned and walked up the street in the direction she pointed. She stood straight and brushed off her clothes. She smiled at me. "You have time to eat, but there will be more." I didn't inquire. The distrust gone like a wisp of cloud.

I ate while she sat in silence and watched me, eating very little herself.

When I finished, I picked up my pack and slung it over my shoulder. She came to me and embraced me, then looked into my eyes, and kissed me full on the lips, caressing the side of my face.

"Go. Find this man." Her eyes beckoned. She had more to say, but stepped away.

"Goodbye, Mia, and thank you." Tears ran down her face and she made no attempt to wipe them away. They dropped onto the dusty floor like raindrops. I wiped one away with my thumb and held it to my lips.

Then left.

I lead Sumu through the city streets, toward the gates past the Grand Bazaar. The sights, smells, and sounds of the bustling town were overwhelming, and I longed for the quiet the desert would provide. I walked past four soldiers, swordsmen of the Herra's Rogues Army, dining outside. They kept me under a watchful gaze, then returned to their food and drink.

At the gates, I stood and looked out upon the foothills. The sun was high overhead. I had enough daylight left to make it through the canyon. I gave the city one last glance, mounted Sumu, and began my journey North along the Black Road.

I approached the canyon as the sun descended to the horizon. There, on the road, stood four men. The same reavers and bandits as before. Head wrappings covered their faces, but I could see the smiles in their eyes, confident, or chaotic, thinking me an easy target. All four carried broad scimitars that glinted in the falling sun, emblazoning them with a wicked glory. Above the canyon entrance, I saw archers poised, ready.

I thought of spurring my horse through them, but it would be a significant risk to him. I stopped, then dismounted and stepped in front of Sumu. I drew both of my swords. Something changed in their expression.

Recognition?

One pointed and stepped back. They parted and moved to the side of the road. The archers moved back from the tops of the canyon. I sheathed my swords.

I heaved a sigh of relief and immediately remounted Sumu. I grabbed my water skin and tilted it, letting the liquid run across my lips and down my throat. I hung the water skin on the saddle horn and snapped Sumuz into a charge.

We raced between the bandits and on through the darkening canyon. We raced past remnants from the attack days before, between high rock walls, and a dry stream bed.

I slowed Sumu as we neared the other end. The stone towers cast grim shadows of near darkness in the canyon as the sun set behind them. I reined Sumu over to the edge of the road to a small trickle of a stream, remnants of the White River back home, which flowed along the bottom of the canyon. He bent down and drank.

The sun fell behind the canyon's walls, and darkness was upon us. We continued past the twin towers of stone and emerged into the night before making camp.

We traveled through the next day, and I reached familiar foothills just before dusk. I could hear echoes of the Priestess in my thoughts and wondered if the madness was returning.

I made camp in the shelter of rock where the night bird sang. My home not long ago on a cold and rainy day. I would camp until dusk tomorrow before I attempted to cross the desert to the village of Ca'Bri. It is here in this alcove I was to meet the man the Priestess spoke of. A former Rogues Army El Friz, a leader, and trainer of swordsmen.

But why, I wondered. And would this chance encounter happen before I left?

"I will give it a day," I said to Sumu, and stroked the side of his face.

I built a small fire and rested next to it while Sumu wandered amongst the fresh sage grass. I thought about the journey and if I could continue to Ca'Bri if I did not meet this man the Priestess spoke of.

I shuddered in the chill and lay down upon the wool blanket which separated me from the dust of the red rock and protected me from the cold of the night. Then I heard a familiar chirp, a short song, then the fluttering of wings, and knew I was not alone.

The next morning I sat in the alcove, sheltered from the sun by my rocky home. I stood and walked out into the warm sunlight. Sumu grazed on the scrub grass nearby.

The excited song of a desert bird made me smile.

I glanced over my shoulder to where the birdsong came from. Atop the roof of my stone shelter stood the peculiar yellow and brown songbird, warming in the sun and singing, unaware of the world around it. I hadn't seen it in the daylight, and the song was different. Was it the same bird? It caught my eye and silenced itself. It tilted its head and looked at me from a different angle. Its gaze froze on me as it surveyed me. I held out my arm, and it tilted its head to the opposite side. Curious. Cautious. It turned its head south, then flew off.

The song was gone, and I was alone again. My horse grunted.

"Not alone," I said and turned to him. He neighed and stomped on the ground.

Someone, or something, was approaching.

I retrieved my long sword from the alcove of rock and mounted Sumu. I surveyed the area and saw nothing. I turned around and again saw nothing. Sumu became more restless, tromping back and forth, and I pulled hard on the reins to steady his gate. I nudged him up a small ridge to get another look from higher ground. I could see the valley below where the river runs after a hard rain, scrub all around, and rocks large enough to conceal oneself. Again, Sumu fidgeted.

I looked around and saw what appeared to be a person on the northern ridge looking at me. They stood for a moment, then continued toward me. I nudged Sumu back to the alcove of rock and sat atop him, waiting. I watched the person make their way toward me. Sumu nickered and shook his head. He stepped back and to the side.

"Easy, easy." I stroked the side of his neck. I could hear the traveler's footsteps and soon saw him coming up the road.

"Ho," I called.

The traveler stopped and looked at me, still too far to make out much in the way of features. He stepped toward me again, and as he got closer, I could see he was wearing a long maroon and brown robe, his head covered to protect it from the glare of the sun. He carried a small pack upon his back, a walking staff in one hand. He wore a sword on his right hip.

He spoke a greeting in the Eastern tongue. I raised my left hand, then lowered it. My sword still grasped in my right. He saw the glint of the steel and stopped, then said something else I could not understand. His eyes peered at me from under the head wrap and looked cold and gray, like the steel of a freshly forged sword. He squinted. I lowered my sword, and his shoulders dropped a bit. He said something and held out his hand.

"I do not understand."

He stepped back.

"You're, a Northerner?"

His words were distinct and clear, with a hint of an eastern accent. His voice sounded aged. My horse sidestepped and whinnied. I patted him again, sheathed my sword, and dismounted. I stood slightly taller than the stranger.

"I am."

He squinted at me.

"You are soldier. A soldier of the Northern Army." Still dressed in Eastern clothing, I was unsure of how he knew.

"I am, or was, I suppose. And who are you?"

"It has been a long time since I have seen a soldier of the North."

"Aye. A long time for me as well." His eyebrows raised, and he looked me over, inspecting, memorizing.

"You are a conundrum, sir, for never in my long days have I seen a Northern soldier in Eastern clothes atop an Eastern horse of royal blood wearing the blue sash of a royal escort. Unless the sun has taken my mind, and I'm seeing things not as they are, you have quite a story."

He blinked and pulled back the hood from his head, revealing short black and gray hair and a wise face partially covered in a beard.

"I am Betir."

Chapter Twenty

Betir El Friz

"Betir El Friz."

"Yes. You recognize the name?"

"I have heard of it. Someone close to me told me you are a rebel with the Rogues Army."

He broke out in laughter.

"I was. Now, just a rebel. Or a rogue. I'm not so sure anymore." He chuckled.

I realized I was laughing as well. It had been some time since I heard the sound of laughter, and an eternity since I heard my own laughter. There was something familiar about the man. His way of speaking in the language was wholly natural.

I sheathed my sword. I remained awe-struck and mystified by the power of Priestess Kristava. I regained some semblance of humanity, if only for an instant.

"Come, would you like to rest?" I motioned toward the alcove.

He bowed. "These tired bones could use a rest, thank you." We walked to the alcove. "Are you sure it is sound having an El Friz share space with you Northerner?" I nodded, and he sat.

"Tell me, Betir El Friz, how long has it been since your time with the Rogues Army?"

"Ha, ages, my friend. If you are wondering if our paths crossed, I spent my time South as envoy for Herra Al Jalali, or as an escort for the caravans. I did not fare well in the company of those militants who follow Al Friz." He chuckled to himself then dropped his pack from his back. He slid it around into his lap, opened it, and pulled out a skin of liquid. He took a drink, then wiped his mouth.

I pulled a flat of bread Mia packed and tore it in half. I handed one half to Betir.

"So you served with those under this new Al Friz?"

"No." His face went sullen and white. "A higher mission was given to me." He cleared his throat and took another drink. "A mission which ended my days as a swordsman for the Rogues Army."

"Mission?"

"Aye, my mission was to kill a man."

"I apologize. I do not mean to pry."

He scoffed.

"No need to apologize. I don't get to share the story much, if at all. In all my time in the Rogues Army, I fought for what was right, for me. But this mission made me a murderer. Despite what the North believes, it is an honor and privilege to be titled an El Friz, and one has to maintain that title with integrity." He leaned back and tore a piece of bread from the loaf. "Nothing to fret about now. My past is in the past, as they say, and so are my days as a swordsman for the Rogues Army under Herra Al Jalali."

He stared at me a moment, and frowned, like there was something about me he couldn't place. He leaned forward and smiled.

"And what about you? What brings a soldier of the Northern Army into the eastern lands? A woman?" He popped the piece of bread in his mouth.

"A story for another day, perhaps." I took a drink from my waterskin. "Maybe you can answer a question as a former Rogues Army soldier. I never understood the suddenness, or reasoning, behind the attacks on our border villages."

He nodding and pulling another piece of bread from the loaf and ate it.

"This bread is from Bin El Omen." He closed his eyes and hummed while he ate it. "There is a manner in the way the bread is made which makes it unique, not just to the Eastern Lands, but Bin El Omen. Am I right?"

I nodded.

"Well, to answer the question. While I cannot speak for recent events, tell me, what was taught to you?"

"Only what I was told, that the only purpose was to steal our women, or pillage, create chaos. But now the attacks are different, more strategic, more military. In the past we resolved it as one would any ordinary pest." My poor choice of words hung in the dry air.

"Pest? Ha!" He shook his head. "I'm sure you are aware that in the old ages, the Eastern borders ran much farther. The Eastern Empire, we called it."

"Yes, the Empire of the Eastern Star."

"Aye, called that because there were two empires. The Eastern Empire which stretched from the Sighing Seas in the east to the Phéta Mountains in the west, north to the Shope'Ta Lakes of ice, and South beyond the City of the Southern Moon to the Seas of Kerenimore. This was all once our land." He laughed. "And your Great Hall was our capital."

He took another drink from his wineskin.

"I am aware."

"Then the uprising came from the South. For many summers, the battles raged on. The south pushed up to the northern ice and forced the resistance east to the desert. The southerners called it the Empire of the New Dawn."

"I still do not see what this—"

He held up a finger, stopping me.

"Then, out of the northern edge of the western lands came the storm. A storm of men, of armies, new to the lands. The force engaged the Empire of the New Dawn, and pushed them south, across the Emerald River. You call it the Sleeping River, though I never understood why. After the age of war was over, the lands settled into the territories we now know. The northern folk, as you are called, are the sons of what the southerners called the *northern darkness*."

The term he used struck me hard. I averted my gaze to the ground, frowning.

He took a small drink from his wineskin.

"You are only a northerner to the people of the south." A slight smirk drew across his face, and I could see in his eyes a soul humbled by ages of conflict. "To the people of the East, you are conquerors of the southern invaders, but... to some, you are intruders, occupiers of the land we lived on with pride, and in peace. Those who still believe it to be *our land* and fight for it are part of some new faction under a self-proclaimed Herra, A'avikon Ha'amu Al Friz. Your so-called *pests*. Your military faction. And their attacks, are strategic. That is the change."

"I have heard rumblings of this so called Herra."

"A man cannot serve two masters," he said, wiping sweat from his brow.

Who they ultimately served and their strategy was clear to me now.

Betir El Friz sighed, took another drink from his wineskin, then offered it to me. I accepted it and noted a portion of his index finger on his right hand was missing. A battle injury, I presumed. Then I noticed my hands were shaking. I took a drink and handed the skin back to him. Eastern wine. I reached over to my pack and pulled out some dried meat and more flatbread, and we sat in the cool shade of the alcove and ate for a moment in silence.

"If our lords laid eyes upon us, we'd have a good laugh," he said.

"Aye." I looked down at the bread in my hands. They were no longer shaking. "The stories, they matter not now." I wiped the sweat forming on my forehead. "My homeland no longer exists."

He looked west out over the foothills. "I have heard stories from some merchants who traveled the Black Road as of late. Stories of voices in the mist. Shadows. The smell of death permeates the land near Karvas Forest outside the Great City. And some have brought stories from the South along the road to Gal Abed. It is a strange tale they bring. One of nightmares and fantasy."

"Please, what have you heard?"

He wiped his hands on his robe, then wiped some sweat from his brow.

"The spiced meats of Bin El Omen," he said, disregarding my request. "You have stayed there?"

"Yes. But not by my choice. I am traveling from there." He peered at me. "Back home." I felt foolish by my choice of words.

"Ah, you ran into some trouble there, soldier?"

"I, yes. I encountered some of your old compatriots. And... it is nothing. As you say, stuff of nightmares and fantasy."

"You are weary, Northerner. Tell me your story. How does a Northern soldier appear in the capital of the Eastern Lands?"

I gave a derisive laugh and looked up at the rock above.

"This is not my first time in this alcove, Betir El Friz. The first time I camped here," I sighed, "I was with a caravan of traveling spice and silk merchants and..." I looked over at him, sensing his reaction. "Their priestess."

"Priestess? I am aware of only one priestess who travels with the merchants. What is her name?"

"Kristava," I offered. His eyes opened wide, and I detected a bit of awe or fear at the name. And possibly... love.

"Soldier of the North, you have traveled indeed if you have had counsel with Priestess Kristava."

"They found me on the edge of the desert, delirious and mad. And half-dead. They saved my life."

"You are most fortunate. There is a higher power watching you, my friend. You have a purpose indeed which you," he pointed a long finger at me, "have not seen or cannot see." He sounded like the Priestess. I gave this some thought. He rested his hands in his lap. "And here I sit, in my numbered days, with a soldier of the North. Me, the great Betir El Friz, swordsman of the Rogues Army. Former." He laughed. "My, what jokes the Gods play on us mortals."

He wiped a tear from his eye and took a breath.

"We, refugees both, breaking bread and drinking wine." He slapped my shoulder and started laughing again, and I couldn't help but join. "There is a reason, no? And now I ponder, what is my purpose in your quest? What is my journey?" I dared not tell him about the Priestess's vision that he and I would meet. "Hmm, a lot to think of as I wander this road alone."

He peered out from under the rock and looked at the sky. "It will be evening soon." He looked over at me and caught me wiping a tear from my eye. I wasn't sure if it was the laughter, or relief, or the great sorrow of my journey lifted, if only briefly.

He reached out and put his hand on my shoulder. And I was comforted. As if I was being comforted by an old friend I'd known all my life.

"Tell me, soldier, what is your name?"

The tears streamed uncontrollably now. Ashamed, I put my hands to my face. The sense of longing for conversation, the chance to tell my story, overwhelmed me. He left his hand on my shoulder, as passing friends in the desert. I took a deep breath and wiped the tears away.

"My name. Look at me. I have failed my homeland. My wife and daughter are dead. I have failed them all. We were to travel West to Gal Abed to visit family. Now, here I cry like a baby from the womb in the presence of a stranger, a stranger from the East, no less, who has shown compassion for me. The merchants also, finding me, nursing me to health..." I looked over at him. "So many years I spent in the fit of battle with an enemy I never knew, acting out some futile revenge out of anger. I am weary of battle and wish to be freed from it. My name. It is meaningless now. The northern lands are gone, decimated by some force from the northern wastes. I, I could not save them. My family. My men. My city." I hid my face as the tears welled. "I am the last, the only one left."

I moved forward and stood up and out of the alcove. I growled and kicked a rock across the dusty earth.

"She took it all from me!" My strained voice echoed off the rock walls and out into the foothills.

Sumu nickered and moved away, finding safety in the sagebrush. I heard footsteps, the crunch of the rock and sand beneath his boots. "All of it. My father, my land, my family." I felt the hand on my shoulder again. "And now I am thrust into the abyss by this... darkness. The darkness of the northern sky, and the darkness now, inside me."

I watched the last tear as it fell from my face and disappeared into the dusty soil, like the blood of so many I have slain here.

"I have failed everyone."

"You have failed no one, soldier." He turned me toward him and stared at me with wise silver eyes. "You only fail them," he tapped his finger into my chest, "when you accept defeat." My breath stopped. Everything stopped. Then I took in deep breath.

"Aye," I managed to say, only half-believing the word myself.

"You have your good name, soldier. And your memories."

I sighed. "What good is a name? I cannot remember the name of my wife or my daughter. All I have are visions and nightmares and so close, their names, so close in the ether right before me, and I can't..."

A rain of tears began again as I became more... broken, crumbling inside. I looked up at the sky. A yellow bird flew overhead, and I watched as it flitted around and landed on a rock an arrow shot away, and chirped a familiar song. I took a deep breath and cleared the rain of sorrow. I looked over to the man, who was also watching the bird. He turned his head to me and I stared at his steel-gray eyes.

"I am Commander General Rini Soltari of the Northern Army. Former." A great weight lifted from my shoulders at the sound of my name.

Speaking my name. Hearing my name.

His hand fell from my shoulder to his side, and his eyes widened. He cleared his throat and stepped back a few steps. I frowned.

"You, you recognize my name?" He turned back to the alcove and retrieved his pack. He paused. "Betir?"

"I must go, friend. I must..." he stopped, stood, and faced me, holding his pack low in front of him. He sighed, then looked up at me, and I could see the brink of his tears. "I am," he cleared his throat, "so, so sorry. I fear for the wage of war, we are both still paying. And I pray we can remember our time spent here, breaking bread, drinking wine, and the sound of our laughter. Not the sound of steel on steel and the cries of dying men."

He pulled the covering over his head, reached down, and picked up his staff.

"May the blessings be upon you in your journey, Commander. Peace be with you."

"And with you, Betir El Friz."

I watched him walk to the road and disappear behind a large rock.

I walked back to the alcove and sat down in its cool shade. I looked over to where El Friz was sitting moments ago laughing, and saw a piece of silver. I picked it up. It was an amulet of some form. I thought I recognized it, but then shuffled that thought away. How could I? I looked over its silver edges and gold inlay designs in the center.

The amulet itself was a circle with two crossed lines etched into it. At the center of the two lines was a gold diamond shape, its points positioned on the crossed lines. I turned it over, and on the back was the stamp of a family crest. I dropped the amulet. I stared at it where it lay on the dusty earth, baffled by its presence.

The side with the family crest, my family crest, stared back at me. I picked up the amulet, turned it over in my hand a few times, then clutched it tightly as the fall of tears came again. His words, *I had to kill a man*, echoed in my mind. Then I knew the burden El Friz carried, and who he murdered. I clasped the amulet tightly in my hand, and the knuckles turned white.

I stepped out of the alcove. I walked toward Sumu, and stopped. My mind raced. Do I follow the man I believed killed my father and avenge him, or continue to Ca'Bri and avenge my homeland? The Priestess's game was just more torment from sorcery I would never understand. I walked to a high rock at the top of the ridge. I caught a glimpse of Betir El Friz in the far distance before he turned and disappeared into the foothills.

I returned to the alcove and placed my father's amulet in the pouch with the purple lotuses.

CHAPTER TWENTY-ONE

Ca'Bri

EVENING CAME AS I made my way to the edge of the desert. Its glow in the twilight sun stretched out before me. Soon, I would be across and in Ca'Bri.

The sun laid itself to rest, and I spurred Sumu into a ferocious gallop and made my way through the dark on a night ride across the desert. The moon did not show its long face.

The shape of the foothills rose in the near distance. I urged Sumu on faster. His gallop was lively, his nostrils flared, and flames of mist announced every exhale in the chill desert night.

He showed no signs of tiring, driven by his desire to get across the sea of sand. I did not fear the desert, or the fires of the desert dwellers whom none spoke of, but all feared.

We reached the foothills just before dawn.

I slowed our pace to a trot. The road glowed in the dawn's light. I continued until I found sanctuary among the rocks and prepared camp.

Sumu found a patch of sage and nestled down into it.

I lay near him, covered myself from the sunlight, and fell asleep.

The sun was bright in the cloudless sky. A cool, gentle breeze touched us. I lay on a green slope of grass overlooking the hills of the Northern Lands. Next to me, I felt the warmth of a body and rolled over. My wife, fast asleep with her back to me, lay as still as the night. I did not disturb her peace. I sat up and saw my daughter curled in her mother's protective arms, staring at the sky.

Her eyes moved. She looked at me. Her sea-blue eyes captured the sunlight, and she squinted.

"Papa," she whispered. "Are you coming home now?"

I put my finger to my lips. "Silence, little one. Soon."

She smiled and glanced at her mother, then frowned at me.

The wind blew across her red hair and twisted it into fiery knots. Her squinted eyes, tired, closed and gave way to sleep, and her soft snores fell into the warm embrace of the wind.

I woke at midday. Sumu grazed near me. His heavy steps pondered the rock. Clouds drifted through the sky. I gathered my things and fetched some of the bread and dried meat I had with me. I sat in the shade of the crimson rocks and ate.

I recognized the low red rock foothills of my homeland. I was less than half a day's ride from Ca'Bri.

A coarse and sudden wind blew, and a foul stench caressed my nose, interrupting my meal. My stomach turned. I recognized the smell. It was the smell of rot. Dead flesh of an animal, putrid and stale in the scorching sun.

I put the food away.

Sumu looked up as he caught the scent. The smell hung in the air like a pestilence. I grabbed his reins, mounted, and we trotted at an even pace along the winding road into the foothills until the miserable stench drifted away with distance. We rounded a large boulder, and I could see Ca'Bri in the distant shimmering haze. It sat overlooking the valley of the desert.

I rode under the arched entryway of Ca'Bri. No guards stood. The post was abandoned. But the village looked alive enough. I stopped in the city square and looked around. There were groups of people here and there. Some traveled by horse. Some gathered around a small fountain. Most shopped at the bazaar, although only a handful of caravans from the east had set up shop. They sat and ate, talking all the while. None looked at me in wonderment. None cared.

Nor did I.

There was something different about the people. Like the spark of life was missing, and they were all puppets doing routine things. It was faint, but there.

I saw no soldiers from the Northern Lands.

I was a stranger here.

I dismounted and walked Sumu closer to the fountain, which was empty. I overheard two men sitting on the fountain wall near me talking about the Great City. The words were grim. The city had fallen. They spoke of moving south to Khor'Akber. They saw me and halted their discussion, peering at me like I was a diseased man. I remembered what I was wearing, and the city where I stood, and smirked. They thought me a madman then and left, disappearing into the village shops.

Ca'Bri was fair-sized. Some considered it a city. And it moved like a city. But with the lack of merchant carriages and water in the fountains, the city seemed quiet. And dead. I made my way to the stables, handed my horse to a stable boy, then walked across the road to the Inn of the Desert Dawn to rest for the night before traveling North to the Great City.

There were only four patrons within the dim bar seated at a table far from the door. They did not turn when I entered. I was invisible, ghostly, a phantom, treading on the fine borders of the spirit world and the real.

I walked toward the bar and saw the barmaid Iliana, a kind and strong older woman who filled out her dress and apron generously. Her hair was pulled back, showing her round face, and the few wrinkles of age. Her usual joyful face was now one of solemnity and foreboding. I stood before her, the two of us separated by the width of the long wooden bar. She said nothing, waiting for me.

"Iliana. So good to see you." She frowned. I cleared my throat. "I am here to acquire a room and food."

Her eyes stared through me, wider now.

"For an easterner?" she snarled. Iliana's age was taking her memory. She would be a little older than my mother, if she were alive.

"No, no." I smiled. I pulled the hood from my head. There then came the brightness in her face. The sorrow was replaced with a sparkle of wit.

"Rini?" she said, then came around the bar and embraced me. She held me and looked me over. "Why are you dressed... never mind. Never mind. I care not about the goings on these days. Come," she said. She took my hand and led me to a table. "I bring you food and wine, yes?" I smiled, a phantom no more, and sat down.

She returned with a bowl of stew, and a cup of wine, then sat across from me.

"You are... you have aged, young man. Are you well?"

I smiled at the taste of familiar food, and being in the company of a familiar face.

"I am better." I leaned back. "I have many questions, and you may have the answers," I said. "Will you be so kind as to share... what has happened here?"

She seemed confused.

"Answers? I have questions as well. I am not sure—"

"The Great City. I have heard rumors."

She stared at the table, then turned a silver band on a finger of her wrinkled hand.

"Aye. A great darkness is over the city. Death. We can smell it. We have heard from some who have escaped that a Queen of some form now sits where Lord Airik used to." She looked up at me. "They are all dead."

I stopped eating.

"I sensed that."

"But there is a great sorrow in your eyes."

"My wife."

"Oh my. Rini. You must be devastated."

"They perished during the first attack. She.. and my daughter. She was to be seven the following day."

She gasped. "Oh, the sweet darling. I am so sorry, Rini." She seemed on the verge of tears. "I wanted to meet them so badly." At that, she wiped away a tear from each eye, then looked at me. "Where have you been, that you do not know of these happenings?"

I relayed some events, leaving out others. I told her of my time in Bin El Omen, and the rescued woman. She seemed to recognize some part of that. I looked into her old eyes. They were solemn. The darkness hadn't spread to Ca'Bri, but she sensed it coming.

Then her eyes went wide.

"Oh! Something I remember, Rini. More of your friends appeared here after word came from the Great City. They were with a few others, not many."

I sat up, my heart skipping a beat.

"My friends?"

"Yes, soldiers. They did not have money to pay for rooms, but I let them stay. They left only recently, I think, could be longer. Days pass by. They looked beaten and weary." And then she put her hand to her mouth, drew it away slowly, and whispered: "One was completely mad."

"Are they still in the village?"

"I have heard rumors of soldiers camped outside the southern gate near the road to Khor'akber. But one cannot be sure of the things heard in Ca'Bri anymore," she said.

I took a deep breath. She frowned.

"What is happening?"

A call from the back of the room for more ale pulled her gaze from me. She smiled politely, then turned back to me.

"I have to return to the Great City."

She leaned back in her chair. "Only death awaits you there, Rini. There is naught you can do." She took my hand and held it, then patted it. I stared at the food and wine before me.

"I made a promise." I looked up at her, and a tear escaped.

"You can have the room off the courtyard. Stay as long as you need to."

"Thank you, Iliana." She stared at me as if she was just seeing me for the first time.

"You have your mother's eye. She was beautiful and full of pride." She chuckled. "My memory may not be so good, but some things are meant to stay."

I longed to hear more of my mother, but the urge to find the soldiers drew me away.

"I—"

"Yes. Go now, young man."

"I will be back."

She kissed my hand, tucked a key into it, got up, and went behind the counter to pour a cup of ale for the man in the corner.

Filth and decay covered the cobbled streets of Ca'Bri. The stone buildings, which used to be colorful, now sat worn and faded. The people smiled as if wearing a mask, but underneath, they were screaming, or crying. It sent shivers through me. I rounded a corner and saw men bartering at a fruit stand. I stopped. They wore the colors, the black leather, the uniform of a Northern soldier. Their hair was long and ragged, as was mine, and their beards rough and swollen. I leaned against the wall of a shop and watched. They bargained for three pieces of fruit in trade for a dagger. Not a fair trade, but the emaciated faces of the soldiers agreed, reluctantly. They turned and wandered down the road away from me.

I walked to the fruit stand.

"I will give you three pieces of gold for that dagger."

The old lady behind the stand peered at me from under a red scarf. Her wrinkled, fat face studied me with eyes glazed over from age. I held the gold out. She looked at the dagger.

"I assure you, woman, that dagger is cursed. I am doing you a favor." She picked it up, handed it to me, and reached for the gold. I curled up my hand. "And ten more pieces of fruit."

She was getting a bargain. The gold was enough for her to close shop for a few days. And she knew it, although she did her best to conceal it.

"Fine, Easterner," she said with a raspy, aged voice. "Have your five pieces of fruit and one cursed dagger. But only northern gold is good here."

Two shadows appeared and covered the woman's face. I turned, and two large men stood there, arms crossed.

"No room for the likes of you here, Easterner."

He spat on the ground. The other grunted. They were about my height, with thick black hair, and carrying a sword at their hip.

I turned away from them.

"Northern gold, madam." I held it out. She spat on the ground, handed me the dagger, and took the gold.

"Hey." The man tapped on my shoulder.

I whirled around and had him by his shirt collar, the dagger point at his neck. The other stepped back and drew his sword. He held it as unnaturally as a new father might a newborn. Unsure what to do with it, scared he would drop it.

"I am no Easterner. But I will strike you down no less and leave you gasping your last breath in the streets of Ca'Bri."

I let him go and pushed him back. I threw back my robe and drew my long sword.

The two backed up a few more steps. One backed into another fruit stand, dumping the contents onto the ground. He held up his hands in front of him, then turned and ran. I moved to the other, who dropped his sword and ran in the opposite direction. I sheathed my sword, picked up the one the coward dropped, and slung it through my belt. I turned to the old lady. She showed no reaction except for a slight grin at the tip of her mouth. I picked ten pieces of fruit, stuffed them in a pack, then walked down the road after the two soldiers. Along the way, I picked up some dried meats and a bottle of wine.

CHAPTER TWENTY-TWO

The Others

I WALKED TO THE southern gateway of Ca'Bri and looked at the cobblestone road that extended beyond it. It continued just beyond the gate, then turned to dirt, a worn path through scrub and rock. I saw smoke on the horizon. They were not far.

I wandered back through the streets amid the curious stares of Ca'Bri.

I entered the inn, proceeded to the courtyard behind it, and toward my room. The courtyard, a once beautiful garden of yellow and orange flowers, fiery red shrubs, and fountains, now lay dead and dormant. Withered. Dry like the desert it overlooked. I entered my room and set the pack of food on my bed.

I grabbed my other pack from the corner and emptied the contents onto the bed. My leather armor, my uniform, and the pouch holding my father's amulet, parchment, and the petals of two lotuses. I stared at the uniform. I ran my finger across the silver clasp that denoted my rank. I slipped off the eastern garb and found myself stirred to put on the uniform and leathers. Anxious, ready. But the weight of it all was still too heavy. By donning this, I once again assumed the role of warrior, a seeker of battle, a bringer of death. A role I resigned before the attack, now forced back into.

I washed and cleaned up, then slipped into the uniform and battle trappings. I attached the clasp, then strapped my long sword sheath to my side, the sword of my father. I sheathed my short sword in the harness across my back.

Glares from the tenants of the village guided me on my walk to the stable. I retrieved Sumu, packed the wares in the saddlebags, and made my way through Ca'Bri. I took a different path through the small village. The road along the southern edge was filled with people living on the street. Their shelters were nothing more than makeshift tents of canvas and blankets. Small fires boiled water for anything they could toss in for a daily meal. Most were women and children. The men were probably soldiers at one time. The children walked alongside me jabbering about kids things, excited to see a horse and rider, and a soldier, swords and such. I stopped and looked into their eyes. They were playful yet carried a heavy burden. I pulled some of the gold the merchants gave me and handed each child a gold piece. In our Great City, such places as this do not exist. It is not allowed.

The children ran back to their mothers or, if they were lucky, fathers, some fortunate to have both, excited at this financial gain. I could see their burden lifted for at least a day or two.

I stopped under the archway, leading out of Ca'Bri, and mounted Sumu. I spurred him on to a comfortable gallop. The sun would set soon and I cared not to travel the streets of Ca'Bri at night.

I neared the smoke from the small campfire and slowed to a trot. The dirt of the path deadened our footsteps, yet the trained ears of the soldiers had picked them up. The sound of steel being unsheathed drifted to me. I rode around a rock outcropping and the small party appeared, seated around a fire. I stopped. They stared.

One soldier, an officer, gasped, lowered his sword, dropped it, then dropped to his knees, staring at me as if the western god Yoomala itself had stepped into camp. Another also dropped his sword and collapsed to the ground. And they all wept. Most stood in disbelief. Some kept their composure, too weary or beaten to show any emotion, or the recognition was slow to set in.

I dismounted and removed the saddlebags from my horse. There were five soldiers. I heard footsteps behind me and looked over my shoulder at two more standing there, swords drawn, hanging at their side. The officer, a captain, composed himself and stood. Behind him, another soldier appeared from around a rock. Eight men. Eight of my brothers from the Northern Lands, and I thought I had entered another dream.

"By the gods, how many are you?" I said to the officer approaching me. He was a tall man, almost as tall as I. His face appeared worn and old, even though I knew he was much younger.

"Commander Soltari?" he cried. "You are alive!" He took my right hand. He knew me, but I did not recognize him. I stepped back. The joy on his face was unbearable.

"Living, Captain, but no more alive than the looks of you."

He raised his head. Tears streamed from his face, writing liquid epitaphs through the creases in his dried and dusty skin. He released my hand.

"Tell me your name, Captain," I said.

The tears stopped, and he let the last roll from his reddened cheek to the worn and beaten leather of his armor.

"I am Captain Adain Fonchesca."

I knew the name.

"You are the son of the former Commander General Fonchesca?"

"I am his youngest, sir." His head bowed in grief. "My father, and my three brothers, are..." The agony unleashed a rainstorm of tears.

Behind him, his men formed up. He wiped the dirt, sweet and tears away.

"These are your men?" He looked behind himself.

"Yes, Commander. These eight, and there are eleven more working to get money for food. We have," he sobbed and dropped his head, "nothing."

"There are twenty of you?" He lifted his head and nodded. "Captain, that is more men than I have seen since the attack at Farwic Outpost." I sighed and held up the saddlebags. "I have brought food and wine, but I'm afraid it is not enough to fill all your bellies." I looked at the saddlebag and felt pathetic. I was not expecting so many soldiers.

I wiped sweat from my brow. I gave nearly twenty pieces to the children of the street, and we would need a fair amount for horses, rations, and beds to sleep in tonight. I could feel the weight of a great, but different burden resting on my shoulders. I did not have enough for the journey for twenty-one soldiers, but I had enough to procure supplies, horses, and a cart. And at least one night's stay at the inn.

"Captain, you and your men will come with me to the Inn of the Desert Dawn. There, you will rest and eat. I have a mission for us, and you will once again get to serve your lands."

He looked up at me, his gaze cavernous.

"Commander, it would honor us to serve you." He bowed his head again.

"Come with me then. We shall discuss my intent while your men gather their things."

We walked to the road.

"Captain, I aim to return to the Great City."

His eyes lit with fear.

"Forgive me, Commander Soltari, that is the one mission I fear most." He was shaking his head.

"We must retake our homeland, Captain Fonchesca. We cannot let the darkness linger, nor let this Queen of Shadows sit in our Great Hall, in our Lord's chamber." He nodded, and his hands were shaking now.

"I agree, commander, but with a force of the size of ours? It cannot be done. Do you have more soldiers?"

I frowned. "No. It is... just me."

He looked at the men clearing the camp.

"These are not all my men. We found a few wandering the road to Ca'Bri and south of the Great City. One we found weeping by the Black River. We later learned his wife and four sons were dead. And two we found mad, gibbering to themselves in the forest outside the city. We barely escaped with our lives and sanity, Commander. I do—" He sighed. "My small force watched as those black husks killed indiscriminately. They wielded horrific black blades. They dragged the dead to the ramparts, dropping them outside the gates. The blades were cursed, Commander." He welled up with tears. "I watched—" He fell into sobs and turned away.

"This is why we must return, Captain. We will soon have our strength. We know the enemy." He was shaking his head. I grabbed him by the shoulders. "I made a promise to my wife that I would return!" I heard my anger and my fear as I spoke the words. He looked at me and winced away.

I let him go.

I have heard this madman speak before... This voice. This anger. And I thought of the look on Igvar's face when he talked about what they found in the foothills of the Black Road.

My handiwork.

I rested my arms at my side.

"Please, Captain, continue. If you can."

He took a deep breath. "The black blades. I watched a friend get struck down by a black husk and, moments later, stand and fight. But he fought against us, and his gaze was black as night."

We stood in silence for a moment. I stared off into the night, trying to envision his words.

"They rose from the dead commander. They killed anyone. Everyone. We were surrounded. We made it to the shops by the North Gate and escaped through the underground passage to the old East Gate, and there—" He wiped his face with a cloth from his belt. "We ran." His head hung. He was shaking. "So cowardly," he said under his breath.

"Captain?" He looked up, then wiped his face again. He stood tall and took a deep breath.

"Commander, I would follow you to battle on any day. But to return to the Great City with our small force is madness." He saw the shock on my face from his words, but remained firm. "Only shadows and death live there."

Then his eyes brightened.

"There are others, like us, who left for Soldier's Pass in front of the gathering storm. We were preparing to journey west when you found us. We hoped to find sanctuary in Gal Abed."

"Soldier's Pass? Commander Versol's force?"

"Aye. They... they never came."

I stepped back, shocked. I pulled on my beard, thinking. Why did they not show? Did they also meet some tragic end like we did?

"Your desire then is to head west, and then what? At what point do we return and vanquish this enemy?"

"Return?"

He thought about this, then shuddered.

"My family is dead. The city is dead. All around it is dead. There is naught to return to."

"We must."

"I will not return to that place without the benefit of strength in numbers. Even then... There are things, Commander, shadows, which now live in the forest around the Great City. They cannot be slain. There is an evil there. Two of the men we found went mad from the nightmares alone."

I put my hand on his shoulder. "We will avenge our homeland, Captain. We must. I know of these things you speak of."

"We could ask the Southern Lands for aid." I lowered my hand.

"Bah, they are not soldiers, warriors like our kin. They dress in fancy armor with decorative swords. They no longer know of battle as we do. They have lost the way."

If what he says is accurate, we will need a larger force, and if there are more of us in Gal Abed... I sighed.

"I hoped to return to the Great City. I made a promise," I said. "A promise to see the head of this queen posted on our North Gate. Now, I fear I may not fulfill that promise if all you say is true." I walked along the edge of the road, and he followed. "My journey from Farwic Outpost has been long. I know of the ill mist in the forests. I, too, lost men to it. We found ourselves in the foothills in the Eastern Lands before..." I frowned. "Madness. Yes."

I stopped and turned to him. The sounds of the night echoed in the distant foothills, and the moon lit his hopeful, yet weary, face.

"We will head south and travel the Kinelot Road to Gal Abed, where my brother lives. There we will regroup and refresh ourselves and collect any remnants of our army along the way, and any who traveled to Gal Abed." He smiled, almost pleaded.

"Thank you, Commander. Thank you."

I reached to my hip and pulled the dagger from my belt.

"Now, who does this belong to?"

We stayed at the Inn for the next five nights. We rested, fed, refreshed, and readied for the journey. The men helped around the Inn to earn their stay with some repairs, stocking, and handling those who had too much drink. The work made them feel alive again. It gave them purpose. A sanctuary from themselves. The courtyard was alive and thrived again with life, and the fountains flowed with water and renewed hope for the men.

I procured the items for the trip and, with Iliana's help, made some bargains through what she called respectable merchants. I said goodbye to her and paid for what I could. She took half and politely refused the rest.

"You have a mission, Commander, that we shall all benefit from."

"I am thankful the darkness has not found Ca'Bri Iliana."

"Aye. Maybe not. But an ill wind blows here, and I am certain it is upon us." Then she took my head in her hands. "Fear not Rini Soltari. You will remember their names." She kissed my cheek and bid me farewell.

We left the village of Ca'Bri and headed south to the city of Khor'akber to travel the Kinelot Road to the City Of the Southern Moon.

My men, now refreshed, prepared for the long journey, their gazes now a mask of prosperity and hope.

The terrain we traveled upon from Ca'Bri to the Krazos Valley was flat, merciless, and barren. A stiff wind blew across the land through the day and night and on it the faint stench of death. Crimson plateaus, which rose from the flat earth, like monuments to a jagged time, flanked the road.

The land soon became tree-covered hills, rocky bluffs, steep descents, and deep valleys across broken creeks. A road from a time passed, barely existing in the rough rock-hewn ground. Our progress was cold across the plateaus, but swift. Here, our progress slowed as horses quickly grew weary in the unsteady terrain.

We crested a steep hill and found ourselves on a high bluff overlooking the river valley. Below, we could see the village of Khor'Akber, shadowed by the bluff. The rock road we traveled led us along the ridge and on a slow decline down to the valley, where we camped before entering Khor'Akber. A swift darkness fell upon us. An eerie darkness, as if the land itself was swallowing us. We slept, but the rest was fitful and unsettling.

A man cried out, then whimpered.

Maybe it was my own voice I heard.

CHAPTER TWENTY-THREE

The City of the Southern Moon

THE NEXT MORNING, WE traveled amidst a deep fog and rode to the gates of Khor'Akber. The city appeared lifeless in the morning mist, but soon took life as it lifted. We resupplied some stock, and fed and watered the horses. We were relieved to find no sense of shadows, or darkness, affected Khor'Akber. The stable hand told us there were more soldiers like us in the city, most camped south of the village. I sent out a small patrol to check the Inns and they returned just before evening with nine more soldiers. We learned some had families who escaped with them from the Great City. They offered to join us, and soon our party grew to thirty.

We left town to the southern edge, where we found a small encampment of about twenty refugee families. They escaped through the western gates, headed south across the plains and open fields, and through the forests to Khor'Akber. They said the darkness was heading west and feared for their families, who traveled the Black Road to Feren Ta or the Western Lands. Of the families, there were eight more soldiers, three of whom joined our party. The others were not well and would not survive the trip.

We camped for the night with the refugees. Strange stories were told. Most a grim reminder of my failure.

The following morning, we traveled south toward the Kinelot Road. The terrain was unforgiving. By evening, we reached the bridge over the Sleeping River and camped. The horses drank from and rested near the water. Soldiers stripped of their clothing and bathed, reveling in the cool water. The river turned brown from the grime and filth.

A light fog from the river covered us the following morning as we crossed the bridge into the Southern Lands. We continued south and reached

Kinelot Road and the dark forests just before the evening. The horses were weary, so we camped.

"We are two days' ride from the City of the Southern Moon," I said. Captain Fonchesca looked at ill ease as we sat next to a fire. He made quick glances into the deep forest. "Captain?" He turned to me, then sighed.

"Aye, two days." He was fiddling with a leather strap on a small pouch. "This forest, I expect to hear voices, sighs, or moans. I am on edge." He set the pouch down, smoothed out his bedroll, and laid down with his back to me, facing the forest. He clutched his sword close.

The forest was alive with the night chatter of frogs and insects. And the occasional sob of someone in torment.

On the eve of the second day, we reached the gates to the City of the Southern Moon, which sat across a stone bridge over a small tributary of the Sleeping River. A high wall surrounded the city. Fires accented the towers of the gates, and below them, archers stood, ready to strike at any outside force. I sat on my horse alone on the bridge. A man peered down from a tower.

"Stand down before the gates to the City of the Southern Moon," he called.

"We have no quarrel, gatekeeper," I said.

The gatekeeper leaned to one side. "What do you seek in the City of the Southern Moon?"

"We seek food and shelter, permitting."

The gatekeeper stood stoic and statuesque. A strapping man draped in polished chain armor with a crimson stole and a silver helmet. He held a long guidon bearing the colors of the Southern Moon, a pointed flag of crimson and yellow.

"You seek the impossible, for we do not willingly and openly admit foreigners into the realm of the Southern Lands without the approval of the Goffs."

The Goffs. Hearing the word jogged a long-lost memory of my father.

"Then I seek council with your Goffs, gatekeeper."

"State your name."

"My name?"

"Your name, sir. Do you not know your name?"

I challenged the thought.

"I am a Commander from the Northern Lands."

"There are no men from the Northern Lands this day, lest they be the walking dead, or under the control of that abomination who calls herself the Queen of Shadows." He spat the words from his mouth.

I looked back to Fonchesca. His eyes reflected that which entered my mind.

They knew.

"The Northern lands, foreigner, are cursed grounds trodden upon only by the boots of the evil ones. Tell me your proper mission, or I shall have an archer pierce your eye with a black arrow, and ye shall know my mission."

"Then we are spirits who have returned to this world, gatekeeper. Think as you like."

"So be it," the gatekeeper said.

He raised the guidon, and I heard the pluck of a drawstring and the hiss of an arrow. I knocked the arrow away with my gauntleted hand, snapping it in two. Sumu did not falter. The gatekeepers' joy fell from his face to the ground to be consumed by the worms below.

"I do not come with bad tidings, gatekeeper. I am Commander General Soltari, of the Northern Lands, known by some as Shaviska! By others as Saka'Ali."

His guidon dipped slightly.

A bird fluttered in the tree above me and squawked, and my horse grew restless and sidestepped.

"Commander Soltari," the gatekeeper said. There was a long pause as the gatekeeper turned and spoke to someone behind him. He turned toward me. "My apologies, sir. We have been expecting you."

"Expecting me?"

"We shall arrange for you to have your council at first light. You may camp there in the grove on the other side of the road."

He raised the guidon straight.

"Do not overstep your boundaries, nor cross the road, foreigner, for tonight our eyes will be upon you. You shall receive naught any foodstuffs nor drink until the Goffs request it for you. It is our way."

I turned my horse and rejoined my soldiers, lost in the meaning behind the gatekeeper's words. I looked into the tired faces of the men and turned to Captain Fonchesca.

"He said they've been expecting you, Commander. What did he mean?"

I shook my head. "I know not. Make camp, Captain, and give the City of the Southern Moon a wide berth. We will consume the dry rations tonight and fill our bellies in the morning."

His reply was a tired nod.

The dawn came from behind a wall of low, sleeping clouds that thought to consume us in their chill, drizzled grace. We crawled. We wept. We were tired, but a new life was coming. The many days on the harsh ride here had taken its toll, and my men barely moved from their slumber.

I stood. The sound of creaking metal and whining steel came from the City of the Southern Moon. The gates rose and birthed a small party of seven men on foot. Six in two neat, straight rows of three and one out front to lead them. They were all dressed in crimson cloaks and dark leather armor. Each wore a polished helm. On top of the lead man's helm was a decorative red plumage. Each man a soldier, each man identical. All tall, all with long, dark hair. The fog parted as they cut a swathe through it while they crossed the stone bridge to the road.

They approached us with an air of symbolic confidence.

They stopped, and the leader stepped out and stood before me. Along the edge of his cloak were strands of silver weaved into the fabric, and he wore a silver badge that looked like a half-risen sun with two horizontal lines above it.

They all had blue eyes, save this one. Eyes, green like the forest, and bright.

He spoke.

"Commander Soltari." His voice was sharp, distinct, and void of accent. It was direct and to the point. Eloquent, like all trained warriors of the Southern Moon. "The Goffs request your company. You Commander. You alone."

"I am ready." I moved to join them.

"You must leave your weapons here, Commander. It is our way." His eyes peered into mine, not wavering for an instant.

I removed my weapons and handed them to Captain Fonchesca.

"Captain, these are my life and all I have in this strange world. You will guard them above all else."

He bowed his head.

"The honor is mine, Commander." His voice was deep, low, and tired. He accepted my weapons and stood next to me.

"I am ready," I said to the man with the forest eyes.

He tilted his head in affirmation.

The six turned and walked toward the city behind the wall. I followed.

We glided through the fog and across the bridge to the large gate of the City of the Southern Moon. We passed underneath the immense stone structure, which housed the iron bars of the gate, under the watchful eyes of the gatekeeper. The gates groaned shut behind us. A grove of moss-covered trees shrouded a cobblestone path that wound through them and led to the city center. A stone building at its heart towered above the others. It was flat and tall, capped with a dome of gold. At each corner of the building grew four very tall spires. Poised atop the covered spires were men armed with crossbows.

The architecture of the domed building was like our Great Hall and the Palace in Bin El Omen. It was true about the Northern Lands. We lived on borrowed land in borrowed buildings. Our history was non-existent. And we were no different from the Queen who now occupies our borrowed hall. I heaved a sigh, and the fog of my breath dissipated and mixed with the morning fog. An icy chill passed through me.

We continued along the path which led to the hall. A small stream ran along the path beside us. Its trickles and the occasional chirp of birds were the only noise in the city. The streets were barren and lifeless. The city was a display, a piece of history forbidden to the inhabitants of the Southern Lands. Like a painting. The only movement was our march to the domed building.

"Where are your people?" The soldier ignored my question.

The doors to the domed hall were massive beasts. They stood three times taller than I and were made from dark solid wood supported by steel plates and bars. They bore no windows. The entire front area of the building was absent of any window, save for those in the spires.

The man of the forest eyes stepped forward and rapped on the colossal door three times. I expected their immense frames to be opened by a giant behind them using all of his might. But a smaller, concealed, man-sized door opened before us.

We walked through the doorway and into a well-lit room. An immense grand hall of marble columns and floor with decorative and complicated inlays in yellow and red onyx. In the center was a massive 8-point star made from gold.

A grand staircase of white marble at one end led up to an open gallery circling the entire hall itself, and from its rails hung flowing vines with blooms of various colors. A level above that and across the roof were casements, angled and set in a way as to illuminate the room in a dazzling array of radiant light. It was a dizzying sight. From the outside, the building appears whole and complete. Inside, its secrets revealed. Shafts of daylight poured through every wall along the ceiling. Without the cloud of the fog to steal it, the light was powerful and bright.

The wonder of the architecture amazed me. Before the invasion, our Great Hall was a proud and tall structure. But it is dark and filled with shadows cast by torchlight save for the crystal dome which shrouds the incoming light in a gloomy yellow haze. It was dimensionless and gray.

Long streaming banners of crimson with a yellow flash, like a sunrise, hung from the tops of the ceiling. The banners reached down and lightly caressed the edges of the wall from a breeze within. We walked to a small wooden door.

The man with the forest eyes knocked once.

The door opened, and the man stepped aside. He motioned for me to walk through. The soldiers were well-trained and well-led, but they had never seen a moment's battle, and I feared for their lives should the wages of war come to their city walls.

I walked through the door. A long table of polished wood sat in the center of the room. Three chairs lined each side of the table, and a single high-backed chair graced each end. Men bearing long, silvery white hair occupied the chairs on both sides. All the same. They all wore white tunics covered with a dark crimson cloak, the edges lined with silver braided cord. At the far end stood a man. Gold braid lined the edge of his cloak. The chair before me was empty.

The room was open at the top with a clear view of the gallery above us under the dome of this great hall in the legendary City of the Southern Moon.

"Commander Soltari, at long last," the man at the far end said.

CHAPTER TWENTY-FOUR

Gallery of Visions

"IT IS SPECTACULAR, IS it not?" he said as he stood.

I nodded, still taking in the wonder of the craftsmanship and artwork around the inside of the dome.

"It reminds me of—"

"Home?" He had a slight smirk on his old face. The word struck me hard, for home was now a lost word with little meaning. "The Dome of Men is a thousand ages old, paid for by the blood of many soldiers. It is in their honor that it was built."

He watched me, looking for some expression.

"In the gallery above us, we have a scene from every major battle known by the Southern Lands. Although the gallery is as old as it is, it is still incomplete."

"Incomplete?"

"Yes. There is one more battle which must be fought."

His words bewildered me. A feeling I was not familiar with, nor cared for.

"Your gatekeeper said you have been expecting me?"

"Sit, please." He motioned to the empty chair, then sat down. "There is much of this land you do not understand, Commander Soltari."

I pulled out the heavy wood chair and sat, my curiosity ignoring the pompous words of this man.

"I am Prime Goff Il'Gavar. You may address me as Il'Gavar." He raised his eyebrows and tilted his head.

"Il'Gavar, we only come to seek shelter. Food and water for the soldiers and horses."

"You look like your father," he said. The others around the table looked at me, one nodded.

My head swam. My eyes darted from each of the Goffs side to side, back and forth, then settled on the one across from me. Il'Gavar's gaze was unwavering. He leaned back in his chair and clasped his hands on his belly.

"I knew your father. I am the one who requested his presence in the City when he was... It was most unfortunate what happened to him."

I no longer cared for the interrogation or the placating banter.

"Il'Gavar, if you please. I have traveled far and still have far to go. We are weary from crossing the Krazos Valley and need—"

"They will be cared for, Commander. I assume you travel to Gal Abed, or will you cross the river here to return to your homeland?"

"West."

He nodded and leaned forward, resting his clasped hands in front of him on the table.

"Commander Soltari, you are a man of action. Your Lord sent you, I'm afraid, to an unwinnable battle in the North. I'm surprised you survived. The force, which your soldiers and your city had the unfortunate destiny of meeting, is led by the Sister Ta'Bedtian. I believe she goes by Queen Ta'Bedtian now."

"I only know of her as the Queen of Shadows. How is she known here in the Southern Lands?"

"She is *from* the Southern Lands, Commander."

I leaned forward.

"She is from the City of the Southern Moon, and she is one of the Sisters of the Whispering Dawn." He saw the confusion in my eyes, and then stood. "Please, join me."

I stood and he led me to a long set of ornate iron stairs at the end of the room which ran up along the wall to the gallery under the dome. He walked up the stairs, and I followed.

"For many ages, the visions of the Sisters of the Whispering Dawn were written on our tablets. The visions proclaimed many things, and they came to pass. Our society of old soon accepted these visions - and their outcomes - as inevitable. Inalterable. We live by them, you see. They guide us."

He looked up to the dome as we walked the stairs.

"The visions of the Sisters were documented, and some of the more relevant milestones, are memorialized in paintings here in the gallery, along with our history. These were, or are, visions of a future foretold."

We reached the top of the stairs. The paintings lined the walls of the vast gallery. The massive dome's dizzying height above the council chambers was uncomfortable. The other six Goffs ascended the stairs to join us.

"There are seven here which may interest you."

We stopped before a large mural.

"The first of the paintings, Commander, is the great battle of the Southern Moon. This is the battle from which our land was born ages ago. This is not a vision of the Sisters of the Whispering Dawn, but our history. It is our beginning."

The painting showed an immense army of what looked like men fighting against beasts. Beasts who once were men, or not men yet, oddly shaped and hairless except for a mane of thick growth down the back.

"Vicious beasts. Our stories describe them as wild and savage, with sharp teeth and primitive weapons of rock and wood. But they fought to the death. They knew nothing else."

He walked toward the next painting in the row, the other Goffs shuffled along behind him.

"Some ages later, during the Empire of the Eastern Star, our people here in the south started to exhibit special gifts. I should say women, for they were all women, all with dark green eyes. They began having visions of things to come. We knew not from where these visions came, and in our misunderstanding, our initial reaction was harsh."

"You killed them?"

He groaned and stopped in front of a painting.

"Yes, and their deaths were not quick or pleasant. As I said, we did not understand, and initially, they were perceived as some supernatural threat. We lost many visions due to fear and carelessness of those in the past."

The painting depicted a woman hung between two stakes, her body flayed and open, fire all around her as people watched.

"Later, we realized those with this special power all had the same vision, even though they were separated by a great distance. They were brought together, educated, and raised together. "

"The Sisters of the Whispering Dawn."

"Yes. No doubt your father mentioned them?"

"No." I took a deep breath. "He never had the opportunity."

"Of course."

The next painting showed the outside of a building, similar to the one in which I now stood, and there in a courtyard stood a circle of ten women of all ages robed in white, with blond braided hair, arms raised toward a blue orb floating above the ground in the middle of the circle.

"The sisters?"

"Yes. We started documenting their visions after realizing some had come to pass. The blue orb is symbolic of the one true vision."

I opened my mouth to say something, then decided best not to. Then said: "How?"

"Clairvoyance."

"Clairvoyance?"

He looked at me and smiled.

"Yes, the ability to see future events."

"Sorcery." Before I could stop it again, the word was out. Goff Il'Gavar grinned.

"Ah, yes. I forgot your lands lack belief in such things. No, not sorcery. A gift." I let it go. There was something peculiar in the painting. Beyond the circle of women stood a row of four younger girls against a building, all blindfolded.

"Are these also sisters?" I pointed to the girls.

"No." There was a bit of malice in his tone. "They have the trait of the dark green eyes but cannot see visions. They have a far deadlier ability. Hence, the blindfolds. They are called the Kur'Ya." A severe chill ran up my spine, and I stepped back. He tilted his head. "Commander?"

"It is nothing." Sweat formed on my brow.

There was something amiss. His eyes dropped to the floor. He took in a deep breath.

"When Ta'Bedtian left, she took with her a Kur'Ya named Pri'Eten. They were friends." He looked up, then reached out, directing me to the next painting. "Shall we?" I held his gaze for a moment, then turned.

He led me to a painting that showed a great battle with horsemen, swordsmen, the dead, the dying, and the victors.

"This battle is the first mentioned by the sisters."

"The horsemen, the soldiers, they all look... the same."

"Yes, this was the battle to establish our right to rule. This battle was necessary to prove who we are or were to become, rather. This is why our flag is crimson and yellow. Crimson for the bloodshed and yellow for the dawn. A new day. A new beginning, if you will."

"The Empire of the New Dawn," I said.

"Aye." The story relayed by Betir El Friz came back to me once again. "When you overthrew your empire and pushed those who fought for the dead Emperor across the desert."

"Yes. That is correct." His head tilted slightly. I could see my response was unexpected. He turned and led us to the next painting.

I stood and stared at it, stupefied. My mouth agape.

"Ah. I see you recognize some aspects of this one. This is when the Empire of the New Dawn found itself defending against invaders from the north."

"Aye. But to see it, here. It looks like... The building, there in the center. That—"

"Yes. Your 'Great Hall' as you call it. The building has seen many changes. I believe you also call it the 'Hall of Fallen Empires'. And for good reason, no doubt."

He turned to the painting.

"After the great battle with what would become the Northern Lands, we settled here south of the river, and became part of the great balance the Westerners believe in." He chuckled. "There were some petty disputes amongst our leadership, and a trade war ensued. Safe passage was no longer guaranteed for Northerners. We built the wall around our city. It is the only safe entry into—"

"If the Sisters had visions of all of this, then why wasn't the Empire more prepared?" Il'Gavar smiled.

"The attack was sudden. Some called it extraordinarily random. The visions started occurring barely a moon's length before your people came from the northwest. We were prepared, just not prepared for the likes of your kind."

He looked at me and his eyes seemed a bit more sinister. The same look the eastern radicals have in their eyes.

"Is my father's murder in one of your paintings?" The question was out before I could mind my tongue.

"No."

He glanced at the painting, then walked past me to another. It showed the sisters in a circle with one standing on the outside of it, back turned to the rest.

"This is the splintering of the Sisters. This one here..." He pointed to the one with her back turned to the others. "Young, smart, highly intelligent. Vision after vision, plus some other... say... unique abilities. And you can call it sorcery. But she was also combative. She would speak against the other sisters. She would argue that her visions were the only correct ones, and so forth. It started when she was a child."

"A child?"

"Yes. As I said, if a daughter is born with the trait, they were brought to the Sisterhood to be raised. She was only a baby when she came to us."

"And the parents? What of them?"

He frowned as if trying to repress a violent memory.

"The trait. The dark green eyes you mention," I said. "Like emeralds on fire?" Il'Gavar shuddered. I remembered the eyes of the girl I rescued from the Rogues Army—the Kur'ya.

"Yes, like emeralds... on fire," Il'Gavar said. "You have seen these eyes?"

"I have."

His face twisted a bit, and he cast a worried look at the other Goffs.

"Commander, if you have borne witness to these eyes, then you have met Ta'Bedtian herself. I can assure you—"

"No. A Kur'Ya. In Bin El Omen."

He scoffed, and chuckled. "There is only the one who left with Ta'Bedtian. However, it has been many ages, and it is unlikely you met her."

"How can you be sure?"

"Because you live, Commander."

"The Kur'Ya drain life with their gaze. That is the far deadlier ability you mentioned. That is why they are blindfolded. Am I correct?"

Il'Gavar stood stunned, then slowly nodded. He turned to the other Goffs and got received no support.

"But... you lived?" He frowned. "Well, that is something to consider. Please, let's continue." He was lost in thought as we walked to another painting, passing a few of little interest to him.

In the painting a tall woman with a gold head adornment stood at the top of a stair, arms outstretched. At her side, kneeling, were eight dark-haired women, four on each side of her, heads down as if in despair.

Before her on the stairs was an army, soldiers of the north by the uniforms, surrounded by the bodies of things similar to the musta kuori, but with red eyes and much larger, and they carried blades of black metal. At the head of the army stood a Northern soldier... with two bloodied swords raised high.

I recognized the swords... as my father's. A sword long lost to me.

Il'Gavar looked at me, then back to the painting and continued.

"At the time, of course, we did not know who this represented, or who the eight women were, or what they represented. Until recently, we also did not know who this man was leading the Northern Lands to victory." He turned to me. "This soldier is the one we've been waiting for. This soldier, Commander, is you." His sincerity was false, his tone of voice stale, as if the speech was planned and practiced. It was a lie. I was sure of it.

But my eyes were drawn back to the short sword. It was not the one I carried. This sword... was lost.

Gone.

"Your painting shows nothing and means nothing. That is not me. That... is my father."

"Your father?"

His words faltered and his laugh was full of unease.

"Aye. That is not my sword. That sword was cleaved in two when my father was murdered by the militants of the Rogues Army. I do not have possession of that sword and know not what happened to it after they returned me to the Great City." I looked at him. This should have troubled Il'Gavar, but his face remained expressionless, like he already knew. "He is the one who was to kill this Queen of Shadows. Not me. Your vision is wrong. According to your... sorcery, it is too late."

Il'Gavar pulled at his face in deep thought.

"It is possible, I suppose, when the Sisterd had this vision, Ta'Betian knew its true meaning and had your father tracked down and killed to attempt to change the outcome. Or fulfill a destiny only she saw." Il'Gavar looked to the other Goffs for support. One had tears in his eyes and was visibly shaking. Something was awry. "It has been over twenty ages since this vision first came to light."

"My father was murdered twenty ages ago." Something still did not satisfy my curiosity. "If Ta'Bedtian had my father murdered to change this vision and ensure her place of power, then this is nothing more than a painting in a gallery." My tone became more threatening and he stepped back. "If you knew of all this, and you know of the Queen, then why not prevent it yourself? Why does my homeland have to suffer and my family murdered?"

Il'Gavar grinned slightly, collected himself, and started pacing. Emotions whirled through my mind like a blizzard, and I reflexively reached for a sword that was not there.

"We are bound by the inevitable. It is our way." He stopped pacing and faced me. "We cannot stop the visions. In our belief, they are bound to the laws of the universe, and even if we tried to prevent the outcome, ultimately the vision would be realized... some other way. There is nothing we can do except help fulfill the vision. And to support the victory over her."

His face was grim and detached. The brilliant color in his eyes went dim as he formed his thoughts.

"Tell me, Il'Gavar, what the visions of the Sisters of the Whispering Dawn say now."

He burst out a short, nervous laugh.

"Nothing, Commander. They are all dead."

He became dark and serious. The Goff, who was whimpering, screamed out, then left the gallery in a mad rush. Il'Gavar straightened, his face now a calm demeanor, uncaring, vacant.

"After Ta'Bedtian left, a long period went by with no visions, no cohesive vision from the sisters. It was as if their power had disappeared. The Emperor had them all burned unceremoniously, no longer of any use, I suppose, and then razed the temple." His eyes were empty as he said this. "The truly startling thing is since Ta'Bedtian left, no daughters have borne the trait."

He turned to his remaining colleagues.

"Not our finest moment, Commander" Il'Gavar scratched at the back of his head. "But the way of the emperor was our way."

"Was?"

Il'Gavar lowered his head.

"Yes, Commander. Emperor Val Distad is dead. And with no son or suitable heir to take over the throne..."

I understood the weakness of the Southern Lands then. The emptiness of the city. It was a shell of an empire long gone. A facade, and the balance no longer existed.

"He had a daughter," I said. "He had a daughter... in the Sisterhood. That is what you are hiding."

Il'Gavar notably shuddered, then tried to collect himself.

"It is true." He looked up at me with old eyes just then. The weight of it appeared hard to bear. "Now you know one of our darkest secrets." He saw the look in my eyes, then scoffed. "Oh, no, no, Commander. The Emperor's daughter is not who you are thinking."

Half-truths, riddles, visions. Even then, something still gnawed at me. The Emperor ordered his own daughter... to be killed? Or she... she escaped... I was anxious to take my leave of this sideshow.

"Come, let us proceed back to the chamber."

Il'Gavar turned and walked along the gallery wall and back to the stairs. The secrets hidden by his words lingered with me as we descended to the room. I put it to rest. We all followed and then sat around the table once again.

"Soltari, we of the Southern Lands offer our help. We will help you regain your homeland, Commander. This will be our greatest battle since—"

"This is not your battle to fight, Primary Goff Il'Gavar. This battle only belongs to the Northern Lands." I stood. "The Southern Lands wasted their opportunity because you live in a world of hallucinations and paint." Il'Gavar's face went red. "My lands, my wife and daughter, my father... all paid the price for your—"

Il'Gavar slammed his hands on the table and stood.

"Commander Soltari, forces you cannot explain brought you here. We've been expecting you."

"You've been expecting my father. And he is dead for twenty winters now." And then it came to me at once. "You. You were going to tell him about the vision, weren't you? That is why you summoned him. And now—"

Il'Gavar angered more.

"She must be destroyed!"

"What are you hiding, Prime Goff Il'Gavar? What is it behind your eyes I can sense but cannot see? Fear?"

"We can ill afford to have Sister Ta'Bedtian sitting at our gates. Her sorcery is more powerful than we have ever seen." I leaned forward on the table.

"There, Il'Gavar, is where she will sit until *our* final battle is won and I post her head above *our* North Gate, for I have proclaimed it. Or shall I paint you a picture?"

Il'Gavar sat, then leaned back and grinned.

"With a force of what? Thirty soldiers, Commander?"

A few of the Goffs chuckled.

"Our army is ready, Commander, and will remain ready. A force of 2,000 strong awaits my command. A battle-hardened leader like you with a force as strong as ours could successfully lead this expedition against the queen. We know her powers."

"You know what she used to be. Tell me, Il'Gavar, what are the black things lying about the stairs in the final painting? Who are the eight behind her?" He stared at me, blankly. "You know nothing."

"It is your best option, Commander Soltari."

"But not my only option. Your prophecy is dead. It died with my father. I am not him. I settle things with my blades, not by waggling my tongue. I decline your offer. I do not need or desire any help from the Southern Lands. And I am not here to request it."

Il'Gavar nodded. "So be it." He stood. "You and your men will be escorted to our western borders. I will guarantee you safe passage. We wouldn't want another Northerner killed on our soil."

His tone was heartless, devoid of any sympathy. The door to the chamber opened, and the tall soldier with the forest green eyes stood in the doorway.

"This is Commander Ghenesta. He will accompany you back to your camp."

I stood. "And to my original request?"

He sighed. "Yes, Commander. We have tended to your people and horses with food and water."

I bowed my head. "Thank you, Prime Goff Il'Gavar." I turned, and as I did, Il'Gavar gave a slight nod to the Goff on his right.

The six soldiers were waiting for me beyond the door. They stepped in front of me and escorted me out of the domed hall, through the city, and to the large gate. They stopped at the bridge and parted into two neat, straight rows. I walked between them.

As I crossed the bridge, Ghenesta spoke.

"Commander," he said in his proud and straight voice, "You are to camp here for the night. In the morning, a small party of soldiers and myself will accompany you to the Western Lands."

He bowed, and the seven of them turned and walked back into the city. The gate made its slow descent downward and closed with a resonant crack, separating the City of the Southern Moon from the rest of the lands.

Chapter Twenty-Five

Torment

I woke before daybreak and started a fire. The men rustled in the early dawn. They awoke one by one, gathered rations, and tended to the horses. The fog was as thick as a chowder on a chilly day, and as damp and cold as the northern wind.

The fog lightened to a dark bluish-white as the sun crested through the trees. The gate to the City of the Southern Moon cut loose a startling crack as it rose into the towers. The city exhaled seven men armored in leather with hooded cloaks of scarlet flowing behind them. Their horses, all black and lightly armored, trotted across the bridge to the road. Their saddlebags bulged with provisions. Each wore decorative swords and carried a variety of other weapons on their person and saddle. Axes, daggers, bows, and quivers with multi-colored feather guides. The horsemen approached. They were the same men from yesterday. Commander Ghenesta pulled the hood of his cloak back.

"Commander General Soltari," he said. "My men and I will accompany you on your journey to Gal Abed, the Mountain Wind. You are ready?"

"Nearly. We will eat together before we leave."

"Very well."

They moved their horses from camp and dismounted. The horses grazed nearby in the wet dew of the morning with ours.

Myself, Ghenesta, and Fonchesca sat around a fire, while the rest built another fire and prepared for our departure.

Silent.

"That is an unusual sword you have." I said, nodding to Ghenesta's blade. The edges curved like waves of water and rippled from hilt to tip.

"Yes, this sword has been in my family for many ages. Like yours, yes? It appears simply decorative, but I can assure you its bite is deadly."

His banter trailed off as thoughts of our journey ahead wandered in from the mist.

We cleared camp and set onto the Kinelot Road toward the Western Lands. Commander Ghenesta led my party while the remaining soldiers of the Southern City rode to the rear. They did not speak. I enjoyed the silence and the lack of conversation. The only sounds came from the low breaths of our horses, and the jingling of their tack. I was in a dark, melancholy mood, and could do well without the usual niceties of getting to know each other. I did not care. I would know in time. I pulled the hood of my cloak over my head and separated myself from the rest.

We rode throughout the morning. Not a single word was spoken. Not even when the fog lifted high in the sky and unleashed the rain upon us. No glimmers of joy were uttered when the rain broke, and the sun peeked through the clouds.

And no one but us traveled the road. The realization sent a shiver up my back. The road was as quiet as a grave.

It was simply, the road.

The road was lined with tall pine trees whispering in the wind. A new fog descended and hung in the air, throwing an eerie glow as the sun moved across the sky, casting shadows in the dark wood. An occasional animal would appear, or make a track through the forest as it ran from the advancing party. We rode for over half the day before we stopped in a meadow nestled in a grove of tall pine that stood like outcasts in the forest of oaks, elms, and ash.

We sat on the ground, ate, and drank water, resting our bodies from the saddle. There were no orders to give. Our mission was a simple one. Travel to the city of Gal Abed. Beyond it lie the mysterious lands like the western plains, and the undying mist. Stories say beyond the mist lies a a land like none other. As a child, I was told the Western Lands were home to strange folk of all sizes. They had clans who were very short and could walk under a horse without tilting their head, and some were so tall that a horse appeared as a wolf next to them. I did not know what the Westerners called these folk, nor did I care. To me, they are the stuff of myth and legend. Fantasy from an over-imaginative father, I suspect.

We camped in the meadow.

For the next two days, we rode in relative silence.

For two days, we saw no other travelers.

On the third midday, we settled once again in a meadow off the road. The horses grazed on the fresh grasses or walked the edge of the Sleeping River, which the road followed, and drank their fill. I sat with Captain Fonchesca.

"We should reach Gal Abed the day after next," I said.

There was a rustle behind us and I looked as a small animal scurried into the forest. I stood. The place suddenly seemed familiar, and a sense of dread came over me.

I knew this place.

The sun vanished behind a dark cloud, and the depth of the forest fell into shadow beyond the small meadow. Another rustle came from our left, then circled us, staying undercover in the forest. Its steps were slow and careful. The sun came out from behind the cloud, and the forest brightened. There, in a clearing beyond the meadow, stood a tall, old and gray, leafless oak, with long branches stretching out from all sides and up. Alone, it sat, lifeless in a ray of sunshine. I walked toward it.

"Commander Soltari," Fonchesca whispered. I raised my hand with my index finger extended. I drew my sword.

I reached the edge of the meadow and saw a small deer path leading to the clearing. I walked along it, quietly, watching both sides of the forest for movement. I heard a click of a twig to my left and saw nothing. I continued the short distance to the tree and stepped into the clearing. I gazed up at the oak.

The tree stood taller than those around it, and the branches reached out the length of several wagons end to end. I walked under it, then around its massive trunk that would take at least five grown men hand in hand to wrap around it. I reached the other side and looked back toward the meadow, but it was gone. I walked a little more around the tree, certain I was looking toward where the meadow should be, but couldn't see it.

I knew the tree. The last time I stood under it, my father was at my side. And the meadow was where I last saw him alive. The ambush came from this forest.

I collapsed below the tree, leaning against its massive trunk. I removed my gloves. My hands were wet from sweat and rain. I pulled the pouch from my belt containing the lotuses and removed one. I held it in my hands, then pulled it close to my face and inhaled the sweet smell. I sat silent in the solitude of the forest...

...as it closed in around me.

Rini...

The voice came from behind me, then all around me.

Rini.

The haunting whispers of an apparition.

"...Father..."

I am here...

It was in front of me now.

"I... I am sorry..."

A ghostly figure in white appeared before me. A woman. I could see the forest through her, and the sun fell behind a dark cloud again, shrouding us all in darkness.

The white became a gray shawl that covered her head and draped the full length of her body. It fluttered in a slight breeze. She floated above the forest floor.

"Who..." I said, my voice broken. A flash of my dead father lying on the forest floor flashed in my eyes. Sobbing came from the forest. A child's sobbing. A child's scream.

You cannot avenge thy homeland, Ssssoltariii...

The voice blew like a breeze, and echoed in my mind. My voice. Fluttering...

A chill on the wind brushed back my hair. Then, the apparition reached inside her shawl and drew a long, thin black sword, and the forest darkened to shadows and moved all around her. Only her outline stayed, reflected on the mist that formed in the air.

"I will avenge my family,"

I screamed at her, but the words disappeared in the wind, the force of them lost. The anger turned to sorrow.

Noooo Soltari. You have failed your homeland...

Her words were a gasp of torment through gritted teeth. My voice. She held up her sword with the tip pointed to the ground. She moved closer.

"I have failed them."

...Yessss...

The long-dead roots of the oak moved like fingers digging into the dark earth.

A biting breeze blew across me.

I looked up at her now hovering above me, sword tip at my chest. She pointed at me with a long, skinny, dead finger.

There will be no retribution...for you...

And she plunged her sword into my heart and the tree behind me, my blood flowing onto its dry, dark roots. They wriggled and squirmed, like worms after a hard rain, then settled into the ground. A flash of bright light blinded me and the apparition was gone and there before me stood my wife and my daughter, their clothes sodden with their blood, and my wife spoke to me. She spoke with the voice of the dead, a crackling whisper.

"What is my name, my love?" Tears of blood dripped from her eyes to the ground.

"I... I do not know," I sobbed. And I looked up at the sky. The branches of the tree became a darker shade of brown, sprouting stems and leaves and becoming full of life from the blood of my torment. I looked at my daughter, who was shivering.

"I'm scared, daddy. Are you coming home now?"

I grasped the blade of the sword and pulled it from me, and the tree. Its sharp edges cut into my hands. I stuck the sword of torment into the ground and used it to pull myself up before my wife and child, and stepped forward. I reached out my hands to them. Blood dripped from my fingers.

"Forgive me."

A blinding flash and a crack, and the sword rose and snapped in two. The light cleared, my eyes cleared.

My wife opened her mouth and spoke to me. I couldn't hear her words. She was voiceless, transparent, mist. They disappeared as quickly as they came, and the sun appeared from behind the clouds and lit the forest around me.

I was lying on the ground under the tree. The purple lotus lay beside me in a quiet beam of sunlight, gently jostled by a breeze. I sat up, picked up the lotus, and put it in the pouch. I leaned back against the tree and tried to shake the visions from my head.

A twig snapped to my right. A fawn grazed in the forest's underbrush. Behind it stood its mother, staring at me, the ghost of a man. Captain Fonchesca approached me. The deer scattered into the woods.

"Commander?"

"I am ready to ride. Let's break camp and leave this miserable place." I stood.

"Aye."

We continued our journey until the sun disappeared behind the tall trees. We found a clearing near the road and made camp for the night. I knew tonight would be a sleepless one. Something foul lurked in this forest, and my vision earlier left me shaken, suspicious, and drained. It was only a matter of time before I slipped down the slopes of sanity again into the abyss. The torment of my vision by the oak weighed heavily on me as I lay under the canopy of stars staring into the moonless night.

At dawn, we rose, ate, and mounted our horses, nudging them down the road. An orangish mist hung in the air in the early morning sunlight. The air was cold and penetrated my leather armor. The soldiers ahead paused, and we stopped. The sound of jingling tack, tapping metal, and the lonely creaks of wood emerged from the mist ahead. The chill birthed two horses pulling a caravan and driver, followed by another, and another. One by one a line of thirty wagons sauntered past us. The drivers gave us barely a look.

Not one Roama smiled or waved. They moved like ghosts as they traveled the Kinelot Road.

We continued through the day in darkened silence. I spoke not of my encounter by the oak, and none asked, each lost in haze-filled thoughts as we made the trip step-by-step to the west.

The forest opened up and before us lay a vast plain. The sun cast flames of red, yellow, and orange across the horizon behind the mountains in the distance. It was nearing dark. I was relieved to be out of the forest.

"We will camp there by the river at the bridge and finish our journey in the morn. We are still a day's travel from Gal Abed," Ghenesta said. I agreed, and we made camp in silence at the edge of the forest.

We rose to a clear day with blue, cloudless skies. A cool wind blew from the west. We crossed a wooden bridge over the Sleeping River. Soon after, we passed the intersection where the Madoran Road runs north along the mountains into the Northern Lands. The Roama call it the *Red Road*.

"We are in the Western Lands now, Commander. My men will camp here and await my return from Gal Abed."

"And you?"

"I have different orders. I will continue to Gal Abed with you."

He kept his gaze ahead and said no more.

By midday, we crossed a large stone bridge across the Sleeping River into the Western Lands. We stopped at a clearing in an open, lush green field. In the distance rose the white Croft Vale Cliffs, and sitting on top, as if hewn from the rock itself, sat the city of Gal Abed.

The city was built with white stone, set against a backdrop of greens and grays, and built along and into the cliffside. Towers braced by parapets sat at each corner. From the center rose The Keep of Gal Abed, broad and square, like a fortress within the fortress. The city blended into the white rock at the base along the edge of the cliffs. A long arched bridge spanned across the Sleeping River, which plummeted over the edge of the cliffs in a grand waterfall they called The Falls of Huol Taya, or Guardian Falls.

A strange and unfamiliar peace washed over me.

Like I was returning... home.

Part Three

INTO THE ABYSS

CHAPTER TWENTY-SIX

Gal Abed

WE FOLLOWED THE WINDING road up the hill to a plateau and to the bridge over the falls. Eight mounted sentries waited at the edge of the bridge, blocking our passage across. The bridge spanned high above the river. A fall from it meant certain death, not from the water, but the rocks below, and the eventual tumble over the long waterfall at the cliff's edge. Behind the sentries at the other end of the bridge sat a large stone and steel gateway capped with two large towers on each side that faded into a long natural rock wall extending along the edge of the city.

"Identify yourself, travelers," said one sentry. He wore chain armor decorated with the colors and symbols of the Western Lands - a red and gold rectangle, with a white tower placed in the middle.

"I am Commander Ghenesta of the City of the Southern Moon, and this is Commander General Soltari of the Great City of the Northern Lands."

The sentry's horse faltered a bit and sidestepped.

"Commander Soltari?" The sentry squinted a bit to see my worn and weary face behind the long strands of my black hair and beard.

"I am." I held my head up. The soldier went white. He leaned over and whispered to the sentry next to him. In an instant, the sentry wheeled his horse around and raced across the bridge to the gate. The sentry cleared his throat.

"State your purpose."

Ghenesta looked at me, then back at the sentry. "We have come for council with your Lady."

"Invited?"

"Identify yourself, sentry," I said. He seemed startled.

"I am Topet, Captain of the Guard."

"Captain Topet, time is of the essence. We have traveled for days from the City of the Southern Moon, and I, along with my companions from the Northern Lands, have traveled for seasons and are weary and hungry. We ask for passage to the City of Gal Abed. Please relay my request to Regent Tass Burnok."

"Heard, Commander Soltari." He spoke with a bit more confidence, borderline arrogance, and nothing else.

"You shall not grant us access?"

He glanced at me.

"I assure you, Commander General, we have announced your presence, and I am awaiting my orders. It is not within my power to grant access, merited, known or otherwise."

The sentry returned from the gates at a full gallop across the bridge along with six more horsemen. One held a guidon with a long gold and red streaming banner flowing from it. I instinctively backed up my horse and saw Ghenesta do the same. However, I felt no reason to distrust the soldiers of Gal Abed.

The sentry turned and whispered to Topet, Captain of the Guard. He looked at us.

"Commander Soltari, our Regent welcomes you on your return to Gal Abed." Ghenesta looked at me.

"Thank you, Captain," I said, slightly bowing my head.

"The honor is ours, Commander General. If you and your men will follow my guards, they will accompany you across the Bridge of Halos, where a party awaits to welcome you into the city."

Two of the sentries turned their horses, the one with the long guidon and another. We followed. The height of the bridge was dizzying. The drop certainly fatal for the fall was higher than the tallest pines, and at the end of it, rocks and fast flowing water.

We passed under the massive stone gateway of Gal Abed. Six men cloaked in red and gold stopped us near a city circle. In the middle of the circle stood a grand fountain. On top of the fountain was a sculpture of a man looking up at the heavens, sword raised in one hand.

Stout and strong, the tall men stood before us. All wore beards of various colors and lengths, all with a tinge of red. The people here forged the best weapons and large machinery used on the fields of battle. Machines that could hurl fire and rocks over city walls. People of warfare. But not of war.

The tallest of the red men wore a cape studded with gold leaf and a silvery white trim around the edges. He wore gauntlets on his large hands. He turned to me.

"By the Gods, Rini. It is true." I dismounted and walked to him. We embraced. "It is good to see you again, big brother." He held me out at arm's length, looking down at me, then to the others.

"You and your party will join us at the Dragons' Cry."

He pointed to the tall, wide square tower behind him. It sat atop a long stone fortress decorated with many flags. They were the flags of the many clans which made up the Western Lands. They were all of many shapes and sizes, but one thing united them: the red and white colors of the Western Lands.

"Come, let us eat and drink. Mostly drink." He roared with laughter, and a feeling washed over me, which cleansed me and filled the dark pockets of my being, and I was suddenly humbled by this man, this child who always towered over me, always laughing.

"You may leave your horses here. Our ostlers will tend to them."

I looked to my right and saw a large encampment of Eastern travelers and the Grand Bazaar of Gal Abed. I remembered the place, and the food.

Burnok guided us toward the tower and the place he called the Dragon's Cry. The tower loomed over the city. The city itself was a sight to behold. Its breathtaking cobbled streets lined with shops. The city folk going through their daily lives as those in the Great City once did. Buying, selling, trading in the bazaar. Food shops, clothing, blacksmiths. Smoke rose from one shop, and the smell of smoked meat hit me. I stopped, closed my eyes, and took it all in, savoring the sweet smell, remembering home. Burnok patted my back and chuckled. He said something, but it was lost to the sights, sounds, and smells of the city.

Atop the corners of the towers, fires blazed, silhouetting the sentries keeping watch. The view must be both breathtaking, and unsettling, from their position looking out over the valley below.

The massive doors to the tower were broad and heavy. They stood open with two sentries posted on each side. We entered. The opposite side of the tower was open, allowing fresh mountain air to breeze through unchecked. Torches blazed, and the smoke whipped up into the air. I followed the traces of it to the top of the tower, which was also open. Stairs along the walls lead up to the next level, then another, and another. Light gleamed in through the various casements. We walked toward the opening at the far end.

The sound of a small waterfall from beyond the opening echoed through the tower.

I stopped and motioned Burnok aside. The others continued, led by the Western guards.

"I know, brother, it has been a long time since I last visited. When I received command of the Eastern forces, I…"

"Is this you apologizing, dear brother?" He smirked under his beard.

I found no comfort from the ground I now stared at.

"I had a wife. And a child. A daughter."

He put his hand on my shoulder. "I am sorry. You must be filled with pain."

"I cannot remember their names, only their faces and…" I watched the trails of smoke from the braziers float up through the tower.

"You have been through much, Rini. I'm sure you will remember in time."

"Aye. In time." He gripped my other shoulder and squeezed both tightly.

"Come," he said, turning me to the opening. He put his arm around me and motioned with the other. "Right now, let us fill your belly with excellent food, and your soul with light-hearted conversation." He let go. "And wine, yes?"

I shook as the chill of the air washed through me.

"Aye. And wine."

We walked past the edge of the opening and back into daylight. I squinted at the suddenness of the change. We were in a large courtyard prepared for dining with covered tables and high-back chairs with ornate carving. Off to one side were stations for cooking. Smoke billowed up from one, and the sweet, smoky smells wrenched my senses. We crossed to the back in a shaded grove, which sat on the edge of an opening in the rock against the cliff face. Water streamed down the cliff-side near us in a fit of miniature waterfalls and down through a naturally hewn hole revealing a spring, green and blue.

"The Dragon's Cry," said Burnok. "Welcome, my guests."

Chapter Twenty-Seven

The Dragons Cry

Myself, Burnok, Ghenesta, and Fonchesca sat at a table near the falls. The remaining soldiers sat at tables set around the open area.

"My land, it is good to see you again, my brother. My heart is filled with joy." I smiled, or at least what would pass for a smile. His smile faded. "I know what brings you to Gal Abed. A most perilous thing—" My eyes went wide.

"A most perilous thing?" I said. He frowned, awkwardly. Not an expression his face was used to.

"I apologize, brother. I do not mean to offend." He met my gaze. "I would like to know my brother again."

I sighed. "Light-hearted conversation."

"Yes. And leave formalities for counsel chambers."

Some servers brought us wine, a plate full of steaming hot meat, and one full of fruit and vegetables.

We talked amongst ourselves about nonsensical things. Burnok told his favorite story of how he saved my life one day camping with our father. Laughter echoed from the other tables as I filled my belly with the smoked meats of the Western Lands.

Burnok let out a hefty belch. He was a large man. Built like a bull ox and as tall as a bear. I wondered from where it came. His mother was thin and small. Our father was stocky, but shorter than I am now. It must lurk in his Western blood.

Burnok sighed. "Alright then, drink and talk business. I have only heard stories about what has happened in the Northern Lands, Rini. I am so sorry to hear. The Roama often fill their days and nights with stories. Some true, some not."

"Time is lost to me, my brother, since the darkness from the northern sky." I relayed the details of the initial attack on the Great City, leaving out my resignation. I told him about the force I took to the Northern Wastes. And of the blizzard.

"I have heard stories of this blizzard. I thought it was some drunken Roama embellishment. But, you were there?" I nodded. He leaned back in his chair, stunned, silent, then wiped his mouth with the back of his sleeve. "By the Gods Rini. I had no idea. I mean—"

"I am here now, and have traveled very far to be here."

A cool breeze rushed through the area.

"I have to ask, brother, why not come here first? I am curious."

I looked at him. "The depth of the snow, the wind. It was easier, and albeit safer, as we now know, to travel through Zhalé Pass. We started for the Great City and reached a grove of trees by the White River. Something... lived, in those trees, in the mist."

"Shadows," Fonchesca said. Burnok turned to him.

"You were there too?"

Fonchesca shook his head. "No, we encountered the same in our escape from the city."

"Escape? Oy." Burnok stopped eating. He leaned back in his chair, taking all this in. He stared at his plate, trying to work it out in his head.

"Stories from the Roama speak of an ill wind, a deadly chill. They no longer travel the Black Road. They say it is cursed."

"Aye. All the merchants left the bazaar before the first attack, like they knew or heard of something."

"And they said nothing?"

"They did not, is my understanding. I had just returned from the East. The attack came within a storm that same night."

"Rini, are you saying some sorcery was involved?" Burnok chuckled nervously. "You?"

"Is, involved, brother." He let out a long, deep sigh. He knew for me, or anyone in the Northern Lands, to mention any idea of sorcery was a serious matter. Northerners did not believe in, or discuss, such things.

Burnok leaned back in his seat, hands on the table, pondering my words.

"We came to a road. The Black Road, I believe. We followed it to the foothills at the edge of the desert where..." I let my thoughts trail. I felt no need to relay the grim details, especially those of murder.

"Desert! My eyes, Rini. Have you traveled East?"

"Aye. There, in the foothills, madness beset the last of us. And there, the last of my men died." Fonchesca stopped chewing then and turned to me, waiting for more, but I stopped.

My heart was sinking deep into the darkness again.

"Some silk and spice merchants found me at the edge of the desert, and I traveled deeper into the Eastern Lands, to Bin El Omen."

"You have traveled, brother. You talk of places I have only heard of in passing." He chewed on a piece of meat, pondering the idea of traveling so far east. "Sure, I've been to the Great City, and the City of the Southern Moon, but never to the Eastern Lands." He stroked his beard in thought. "The merchants though, they travel far. It defies comprehension. They travel even beyond our western borders. I know not where. They talk of great and absurd things, and the edge of the world. I care not to see such things." He shrugged. "I am happy with all the comforts." He chuckled and leaned over to me. "But my axe and sword could use some time on the battlefield." Then he burst into laughter, momentarily silencing it with a swig of wine. "Bin El Omen, eh?"

"Aye."

"Isn't that where those brigands you talk about are from?"

"Some. A new Herra announced himself some time ago, calls himself an Al Friz, and formed some of the Rogues Army into a radical faction. They are the ones we quarrel with on the eastern borders. Most of the Rogues Army in Bin El Omen are part of the royal guard, allied to the Herra. Some are paid mercenaries hired out from the guard. It is not uncommon for them to escort merchant caravans either. They escorted this caravan, probably because of who traveled within it."

I had everyone's attention now. The only sound and movement was the slight fall of water behind us.

"And who was this person?" Burnok said.

"The Priestess Kristava."

He coughed and nearly choked on the food in his mouth. His eyes were wide.

"Well," he said, then took a drink.

"It matters not. I fought alongside men of the Rogues Army when the caravan fell under attack in Kaksoset Canyon. I also fought against them in Bin El Omen, saving a..." I trailed off at the thought. "A young woman."

"A chivalrous bastard to the end, eh?" Burnok said.

"And daring. Killing Rogues Army in their own city?" Fonchesca added. Everyone laughed.

"It did not go unnoticed," I took a sip of wine.

Burnok stopped laughing and let it trail off.

"It was eastern brigands who slew our father," Burnok said. "Four of them. The one who murdered him escaped," A silence fell across the table. Everyone knew the story.

"Do you remember Lt. Estarenza?" Fonchesca said. My eyes widened, and my stomach welled up into my throat and choked me. I coughed.

"Aye. Why do you mention him?" Fonchesca looked startled.

"Commander?" I realized the rage in my voice and cleared my throat.

"Apologies, Captain. I remember Lieutenant Estarenza well. He was with me on the journey from the frozen wastes to the—" I cleared my throat and looked at my now empty plate. "Why do you mention him?" I asked, calmed by the sorrow and horror.

"No, I apologize, Commander. I did not know. I—" He sighed. "I am sorry."

"Please continue, Captain," said Burnok. The voice was soft, like the wind that blew through the courtyard. A voice which did not match the man.

"His father was with your father on that day, Commander."

"I am aware."

"Of course. I remember Uri telling me the story his father used to tell him when he was teaching him the way of the sword. His father regretted the day your father was killed. It weighed heavily on him until the day he passed."

"He never shared this with me. Why would he regret that day?" I said.

"He felt he allowed the one who killed your father to escape. The story is three of the four attackers were dead, and Estarenza's father was involved in a duel with the last of them. He called him a master swordsman, none like he had ever seen. Uri thought his father admired him somewhat. For his skills only, he meant." His gaze dropped to the table.

"Continue," I said.

"Estarenza's father was wounded, but at the end of the fray, he managed to get a hit on the Eastern swordsman, a good one, too. The swordsman dropped his weapon. Unfortunately, after that, he escaped. Estarenza's father kept that sword. He said he would tell Uri to remember, no matter how masterful you are with this weapon, there is always one better than you, so ensure you are the best at all you do."

I was sick.

"Uri Estarenza was a fine swordsman. And soldier." I said. "I remember the two in a heated dual and the sword fall. I was being coddled by one of the other soldiers, a horseman, as I stared at my father's motionless body."

I was heavy.

"Father was a good swordsman, Rini. But his weapon of choice was his tongue. He was a crafty speaker, and because of our father, the alliances within the lands exist. It no longer matters what anyone says. What we have is now, with the beauty of the future, and—"

"The weight of the past." I looked over at him. "Papa used to say that. He used to tell me that as a boy when I felt sullen." I smirked. "Beauty of the future." I laughed, and Burnok quickly joined. "What a horse's ass of a thing to say." My laughter turned hearty as the weight of my past briefly slipped away. I poured some wine into my cup and drank. The laughter soon died down. "If only he could have seen the future." And then I became stone as my thoughts turned to the Queen.

"Tell me Fonchesca, you said this Estarenza's father got a hit on the brigand and loosed his sword," Burnok said. "How did the man escape?"

"The swordsman moved to parry, and Estarenza's sword came to the hilt instead of sword. I remember him showing me the mistake. His father, remembering every detail, knew where this swordsman erred. The sword came to hilt and loosed not just the sword, but the swordsman's finger. This finger." He pointed to his first finger. And then my heart filled with trepidation and rage all at once and I slammed a fist to the table and stood.

"Easy Rini! What—"

"It was him. Even after watching him leave, I sensed it, and did nothing."

"Who, Commander?" I slipped my hand into my belt pouch and brought out the amulet Betir El Friz had left. I tossed it onto the table. Burnok stared at it, then picked it up.

He looked at me. "Where did you get this?"

"A man named Betir El Friz, whom I met in the desert on my way to Ca'Bri."

"El Friz?" said Ghenesta.

"Aye. This was my father's. I remember it. He must have lost it the day they murdered him, and Betir El Friz picked it up, maybe as a trophy." Burnok held up the amulet and turned it over in his hands.

He looked up at me.

"He left it behind after our counsel in the foothills. I wondered why he went pale after I told him my name. He packed up his belongings and dropped it. Or left it. He knew. He knew me no longer as the young boy weeping over his dead father, but of the man I have become. A soldier."

I leaned back in my chair.

"And he was missing the very finger you described, Captain."

Chapter Twenty-Eight

Commander Versol

WE FINISHED DINING AND Burnok led us down the road from the Dragon's Cry through the center of the city. We walked along the white cobbled streets lined by white stone houses with thatched roofs and shops. Children watched us from windows and iron balconies or ran giggling ahead of us, most eyes on Burnok as he smiled and laughed and greeted townsfolk along the way.

We came to a large garden area lined with white and red flowering trees that towered over us, the fallen petals soft under our feet. Iron fencing lined the walkway, and lush green grass filled the expanse. The trees opened, and the path veered westward toward the mountain and an immense white stone building the size of a small castle built out of the cliff-side. Along the parapets high above, soldiers stood watch, and red and white banners inlaid with a golden dragon, hung. Above a large arched doorway wide enough for wagons and horses to enter and exit, a row of flames burned with a distinct reddish color.

"Welcome to our mountain fortress, home of the Lady, and Lords, of the Western Lands."

"It is a sight to bear witness to again, my brother. I have not seen it for so long." He looked down at me and grinned.

"Aye, it is indeed." He turned and pointed behind us. "Look."

We all turned. We could see the lush valley below, which we crossed earlier that morning, and the Sleeping River winding off into the forests. The ridge line of the mountains stretched out to the north and south. We could see the two roads which lead to Gal Abed. The Kinelot Road, the one we came to Gal Abed on, and the one which runs along the river a piece and heads north to S'Ruh, called the Madoran Road. What the Roama call the "Red Road".

"The road to the Great City," Fonchesca muttered.

The air chilled, and a breeze blew through the garden, swirling the red and white petals into a macabre sort of dance. The view from our precipice was breathtaking, and seeing the road to my homeland filled me with dread and sorrow.

Burnok smacked me on the back, knocking me forward a half-step. "Come, there are some people you should meet."

We turned and walked through the grand portcullis into an open area and followed the stone road leading to the fortress built into the mountain.

"This is the Keep of Gal Abed, where we will go presently, but first come with me." He followed a path to the right to a barracks building at the far end, where guards, staff, and other military members were housed. It, too, was of white stone and stood three stories. The front was lined with windows.

We entered into an open chamber. Sunlight streamed in through a window above the doorway. Lanterns and sconces lit the room on a far wall, and stairs on the side led up to the next level. We walked past the stairs, the footfall of our boots echoing across the wooden planks of the floor. We came to another door with a guard posted on each side. Burnok stopped and turned.

"I will show you where your men will quarter." He grinned. "I believe they will be most comfortable here." He turned and nodded to the guards. One reached over and opened the door. We entered a large room with enough beds for 200 people, all in neat rows. Windows lined one wall, and light and cool air streamed through them.

The room was occupied.

Fonchesca stood wide-eyed, and a slight grin crept from the corner of his mouth.

A few of the occupants near the door saw us and stood. One mumbled something. Another dropped to his knees and wept. Another called out, and more occupants appeared from around the beds and gathered before us. Soon, there were shouts amongst the groups, and even more appeared. Most were in the plain clothes of the villagers, but some wore the black uniforms and insignia of the Northern Lands.

"It is true," I said. I felt a heavy hand on my shoulder. Fonchesca wandered over to the men, and laughter, and tears, and murmurings of conversation quickly filled the hall. A face stood out. A face I knew.

"They showed up in small groups, some worse for wear. They came in from all over."

"How many?" Soldiers behind me streamed past and into the throng of the gathering.

"Enough to pick a fight," Burnok chuckled. "Not enough for an army." I left him and walked over to the face I recognized.

"You." The man turned and smiled, tears streamed from his face. "Captain Astonzi."

"Commander. It is so..." he sobbed. "It has been so long since anyone has shown, we assumed."

"I understand. Our force is small. Barely thirty of us traveled here."

"You, you are here, Commander. Praise the blood of the fallen." I put a hand on his shoulder.

"It is good to see so many of you, Captain. So good." I put my hand on Fonchesca's shoulder and the three of us stood for a moment, smiling. Seeing so many soldiers from the north gave my soul a glimmer of hope. "How many are here?"

"At last count, 82," Astonzi said. His face went grim. "Commander Versol is here."

"Versol? This is great news." I looked around.

"He is here in Gal Abed but not in here, Commander. He is in the stronghold being cared for."

"Cared for?"

"Aye. He is wounded, and very ill. I fear he may have the bla—"

"I must see him." I walked over to Burnok. "I need to see Commander Versol. Where is he being cared for?"

"Follow me."

I looked back at Fonchesca. He was in the throes of conversation with the others. Some strange pull within me told me not to let them from my sight, some sort of new... dependence upon my brothers in arms. My soldiers. My family.

Burnok led me from the quarters and through the courtyard.

"I will not lie, brother. It is good to see more soldiers of the North."

"Aye."

"I have a question, though." I stopped and looked up at him. "Have any people arrived, non-soldiers, refugees of the Northern Lands?" He tucked his lips in, creating a strange effect on his bearded face.

"Not as many as you wish, I'm afraid. Less than 200. Come, we have news for you, but first, you will talk with your commander. I'm sure he will answer your questions."

We walked through the courtyard to the Keep of Gal Abed. The gatehouse opened like a gaping maw filled with teeth as six guards, three on each side, stood tall and watched us approach and enter, while another four watched from a parapet above.

"This truly is a fortress, Tass. We have no comparable structure in the Northern Lands."

"Aye. This city is very old and was built out of necessity, so I am told. Tales told by old men for wives and children." He laughed and slapped my back. I winced at the *brotherly love*.

We crossed a small bridge over a rushing stream and into the main keep. The room was dark, and it took a moment for my eyes to adjust. Torches burned, lighting the grand hallways and stone stairs. We turned and entered a room to the side. There were several beds in two neat rows. Nursemaids tended to the people occupying some of them. The room was long and narrow.

"We do not know what is wrong with your commander, Rini. Prepare yourself."

Commander Versol lay in a bed at the far end of the room. He looked old, older than I remember. His eyes had sunken, and the whites were gray. He was half my weight, if that. His head rolled over to me. His gaze, vacant and distant, caught my eye, and a light glimmer of a smile appeared at the corners of his mouth.

"My word," he said in a voice rough and leathery. "The great Saka'Ali. You live." I walked over and knelt by his side. I took his hand.

"Aye Voitto. I live." He coughed.

"And I die. So, sick." Burnok's face was grim, and he shook his head.

"He's been here for two seasons. He came with ten men, worn, weary and—"

"Half mad?" He nodded.

"Shortly after he arrived, he became ill. He is injured, brother, and the wound, albeit a scratch, festers. There is nothing we can do."

"Tell me what you can."

He coughed and winced. "We left for the Great City from Tinas Brigh when we received word of the attack. We could also sense and smell it on the wind. The morning we reached Karvas Forest outside the city, you could see it. A darkness in the northern sky. The wind would chill to the bones, Rini. So," he coughed again. "So cold. We were almost to The Great City, and you could see them, coming from the storm. So many. Blacker than the darkness." He reached out and grabbed my arm. "Water?" I looked to Burnok, who clapped his hands once, and a nursemaid came over. She helped Versol with water from a skin kept near him. He eased back into the bed, his eyes wide.

"They... they attacked and swept into the city. The dark ones, mis-shapen, they were unskilled. They carried crude weapons used to maim and destroy. Easy kills for a swordsman, but a hearty strike of their weapon was certain death." Then he looked at me. "And if they only drew blood, well... the wound would fester, turn black." He reached up with one arm, pulled the cover down, unloosed his gown, and revealed his shoulder. I turned away.

"But the worst, Soltari, those they killed with those blades, they would... would." His face tightened, and he sobbed.

"You are safe here, Commander Versol," I said. He took a deep breath.

"They would rise and fight." He turned away and stared at some lost memory.

"Go on."

"All of them, not just the black husks, but women. So beautiful, and deadly. Their gaze." I thought I knew who and what he meant by the gaze. Knowing there was more than just the one called Pri'Eten sent a shudder through me. "But then, I saw her. I saw the..."

"Queen?" He breathed out a long breath.

"Yessss. Her green eyes, in the clouds." He patted my arm. "I, we turned around, overwhelmed by the force of the attack. We fought, but had no choice but to retreat to Feren Ta. There were so many of them. I lost over half my men there on the Black Road. After a short ride, they no longer pursued us and we made it to Feren Ta." He looked over at me. Tears streamed from one eye. "I've betrayed our people, Commander."

"No, Voitto."

"We ran like cowards from our Great City as this vile, wretched thing took over. And the cold, so cold. Everything frozen. Soon, they came again for Feren Ta." He looked around. "Rogues Army soldiers were there. They called the black things, musta kuori, or something like that. The black blades inflict something they called musta kuolema. I remember this from one of them we captured. We went south from Feren Ta across the lands. We stayed off the road. Most of my men were turned in Feren Ta by the kuolema. The Rogues Army called the turned ones, Var'Yo. They can..." he stared at the ceiling. "The only way to kill them is to slit their throat or remove the head. The blood. So black." He coughed a fit. His eyes were losing color, the whites slowly turning a darker gray. "The blood is the sickness." He turned to me and grasped my sleeve.

"I, I cannot Voitto. Please..." His eyes widened as he stared off into the distance beyond me.

"Oh...," he said in a hushed whisper. "Something even more vile came to Feren Ta. It looked like... a woman, but hunched, with long claws, black hair, and a mouth filled with flesh-ripping teeth." He winced, and black spittle ran from the corner of his mouth. "The Rogues Army soldier we captured called them *R'Uma*. The 100 souls you see here are all that is left after we crossed through Soldier's Pass and made our way to Gal Abed." He tightened his grip on my sleeve, then arched in pain. He looked at me, his eyes completely black now.

"Kill me..." he groaned. "You... must... kill..." Then his movements stopped, and his body went limp, relaxing into the bed.

I stood. "You are free now, Commander Voitto Versol. You have earned your place in the afterlife."

I turned to leave the room. Burnok grasped my shoulder.

"Brother." He was staring at Versol, eyes wide. I turned around. Versol was sitting up, his face now a vile expression of madness. He growled, and more black fluid drained from his mouth. I unsheathed my short sword and slit his throat. Black blood, as black as the night before dawn, spilled from his gullet, but seemed... alive, like an infestation of black ants looking for a new home. A wisp of air escaped, and he fell back onto the bed. Burnok quickly grabbed up the coverings and wrapped them around Versol. He directed the nursemaid to take the bed, covers, and body and burn them all.

She ran off in tears.

I walked out and into the grand hall of the keep. Burnok close behind.

"Brother," he called out. "Come," he placed a hand on my shoulder. "Join me. This way."

"I cannot. I have to return to the barracks. I have to return to the Northern Lands, to home. I have to keep my promise!" He sighed, then stepped away and looked at me.

"Brother, what can you do with 200 men? Hmm? Come, we are expected in the counsel chambers shortly." He provoked a half smile on his face. "Please."

He lightly guided me toward the back of the stronghold to a pair of large doors at the rear.

Chapter Twenty-Nine

The Council of Gal Abed

T HE TWO GUARDS POSTED by the large, dark wood doors stepped aside and opened them as we approached. They stood tall and straight as Burnok and I entered. The hall was open and immense. Arched columns lined the sides. From the columns hung the banners of the Western Lands. Posted at each column stood a guard, bearing gleaming silver-tipped pikes in hand which sparkled in the sunlight streaming in from the windows above. The floor appeared to be the same white stone as the cliffs. Inlaid in the center was a large red dragon made from a mosaic of crushed ruby and marble, a tribute to their deity, Yoomala.

Our boots echoed in the empty chamber. At the far end sat a dais, four stairs high, and wide enough for an entourage. Curtains of red and white hung behind it. The dais was empty save for two guards, one on each side.

Burnok stopped before two ornate doors carved of the same dark wood. On the doors was carved the same dragon as on the floor.

"The chambers of the four Lords of the Western Lands. Well, three Lords, and the Lady Linnoitus who is chief among them."

"And Lord Linnoitus?" Burnok shook his head.

"You have spent too much time eating the spiced foods of the East, brother. He is dead, some two summers now. Lady Linnoitus rules over the Western Lands." He signaled, and a guard stepped from the shadows and opened the door. "Oh, and watch yourself with Lord Westval. He is an ass. Something has changed in him of late. Just be on your guard." Burnok did not grin.

"Understood."

The guard bowed as we entered the room. A long polished wood table of a deep red, which appeared to be cut from the length of a single tree, sat in the middle upon ornate rugs. High-back chairs lined the table on each side. Light streamed in from high casements near the ceiling. Braziers lined the walls. The door shut behind us.

"You carry some distinction here, brother," I said. He chuckled.

"Aye, being Regent to the Lady Linnoitus comes with some perks." He stopped and turned to me. "And just because she's family, you may not call her *auntie*." He winked and spread his arms. "This is where the council meets, deals are made, and where wars are waged before they are fought with soldier and sword. Come."

"I have been here before, Tass," I said. "But it has been many ages."

"Aye, but this time, you have a seat at the table as an honored guest." His statement gave me pause.

"Why are we meeting with the council? I have found what I came to Gal Abed for."

He led me to a small table at the rear. Upon it were bottles of wine and water, fruit, and bread.

"They will be here shortly."

He filled a small goblet with wine and handed it to me. He poured one for himself.

"The council has some interest in what has happened in your lands, naturally. And you are here to request assistance, are you not?"

He picked up an apple and took a large bite from it. Juice stained the top of his beard.

"I—"

The door opened again and two guards entered, followed by Commander Ghenesta, Captain Astonzi, and Captain Fonchesca. The guards stopped and stepped aside. The group saw us and walked our way. Burnok waved his hand, letting the guards know they could leave, and they did.

"How is Commander Versol?" Astonzi said.

"He is dead, Captain." I would spare him the details.

He hung his head, and Fonchesca put his hand on Astonzi's shoulder.

"So many lost," he said.

Another door at the far end of the room opened, and three men entered. Lords of the Western Lands. Two of the men were dressed in long-sleeved, buttoned white shirts with high collars, doeskin breeches, and high-calf leather boots. The third was dressed as Burnok. A soldier.

Two ladies dressed in flowing gowns of white with red decorative stoles walked behind the Lords, followed by two guards who shut the doors and posted in front of them. The Ladies both wore a thin sword on their left side and one red leather glove on their right hand. They were alike, mirror images of each other, save for the headdress they wore. The Lady of the Western Lands, Lady Kivi Linnoitus, wore a thin gold band. The other, her sister, Lady Veri Burnok, wore a silver band. They had long dark hair, blue eyes, and fair skin. They sat at the heads of the table. The man dressed as Burnok approached us.

"Regent Burnok, these are our guests?"

"Aye, Lord Åkerfeldt. Captain's Fonchesca and Astonzi of the Northern Lands, Commander Ghenesta, whom you know, and this is my brother, Commander General Soltari."

"Ah, Commander, we finally meet again. My, how you have changed, I say."

"Changed. Yes," I said.

"Please, you and Commander Ghenesta, join us." He eyed my Captain's, smiled, and motioned to the food table. "Help yourself."

I was suspicious of why Ghenesta was being given a seat at the table.

The four of us sat at the table with the others. Burnok near Lady Linnoitus. I looked at the ladies, unsure of the proper customs, and noticed Burnok lean over and whisper to Lady Linnoitus. Her eyes lit, and she smiled, then spoke.

"Commander General Soltari, welcome again to Gal Abed. I trust your brother is treating you well?"

"He is, my Lady."

"Well then, without haste, I will ask my sister to begin our counsel." I turned to the other, whom I had known since I was a young boy. She smiled at me and the sunlight from the other end of the room shone in her eyes, revealing a hint of joy mixed with sorrow.

"Greetings, Counsel members, and our honored guests. Times in our land are prosperous and plentiful but are shadowed by the upset in the balance and the grim news from the Northern Lands. We have heard fact, and rumor, and both are concerning." She turned to me. "Commander Soltari, have you news to share from the Northern Lands?" I squirmed a bit in my chair. I fought battles with swords, not tongues. I heaved a heavy sigh.

"Aye, I do. Our Great City was attacked without provocation from an army that came in from the North." I continued to relay the details of the first night, the storm, and information about the Rogues Army and the musta kuori. "They were not there to claim, take, or plunder, but to burn and murder, and to warn us. It was under this siege that I..." I took a deep breath. "I, um."

I became dizzy, then I cleared my throat. I gazed at the table and the intricate details of the wood, and lost myself in the lines. Words fell from my mouth, out of my control, out of my grasp, mumbled like a madman talking to himself.

"Lost my family, my wife, and my daughter."

There was a gasp from somewhere. My eyes remained transfixed on the lines of the table. A reflection of a desolate stranger showed in its polished surface. I looked up at the complex and detailed art on the ceiling that I only now noticed. I took another deep breath, then looked around the room.

"We were told by a captured Rogues Army extremist that another attack was imminent and that it would be unlike we had ever seen. I led the army to Farwic Outpost near our northern borders. We were to march into Ro Ista Pass where the Rogues Army extremists, who serve this new self-proclaimed Queen, occupied an old fortress. Commander Versol was returning from the west and would secure the city."

The Lady Burnok's eyes welled slightly with tears. Were they tears of concern, or tears of a mother? I could not tell. A solemn voice came from my left.

"Go on, Commander. If you please," Lady Linnoitus said. Lord Westval sighed and crossed his arms. I looked at his vacant eyes, his meaningless expression.

"It was there my force succumbed to a blizzard which lasted three days and destroyed the outpost, and all but myself and about twenty others survived. Horses, soldiers, buildings, gone." I leaned on the table, tired from the memories and the weight of the journey. I felt a tap on the shoulder and looked over. A servant stood with a glass of water. I took it and drank.

The smug voice of Westval broke the silence. "And was there an attack on the Great City?"

I looked at Fonchesca, who was standing beside the table with the food.

"Yes."

I relayed the story of finding Fonchesca and his escape, and traveling to the City of the Southern Moon, what I learned of the Queen, and what I learned from Commander Versol. I felt no need to tell them about my time in Bin El Omen, or my journey from Farwic and across the desert. I stopped. Their faces were aghast, save for Westval. He carried a slight smirk and held his arms crossed. My blood boiled.

Commander Ghenesta then spoke and provided additional information about the self-proclaimed Queen. Information I knew, but cared not to share.

Then he stood.

"I stand as consul for Southern Lands, and the Council of the Goffs, Keepers of the Gallery of Visions. The Goffs request the support of the Western Lands to purge the self-proclaimed queen from the Northern Lands and restore the balance. We have provisioned horsemen, soldiers, equipment, and supplies to defend ourselves should it come to that. My men await at the border for my return with your response." He turned to me. "We offered our assistance to Commander Soltari. He refused."

Then he sat.

"I did not seek help from the Southern Lands, nor do I seek aid from the Western Lands. Commander Ghenesta's remark to *purge* the Northern Lands sounds like an act of—"

"Commander Soltari," Lady Linnoitus said. "Choose your next words carefully. We are not at war. We come together here at the counsel table to avoid such foolishness."

"I apologize, my Lady. I sit at this table because I was summoned and requested to provide information, which I have done. I did not request this counsel." She turned to Burnok, then back to me.

"Then, Commander, why are you here?"

"I learned that some of our forces may have fled West after the second attack, or remnants of Commander Versol's force may have been pushed westward. I came, Lady Linnoitus, for my soldiers." Her face folded into a frown.

"Do I understand, Commander, that you intend to take these soldiers back to the Northern Lands and fight?"

"You understand correctly, my Lady. It is our duty. We are warriors. It is our home." Ghenesta was staring blankly at the ceiling. She tittered, then cleared her throat. The momentary smile faded fast.

"All that remains is shadow. She has destroyed my home, seized my lands, and killed my family. Our father was murdered in the Southern Lands, perhaps by this wretched Queen."

"Murdered?" Ghenesta said. "Are you suggesting the Southern Lands had a hand in your father's death?"

"Rini," Lady Burnok said, her voice soft, like a passing memory. A memory I had not heard for some time. "That was so long ago. Why?"

"To prevent some prophecy, some vision of this Queen and the Sisters of the Whispering Dawn from being fulfilled."

Westval blurted out a laugh and was hushed by the gaze of Lady Linnoitus. He turned away from her glare. Ghenesta stared at his hands on the table.

"She now sits on the throne of my Lord, my cousin." I followed the Lady's gaze as they traveled to her sister across the table.

"Lord Airik was your cousin?" Westval blurted. I faced the Lady Linnoitus.

"As you know, my Lady, my mother, and the mother of Lord Airik are sisters."

"Which makes you, by blood, by rite, heir to the lands, if he is dead," she said. The palms of my hands became sweaty, and I rubbed them together.

"What lands? There is nothing." I wiped the sweat from my forehead. The banter made me weary. "I am a soldier of the Northern lands, not a Lord, not a... what's the word? Diplomat. I was born without my father's sense of negotiation and mediation. Only with my ancestor's thirst for battle."

"And what of your mother?" I startled and turned to the voice. A male voice. Westval, again. A slight snarl formed on my broken face.

"My mother?" I said. "My mother died giving me life. I have no memory of her, only stories. Stories which stopped after my father was murdered." He all but shrugged away the words.

"Commander, you yourself just said you were in charge of a force 2,000 strong and lost them all to a... a supernatural blizzard?" He chuckled.

"I never said it was supernatural." I frowned at Westval. Something...

"And now you think you can march into the Great City and defeat the Queen with a force of 200?" He guffawed. "I have to know, Commander, are you mad? Or—"

I jolted from my seat and drew my sword as I lunged across the table. Burnok grabbed my leg, but I broke free. I grabbed the puffed-up politician by the collar of his robes and had the blade of my short sword across his throat. His smug eyes were wide with fear. Terror is all he knew now. His condescending eyes reflected my mad visage.

"I will do all that it takes to see her blood spilled, you wretched piece of—"

"Commander Soltari!" Lady Linnoitus said as she stood. "Stand down, sir!" I held my sword to Lord Westval for a moment as he stared into my eyes and saw the madness, the pain, the torment within me and turned away in disgust. I let him go and was dragged back across the table, his smug expression grimacing from the horror.

I screamed in his face and he jumped from his seat and ran to the chamber doors, the front of his pants dark with piss.

"Weak," I said. The chamber doors slammed, the sound booming in the large hall.

I stood and shrugged off the grips of Burnok and Captain Fonchesca. I sheathed my sword. Burnok stood by me, his hand on my back. I looked at him. He was grinning under his beard. His back turned to Lady Linnoitus. Her face remained expressionless. She gestured for me to sit, and I did. Burnok followed.

"Well, now, Commander. There will be no more of that." She brushed off her gown, pulled it around her legs, then sat.

A silence hung heavy in the room as the sun slipped from the sky and cast dark shadows across the table.

"My lady. I am a man without a land or family. I am a refugee. I must return with my soldiers and redeem our lands, to restore our home. Not waste time—"

"And then what, Rini?" Lady Burnok said. Her soft voice carried a heavy weight. It had been ages since she called me by my name. "What happens after you have enacted your revenge upon this sorceress Queen?"

Her piercing blue eyes carried me to a distant memory of her and my father. I felt trapped in a mirror between the two of them.

"You have family, Commander," she continued. She motioned with a graceful gesture toward Burnok. "And you have a land. You and your people are welcome here. Your father forged relationships which run deep, even among us here at this table." My head was swimming, and I looked at her through the haze, through the sunlight, to her eyes.

"And leave the Northern Lands in possession of this... unnatural..."

"Commander." Another distant voice echoed. A male voice.

"I have nothing. She, she has taken everything from me!" I slammed both hands down on the table and stood. "EVERYTHING!"

"Please," Lady Linnoitus said. Burnok stood and came to me. He put his hand on my shoulder and whispered in my ear, but I heard nothing, only the warmth of his breath on me as he spoke.

"I am the one they call Shaviska! I am the Saka'Ali! And I will ride with all the rage and sorrow and torment within me to the Great City! I will face this Queen Ta'Bedtian and plunge my swords through her eyes so she can see and feel all the pain and misery that has become me as my steel pierces her skull and the echoes of her final screams are consumed by our Great Hall! This black witch must die! And by my hands, she will. I will remove her head and post it at the North gate for all to bear witness to the fury and wrath in my blood and that of my people! I am death!"

I walked around the table to the door. I heard another pair of boots coming from behind and I whirled, sword drawn, and through the haze, there was... my father, arms outstretched. With the sunlight glowing behind him, he was shadow, a silhouette, beckoning me. Sounds, words, a voice. A calm voice. I dropped to one knee, laid my sword on the ground.

"Father?"

"Rini," the voice said, and I felt a hand on my shoulder and then was cast in shadow as they knelt before me. "Rini, are you ok?" I looked up, and there was my brother, fear in his eyes, on his face. "Rini, by the Gods, look at me."

A lady appeared. A lady with long dark hair and radiant blue eyes. She reached out to me, put her hand on my face, and held it there.

"Rini," she said in a voice, soft, pleasant, and motherly. Her touch a shock, tormenting, and caring, like a ray of sunshine through a break in the storm.

"I... I am sorr—" I collapsed, and the void once again consumed me. "—ow."

CHAPTER THIRTY
Awakenings

T HE SUN DRIFTED ACROSS the sky, and a cool breeze caressed my face. I looked over the rolling green hills of my home. A shadow ran across my field of vision and I glimpsed her out of the corner of my eye as she passed. Her giggle trailed upon the wind.

I turned, and she stood before me, my child, my daughter, her mass of reddish hair covered her face. A shadow moved across me, across us, and it enveloped us, cast us in gray. I looked to the sky as the sun disappeared behind dark clouds, mustering into one monstrous black formation.

My daughter parted her hair from her face revealing darkness, a featureless black face of onyx, her deep blue eyes set as jewels, which faded and changed to green and my daughter shifted, and grew tall, her hair flowing out like a fountain from red to white, her onyx face formed and shaped into a new face, a face I saw in a painting once...

And she leered at me as her body writhed.

Soltari... the wind whispered.

I opened my eyes. I was alone in the priestess's caravan. The pungent aroma of incense only a memory, replaced with rusty air. I peered into the darkness and saw nothing behind the veil. I stood and felt my way to the door, opened it, and stepped into the light.

Gal Abed sprawled before me. The streets, devoid of the living, ran crimson. The Keep was a crumbled smoking ruin. Bodies lie stacked. The river now flowed with blood. The caravans were burned to ash. The remains of a charred easterner lie from one, reaching up and out, beckoning for help which never came.

I stepped onto the ground and lost my footing as I sank deep into the earth and fell from the caravan into the liquid ground beneath me, consumed, drawing. I slipped under and fell into air, the world around as black as the moonless desert night, falling, falling...

I screamed and there was only silence as my body tore apart and flashes of white light blinded me. A distant rumbling, then a louder crack of thunder near me, and another flash, then another crack of thunder. Millions of glass shards shattered around me. A flash and another break of thunder exploded as I fell deeper into the black abyss.

Flash.

Thunder.

I walked the streets of Gal Abed and pulled my cloak around me, turning myself into a faceless shape. Someone called my name. All eyes upon me, upon this dark visage.

I wandered past unfamiliar sites, unfamiliar faces. Bodies lay strewn on the streets of the city. Blood flowed from cobbled faces. My name, called again from somewhere. Above, dark clouds rumbled, preparing for battle, and flashed menacing streaks of light. Smoke filled the air from unquenchable fires.

More rumblings, more streaks of light. A horse rushed past me, dragging its dead rider through the streets, painting a long streak of crimson on the black road. I saw the gates ahead, and the bodies of the Guards of Gal Abed, heaped in a pile, some strung from the Bridge of Halos.

I dropped to my knees and closed my eyes. The thunder, the screams, the crackling of fires, the footfalls of people running, and the clang of steel echoed off the rock walls of the city. An acrid smell of burnt offerings assaulted me.

A horse screamed. A gray horse.

"Sumu!"

Flash.

Thunder.

I opened my eyes.

The vague sound of thunder rumbled in my head. I lay on a bed of soft pillows. I sat up. A heavy rain fell outside.

I took a long, deep breath. Her wicked spirit knew me. She watched me. *Fear not this Queen, young Soltari...*

The voice echoed within me and without me. In the room was a candle, faintly dancing. And in the candle's light, a shadow.

"She is here, in Gal Abed," I said.

In spirit only. She is far from the fortress of the Western Lands.

"I must go."

You must sleep...

My eyes grew heavy, and the candle and the thunder slipped into darkness... silent... ethereal...

Sunlight streamed through the windows and cast unfamiliar shadows in an unfamiliar room. The ceiling was barren, stone, white. A thin crack held my vision. I was alone, lying on a bed. Someone had undressed me and draped a long shirt around me. A melee of birds chirped outside the window. I sat up. The room was furnished well with rugs, draperies, a wardrobe, two sitting chairs, and a table. Banners with various patterns and symbols hung from the walls. Nothing recognizable. At one end was a wooden door.

The door opened, and a servant girl came in carrying a large bowl and pitcher of water. She wore a white and gray dress. Simple. Her blonde hair streamed down her back. She looked up and saw me staring at her.

"Oh. Excuse me, my lord."

She bowed her head and stopped and stood there.

"What time of day is it, miss?" I said.

"Morning, sir."

"Please. Continue."

She brought the bowl and pitcher to my bedside, and set it on the small table. She poured water into the bowl, then turned and scurried from the room, closing the door behind her.

Morning. How long have I been here?

The door opened again and Burnok walked through, followed by two servants, one of them the girl who just left.

"Rini! You are alive." He burst into laughter. He walked to me, grabbed a nearby chair, and sat beside the bed. His beard a wide smile. "That was quite the show, I will say. You gave us all a start, brother." The servants stood idle at the end of the room, waiting for orders. "Do you need anything?" I shook my head. He waved his hand, and they left, closing the door behind them.

"How long?"

"Only since yesterday."

"Where are my clothes?"

"Being tended to." He pointed to the wardrobe. "There are clothes in there, some less formal than others."

"Look at me. Bedridden, like an invalid."

He leaned forward. "You have experienced so much. I hope you rested?"

"My body may be."

I moved to get out of the bed, placed my feet on the cold stone floor, and stood.

"This, this quest of yours, this journey to vanquish the Queen. Is it a foolish endeavor?"

"It is my home you speak of Tass Burnok. Taken over by some vile sorceress. I cannot sit idle. Or quit."

I pulled some clothes from the wardrobe and my pouch fell from the top shelf. There was a metal clink on the floor and the amulet left behind by Betir El Friz fell out. I picked it up and placed it into the pouch. I peered into the small bag and heaved a heavy sigh.

"All I have left."

"Sorry?"

"This pouch. Symbols of memories. It's all I have. Reminders of a promise I made." I held up the pouch. "Two remnants of purple lotuses, a slip of parchment, and our father's amulet." He stood.

"Lotuses? May I see?" I opened the bag, and he peered inside. "The flower of the Northern Lands?"

"Something like that."

"A reminder of home?"

"I brought these home for..." The names touched my lips and slipped into the ether. "My wife, and daughter."

"And have you... remembered?" I shook my head. Burnok sighed. "Tell me about them. What were they like?"

"My daughter, she was rambunctious and full of good energy. Always a smile on her face." I looked at him. "You would have loved her. She had flame red hair." He grinned. "Like her mother."

"Ah, she must come from good stock." He winked.

"She had the most beautiful eyes and was such a good mo—" My voice cracked. I swallowed, and took a deep breath. "We had just made plans to travel here, to Gal Abed. We were to leave the following day, to come see you." Burnok sighed. "Instead, that night, I rested these lotuses on their shrouded bodies before I set everything alight." He placed a hand on my shoulder, then caught what I said and his eyes opened wide.

"You burned... everything?"

"The home, yes, with their bodies inside. I only have one purpose, brother. To keep the promise I made to them."

I looked into his eyes, and he saw the depth of mine, and he nodded.

"I understand."

"I think I know what her plan is."

I walked to the bowl of water and washed my face, then dressed and buckled my swords to my side.

"In the City of the Southern Moon, at their gallery, the paintings and—"

"Visions, prophecies, all fantastical pig dung, brother. You believe this?"

"It was our father in the painting, I'm sure of it. It was his sword, the sword which was broken the day he died. A sword I have not seen since that day. When she realized it was her in the vision, and saw her defeat at the hand of our father, Taivas Soltari, she had him killed."

"Betir El Friz acted alone, brother. They knew our father was summoned to the Southern lands. They hunted him down, and killed him." He looked out the window, watching the rain roll down the panes. "Brother, this queen is a rogue, acting for herself."

"Forgive me, little brother, but you are wrong."

He harrumphed and turned, standing tall with his hands on his hips. He looked down at me.

"Little brother, indeed." His beard split into a smile. He couldn't help himself. "Fine, go on with your tale of witchcraft and magic if you must. But make it quick. I am getting hungry, and when I get hungry, I get grumpy."

He sat and rested his hands on his knees.

"With the emperor dead, I think the queen invaded the Northern lands to position herself for an invasion of the Southern Lands," I said. "She intends to claim them as her own."

"Emperor Val Distad is dead?"

"Aye. According to Goff Il Gavar."

I walked to the window and peered out. I could see the barracks where the rest of my force was. In the courtyard I saw Commander Ghenesta talking with someone, the polished silver helm unmistakable amongst the others.

"Still, Rini. I don't see where her vengeance lies."

"When she left, she may have traveled east and made deals we do not know about."

"Her work would have been difficult as a Southerner, given their history," he said.

"Aye. But not if she promised them something. Which she did."

I moved to the bed and sat down.

"About six or seven ages ago the attacks on our Eastern border became extremely consistent. Not like the bandits of the far past, but a new militant faction of the Rogues Army. Organized. This new faction formally split from the true Rogues Army and General A'avikon announced his title as Al Friz, as a new Herra. They are allied with the Queen of Shadows, this we know. The attacks started around the time that people claim a darkness came into the eastern lands, from the south. Shortly after father was murdered. About the same time she... left..."

It came all at once like a mad rush.

"You said she promised them something?"

"Aye, the Great City. The former capital of the Empire of the Eastern Star." I looked at him. "And the Northern Lands."

"That is huge, Rini, that could establish this General as a new emperor and... no. I do not believe her intentions are true." He chuckled. "If I were a gambling man, Rini, I'd also say she used her powers to trick them and has no intent on sharing the spoils."

"Agree."

"But this still does not explain where her vengeance lies."

"Her vengeance must be personal, something that has to do with the Southern Lands."

"Or she's allied with someone in the Southern Lands. Who benefits from the Emporer's death?"

His words hung in the air like a thick fog. A face came to me. The smug face of an old man and his openness to inform me of all that was and is in the Southern Lands. Too happy to share after ages of isolation.

Burnok cleared his throat.

"Come." He stood. "We will join the others. They will be happy to see you."

I stood and wandered to the window.

"I would prefer to wander, alone. To think on this more."

"I understand."

"Have you spoken with Ghenesta?"

"Aye. He is the one on a fool's errand, brother. He has sent word to the Southern Lands. He will stay here, he hasn't said why. The council denied his request."

He walked toward the door.

"Oh. You said something at the council yesterday. Some word. Shavesta or—"

"Shaviska."

He burst with excitement.

"That's it! What is that word?" I walked to him.

"A word a priestess with the spice merchants gave me. It means, *risen dead*."

He laughed. "It suits you, brother," He left me to my brooding.

CHAPTER THIRTY-ONE

The Streets of Gal Abed

I SAT AT THE edge of a stream in the city. The diversion of water here was a necessity, and a virtue, adding to the beauty of the city. I found strange comfort sitting on the flagstones at the edge of the stream. Comfort I did not welcome. Across from me, merchants sold their wares: silks, spices, meats, trinkets. The city was rich with them. Most bartered for goods they could take and trade back east. The smells of their cooked foods wafted across the air and took me back to Bin El Omen, and my home, for the same smells drifted around and through the North Gate.

I stood and walked the cobbled streets of Gal Abed, along its clean flagstone surface, its unique architecture, its gardens, and wondered how they have been, so fortunate to be free of the sadness, free of the sorrow of the Northern lands, and the rage of the South and East.

I walked past the street shops in the central bazaar, touched the fine silks, and smelled the savory spices. I stopped at a shop selling trinkets. Small playthings for children. I noticed a doll sitting on a table next to so many like it with green button eyes and hair made from red string. I picked it up. A doll my daughter played with, slept with, and never let leave her sight.

A doll she died with.

I looked at the shopkeeper with tears in my eyes. Her face was a happy brown face. She was old and wrapped in colorful silks. Jewelry pierced into her face, a thin silver chain strung from nose to ear. I remembered this shop in the Great City when I got this doll. And maybe this same shopkeeper. Fragments of a memory slipped with time.

I touched the cloth face, the blue and green clothing. I set the doll on the table and nodded to the old woman. She smiled, her brown eyes full of pureness and happiness. The face of a life without war, I thought.

Distinct and familiar wafts of smoking meat drifted past, and I followed it to the end of the row of merchants. I recognized the smell and the specific spices. A man hovered over an iron grill full of sizzling meat, licked by flames, as smoke surrounded him. He was slicing the meat from a tall spit, then folding and rolling it in a mixture of spices and placing it on the grill.

He looked up and saw me and a broad smile stretched across his face. He recognized me. He motioned me closer, nodding his head and beckoning me. I stood before him, this old man from the caravan in the desert. He spoke, and although I couldn't understand what he was saying, I nodded, and put my hand on his shoulder. He was not a vision of the past.

I gave him some coin, and he motioned me to a table. A moment later, he brought over a wooden plate with a flatbread covered in meat and grilled vegetables. Next to the plate he set a bowl of spiced rice. I sat and bit into the food, and the spice, the warmth, the taste, all flowed through me and returned me home to the merchants who found me in the desert, and out from my body drifting away with the smoke of his fires. The old man chuckled and patted me on the shoulder.

"Ah, my brother. I see you've found the best place to eat here in Gal Abed," Burnok said as he approached, then laughed his hearty laugh. He turned to my friend... my friend. I had not thought of anyone in that manner since Igvar. Burnok said something in the old man's language. The man bowed and handed Burnok a wooden plate with two flatbreads piled with meat and vegetables.

"You speak their language?" He chuckled.

"Enough to understand, and get what I want, brother," he said and sat across from me. "Do you not with all that time you spent in the East?"

"No." I averted my eyes to my plate, then to him. "What brings you here?"

"I said, this is the best place to eat here in all of Gal Abed." He smiled. "But don't tell anyone I said that."

Burnok took a bite and juices spilled out the open end of the rolled bread. He eyed me the whole time he chewed. He set his food back on the plate and wiped his mouth with a cloth.

"Alright, tell me, what has your thoughts so consumed? You've hardly touched your food. It'd be a shame for it to—"

"You are correct, brother. I have a lot on my mind." I picked up the folded bread with the meat and bit into it. I swallowed and wiped my face with a cloth. "Have you wondered where the Northern invaders came from and why?"

"Deep. Too deep for casual conversation. Besides, Rini, these questions have gone unanswered since well before our time."

"Aye. At some point, the Northern lands became complacent and oblivious to the world around us. And now we have paid dearly for that complacency."

Burnok grunted.

"We have nothing to offer. Nothing to trade. No craftsmen. All we know is war and battle. Death is all we have dealt, and in return, all we have received. We get our best weapons and armor forged in the city of Ahjo, here in the west. Our spices and fabrics come from the East. We have no true origin, no story, no roots, no history except as invaders and takers. Takers of a land which was not ours." I leaned back. "Am I no better than the Queen?"

Burnok choked on the food he was chewing, then swallowed hard.

"By Yoomala, brother, are you trying to kill me."

He coughed, then took a drink from his cup. He pounded on his chest and caught his breath.

"Rini, you are better than that hideous self-proclaimed Queen. You have a true and honorable purpose, brother. Hers is selfish and bent on destruction, chaos, and death."

"Do I? My only purpose is vengeance. Vengeance for my family, for my lands. Also selfish and bent on destruction and death."

"Aye, that is true. But you do it out of necessity, with a motive. And you have 200 soldiers behind you, following you, to do the right thing, the sane thing. She is insane. You at least possess a reasonable mind."

I shuddered at his words.

He poured water from a pitcher into his cup and took a drink. "She does this to gain power, for advantage, for her own selfish desire to rule and destroy."

"Aye. I'm not sure I have the will to fight, this fight, or any others. It is why I resigned my commission in the Lord's service bef—"

"You did what?" I looked at him and shrugged, then picked up the last remnant of meat on my plate.

"I resigned my commission as Commander General of the Eastern Borders, the day of the attack." I pushed the food around on my plate. "I have grown weary of fighting, of bloodshed, and realized I could die and never see my family again. And to what purpose? I no longer knew why I fought the Rogues Army or why..." I sighed. "This is the reason we were going to travel here to visit you." I sighed. "You would have loved them, brother."

"Rini?" I looked up at him. "I... I have no words to say. I am heartbroken that..." His voice trailed off and his gaze dropped to his plate. I sighed and looked at the old man turning meat on the grill.

"Do you know his name?" I nodded toward the old man. Burnok frowned a bit. An unnatural expression for him.

"Some names are best left unsaid, my brother," he said, biting into the food. He picked up a cloth beside him and wiped his hands, then mouth. "But I can see something in your eyes that tells me you want to know. Why?"

"I know him. His clan was the clan that saved me in the desert. We spent a day together outside camp sheltered in a rock alcove from a hard rain." The same alcove in which I met our father's murderer, I thought. And a bird chirped somewhere, the sound somewhat familiar in the haze of memory. I sighed and leaned back in the chair.

"His clan—this clan?" He spread his arms to indicate the merchants around us. I looked around and realized most of the faces seemed familiar. In the pottery shop across the street from us sat a mother in a black headdress with two small children near her, a boy and a girl. They were staring at me as if I were a ghost. I looked around and there were more familiar faces. The old man glanced up from his work and smiled in a way to say "you like?" Or "you remember?" I smiled and nodded.

"Aye. This clan. They are the ones who found me in the desert." I took to the streets of Gal Abed to escape my past and wandered into its midst. I set the folded bread onto the wooden plate. "And if they're here, then that would mean..."

He stared at me. "Would mean what, brother?"

"That she is here too."

"Who?"

"The Priestess, Kristava."

Burnok bit into his food and half the meat escaped the other side of the folded bread and dropped to his plate. He swallowed hard and followed it with a full cup of water.

"Here?"

He wiped his mouth with the back of his sleeve and leaned back. He shook his head.

"I would have been notified, brother. This clan may be here, but the Priestess is not."

I picked at the remnants on my plate.

"One of the last things the priestess said was that I need to seek a man named Betir, and I would find him where the yellow bird sang. The day I spent in the alcove with him," I gestured to the old man, "there was a yellow bird, a night bird, singing. She said he would have the answer to a question I longed an answer for."

I wiped my hands and face with the cloth.

"It's the place I stayed on my journey back, and where I met Betir El Friz, as she said I would."

He grinned. "That place is part of you now."

I stood and went to the old man.

"What is your name?" I pointed to my chest. "I am Soltari." I pointed to him. "Your name." His face changed to understanding.

"Amir."

"Amir?"

He nodded.

"Amir, El Friz."

I froze, and a large hand fell on my shoulder.

"Come. As I said, some names are better left unknown." Burnok said something to the man, and he bowed to him.

The man replied, and the word "Shaviska" floated out amongst the other unrecognizable words. He bowed to me. We left and walked up the street. The eyes of the merchants followed me as I passed by.

I thought of Igvar again, and a heavy sorrow came upon me.

We walked past the merchants to a camp filled with the ornate wagons of the traveling merchants. Off to the side, a small stable of horses stood. I stopped, took a deep breath, and swallowed hard. A rush of panic swelled in me. At the center of the caravans sat the wagon of the Priestess Kristava. I rested my hands on my knees, trying to catch my breath.

"Brother, are you well?" He knelt beside me.

"No. But I will be fine," I said in between gasps. "She is here."

The sight of her caravan put fear and dread and panic and happiness into my heart. I could not explain. I stood, drawing in a deep breath. I closed my eyes and let the breath out, long and slow.

Shaviska...

I opened my eyes.

We walked to the caravan and a man approached us. He was tall, gangly, like a puppet on strings. He wore a tan robe that hung on his body. His white head covering was partially stained yellow with sweat. His long, bony fingers reached out to clasp my hand, and he bore a broad cheerful smile. His eyes were content and welcoming, and he spoke with a clear, crisp voice.

"Regent Burnok, to what do we owe the pleasure of your visit?" He was smiling, then saw me and his smile faded into recognition.

"Counselor Farir. We seek counsel with the Priestess."

The Counselor bowed, then peered up at us.

"I apologize, Regent, but the Priestess is unable to accommodate. She has informed me there is another pressing matter." He looked at me. "A matter which you will be called to momentarily."

Two Western guards approached us.

"Regent Burnok," said one. "The Lady Burnok requests you and Commander Soltari to join her at the council chambers." Burnok turned to me.

"Still don't believe in sorcery or magic, Rini?"

He chuckled. He bowed to Counselor Farir, who returned the bow, then glanced at me with a smile.

"Right. Let's go," Burnok said.

We walked to the council chambers, and the guards followed us. When we entered the Keep, Lady Burnok stood outside the chamber doors. A smile dawned on her face. Two guards were posted near her.

"My boys," she said.

She walked over to me and put her arms out, then embraced me. The move was distressing, caring, confusing. She released me and touched my cheek. Her eyes shimmered in the sunlight creeping into the Keep as the sun lowered.

"Come. I have something for you, Rini."

Chapter Thirty-Two

Lady Burnok

Burnok and I followed her through the grand hallway of the Keep and up the stairs to the landing carved straight from the stone of the mountain. The walls were hewn rock, and at the far end, a small waterfall from a passageway outside filled a natural pool of water. From within the waterfall, a single small tree grew from the rock, green and bearing white and red flowers. We turned and followed her across the landing to a double-arched doorway with Gal Abed guards posted outside. They stood tall and straight when she approached. A guard opened one door, and we entered a large chamber. Tapestries hung from the walls, and ornate rugs covered the floor. On one side was a bed, tables, and dressing chairs. Light streamed in from two windows at the far end. The walls were smooth on two sides and cut rock on the others. I walked to the windows which overlooked the bridge, the courtyard with fountains, and the merchant squares. The bazaar bustled with citizens of Gal Abed, and rows of wagons filled the area where the caravans of the eastern travelers parked. As I watched, three wagons crossed the bridge into the city. I looked across the bridge and noted three carriages sitting off the road. One was black as night, the others green. None had windows.

"Odd, that black carriage," I said. Burnok grunted in agreement. "Do the tradesman have free passage into Gal Abed?"

"No, except a few, like the Priestess Kristava. Some travel here often enough and become a part of the city. Some, like those crossing now, I suspect, come and we'll most likely never see them again. The guards at the gates will deny entry to any suspicious riff-raff. These may have been under gate watch for the last two days, like those."

He pointed to the tree line across the river where the three strange caravans sat. Next to them was a row of seven carriages where other travelers made camp while they waited for entry. I could see children running and playing. One merchant had set up shop for those leaving the city.

There was some shuffling behind me, and I turned. Lady Veri Burnok walked over to us.

"Look at you lads. My, how time has shaped the both of you." She turned to me. "Rini, do you have many memories of me?"

"Of course, though the days have been long. I remember camping in the mountains, fish hanging from my father's sword. This one." I touched my long sword.

She smiled and caressed my cheek. "Your father, Rini, would be most proud of you."

I looked into her shimmering eyes. "Proud? I am but a shell now, Lady Veri. A wellspring of failure."

"Failure? You are no failure, Rini."

My sorrow conflicted with my madness and my heart screamed. I closed my eyes to keep them from bursting from my skull. I shook my head.

"Rini," her voice once soft, now stern. "Look at me."

I opened my eyes and two tears escaped into the wilderness of my face.

"You are no failure. You are still here, fighting. You have stood before the counsel and my sister, the Lady Kivi Linnoitus. You have faced tremendous forces which have robbed you of memory, of life, of your soul. Yet, here you stand in the halls of Gal Abed, a man destined. Until you walk away in defeat, you are no failure." She smiled. "I say again, Rini, your father would be most proud of you." She turned from me and walked across the room to the bed on the far wall. "Come." I glanced at Burnok, then followed her. Burnok's footfalls behind me fell heavy on the large rugs.

On the bed lay a sword in a black scabbard and I stopped. My breath taken. I knew this sword. I looked at her, my face a shadow of a child. A memory came of me as a boy in the wilderness with my father. A fire with fish cooking in the morning chill air, and of my brother's laugh, and a woman peering from behind my father, smiling at me. And resting near my father, this scabbard and this sword within.

The black leather bindings, the gold and silver pommel, the gold hilt, and the family crest inset in the center of the crossguard. I looked at her, her face bright with a wide, sad smile.

"This," I touched the sword, "is my father's sword. The sword, I remember. But…"

"It is the sword Taivas carried with him. The sword he carried into battle, as it was."

I picked up the blade and scabbard. Its weight felt good in my hands. It felt… complete. I gripped the hilt and scabbard and slid the sword from its sheath. I held it up and there on the gleaming blade, a reflection of my father staring back at me. His face always bore a smile, but you could see the pain behind the eyes, the weariness of life. The face in the sword. His true face. World-weary, battle-hardened, sorrowful, but happy. I turned the sword and rolled it through the air.

I frowned.

The blade was too clean, too perfect, without blemish, blood, or flaw. I looked at Lady Burnok.

"The blade."

"The blade is new, Rini. Re-forged in Ahjo by our master smiths. The blade on this sword was—"

"Broken. I remember."

The tree, the sudden attack by the Rogues Army, the clang of swords, my father fending off one attacker and killing him. Then another attacker and his sword went up to block the swing of his assailant and… the blade shattered. The attacker kicked my father to the ground, my father laying there with half of his short sword in hand just as the militant's sword lunged into his heart, killing him. Another soldier came and fought the attacker. An awkward hit from the soldier and the attacker's sword fell, then the attacker fled holding a bloody hand and the other's giving chase while my father's body lay motionless on the ground, the hilt of this sword which I now held, with its broken blade, lying next to him. I tore myself away from someone holding me and ran to his horse and drew a sword, the sword I carried at my side, to give chase and kill the man who slay my father.

I opened my eyes. I was on my knees, the sword in hand resting next to me. I was sobbing. A gentle hand touched my shoulder, and then an arm wrapped around me, a warm body knelt next to me, and gave a slight squeeze.

"I miss my father, my wife, my daughter, all that has been taken from me..."

We sat embraced as the shadows cast by the sun moved across the walls of the room. I took in a deep breath, and stood, weakened by the weight of my grief. I sheathed the sword and lay it on the bed. I leaned against the bed frame and drew in breaths until the pain subsided and some semblance of composure helped me stand straight. Lady Burnok still knelt on the floor, and I thought about the weight of her grief after losing my father. A grief we shared. I held out my hand. She looked up at me, smiled, and took my hand, and stood.

Burnok was standing by the window, looking out. He, too, shared in this pain. This, my family. My father's family. He glanced at me over his shoulder and nodded, then returned to gazing out the window. Lady Veri stood on her toes and kissed my cheek, then reached down, picked up the sword and scabbard, and handed it to me.

"Take this, your father's sword. And with this sword, make yourself whole again. It will bring you balance."

I took the sword from her and bowed my head. Then, a memory flashed through my mind. I stumbled, then sat on the bed rail.

"Rini?" Lady Burnok put her hand on my shoulder, and Tass came to me.

"It is nothing." I looked at Tass. "The painting. In the gallery." I looked at the sword. "This was the sword depicted, the sword in our father's hand. The sword that..." I shook. "It is me," I said in a hushed whisper. I stood. "I must go." I turned to the Lady Burnok, tears trickled from my tired eyes. "Thank you." I clasped the sword to my belt. My time in Gal Abed was done.

A piece of art on the Lady's bedside table caught my eye as I walked past. A lotus, crafted in white and purple marble. I walked over to it and stroked its smooth edges.

"Your father gave that to me. I told him I loved the purple lotus of the Black River. He brought me this, and said that it would be more permanent." She giggled. "He also brought me the actual flowers, too. He told me some story of their origin."

"Story?" I said, staring at the lotus, thinking of the remnants of the purple lotuses I carried with me.

"There is a story of a creature, a mystic named Unel Moya, who lives across our land in the western mists, and that he is the grandfather or creator of the Roama people." I looked up from the lotus. "They say he weaves the weather and creates the mist and forever lives in a dream state because his favorite food is the lotus."

She laughed, and I laughed with her.

"Stuff of myth and legend, eh, brother?" Burnok stood, arms crossed. Lady Burnok shushed him.

"Well, be that as it may, my sons, there are certain medicines, healing salves, and whatnot made from the purple lotus. There are special properties within it." She looked into my eyes, and I hers. "Some say it has the power to reveal your inner being, your one true self." She reached out and grasped my shoulder. "The council wishes to help you, Rini." I stepped away from her and into the open room, feeling like a trapped rat. "Please consider this. I'm worried about you, my son."

I spun around and glared at her, then relaxed. The move startled her. She walked to the end of her bed and stood next to Tass, who stood like an extra pillar in the vast room.

"Lord Åkerfeldt will bring a force of 2,000 men, supplies, and equipment through Soldier's Pass in the north and meet you on the Red Road, the road you call the Madoran Road," she said. "Even Lord Westval gave his blessing. He is the one who championed the idea of aid for you to the council."

I glanced at Burnok, who was frowning. He turned and looked down at his mother, then to me.

"Forgive me, Lady Burnok, but I do not trust your Lord Westval. Besides, if this Queen is some almighty sorceress, what does it matter if my force is ten men or 10,000?" I gazed out into the final shine of the day as the sun gave way to night. "I thank the counsel of the Western Lands, my Lady, but this fight belongs to the Northern Lands."

Her face sat in a flickering shadow from the braziers on the wall. She looked up at her son, then grasped his arm and held it to her.

"Please, Rini, think about it," she said, her voice barely audible over the many in my head screaming to get out, run, fight, break free.

"I must be alone," I said, walking to the door. I paused. "Thank you, my Lady. For, everything."

I opened the door and left the room.

CHAPTER THIRTY-THREE

The Black Caravan

I WALKED THROUGH THE keep and out into the night. I made haste to my quarters. I lit the braziers in my room from the tinderbox near the door and found my uniform and leathers on the bed as if expecting me. I changed and once again donned the burden I tried to shed so many times, what now seems like ages ago. A different lifetime. I hooked the clasp on the front and slid my father's sword into the sheath on the back of my harness. I clasped its empty scabbard on my belt, then clasped my long sword next to it. My old short sword lay on my bed, beside the pouch with my few treasures. I stared at the sword. All these years with it, all the memories, all the lives it took. I picked it up and clasped it to the other side of my belt. I carefully lifted the pouch, opened it, and looked at the lotuses inside. Crushed and broken, a pile of petals lay on the bottom. I put the pouch in my pack, slung the pack on my arm, and left my quarters.

I made my way across the torch-lit gardens to the barracks and found Fonchesca and Astonzi outside with Ghenesta.

"Captain Fonchesca, get the men and horses together and prepare to leave. We ride tonight."

"We are returning home?" Fonchesca said.

"Only those willing to reclaim it, or die trying. Now, make haste. I wish to reach Opet by dawn." My cadre left, and I looked at Ghenesta. His words during the council meeting still fresh in my mind.

I walked away.

"Commander, you need our help."

I stopped. "I have not asked for any aid, Ghenesta, nor do I seek it. This is our fight."

"With a force of less than 200 broken soldiers?"

I turned and faced him. "Broken?"

"Please, Commander, even you can see the anguish and exhaustion—"

"My soldiers are my concern, Commander Ghenesta, not yours. If they have the will to fight, so be it. I will give them the opportunity to die gloriously in battle over withering away in comfort and solitude on a mountaintop."

"This is a fool's errand, Soltari, and even you know it. You do not know who you are dealing with."

"I know she is flesh and bleeds like the rest of us. And I know the Southern Lands had an opportunity ages ago to quell this force and did nothing." His eyes went to the ground, and he brush dust from his uniform sleeves. He nodded, then looked at me again, eye to eye.

"Then let us help now, Soltari."

"I made a promise to my dead wife and child, Commander, and that promise was not to help the Southern Lands make amends. Good night and farewell."

"Then let me help." He stared at the ground again. "The counsel... they have declined favor with us. I—"

"Why do you wish to join us, Commander? This is not your battle. You should be with your own army."

His eyes narrowed. "My army?" He laughed. "My army is weak, Commander. They rely more on presentation and baubles than training and battle. Not one soldier in that force has seen the likes of battle in ages. I cannot just stand by polishing my buttons whilst she lives," he said through gritted teeth. But there was something more to his story.

"We ride tonight." I walked away and into the garden, surrounded by the night song of the nocturnal critters of Gal Abed.

I made my way to the stables and found the groomsman. He led me to Sumu. There were several of my men tacking the horses and gathering them together.

"Sumu, old friend."

The horse nickered and pawed at the ground. He nuzzled close to me. I strapped my pack to my saddle, took the scabbard for my father's sword, strapped it next to my pack, and sheathed the sword in it. I led Sumu to the end of the long row of stables.

Burnok stood there, tall and arms crossed.

"Leaving?"

"Aye." He dropped his arms.

"No chance then to knock some reason into that thick skull of yours?"

"I made a promise, brother. I intend to keep it."

"Rini, you — by Yoomala, you are marching to your death."

I mounted Sumu. "If that is my fate, so be it."

Burnok grunted, then looked away. In the firelight, the genuine concern for me hid behind his gruff beard. It was in his eyes. He rubbed his forehead, then held his head high.

"Then, so be it. If that is your fate." He reached out his hand and we clasped arms. "It was good to see you, brother. I hope to see you again."

"You will, according to the prophecy of the Southern Lands." He chuckled, and pulled me into an embrace.

On a hill behind him stood the Lady Burnok, and two guards. She held her hands to her mouth, then pulled them away toward me, turned, and disappeared into the darkness.

I gathered my force at the gates of Gal Abed. There were just under 200 of us. The Lady Burnok provided six carts for those without horses and for our gear and rations, which I accepted out of necessity. I nodded to the Captain of the Guard, and the gates opened and we passed under the stone archway. We crossed the bridge under firelight cast by the fire pits burning on pillars along the bridge. Crossing was not as daunting under darkness, unable to discern the dizzying height of the bridge. The sound of the raging waters and the distant falls filled the night air as we crossed.

We reached the other side and turned east on the Kinelot Road. A short time later, we reached the Madoran Road which would take us to Opet, then S'ruh outside Serpent's Pass in the west, the region reigned over by the coward, Lord Westval.

When we turned north to Opet at the crossroads and crossed the bridge over the Sleeping River, we would be back in the Northern Lands for the first time since leaving Khor'Akber in the East. For some of us, the last time their feet rested on Northern soil was after escaping the forces of the Queen.

We guided our horses through the pitch of night and came to the bridge crossing the Sleeping River, and there in the center was a horse and rider, lit by the high moon. I halted our force.

"I request again, Commander, to offer my sword in your service," the horseman said. "I have sent my men back to the city with the message from the Western counsel."

"He's persistent. I'll give him that," Fonchesca whispered.

I nudged my horse to the edge of the bridge.

"If it is your wish to die in the service of the Northern Lands, Commander, so be it. I will accept your sword in service."

We pushed on across the bridge, and the men took a moment to touch the dirt of their homeland. As we progressed on the road, the night became blacker as the moon disappeared behind the thick canopy of the forest. Only darkness loomed ahead.

Something told me our return home would be dark, and unwelcome...

We crested a hill at the break of dawn. The village of Opet sat silent in the fading dark. Tall fires bloomed against the low clouds, casting eerie reflections. Shadows danced in the forest around it from the flickering flames.

We halted.

The scene was too familiar, reminding me of the village outpost Tasa-Arvo on our journey from Farwic. I ordered Astonzi to bring a few men, and ordered Fonchesca to stay with the rest as we went in for a closer look.

Figures roamed the streets. Long, heavy black blades hung from their hands and dragged on the road, making an unsettling scraping noise.

"Husks," Captain Astonzi said.

"Aye."

"Those blades are cursed, Commander. They—"

"I am well aware of what happens, Captain." I looked at him. His eyes shone wide in the firelight. "Captain?"

He turned to me, then blinked and swallowed hard. He caught his breath and let out a long sigh. "Commander, it is not the kuori I worry about. It is the queen's daughters."

"Queen's daughters?"

"Aye. A name we gave the R'Uma. They are something that will forever haunt my dreams. They look like beastial women, with a mane of long black hair down their back, and black eyes."

"Commander Versol mentioned a creature with long claws, and mouths full of sharp flesh-ripping teeth."

"Aye, the daughters. They only know one thing… to kill, and they go for the throat. Every time." He turned to me. "You'll know them before you see them by the wretched stench." He turned his blue gaze back to Opet. "Foul beasts. More foul than even those kuori."

"Right. We will approach slowly and draw out the kuori before moving in hard and fast."

I turned Sumu and we returned to the others.

As we approached Opet and were quickly spotted by Kuori. They galloped on three legs, wielding their heavy black blades high. They hissed, then the first two launched themselves into the air, and were quickly smote down. More came and were easily dispatched.

We charged into Opet, the men smiling, rage and madness in their eyes. With redemption at hand, we stormed the village, and before mid-morning, it was ours. There was a hiss behind me. Fonchesca and I both turned, startled by the sound. A northern soldier with eyes of black ran our way. He had a black blade protruding from his chest.

"Remove the head," I said.

The dead soldier turned to swing at Fonchesca, and before he could, his sword dropped to the ground next to his body. His head tumbled soon after. Black blood poured from the wound and found no purchase save the dirt road of Opet.

We spent the rest of the morning salvaging supplies, then rested. Not all the buildings were burned and we could have quartered in the village, but the men chose to press on to S'Ruh, away from the death and the dead husks lying in the streets. We lost ten men in the battle. We found no other sign of life.

"My hope is they made a fair escape," Astonzi said.

"Agreed," Fonchesca said wiping black blood and grime from his face.

We made camp off the road in an open field as dark clouds moved on in an absent breeze. I noted that some of the men listened to the forest, and were relieved there was no mist, no shadows, and no voices.

At dawn, we broke camp and traveled half the day before we had S'ruh in sight. We stopped on the road and Fonchesca, Astonzi, and I rode up a small hillside on the edge of the foothills to survey what we could. S'ruh sat on the other side of Forge River.

"No fires," Fonchesca said.

"Aye. No fires of any kind, and no smoke to indicate life," I said.

"It looks dead," Astonzi said. His voice trailed off. We sat in silence. Not even the horses made a sound.

The gray clouds continued to hover in the air, and an ill wind blew through.

"Come, we ride to S'Ruh."

We rode back down the hill and joined the others. We crossed the bridge over the Forge River.

Nothing.

No wind. No fires. No life. The only movement was from the river, the river which for eons has cut through the Mountains on our west, creating Serpent's Pass. On the other side of the pass was the city of Ahjo, where the finest weapons are made in their forges. We continued slowly into the village.

We searched S'Ruh for the remainder of the day and found no life. No villager, soldier, kuori, or Rogues Army, and no sign that anyone had been in S'Ruh recently.

The men traded looks. Looks of worry, and defeat. The morale was sinking. They were looking for another victory, yet were handed nothing.

Nightfall was coming quick.

I told Fonchesca and Astonzi to set camp north of S'Ruh in a clearing on the edge of the forest meant for carts or caravans and travelers. A low thunder rumbled in the distance.

"We could stay in the shelter of S'Ruh," Fonchesca said. "Maybe that would lift some spirits? A bed, and—"

"No. This is a foul place. A foul place of death now. It exists only in shadow. If we stay here, we will all reek of madness come daybreak. No, we make camp here."

We set up camp as night fell. A dark night. A darkness unlike any I have experienced since my night on the White River. Lightning flashed in the distance, and tiny droplets announced a rain. In the forest around the clearing, the whispering began.

"It is here," Fonchesca said.

"Mount up and prepare your men."

Lightning flashed again, and a sentry from the south of camp shouted.

"Captain!" he called.

Astonzi came running. There on the road stood four women. Lightning struck again, flashing across the sky, lighting the scene as if it was day. They wore gowns that flowed behind them in the storm's breeze. Black armor with gold filigree encased their left arms. All stood pale in the grim flashes of light, draped by long black hair and masked with baleful grins.

"Kur'Ya," I said. So there were more. The lightning flashed again, and a sentry faced them. "No!" I yelled, just as the man stopped moving, then writhed in some weird contortion, before dropping to the ground. Dead.

"Shield your eyes, turn your gaze away from them!"

Another sentry dropped. The lightning flashed again as thunder rumbled overhead, and behind the four women sat a carriage, black as night. The carriage from Gal Abed. I was sure of it.

Then the rain came down, but did not appear to affect the four Kur'Ya standing on the road. I instinctively drew my old short sword just as a bolt of lightning shot from the sky and hit two of our carts. They exploded, throwing debris and supplies everywhere. Horses and men ran around in the storm, trying to escape this new unreality. Some soldiers moved to attack the Kur'Ya, stumbling and dropping to the ground motionless as their life force was drained. One Kur'Ya raised her gauntleted arm and from it shot a bolt of bluish purple lightning passing through one man, then another, before settling on a horse. All three dropped to the ground. The purple lightning diminished and became a glowing black sword.

Another carriage came into the light behind the black one as lightning from the sky shot across again. One of the green carriages. I could see the driver climbing on top and pulling some sort of rod, opening the doors, then hunching down.

"Commander!" yelled Astonzi from my right. He was pointing at the green carriage. There we both stood, still as the dead night, as the foulest putrescence moved across us. Astonzi's eyes went wide, and he crouched, looking around him. Then, out of the black, the vile beast came, with a mane of black hair, and longish arms ending in long nails. It leaped from the darkness onto a soldier, her mouth full of teeth wrapped around the man's throat. His scream was cut off as the beast ripped the throat out, blood splaying all over her face, and the road to Feren Ta, then washed away by the rain.

"Captain Fonchesca, you focus your men on killing those!" I pointed to the R'Uma who was stalking another soldier. Astonzi's men had scattered.

"Fonchesca, archers now!" I pointed to the Kur'ya. Four men ran up to the crossroad and kneeled. They raised bows and arrows flew, two of them striking Kur'Ya in the throat, another striking the driver of the carriage. The others flew into the air as a R'Uma leaped nearly two carriage lengths onto him and wrapped her vile jaws around his neck. She ripped at the throat so hard that when she looked up, the soldier's head was hanging from her mouth. Another soldier ran up behind her and swung, and her head went tumbling, the soldier's head still in her bloody maw.

The thunder cracked, lightning streaked from the sky, and the storm died. The rain let up only for an instant. The stench of death, blood, rain, and the R'Uma filled the air. I heard a hiss behind me and turned just as a R'Uma leaped from the dark. She landed on the point of my sword, and her weight dragged me to the ground. I landed awkwardly, and my sword fell from my hand. I stood and one of the Kur'Ya was there before me. I turned away, but it was too late.

The screams of my dying soldiers, the shrieks of the queen's daughters, the whining of scared horses, the thunder, all a cacophony of chaos in my mind as my energy gave way. This was my doom. The end of my days, caught in the gaze of this foul creature. It wasn't the one called Pri'Eten, but it mattered not.

I dropped to my knees.

I looked for Captain Fonchesca, but he was caught in the melee. My eyes found Astonzi.

"Captain Astonzi!" He turned. He moved toward me from the cross-roads. "No! You... return to Gal Abed! Get..." The pain of my energy waning became unbearable. I dropped to all fours. I covered my eyes, but I knew it didn't matter if she no longer held my gaze. Once she had it, it was all she needed, and only she could break the spell.

"Get... help!" I sent my dying words into the air. I know not if he heard them. "No..." I said. "I... made a... prom—"

Laughter. Somewhere. On the wind? No. Somewhere... My head exploded in a searing blast of pain, and my face, body, and soul fell onto the wet road of S'Ruh to be washed away with the rain.

Chapter Thirty-Four

The Veiled Man

I WOKE TO HEAVY shackles on my wrists and legs. My body burned from the inside. I laid in a heap, feverish, stripped clean, in a pitch-black void. I shivered. There were faint sounds of conversation, distant and unnerving, in a language I did not understand, but recognized. I tried to sit up but was too weak. I lay there, eyes wide, staring into the black. I beckoned for a vision to haunt me, to see her face, to see... anything.

But none came.

I rolled over onto my knees, my stomach roiled. Cold sweat dripped from my body and I retched. A dark poison escaped my body, a reeking liquid, and I retched again. The world spun out from under me, and I fell over and into the blackness.

When I woke. my breathing was heavy and labored. The stench of my vomit-filled prison was thick. I had relieved myself in my unconsciousness and now lay in a pool of my body's waste. I coughed at the vicious assault on my senses.

The floor beneath me rumbled, and the sound of leather, metal, and wood intertwined with the jingle of a harness. Footfalls crossed above me, then the whole of my body and everything around me lurched, then lurched again. The salty liquid on the hard floor rolled to my mouth as I lay there. I sat up, and a sudden jostling of the wagon threw me down onto my back. The sound of a horse's footfalls on stone knocked behind me, and I knew where I was and who my captor was, and with a feeling of both dread and excitement... knew I was returning home.

I grinned as the ambling of the wagon lulled me into sleep.

A fierce flash of light pulled me out of the slumber. The fury of the sun smashed through a doorway and blinded me. I held my arms over my eyes to block its wrath and heard voices, whispers. A soft, but heavy thing hit my head and at once the light vanished, casting me back into darkness, but the light lingered in my blinded eyes, then faded into the ether.

I reached for the thing thrown at me. It was a wineskin. I sat up on my knees as the wagon lurched again and sent me forward. My heavy shackles pulled me down and I crumbled to the floor, too weak to withstand the lurches of the caravan. I pushed myself back across the slick, wet floor, and sat up. I found the wineskin. I opened it and sniffed its contents, but the pungent smells of my body's waste overwhelmed any scent I would get from the inside. I put it to my lips and tasted a bit of the liquid.

Wine. I drank. The wine refreshed me at once and filled my empty stomach. The effect of the alcohol quickly took hold, and I passed into a dreamless slumber.

I awoke to a deathly stillness. The carriage had stopped. There were no voices, no horses whinnied. It was as if the wagon had passed into a void. I sat up on my knees then shifted to a wall of the carriage and sat against it. My head throbbed. I lifted my weighted arms and reached to the back of it. There was a mass of dry blood in my hair.

I moved to a corner, away from my urine and vomit and excrement. I took a sip of the sweet wine and relished the liquid on my lips. I heaved a heavy sigh. My stomach rumbled, beckoning for food, and tightened.

My head was in a constant, dizzying spin. A warm trickle came from my nose and I instinctively wiped the blood from my face with the back of my shackled hand, smearing it across my cheek. I realized with a pang of pleasure I was smiling. I laughed. I knew my sorrows, my grief, my pain, were all at an end. The only thing left for me now was the relief death would bring.

"Take me then, I am not afraid," I said to the void.

My head exploded into a fury of pain and I screamed and fell to my side. The pain was like a jagged dagger thrust into the side of my skull, then twisted. I screamed again. Among my screams, a woman was laughing. I writhed on the floor, the wineskin lost, its contents spilling out, mixing with my own fluids, and more laughter came, sinister and threatening, and coalesced with my screams.

My gut exploded, and I doubled over as my insides let loose their contents. I reached out and pulled myself across the floor of muck and filth, twisted, deformed, writhing, screaming, and I choked, gasping for air as my throat felt like it was being crushed under the weight of a foot, and through it all, the warm trickle from my nose ended at my lips as my blood sat wavering on my mouth, then dripped to the floor with the rest of me.

The throbbing war inside my head subsided, and my stomach settled. I stood gasping on the edge of the void, on the cliff's edge of sanity, peering into the nothingness beyond, fearing the world behind me and welcoming the fall before me.

A soft hand fell upon my shoulder, and a beam of light shone behind me. I turned and stared into her eyes. Her smile. Her face. She was close, and the warmth of her naked body to mine calmed me as she touched my face and kissed me. An intoxicating warmth flowed through me, and I shuddered. I embraced her and pulled her close. She pulled away and looked at me, stroked my face, said something lost in the darkness, then stepped back and in one swift move... pushed me over the edge and into the fall.

My eyes opened to pitch black save for a tiny pinhole stream of light etching its way through the darkness from a crack in the caravan's sidewall. Every sharp hit from the rough terrain we crossed jostled me and rattled the chains on my hands and feet. With an ember of strength, I pushed myself to the sidewall and sat against it. The light struck my hand, casting a pinprick of warmth. The shackles on my wrists reflected the light to my face, and with eyes closed, I basked in its small ray of heat, a gateway to the outside. A hard knock on the road sent me back to the floor of the caravan and into the darkness.

We stopped. Voices argued outside, and my stray beam of light disappeared for an instant, then returned as the voices made their way around the caravan. I sat up and leaned against the wall. I listened. The voices carried back to the front. The carriage jostled as someone climbed on, then, with the snap of reins, we lurched and were moving again.

My stomach tightened and nausea tore through my body as hunger pains came on swift and sudden. I banged the back of my head against the wall, then turned and pounded on the wall under the driver with my shackles. A distant curse and another snap of leather reins. I pounded some more. Another curse and the wagon lurched to a stop. More chatter came from outside as the driver called out and a faint response floated in. My answer was a quick stomp against the wall with a boot right by my head. I beat on the wall some more with the chain. The reins snapped, and we lurched forward and I braced. We were moving faster than before. Another swift kick from a boot came. Weariness set in, and I collapsed to the floor.

I stared over at the flickering light from the pinhole and focused on it. The pinhole came from a knot in the board. I stared at it in trance, then remembered the promise and knew, this was not my end.

The slow pace and odd jostling of the caravan told me we traveled over rough terrain.

Using the wall as a guide and support, I stood. We hit a large rock, and the impact knocked me to the side. Shouts came from outside. I straightened. My legs wobbled. I focused on what little strength remained in my starved and beaten body and made my way to the wall where the pinhole was. I hobbled to the other side of the caravan and a quick jerk from another rock sent me headlong against the side. I stabilized myself and took a deep breath, then lunged toward the light and smashed into the wall with the whole of my body. There was a crack as the wood splintered. Surprised voices followed. Light flooded in. Outside stood the trees of a forest. We sped up, and the rocky terrain flung me left and right. I stood against the side again and lunged at the now weakened wall and felt the wood splinter again and give under my weight. The cart swerved and sent me flying back across. The impact of my body knocked the cart off balance for a moment, then it swerved again, and straightened. With each turn and swerve, I was tossed about but stayed on my shackled feet. Frantic shouts and light flooded in. A hole now gaped in the side of the black caravan.

Driven by madness, I lunged at the broken boards and smashed through, falling hard onto splintered wood as the wagon rolled onto two wheels. The carriage to tipped and smash apart as the horses, spooked by the suddenness of it all, bolted, dragging the driver and the remains of the cart across the rocks. One of the green carriages was ahead of us and the horses charged into the back of it. The impact awkwardly twisted one horse's neck, and as it fell dead it pulled the other horse down with it, snapping three of the horse's legs.

At the sudden jostling of the green caravan from behind, its horses screamed and bolted. The driver braked the wheels, but the force of the drag was too much, and the front split apart; the wheels cracked on the rocky terrain, and the hitch snapped, yanking the driver with it. He hit with a crushing sound like thin ice cracking as he went face-first into a boulder at the side of the road. The rest of the caravan hit a rock and flipped end over end, landing on its top, then slowly collapsed to its side.

When I fell, there was a snap from my shoulder. Pain shot through my body as I writhed there, broken, naked, and shackled. The cart behind us stopped, the drivers yelling. I staggered to my feet and was attacked from behind with a blow across my back, sending me reeling into a tree. I turned, and a tall, large man came toward me, and we grappled. I entangled his wrists with the chain of my shackles and wrestled him to the ground. I grabbed a dagger from his belt and stabbed him in the throat.

I stood, and a big, burly man grabbed me, picked me up, and tossed me to the hard dirt. He reached down and yanked the chain on my wrists. He tossed me against a large tree. He growled.

And then the smell came. The smell of rot. The rank smell of death.

"Nobody help you now, little man," he said .

I caught movement in the woods behind him as one of my captors ran toward the back of the green caravan. The burly man grinned and reached for me. I sliced his arm with the dagger. He grunted, and his face turned red. He launched at me again and I sliced his other arm. He grabbed me by the throat. There was shouting from someone standing behind the big man. My vision blurred as he choked the wind out of me. I lifted the dagger, then watched the man's eyes go wide as he caught a glimpse of the horror to his right. I jammed the dagger into the side of his large head and his eyes rolled white and we collapsed to the ground together, him on top of me, just as a R'Uma attacked and caught a mouthful of the dead man's throat.

Blood erupted everywhere.

The R'Uma ripped the man's head off like a rabid dog with a piece of raw meat. Blood and torn flesh covered me. She let go of the head and it dropped near me with a dry thump. Then, in one sweep, the R'Uma grasped the man's body and pulled him off to the side. She crouched on top of me. My stomach turned at the stench of the odious horror and my mind snapped in terror, staring into the face of a certain, vile death. There was a whistle on the wind and a brief scream came from the forest. The creature opened her mouth, revealing her rows of blood-stained fangs. Blood dripped on me. Nausea grabbed hold, and I vomited to my side from the stench and found myself staring into the eyes of the dead man's head, the dagger protruding from the side.

She hissed.

I lifted my arms and shoved the shackle chain into her mouth, then pulled down, wrapping the bottom jaw with it. Guttural sounds came from her as she tried to close her mouth. I yanked on the chain as hard as I could. There was a snap, and the chains fell loose. She screamed, choking on the blood in her throat, unable to close her mouth. She coughed, and blood and mucousy spittle drained from her open maw.

I reached over and pulled the dagger from the head and slammed it into the side of her head, just as the sound of a galloping horse came near and a rider rode behind her In a glint of steel and her head exploded at the back as the rider struck a fatal blow. The creature went limp, the head partially removed. I coughed and gagged at the stench and visceral ooze coating me. The horse whinnied, followed by the unmistakable sound of steel striking through flesh and bone as someone screamed, and died.

I lay there, covered with the remnants of one of my captors, and his revolting beast. Moments later, the shadow of a horse appeared before my blood-covered eyes. The rider was silhouetted in the sun. He dismounted. A tall man in a dark robe leaned over me. His head was covered, and a veil masked his face. He pushed the carcass of the R'Uma aside, then grabbed me by my arms and pulled me over his shoulder. I screamed out. He stumbled on the rocky path, then regained his balance. He carried me to the back of an empty cart and set me on the edge of it. I fell back and screamed as I landed on my torn arm. I coughed and gagged and saw red spray from my mouth across the dry, gray wood as I did. He tossed a few things in the back with me. A horse nickered nearby. I closed my eyes, spent from the activity, and slipped into darkness, both horrified, and relieved.

CHAPTER THIRTY-FIVE

The Abyss

A VOICE, DISTANT AND familiar, spoke. The words echoed around my dazed and confused mind. Voice. Liquid. A shadow appeared and disappeared.

I sat at the edge of the Black River and drew some water in my cupped hands. I drank. The hands are not mine, but hers. The water glistened in the bright sun. Bright, white, the glare, the sparkles. A white shadow stood before me. My wife. The aroma of the purple lotus surrounded us. The scent is - part of her.

"Rini," she says, but her lips do not move. She drew more of the clear water in her hands and raised them above my head. She lets the cool water drain onto me. It rolled down my face, and the back of my head. I shivered. She placed her hands on my cheeks, then pulled my lips to hers and her voice echoed somewhere...

"Rini..."

I closed my eyes and the bright glare, the shimmering light, disappeared and all became black. Her lips, soft, wet, and warm against mine. I became lost in her, knowing only her touch on my face and lips. She pulled away and all that remained were her eyes, as blue as the sky - glassy, crystalline, bright. A pair of eyes in the black of the abyss. Her touch still upon my face.

"Rini..."

The pair of eyes blinked and turned green. Emeralds afire. Dark and sinister. Captivating. Cold. Her touch now like fire upon my skin. Burning. I pulled away but could not escape the grasp. My head, my face, my body all alight with the fire from her eyes.

I lay on a stone floor, curled like a babe in the womb, naked and shivering. A withering torch burned in the distance. The light danced.

"Soltari..." It called my name. It's name. Someone's name. I know not. I have no substance. I was a shadow in the abyss, with no light to cast me out.

The torchlight flicked and flickered and died. A single fine ember hung on the end and a wisp of smoke trailed up into nothing above me. The warmth of her touch, of the fire, both gone.

"Rini..."

"Who?"

"Soltari..."

"Who am I?" A warm breeze blew across me and I shivered at its fleeting touch. The single ember glistened, brightened, and a torch lit near me.

Shaviska... something said. Someone. Woman. A warm breeze. The torchlight flickered, then erupted into flame, burning hot and bright. In the far distance, a door. Black. Windowless, with a handle shaped like a dagger, black as shadow. I stretched out, bones cracked, muscles contorted. Something screamed. More bones cracked. I lay prone on the flat stone floor and stared up into the black; the firelight bounced somewhere above me. Beyond me. Around me.

I rolled to my hands and knees. Someone screamed. Closer now. From my body escaped torrents of water, black, in the black, on the black... into the black. I crawled to the door, to the fire, to the warmth. I shivered. Muscles worked in short, broken, choppy movements. I reached the door. I reached for the door.

I screamed.

I stood before the door. Something moved by my side, under the torchlight. It is a girl. Young, with red hair. Color. In the black. She looked up at me with a child's eyes, hopeful, wistful, but her face was full of worry. Scared.

I know her.

Someone's screams echoed in this abyss. Her mouth opened, and she spoke...

"Are you coming home now, Daddy?" A single, wet tear escaped from my eye. The torch flickered.

"Not yet, my angel," I said, and reached out to touch her face, but she was gone. The torch crackled near me and brightened. I grasped the handle on the door and pushed it open and was blinded by a burst of white light.

Hot.

Sweat poured from my face. Blinding light shined above. A shadow interrupted the light and wiped my brow. The light disappeared as a cool, wet cloth covered my eyes. There was a murmur next to me and the jostling of something, the sound of water dripping, then drops, cool drops on my mouth. I tried to speak, but my throat was barren. The smell of spice passed by me. Eastern spice, something... familiar. A voice...

Shaviska...

Her voice. A whisper. A mutter in my ear, like a slight rustle of leaves in an autumn breeze. There is nothing. No black, no light, no sun. I'm neither hot nor cold.

I am nothing.

Shaviska... see me.

I opened my eyes to the gray emptiness.

"I cannot."

You must...

"I want to see her again. Touch her. Hold her."

You cannot... open your eyes. See me...

"My eyes are open."

A wisp of smoke threaded its way across the gray, barely visible. It came to me, wrapped around my wrists, and then pulled me into the gray void. I was floating.

Come to me... see me...

The gray turned darker, and darker, as night fell on a cloudy day. Darker, and into the black.

"No. Do not take me back into the abyss..."

The wisp of clouds became like rope around my wrists. I struggled, but they tightened. I pulled again, but I could not break their grasp. The rope changed to hands, a woman's hands, bejeweled and frail hands with long painted nails. Gentle, tattooed hands.

Her hands.

"Shaviska," she said and opened her eyes. Gold with silver fleck surrounded by a silk scarf. A glint from the ring in her nose, and a jingle from the charms on the chain connected to that ring, then a smile.

"I see you," I said. A child in its mother's unrelenting grasp. "Where am I?"

She smiled, and let go and I fell, fell, floated, flew, then landed softly on a hard surface. Wood, old wood. Wet wood. Movement. I'm being moved. The rattles from chain and tack and hoof falls. Birds singing. Flashing, flashing, in my closed eyes.

I opened them.

Trees. Trees glittered as I passed underneath them and the sun broke through here and there. I was in a cart, on a road.

Alive.

The smell. The smell of death and rotting, festering flesh. Of urine. Of sweat. Roiling. Then a refreshing breeze and the smells of the forest, fresh and clean after a rain.

I groan.

The cart stops. The cart rocks and then footsteps, then a face.

The veiled man.

He grunted, no doubt at the smell.

The sky, blue and cloudless, hung over me. Birds chirped an early morning song as they flitted about. A killdeer and mourning dove called from a tree. The sunlight glistened in the treetops as the trees danced to the breeze. The cool air was refreshing upon my chest and on my body, then my whole body lurched and a fit of coughing took hold. He placed a cloth near my face. Spice. Sweet spices. Gentle... The coughing stopped. The trees disappeared. The sunlight died. The forest went silent and black.

I fell through the blackness. Cold air rushed past my naked body, then rain, and the rain cleansed me, washed me, refreshed me. The pain that wrecked my body disappeared. A sweet voice disturbed the darkness. A once familiar voice. A female voice. Her words drifted over me, wrapped me, and carried me down to the soft green grass under a tall oak tree. A clear stream babbled nearby. The smell of fresh blooms from the tree drifted into the ether, this green island in the blackness.

A light appeared and shone upon me, warming me. Her voice continued. Words. Healing words. Touching words. She called me 'her love' and 'dearest', and her blue eyes appeared in the blackness above my tree island, large and inviting. A swirl of orange-red drifted down between them. The eyes shrank and moved towards me and became a silhouette of a shape from the swirl of red and she walked out of the abyss onto the soft grass. Her form, her body, dressed in a white flowing dress tossed about by the breeze, her arms outstretched, her red hair flitting about her, her gaze steady and bold.

Her voice carried me, lifted me, and I stood before her, and she looked up at me and whispered then embraced me and I wrapped my arms around her and her dress became mist-like, dissipating in my hands, and drifted away like clouds do on a warm summer's day. I stepped forward, then fell to my knees begging as the clouds disappeared into the black, and my tears fell like raindrops upon the ground, softening the grass. The dirt below me became muddy and I fell away from my island once again into the abyss. The sunlight fell away from me, further and further until the abyss consumed it whole and I fell and landed on hard ground knocking the wind from my body.

I sat up, gasping, then collapsed.

The cart hobbled along the dirt road. Clouds formed above. Black clouds. I wore a dressing gown. By my side lay my battered short sword sheathed in its leather scabbard next to my armor. I caught my breath. The sudden realization that both Sumu and my father's sword were gone washed over me like a leaden bull. Blinded by my brazen rage, I had lost everything. My pouch, my sword, my horse. My homeland. Anger filled me. This is not the handiwork of a commander in the army of the Northern Lands. This is the result of a madman.

Around me were a few boxes of supplies. The man in the dark robes sat in the driver's seat. I sat up and groaned. Pain shot through my left shoulder. My wrists were cut, but wrapped, the wrappings stained with blood. As were my ankles. I leaned against the side rail of the cart. I knew not where I was, or who the man was.

Up ahead, there was another road, and the cart slowed. On the road were people. Not people, but soldiers. Four of them. They were soldiers of the Northern Lands. My salvation was at hand.

"Ho there," one yelled. The cart slowed, and the driver reined in the horse to stop us. I went to speak, but my throat was parched and useless.

"Where are you coming from?" asked the soldier. The man spoke, the sound muffled by his face coverings.

"Where is your commander?" he said.

"My Captain is there, up the road a piece."

"Bring him to me. I will speak with no other," the man said. The voice seemed familiar, but I could not place it. My thoughts clouded.

The soldier nodded to the other, then that soldier left. The third soldier was making his way to the cart, then thought better of it. Something turned him away. By the looks of it, the smell of whatever was wrapped in the canvas near me.

A soldier on a horse appeared, a captain, and my smile widened.

"I am Captain Fonchesca. Identify yourself."

"In this cart, Captain, are two things you should see. One of those things is dead. The other, barely living." Fonchesca tilted his head to see if he could see in the back of the cart from his vantage point. He motioned the soldier next to him to look.

The soldier walked up next to the cart and gagged at the foul stench. He turned and retched. The man in the cart chuckled.

"What foul wretchedness is that and what is your name?" Fonchesca said.

"My name does not matter. The foul wretchedness is courtesy of the Queen of Shadows. And hurry Captain, the other is a gift for you and there may not be much time."

The Captain turned his horse and had to nudge it close to the cart. At the same time, the other soldier appeared around the edge. Both saw me, broken and worn.

"By the — Commander Soltari!" Fonchesca said. "Go, now. Get the medic and inform Regent Burnok the Commander is alive." Fonchesca looked up at the man. "Who are you?"

"Just a passing traveler who found the wreckage of a black caravan and saved this wretch from the jaws of that foul thing." He pointed to the wrapped canvas. I went to speak but failed. My eyes drooped. Fonchesca dismounted and climbed into the back of the cart. He looked me over.

"You are alive."

"Only barely, Captain," said the man. "I have done all I can with what I have. You must make haste, for I've nearly lost him twice already."

Fonchesca looked at the driver. "Of course." He ordered someone to bring up one of the supply wagons.

"You can have this one, Captain. It is not mine. It belonged to his captors."

"And what of them?"

"Dead. Those who were not killed in the crash died by my sword. And his hand." He nodded at me.

I knew the voice now. I looked at Fonchesca and said nothing. Only raspy, broken air escaped me. My eyes grew heavy again.

Nightfall was upon me when I woke, and the air was cool with a low-hanging fog. The song of tree frogs and crickets played in the distance. I sat up, alone, now in an open cart, reminiscent of my time crossing the desert. The empty road disappeared into the mist. I coughed and rolled onto my hands and knees, and drew in a deep, aching breath. I grabbed hold of the front boards and pulled myself up to stand. The horse was still harnessed to the cart. Everyone, and everything, was gone.

I picked up my short sword and sheath and placed it in the seat before me. I unrolled my leather armor, dressed, and strapped the sword to my belt. Lightheaded from the exertion of strength, I eased my way from the cart and walked to the front. I pulled myself onto the toe board and into the seat.

I grabbed the reins and gently snapped them, and the horse moved into a walk. I wiped the mist and sweat from my brow and caught myself from tumbling backward into the cart.

We reached the crest of a hill. I gasped and pulled the reins to stop. The horse whinnied, then went silent. Still, like a statue.

There in the distance lie the Great City, aflame. Black twisted towers around the Great Hall stood with flames atop. Flying things swooped around. Screams of the dying echoed through the valley. Around the Great City stood 2,000 men and horses armed and ready to attack and a heavy dark cloud descended upon them with eyes of green in the sky.

Then a flash, and across all the fields lay the bodies of horses, men, women, and children. The village at the West Gate burned, the flames shooting high and casting the shadows of the black husks on crumbling walls. The forest near me came alive, and the low moans carried on as the shadows walked through the trees.

The horse snorted, and back-stepped, then waved his head side to side. A body came from the forest and stood on the road. It's hair a hungry flame. Its face melted to a solid black featureless stone, yet a voice came from it as it raised an arm and pointed to me.

"You! You did not keep the promise!" I closed my eyes and shook my head, but the vision persisted. "You! Commander Saka'Ali! Our blood is on your hands!"

A breeze blew past, bringing a foul stench of death and rot. I tightened the reins, and the horse calmed a bit, then reared up in the harness as shapes blacker than the night moved across the road. The body disappeared as it burned into a pile of ash. The air chilled, and another breeze blew past, scattering the ashes.

Shaviska, the wind called out. The horse calmed and a sweet fragrance drifted in the mist.

Shaviska, the time is short.

"Priestess, what foulness is this?"

Time.

The horse had calmed almost to a sleep. Still, as death, it stood.

A glow appeared on the road and from the glow emerged a spirit creature shrouded in blue-green light. Her eyes shimmered beneath the hood of her silk robe.

You are in the world between dark and light, Shaviska. Come to me. Hurry!

She spoke without moving. Her spirit hovered above the ground, arms outstretched.

I dropped the reins and climbed from the cart. I drifted over to her, towering over her, and fell into her embrace.

Shaviska.

The word drifted in the still air. The word drifted through my thoughts. The word brought a light. A bright light that blinded me.

"Brother!" The voice yelled. "Brother!"

My eyes opened and were burned by torchlight. I winced and turned away.

"Oh, thank Yoomala." Burnok chuckled nervously, unsure, but tears flowed with joy.

He leaned back and fell into the straw on the cart, sitting, hunched over, murmuring something to himself. He handed the torch to a soldier standing near him.

"Where were you, brother?"

"In shadow." The word escaped. My head still lurked in the misty night. I rolled over and sat up. No pain wrenched my body. I stared at the lantern at the end of the cart, focusing on the light. "How long?"

"It is almost dawn." The dark blue-black of the twilight hung on the horizon. Blackest before dawn, I thought. "Two nights since you returned to us."

"Two nights?"

"Aye. How are you feeling, brother?" He was trying to put me at ease. Mothering me.

"I have no words."

He placed a hand on my knee, and I flinched. He withdrew his hand.

"My apologies."

"No need."

"Are you feeling alright?"

"Aye. I am breathing." This time, he laughed. "Where are we?"

"Outside Soldier's Pass, near Feren Ta." I glanced west and could see the tops of the mountains coming into daylight. "Lord Åkerfeldt is on his way through the Pass with a mighty force and supplies." I turned to him, angered, then nodded. I no longer carried the strength to argue.

The song of a killdeer echoed as the forest awakened, and I knew I was no longer in shadow, lost in the darkness.

"Here is some food and water, and wine."

"Thank you," I said.

I cared not to be nursed, to be a burden. But the action humbled me. A horse nickered behind. I sat up and turned. There stood Sumu. He brought his face to mine and nuzzled me. Burnok laughed again.

"We found him standing on the road. Just standing there, not a care in the world, as if waiting for something. Or someone."

I leaned on the edge of the cart and looked at him. Strapped to the saddle was my father's sword . I reached into the pack and pulled the pouch from it. I collapsed into the cart and heaved a heavy sigh. My stomach rumbled, and then a memory rumbled through my head.

"The man. The man in the veil, where is he?" Burnok frowned.

"He is camped just over there. He asked to stay with us until you recovered. Or..." I looked at Burnok.

"That man, brother," I said. "That is Betir El Friz, I'm sure of it."

"The man you say killed our father?" A man emerged from the tree line into the torchlight of the cart.

"I am not that man, young Soltari." He stood at the end of the cart and removed his veil and hood. "I have prayed each day for your return."

"If you are not that man," I said, reaching into the pouch and pulling out the amulet. "Where did you get this?"

I tossed the amulet onto the cart in front of him. Betir El Friz reached down and picked it up.

"Your father gave this to me."

CHAPTER THIRTY-SIX
The Sun Warrior

He rolled the amulet in his fingers. It was the way he looked at it that aroused suspicion in me. He admired it, almost as if it were a trophy.

"Betir El Friz, you may soon get your wish for one last fight." He looked up at me in the cart. His deep-set gray eyes, clear like crystal, gazed at me. Then he grinned.

"You, young Soltari? You think you can best the greatest swordsman in the Rogues Army and far better than any blade of the Northern Lands?"

"I do. And I will." I kept his gaze. "To avenge our father." His eyes widened a bit.

"Our?" He looked over at Burnok and studied him. "Yes, I see it now. The red beard, the blue eyes. The bent nose." He laughed. Burnok humphed.

"You may be the greatest swordsman traveler, but I'm certain you cannot beat my axe, nor both of us at once."

"Don't be so certain of yourself, red giant. Many have died by my blade, thinking as you do. Tell me, what is your name, son of Soltari?"

"Regent Tass Burnok of the Western Lands."

"Burnok. Son of the Lady Burnok, Consul of the Western Lands?" Betir frowned.

"Banter. That's all this is. I will not share information with a stranger and a murderer."

"Murderer? Hmm." He looked at me. "Do you think of me as a murderer?"

"Aye. I do."

"Well then, you would be correct. I have slain plenty, but I have only murdered one." Burnok growled at him.

"So it is true?" I said. He turned to me, then frowned. Then his eyes went wide as the realization came to him.

"Ah... you believe it was by my sword that your father died?" He laughed. "I see. It is clear now. Thank you, thank you sons of Taivas Soltari."

"You dare say our father's name? I do not think of this as a laughing matter, wanderer," Burnok said.

He put his large hand on Betir's shoulder and turned him around. Betir stopped laughing, and as quick as a rabbit, he had Burnok's hand, then pulled Burnok to him, and set a dagger to his throat. I made to stand and fell back against the cart, my strength still spent.

"Be wary, young lad, of who you place your meaty hands upon. It may very well be the thing that kills you."

Burnok jerked his hand away, grabbed the hand with the dagger, and yanked the old man side-wise. He grasped Betir's throat with his other hand.

"It is you who should be wary old man than to mess with these meaty hands for they will crush you like a bug." Burnok snarled. Betir El Friz was gasping for air.

"Tass!"

Burnok growled, then let go. Betir bent over, coughing and gasping. He composed himself, then stood.

"I," he coughed. "I did not kill your father." He looked at me with solemn, yet serious, eyes and took a deep breath. "But I killed the man who did, and for that, I apologize."

"Apologize?" I said.

"Aye, for robbing you of your vengeance."

Tass and I stared at him, then at each other. Burnok crossed his arms in front of him. Betir El Friz's eyes beckoned to each of us.

"Please. Join me at my camp, and you can hear the tale of Betir El Friz." He pointed in the cart. "And bring your food and wine." Burnok looked at me. Betir turned and walked back to his camp in the misty forest.

"Rini, how sure are you he killed our father?"

"We will listen to him, then decide for ourselves. He has the amulet, the missing finger, and he was Rogues Army. But..."

I crawled to the edge of the cart, then sat, and slid off, balancing myself on the end to stand straight. Burnok reached out to help, but I held up my hand.

"But?"

"I'm not sure. There's something... I can't explain, brother. When we met, we talked as if we had known each other for ages."

He grumbled and put his hand on my shoulder. "If it is your wish, let's hear him out."

Betir sat by his fire. He had tossed an extra log onto it and it roared nicely. The flame kept the mist away just enough to quiet the moans from the forest. We sat across from him.

I took a sip of the wine. "How did you know our father?"

"I have known your father since the day I was born." He looked at us. "He was my brother."

"Brother?" I said. My belief in his words trembled. Then he looked at me, and I could see a semblance of my father behind the leathery mask and cold steel eyes. "Brother," I said again.

"He's lying to save his hide, Rini. He's a murderer, and a thief. It only stands to reason he's a liar as well. He's an Easterner for Yoomala's sake." Burnok laughed. "Brother indeed."

Betir El Friz looked at me, deep into my eyes.

"That coin you have, my brother, your father, gave it to me when I left for the Eastern Lands. He told me to never forget where I came from, or who I was. Our father had disowned me, disavowed me. We had traveled to Bin El Omen when I was young. I found a book in a shop about the history of the two Empires, notably the Empire of the New Dawn. When I was older and still bearing that knowledge, I no longer desired to be in Lord Kesto Strome's service, fighting on the Eastern borders. The border villages of the Northern Lands were being raided by Eastern bandits then, not militant Rogues Army, to be clear. The idea of being a part of the Northern Army made me ill. Our ancestors came through the mountains, there," he pointed northwest, "and pillaged everything. Burned everything. In the process probably committed more heinous violence in the name of warfare, not on record of course. We stole, and occupied these lands."

"As did the Southern Lands, Betir El Friz," I said.

"Debatable. The rise of the Empire of the New Dawn was strategic and meant to better the lives of the people. Remember, the people of the Eastern and Southern Lands were one people. There were no borders to divide them until the uprising from the South. There were only the people east of the mountains, and the people west of the mountains, you understand." He looked at Burnok, who turned away. "The Eastern Empire was caught off guard at a weak military and political time. It was crumbling. It was presumed their emperor was dead, and it was true. He had no rightful heir. He died before the southern raiders came. It was strategic growth and necessary. But our ancestors were barbaric, with no strategy. Just a massive killing force who only became civilized ages later and accepted our place in the balance. But others have not accepted their place, or yours. The balance teeters on the brink of collapse at any moment."

"Rini, are we going to sit and listen to this history lesson? You don't believe as he claims, surely."

I raised my hand to silence him. He grunted.

"Once I discovered this truth and the lies we were told as children, I took up my sword and moved to the Eastern Lands and joined the Rogues Army in the Herra's service." He brushed off his robe, then tilted a wineskin to his lips.

"So you were part of the militants under Herra A'avikon Al Friz?"

"As I mentioned in the alcove, only briefly. I didn't agree with their cause and he wasn't Herra or an Al Friz, as he calls himself now."

He picked up a small twig and turned it in his hands.

"We lived outside of the Great City on a farm. We owned the land. The house sat atop a hill in the lush green countryside. In the distance beyond the trees, we could see the towers of the Great City and the spires of the Great Hall. It was just the four of us, my mother and father, and my brother and I. Our father was counselor to Lord Kesto Strome." He smiled as he stared into the fire. My hands were trembling.

A man my father admired sat before me. The master swordsman he always spoke of. A shadow from my past. The one the priestess said would answer a question long held in my heart. Betir tilted his head and stared into the fire as he recalled his memories. My father did the same when he spoke of my mother. I clasped my knees to dissuade the trembling.

"There was this girl. A very beautiful girl. She had a sister. Two of them, actually. Her name was Reginia. My brother was very much in love with her and I knew someday they would unite. And her sister, well, her sister stole my heart. A beautiful woman, and alas, it wasn't my heart she wanted. But my calling was to the East. My father discovered the books and learned of my desires. He banished me from the farm and disowned me for sharing Eastern sympathies. Tensions were high at that time with the Herra and Lord Strome. We were on the brink of all-out war. That is when I left. Thankfully, after much bloodshed along the border, cooler heads prevailed, as they say. Or maybe it was some higher power that killed Kesto Strome. With him, some of the old barbaric ways died."

He tossed the small stick into the fire and it cast embers into the trees above us.

"I was able to keep my past a secret. I lived in El Oton in the north for two summers and learned the language, then moved to Bin El Omen before joining the Rogues Army. I had become an Easterner."

He looked at me and Burnok across the fire. His gaze appeared genuine.

"Ages later, when I heard members of the Rogues Army were hired to murder my brother, I swore by my sword that my only purpose henceforth would be to find the one who escaped, and the one who directed them to kill him, and slay them both.

"And as it happened, in the city of Dagsoud Salam, I heard a soldier while at an inn boasting of killing some envoy of the Northern Lands. I called him a liar, and he told me the story. He was there, and that was the last story I heard of my brother. Later that night, I pulled the jackal to a dark alley in the village and slit his throat. He knew who I was before he died. He did not get to die a valiant or honorable death. I stripped him of his Rogues Army clothing and left him in the street to be burned without memorial with the other dead." He hung his head. "After that, I left the Rogues Army looking for the one who ordered my brother's death. The day will come when they too shall look into my eyes and see their end."

Burnok turned to me.

"Lies," he said. "Rini, you don't believe the words of this man, do you? That's all they are. Words."

"Tell me Betir El Friz, why not return to the Northern Lands after leaving the Rogues Army?"

"I am a strong and brave man, young soldier, but not brave or foolish enough to return and look my father in the eyes. Of course, he is long dead now." He sighed. "Honestly, until you and I met, I did not have a reason to return. The woman I loved united with the son of Kesto Strome and I'm told had a sickly son who is now Lord of the Northern Lands."

"Was," I said.

"Yes, of course." I dared not tell him my thoughts on his love, Hellenia.

"Is it possible those who attacked and killed our father were acting alone, say, trying to start a war with the Northern Lands by killing an envoy? Or maybe between us and the Southern Lands?"

"That is not possible. Militants they may be, they still live by the code. They would only do it if they were hired and paid. Acting the way you mention under the guise of the Rogues Army would mean a fate worse than death within their ranks. No, they were hired, and given the command to kill your father explicitly. The others did not matter in their eyes."

"Like me."

He nodded. "Yes. If they slew you in the act of their mission," he shrugged. "This was well before that faction commanded by Herra A'avikon Ha'amu Al Friz and his son A'avé, the Ghost. The orders, I can tell you, did not come from the Eastern Lands."

"One thing I don't understand," Burnok said. "Father never mentioned to me he had a brother. Why would he not tell his own flesh and blood? Hmm?"

"The day I left, Taivas swore he would keep my secret. He was being groomed to take the place of our father on the Lord's counsel, and nobody needed to know I was an Eastern sympathizer. When anyone asked about me, he would say I moved west to Feran Ta or found a hearty Western woman beyond Soldier's Pass. My father kept the burden of his son to his grave. So it does not surprise me your father never mentioned me. And he was a man of honor and integrity. He would not lie to his sons."

He cleared his throat, pulled his wineskin, and drank from it.

"He mentioned you," I said. Burnok turned to me. "Aye. He said you were out west past the mountains."

"Well, disregard what I said about not lying to his sons, then." He chuckled. "I saw your father last in Khor'Akber. He told me he had united with Reginia and she was bearing their first child. I assume it was you. I never heard from him again after that, and any requests for counsel went unanswered."

"You requested counsel as a member of the Rogues Army?" I said.

He laughed.

"No. As his brother. I am still from the Northern Lands. I had my ways." He took another drink and turned to me. "Tell me, what became of your mother?"

"My mother died giving birth to me."

"Oh." He set his wineskin down, then clasped his hands. "I understand. It makes sense now why he never saw me again. And her sister?" I paused. His eyes still gleamed when he thought of her.

"She raised me after my father was murdered."

"Of course."

"It was you," I said.

He looked at me, his eyes filled with questions.

"My father and I traveled to Bin El Omen. He was looking for someone, but never found him. It was you he was looking for." Betir El Friz became solemn, then turned away. "It must have been because it was shortly after his mother passed. He must have wanted you to know."

Betir wiped his face with a cloth, then turned back.

"Aye. Possibly," he said, his voice cracking a bit. "I wondered about your father every day. I even once traveled to the Great City after we last met, but didn't make it past Ca'Bri. I still could not bear to face my father."

Betir mumbled something in the Eastern language, then wiped his face again.

"Well. So it is. Things are as they are." He looked to Burnok. "But the tale doesn't end there, Burnok of the West. I see you got the burden of the red beard and hair." He laughed. Burnok frowned. "So Taivas traveled west and met a beautiful girl, is that it? He always liked going to the Western Lands with our father and being out of the city, among the trees, the river, and the fresh fish he would pull from it. I know your mother. I have met her. I just... never knew..."

He passed the wineskin to Burnok. He shifted his body, grumbled, then took the wineskin.

"And that would seem like him, moving on after a tragic loss. He had this saying..." He put his hands to his lips, thinking. "Ah yes. All we have is now, with the beauty of the future, and the weight of the past."

Burnok stood hastily, nearly falling into the fire.

"Rini?"

I looked up at him, and his face was contorted, on the verge of tears, like accepting the truth was a fate worse than death.

"Aye, brother." I motioned for him to sit back down.

"You have heard that?" Betir said.

"Yes. He used to tell me that when he left for long periods."

Burnok sat down next to me, trying to hold back the sobs bursting inside of him. I put my hand on his shoulder. We all sat in silence for a long period, each of us lost in the thoughts of our father and brother. The fire was low, and Betir put another small log on it. I looked at him. The firelight cast eerie shadows on his face. But he was solemn. Content.

"There is one other thing, Betir El Friz. The man who killed our father lost a finger during the fight. And—"

"I have a missing finger. Yes, well, that is true. The man I killed was missing a finger on his sword hand. His right hand." Betir held up his right hand, the one with the missing finger. "I am also missing a finger on my right hand, so I can see the confusion."

"I don't understand."

"I am left-handed, Commander." He grinned. "Another misfortune, according to my father. This," he said, still holding up his right hand, "I lost as a boy, thanks to a wild buckskin horse we were to break." He lowered his hands. "The rope was hooked under my finger and that no good animal reared and jerked me forward. The length of rope slipped and burned through, cutting my finger nearly clean off as the horse took flight. The force of it snapped my finger back against my hand. Father had no choice but to remove my finger and burn the wound shut. Something he would have enjoyed doing later in my life, as punishment, I'm sure." He looked at his finger, then at me.

"His story is just that. A story," Burnok said under his trembling breath.

"No, brother Burnok. I believe this man to be the brother of our father. I have no reason to doubt him."

"I do. It's too easy, too convenient, Rini. For all we know, he's some spy for this Queen Ta, Ta, whatever." I smiled, and Betir laughed. "How is he here? Was he traveling with the ones who captured you?"

I looked at Betir.

"Did you follow me, or were you an escort for the caravans?" I said.

"After our meeting in the desert, I returned to Bin El Omen and purchased a horse. I then hired myself on as an escort for a caravan of merchants. Something you said during our conversation led me to believe you were traveling to Gal Abed. There was also something I wandered upon in the desert before we met. Something I care not to talk about." His eyes turned to meet mine and held my gaze. He knew the darkness that lurked within me. The truth of the past. The weight of madness.

I turned away.

"I knew you were not traveling the Black Road nor returning to the Great City alone. Only a fool would be so bold." I stared at the ground, squirming a bit. "And I decided it was time to introduce myself. I have wandered alone for too long. I camped outside the gates of Gal Abed with the other merchants. I was there when you entered the city with that Southern soldier. When the merchants I was with were granted access, I stayed until I saw you call your force to arms and rally by the gates. When you left, I prepared for my leave. I knew you were heading to S'Ruh, and so forth. Well, assumed. That's what I would do.

"Then... I saw the black caravan leave with the other two and knew something was amiss. They had only just arrived. I followed them. During the storm, they disappeared. Then I saw three of your men riding hard toward me, and pass by without a glance. I knew you were in danger. I made it to S'Ruh and saw the carnage of battle, and the remnants of your force huddled in the shops, shaken, and defeated. You weren't on the main road after that. I was fortunate to find you when I did. I happened along a clearing and heard the shouting and horses screaming. I found the makeshift path they were following and, well, the rest, you know."

We sat in silence, listening to the crackle of the logs in the fire. I stared into the blaze, wondering about the aftermath, and my brush with death. I would surely be dead on some unknown path in the forest, if not for him.

"I, I thank you for all that you did." I glanced up at him. He tipped his head and smiled.

Burnok broke the solemn silence.

"If you are my father's brother, then what is your name? Your Northern name?" he said.

Betir El Friz stood before the fire and, in a proud voice, as if by proclamation, said, "I am Betir El Friz of the Rogues Army, former. But I was born Aurinko Soltari, younger brother of Commander Taivas Soltari and youngest son of Commander General Nikolai and his life-mate Enkeli Soltari. Self-exiled from the Northern Lands." He bowed.

The blood rushed from my face, and dizziness swept in like a bird of prey. Burnok noticed.

"Rini?"

He grasped my shoulder to prevent me from falling into the fire.

"My name," I said. "Aurinko. That is… my name."

I took a deep breath, and Betir came to my side. I looked up at him as they laid me down on the soft ground, breathless, on the verge of…

"That is… my birth name."

Chapter Thirty-Seven
An Exile Restored

The trees whispered as a cool breeze blew through, and the scent of dried, smoked meat and sage drifted upon it. The late morning chirps of birds, and the distant rustling of horses, leather, and tack. The smell of wood burning wafted across me. There were voices. Laughter. I opened my eyes. I was lying on a blanket on the floor of the cart. There was no gloom of the day, nor a sign of darkness in the forest. The sunlight flittered through the tops of the tall whispering pines.

I sat up and rolled to my side, then edged my worn body off the cart. I stretched my burdened flesh and bone and grabbed my gear. I removed the robes and slipped on the chilly clothing, uniform, and leathers. I fastened the clasp at the top. The honor and the pride I used to feel when I wore the uniform now left me empty, and cold.

Sumu stood near the cart, eating from a feeder bag. I unclasped my father's sword from my saddle and strapped it to my belt. I pulled the pouch with the lotuses from my bag and attached it to my side. I touched the pouch and thought of the moment I opened the trunk, and there it lay as if waiting on me, waiting for some purpose.

I wandered to the Betir's fire to break the morning chill. Burnok sat near the fire, eating.

"Oy, he awakens," Burnok said, laughing. "Come, brother. Eat." He stood and handed me a small plate of food. He grinned, then sat back down. I sat across from them.

Betir El Friz was also smiling. His leathery, aged face glowed in the firelight with a calm bearing. In the morning light, his skin was dark, and tanned. There was a likeness to my father in his eyes when he smiled, and I understood why he looked familiar in the alcove.

"We were discussing your father, Commander," Betir said.

I took a bite of the cooked meat, and glanced at Burnok. He was smiling behind his beard.

"Rini," I said. Betir looked up at me. "Call me Rini, not Commander."

My stomach roiled at the pangs of hunger. The food was good and warm. But the word Commander stuck in my throat. I have only commanded heartbreak and sorrow. I have left children fatherless, killed or murdered my own men, and left the Northern Lands for dead. And for what? What have I achieved since the attack?

I took the clasp from my uniform, looked at its worn exterior, then tossed it in the fire. I glanced up and saw Betir and Burnok paused in their eating, watching me. I lowered my eyes and focused on that which I could control - satiating my hunger. My uniform was only a facade now for the imposter inside it.

"Anything you'd like to discuss, brother?" Burnok said.

I stared at my plate and swallowed what was in my mouth. I set the plate down, then looked over at the two figures shimmering in the heat beyond the fire.

"I — no." My mind raced with emotion, visions, and emptiness. It was the emptiness where I lay. The vastness of the abyss. Betir filled the emptiness with noise.

"That sword," he said, pointing to the sword at my side. "That is your father's sword." I pulled it a little closer to me. "I remember when he first acquired it. He was so proud of it. Forged in Ahjo in the great forge of Yoomala," he said. "The best forge in all the lands."

Burnok grunted with a proud smile on his face and nodded.

Betir stood and extended his hand.

"May I see it?"

I shuddered, then held the sword and scabbard close, like a newborn babe. I sighed, stood, and handed it to Betir El Friz. He unsheathed it and lifted it high, tilting it side to side, then he waved it around in the air in some dual only he could see. He sheathed it, then handed it back to me.

"I must say, of all the swords I have seen and wielded, son of Taivas, there is no finer blade. You'll find none like it in the Eastern lands, unless picked up by the Roama, of course." He sat and resumed eating.

I sheathed the sword and sat.

"Tell me more about the man who killed our father?"

"He is not worth the breath or time. It was about the same time I ended his life that the darkness came."

I looked at him. "Darkness?"

He took the last bite and set his plate aside. He finished chewing, then drank from his waterskin and wiped his mouth with the back of his sleeve. Burnok reached over, pulled the meat from the fire to his plate. He glanced at me and Betir.

"Aye, what the people called *musta ha'marra*, the darkened twilight. It came from the south." He cleared his throat. "Not a literal darkness, but you could see faces change. The leaders would make sudden and irrational decisions. That's when the Rogues Army formally splintered and General A'avikon El Friz declared himself Herra of the new Rogues Army and changed his title to Al Friz. The Rogues Army had splintered well before that, informally. As I said, the belief was based on an idea but had no formal leader. They were easily swayed by the idea of destruction, terror, that sort of thing."

He took a drink, picked up a stick, and nudged the coals back to a hearty flame.

"But then the faction grew stronger, more militant. They made alliances with outsiders, unreasonable things, like building a force along the borders with the Southern Lands, as if preparing for an attack, only to disband in a moment without explanation. That's where it started, along the deep borders with the Southern Lands. People were told the southern raiders were coming as they had ages ago, then once preparations were made, forces allied and set, word came to disband, that there was no threat. That's when the City of the Southern Lands shuttered their gates and no longer accepted visitors."

He drank.

"There was one thing that stood out in my memory, I do not know why. The militants, some of them started wearing these odd black daggers."

I shivered.

"Myself and a few other leaders in the Rogues Army became suspicious. We would meet in secret to discuss, and then they would act as if there was nothing wrong, that they had been foolish to believe so. Something consumed their thoughts. Something dark. I found myself alone. After I avenged my brother, I left for the foothills outside of Dagsoud Salam. On the way, in the distance, I saw a mass of an army moving across the desert.

They traveled northward to El Oton and Zhalé Pass. I remember because clouds stretched across the sky and it appeared as though something in the clouds lived, watching."

"Like a pair of green eyes?" I said.

Burnok coughed and beat on his chest. He cleared his throat and glared at me.

"Aye. You have seen this?"

"Yes. You say this was five summers past?"

"Hmm, when I saw the movement of the Army was…" he thought for a moment. "Three summers, there about. After that, it seemed as if the darkness vanished. And there was no memory of it."

I looked at Burnok. He was wiping his face with a piece of cloth. His plate was empty.

"Ta'Bedtian," I said. "It has to be. She must have hidden deep in the Eastern lands after she escaped from the Sisters of the Whispering Dawn."

"If she did," Betir said, "she may have crossed the Eastern Lands to the far edge along the Sighing Seas and—" His gaze changed to a wonder of fear. "The Isle."

"Isle?"

"Yes, the Isle of the Mystics. She must have been accepted by them and studied there." He looked hard at me. "If this Queen did study with them, Rini, she would, by now, be a great and powerful force. Her powers would be… unfathomable. This, this all makes sense now."

Betir searched for some meaning in the fire, and then in the trees as he looked around. He stood and began pacing.

"Yes." He rubbed his face, thinking. "Yes, of course."

Burnok looked at me, curious.

"Has he gone mad?" he whispered.

He stopped pacing and looked at us. "I am not mad, Tass Burnok."

"Earlier you mentioned A'avé El Friz. When they first attacked the Great City, we captured three of the Rogues Army. Two of them were decoys. Idiots they must have pulled from the streets. They knew nothing. But the other, he knew me, and he told Lord Airik of the promise she made to A'avé El Friz to give him The Great City. The Queen doesn't want the Northern Lands Betir El Friz. Or the Great City. She's moving south." He sat and turned to Burnok.

"If this is true, Tass Burnok, the Western Lands may also be in danger. They may be trying to restore the Empire of the New Dawn, but this time... yes." He rubbed his face. "Just before the Eastern Empire crumbled under the Empire of the New Dawn, they were preparing to disable Gal Abed, then attack from the east and north."

Burnok laughed. "Disable? Attack? Unlikely."

"I've been to Gal Abed, traveling with the spice caravans. Tell me Tass Burnok, what would happen to the city if the river say, ceased to flow? Or the waterfalls you pride yourself on were to be poisoned? Or what if the caverns below were to collapse?"

"Caverns?" I said.

"Yes, the legendary caverns of Yoomala. Gal Abed has her weaknesses Tass Burnok. It's only a matter of time before they're tested. And if I can think of ways here at this fire to crumble your great fortress, what do you think a force intent on bringing down the Western Lands could think of?"

Burnok rubbed his beard and looked at me. Until now, I'd never seen Burnok worried. Betir El Friz broke the silence once again.

"Another possible way. A more indirect and tactical way to bring Gal Abed down, is from within," he said.

Burnok shuddered. He stood and walked off, the thoughts trembling through his head. He stopped and turned to us. His eyes were wide, this time with fear. And I knew not the man who stood before me.

"Those caravans, with those... things. They were inside the walls. Rini, we watched those caravans come in through the gates. They..."

"The queen must have an ally inside Gal Abed," I said.

Burnok grimaced, then shuddered again. His beard shifted, and his eyes narrowed. He came back to the fire.

"Westval," he said.

He walked a few steps from the camp, picked up something from the forest floor, and threw it into the trees. He pulled his hand down his face, and his breathing became heavy. He turned and looked at me.

"And now a large force of Åkerfeldt's is coming to aid the Northern Lands, leaving Gal Abed exposed to the will of The Queen's pawn, Westval."

I stood.

"Brother, are you putting the burden of this on me?" He grumbled. "When I came to Gal Abed, I was not seeking aid. It was offered." He stepped closer to me.

"And your refusal almost got you killed," he said. He stared at me for a moment. "And now almost half of what little force you had are dead. You always were pig-headed, Rini Soltari. Your defiance is costing lives and livelihood."

"Anger does not suit you, brother Burnok. It loosens your tongue too much."

His fists clenched. I held my ground. Betir stepped up to us.

"Burnok, while all this may be possible, or probable, defeating the Queen would serve the higher purpose and save Gal Abed," Betir said. "Without the aide of the Queen, Westval would be a traitor and put to death, no?"

Burnok peered into my eyes. They narrowed. Then relaxed. His hands opened, and he stepped back. He returned to the fire. Standing behind him on the road were Captains Fonchesca and Astonzi.

"You will join us in this fight," I said to Betir.

Betir smiled.

"Me, Betir El Friz, exile of the Northern Lands, now asked to come to her aid." He laughed.

"The name Betir El Friz will only remain in legend now, Aurinko Soltari, Master Swordsman." He leaned back, hearing his name called out.

"No, young Soltari. I will remain Betir El Friz. You are Aurinko Soltari, warrior of the north." He tossed something to me and I caught it. "I will carry my name as both an honor and a burden."

I opened my hand and saw the clasp I had tossed into the fire. I closed my hand again, holding my own inescapable burden.

CHAPTER THIRTY-EIGHT

A Little Wisdom

THE EARLY AFTERNOON AIR was crisp. A cool breeze came through Soldier's Pass and across the peaks of the Western Mountains. I walked from the fire to Captains Fonchesca and Astonzi.

"Captain Astonzi," I said. "I owe you a debt of gratitude for…" He bowed his head.

"It is my duty Commander."

"Yes. Of course." I looked at Fonchesca. His gaze was ages away. He caught my stare and turned away.

"Captain?" He looked up and straightened.

"Commander."

"Come. Both of you. Join us." We walked back to the fire and sat with Betir and Burnok.

"Tell me, what happened in S'Ruh after…" I said. Fonchesca looked up.

"We, we cleared the town and held our position until Captain Astonzi returned with Regent Burnok and the others. We knew not where you were, or what happened. We thought we'd find you among the dead after the attack, but we did not. Thankfully. Nobody knew what happened to you with the storm, the rain, and the…chaos. We knew not where to look, and no one saw you captured."

"I understand. To get here, you came through Vasara, correct?"

Fonchesca went white and shuddered, then lifted his eyes to Astonzi.

"Vasara, brother, you don't want to know about," Burnok said. "Stories best left to the wind."

Captain Astonzi let out a long breath and said, "We were able to at least re-supply some of our provisions. And we also found a small group of refugees in hiding, about six soldiers, and a handful of horses."

"Our force is down to about sixty soldiers," Fonchesca said. His voice was now more in control. "The village leader, who was part of the small group, had many questions for us. We camped in Vasara for two days. The men weary from the travels, and the battle." He sighed, picked up a stick near him, and tossed it in the fire. "Not all the soldiers we lost were lost in battle. Some wandered off in madness and disappeared. And some from—"

"We left Vasara," Burnok said. "A half day into the march north to here is when Betir El Friz approached our soldiers."

"Was there some new enemy of the Queen's in Vasara?"

Fonchesca shook his head.

"No. Vasara was mostly husks."

"I do not understand. Tell me, what is it about Vasara that you do not wish to talk about? If it was husks only, not Kur'Ya or R'Uma or—"

"The dead," Burnok blurted out. "The not dead, the—"

"The shadows? Var'Yo?"

Fonchesca nodded, on the verge of tears. My patience was dissipating, waning. My tolerance for these games was now gone.

"They were mostly, um," Astonzi coughed to clear his throat and keep tears at bay. "Women, some children. The dead, mostly men, were piled at one end of the village. The smell from the... And having to free the..." He was breaking down.

"I understand now, Captain. No need to continue."

I looked at Betir El Friz. He was staring at me, his face taut and concerned. His eyes narrowed. I stood and walked from the fire. There was a shuffle behind me and then footsteps upon the dried pine needles. I turned. Betir El Friz stood there.

"We must prepare for our advance on Feren Ta," I said.

"Son, you have to realize - and accept - this one thing. You are not alone. You are not the only one on this journey. We are all here. Your brother. Myself. You are our family. Your soldiers are here because they believe in you... and want to go home. The Priestess Kristava didn't have to accept you into her fold, but she did because she also believes in you. You are serving a high purpose." He took a step toward me. "But understand this, and here's what you need to consider, young Soltari." He stared into my eyes. "We are all here, despite one thing you have not done."

"And what is that?"

"Asked."

My mind cleared, and we stood in silence for a moment. I knew I was right. I felt no need to ask for, nor have I wanted help. Yet, here they all were. The damned fools.

"We must leave. Waiting around gives her more time to—"

"Mind your tongue," he said.

I frowned and spun around. He stepped back, then, relaxed his shoulders. He took a deep breath.

"My apologies Rini," he said. "My old ways sometimes return without notice." He took a step toward me, and I stepped back. "Ask yourself this. What has your haste brought you and your men so far?"

I thought about the words Burnok said, about my defiance costing lives. He was wrong.

It wasn't my defiance; it was my impatience. No. My reluctance. My reluctance to accept help when it was offered and to accept the help with me now. And by not thinking this through as a true commander would.

Like my father would.

But I did not have the benefit of consulting him. I was not mentored by him as my brother was. I was raised by a brash woman who later blamed me, and all Soltari's, for the death of her husband and her sister.

I looked at Betir El Friz, and nodded. What he spoke was truth. He stepped forward and grabbed the back of my neck in an odd embrace.

"You will find, or maybe you have, that the harshest and worst enemy any man can face is himself. You overcome yourself, and you become a great warrior. A skilled leader. Better than your father." He laughed. "Maybe better than this old man who stands before you."

I grinned.

"Come, you must sit with your cadre, and family, and discuss this plan for Feren Ta."

"And Tinus Brigh. I want to advance on both at the same time and converge at the crossroad in Karvas Forest."

He smiled. "Now you think clearly. Death has changed you."

"No. Not death. Only my reluctance to wear this uniform." I raised my head high and took a deep breath of the cool forest morning. "But, I am still a Commander in the army of the Northern Lands."

"Not just a Commander, but a Commander General. Son of Commander Taivas Soltari, and nephew of the greatest swordsman who ever lived, General Betir El Friz, former." He winked.

"Aye. Of course."

The sun hung high above us. The forest was alive with bird chatter and the playful scampering of small animals. There were flurries of as the force maintained the camp and horses, some trained, others swapped harrowing stories, some true, some embellished.

"What are the chances, Rini? What are the chances we can succeed against this Queen of Shadows?" Burnok said.

I shrugged. I thought about my earlier conversation with Betir El Friz.

"After recent events? I—" The words escaped me. The last few days in the abyss, the grips of death, and all I had envisioned weighed heavy on my mood, and my confidence.

"What we face ahead is dire," I said. "Some of which will drive men mad. Has driven men mad." I looked at Fonchesca, who was staring into the sky.

Burnok shifted uncomfortably. "Like the dead thing that was with you in the cart?"

"Aye. But those can be killed easily enough. They use no sorcery. They are weapons of the Queen, but of flesh and blood and can be slain by sword. I believe they are the beasts we learned about as boys, the ones that come from the dark forests around the Southern Lands."

Burnok was pale, staring into the fire. Fonchesca had shed tears but was now sitting, listening, head up. Nodding. I looked at Astonzi. Nothing. A soldier to the last.

"The Kur'Ya, though, will have to be killed from a great distance," I said.

"That is not entirely true," El Friz said. He was grinning. He pulled the hood of his robe over his head, then from it, drew a veil across his face, covering his eyes like the women of the Eastern Lands wore. Like the men of the Rogues Army. The veil was thin enough to break the spell but still see through it.

"They had veils like that," Astonzi said. "We found a dead Rogues Army soldier on our escape from the Great City, outside Feren Ta. He was an El Friz, and wore a veil. He also carried a black dagger. A dagger that—"

"Was as black as shadow?" Betir said.

"Aye," Astonzi said.

I shuddered and unconsciously rubbed the old wound on my side.

"The dagger of the desert ghost. Those who serve the self-proclaimed Herra called A'avikon Ha'amu Al Friz. Father of the Ghost. They must serve the Queen."

"It makes sense, given all we've seen," said Astonzi.

"The Rogues Army soldiers I killed in Bin El Omen also had the veils," I said. "They had blindfolded that girl. I've seen it before, in a painting. They knew about her."

Burnok looked up.

"Those soldiers were working with the Queen, then," Betir said.

"I'm not so sure anymore," I said. "It is possible they—"

"There's no other explanation," he said.

Burnok tossed a small log onto the fire, leaned back, and let out a long breath.

"I have wondered," I said. "Why not just kill me like she did my father? Why not send out some mercenaries and have at it?"

"Maybe, and I mean no disrespect," Astonzi said. "Maybe she wasn't the one who killed your father, Commander." Burnok sat up now. He looked at me.

"She did send a force to capture you." Everyone fell silent at Fonchesca's words. "A force that was in Gal Abed, so she knew you were in Gal Abed." I had no argument. My mind rambled.

"Westval," Burnok said.

"Unlikely brother. My visit was not announced."

"Which means only one thing," Betir said. "They were already there."

"Burnok and I watched the black carriage arrive with the others. She knew I would be in Gal Abed. They came for me, and only me." I stood and wandered around the fire. I stopped. "The vision. If it is to be me that defeats her, why toy with me then, keep me alive, take me back to the Great City? Why not use some sorcery, conjure a storm, or some other force? Unleash some power to slay me and change the vision in her favor."

The fire crackled as if our thoughts fueled the flame.

"Maybe she is unable," Astonzi said. I sneered at the thought.

"She's capable."

"Capable, maybe," Betir said. "He said, unable. Maybe she no longer has the ability. She must have limited powers. She must be using those powers now for something else."

"I have seen the capability of her powers firsthand. She drew a blizzard from the north which decimated my forces. It wiped out nearly 2,000 soldiers, horses, and buildings. Gone. For three days that blizzard carried on—"

"Right. Because that was the only thing she was using her powers for. Now, maybe she is using them for something else and cannot spawn a storm or conjure some other sorcery. She must use other methods, methods that do not interfere with where she is focusing her magic. She is conjuring something... else."

His face went dark at the thought of what sorcery the Queen may be spawning.

"Maybe she is watching," Fonchesca said, breaking the silence. "Maybe she can see, or has eyes watching for her."

"She must know something given what happened at S'Ruh," Astonzi said.

I sat back down. "Aye. Let us presume she can see us, or knows that some force is here killing hers. That may be all she knows."

"She may not even know that much," Burnok said.

"Aye. But I am certain we will see much heavier resistance within Feren Ta. Or Tinus Brigh," Betir said. "I believe the closer we get to the Black Road, and the Great City—"

"The more of her forces we shall see," I said.

"Aye." There was some logic to his words.

"Gentlemen, we must prepare for this battle," I said. "Captain Astonzi, find material to use for veils. If we have none, we will get some if possible in Feren Ta and hope we don't run into any Kur'Ya there." He nodded. "Captain Fonchesca, pull the troops together and prepare arms and horses for what lies ahead. I want all souls to know what to expect. I want them training if they're idle."

"Aye, Commander."

"Where is Ghenesta?"

"Probably polishing his fancy sword," Astonzi said.

Burnok chuckled.

"He is with the troops," Fonchesca said.

"Keep an eye on him," I said. Fonchesca nodded, stood, and left. Astonzi rose and followed Fonchesca.

"How long until Åkerfledt arrives?"

Burnok pulled on his beard. "They will come through Soldier's Pass, possibly three days, maybe four."

"Three days?" I said. He looked at me.

"Possibly."

"I cannot sit idle for three days. We must take Feren Ta immediately."

"You cannot with the force you have," Betir said. "We have to assume much greater numbers reside in Feren Ta. And Tinus Brigh."

"Then we will scout. We cannot fight on assumptions."

Betir shifted his weight, picked up a stick, and started tending the fire.

"If you have some insight or wisdom, I should know, Betir El Friz, then out with it."

Burnok was chewing on his bottom lip, which made his beard move in a strange way.

"No wisdom, no insight." He stared at me with his cold gray eyes. "You are forgetting the one element we haven't seen yet, but I expect we will see them soon enough." He put the stick down and looked at me. "While a good idea to send the scouts, what they see and relay may not be wholly accurate. Or complete."

"I trust my scouts."

"Do you? Are they the only ones you trust?"

"I do not have time for—"

"You have time to listen, Commander General Aurinko Soltari. Your soldiers depend on it. Your impatience is clouding your judgment again and will cost more lives. Maybe even your own this time."

He tossed something in the fire and looked around him.

"Your father and I camped on this road before we crossed through Soldier's Pass." He sat on the ground and leaned against the fallen timber he had been sitting on. "That was one of our last trips together."

I stared into the fire thinking of the last time I camped with my father, Tass, and his mother. Betir leaned over and rested his hand on my knee.

"Ahjo," Betir said. "Have you been there?" I shook my head. "I was with him when he had that sword forged. It was symbolic to him. He sold his prized stallion, one he raised from a colt. A prideful beast that one was. Black as night. Long mane and tail. He called it 'Koonnia'. From that horse, he bred four colts. Father was proud of him. Those colts bred more for father after and he sold some of them to the Eastern merchants." He sat up. "He took the purse made from that horse, traveled out here, and had them forge this sword, one of his own he designed with the help of the smiths in Ahjo." Betir chuckled. "Then, being the romantic he was, traveled back home, presented himself with his sword to Reginia's father, and announced his intent to join with her. He proposed to Reginia on the hillside by the farm, with that sword by his side, as the symbol of his honor. And had it at his side when they joined shortly after."

Betir dropped his hand away and stood.

"And when he died," I said.

Betir wiped a bead of sweat from his brow. "Of course. That sword Rini is a symbol of honor and dedication."

"It was shattered by the blow that killed him. It came into Lady Burnok's possession and she had it reforged."

Betir's eyes drifted from me to the sword.

"This sword has been reborn from the fires of Yoomala for you to bear then," he said. "And by wearing it, you honor not only your father's legacy, but your own." He paused and looked around. "The question is, what will your legacy be Aurinko Soltari?"

Chapter Thirty-Nine

She

THREE DAYS PASSED, AND still no word from Lord Åkerfeldt's force. The previous day, Burnok left with three others to the Tower of the Guardian in Soldier's Pass to see if there was any news. He has not returned.

"Are the men ready?" I said to Fonchesca.

"Yes. They have seen what we fight. I am confident in their ability."

"We fashioned the veils and attached them to the uniform," Astonzi said. "Some soldiers even fashioned it into a hood so they could draw up the hood and the veil would fall across their eyes."

"The both of you have done a fine job leading these soldiers."

"Thank you, Commander."

I dismissed them to their duties. Idle time did not sit well with me.

"Commander!" a voice called from behind me. I turned. A young soldier, one of our sentries, was pointing to the West. "Horsemen, sir, eight of them, out of Soldier's Pass." The horsemen appeared from behind a rock outcropping and rode up onto the crest of a hill. I could see the guidon bearing the colors of the Western Lands.

"Burnok." Finally, I thought. "They will be here by midday. Ready the groomsmen. Their horses will need tending. And bring some food to my camp." I looked at the sentry. "Have my brother meet me at the council fire."

"Yes, Commander."

I wandered along a small deer path, consumed in thought. Word would come soon of Åkerfeldt, and our campaign would begin anew. I found a clearing. The sun's rays peered through the treetops onto a small pond that shimmered like tiny crystal beads. I sat down upon a fell log and gazed out at the pond. I let out a deep sigh and closed my eyes.

In two days, at dawn, my force of Northern soldiers, the remnants of my army, will head north to Tinus Brigh while Burnok and Åkerfeldt's men leave for the village of Feren Ta. I thought back to the blizzard. A lifetime ago. A blizzard the Queen conjured from the world of snow and ice to decimate us. I pondered why she has not used her powers to stop us now.

"She is weakened Shaviska."

The voice was sweet and filled my brief solace with relief and a respite from my thoughts.

"Priestess?"

"Open your eyes, young warrior."

She stood before me at the edge of the pond, her white and blue gowns shimmering, drifting around her in a cool breeze. Her blonde hair was braided and wrapped in scarves and beads of lupus lazuli and onyx. The charms from her necklace and facial piercings sent tiny, blinding flashes of light. Beyond the glow, her distinct yellow-gold eyes stared at me, captured me. In trance.

I stood. "How?"

She stretched out an arm and bade me to sit down. Her wristlets jingled as she did. I sat and bowed my head.

"I... I am comforted, Priestess, by your presence. And humbled. How—"

"You have changed warrior of the North." The breeze filled the air with the scent of incense and sweet flowers.

"They say death has changed me, Priestess."

"No, you have changed. You have life." She moved toward me. "I see it. It grows within you." She reached out as if to touch my cheek. The frame of her silhouette glistened in the sunlight. A cool breath of wind caught us, and the fragrance of her wandered around us, the smells sweet and vibrant.

She sat next to me and laid a hand on my shoulder, her touch like the light brush of a spider's web. A flood of anguish from the last day with my wife and daughter exploded from me and I wept, the force of it all too much to bear.

I crumbled.

Her silky embrace was as a mother embraces a lost child who has returned home. An embrace I've never known. An embrace warm and comforting. An embrace of a child for no reason. The tears from the sorrow of being lost, mixed with tears of joy of being found, flowed from my being and drained to the forest floor.

We sat as the sun crossed the sky on its lonely voyage.

And still, I wept.

The fog in my head cleared, and my eyes dried. I stood. The pond was still, and the forest had darkened somewhat. I faced her.

"I do not know what to do," I said before I could stop the words from slipping from me. I sighed and hung my head, then shook the shame from my body. "I... I need your help, Priestess Kristava. I know—"

She nodded, stood, and took my arm in hers, the touch like a feather, almost non-existent. She led me to the water's edge.

"Look," she said, motioning to the pond. "Look into the water and tell me, what do you see?"

I did not recognize the face of the man staring back at me. He looked older, weary, worn, and beaten. A broken man. A madman. His vacant stare peered back at me. On the streets of the Great City, I would have thought him a drifter, a vagabond, and rustled him out the city gates. Our city's values vehemently intolerant of street dwellers.

I would not be welcome in my own home.

"I see a broken man."

"Look deeper. Focus beyond what you see."

Riddles. I still had no tolerance for them. Put me to battle, strategize, make it real, tangible, with force and might, and I prospered. I had no sense of this realm of internal thinking.

"Close your eyes and picture the man you know as Rini Soltari, father, helpmate, and son."

I closed my eyes and saw a man in black leather armor and arm plates, two swords hung from his belt, and gloved hands, standing next to a horse, with arms outstretched and then embracing his daughter. I saw a man kneeling before a sickly Lord, ready for battle, a man charging down upon Eastern bandits, a man standing victorious with a bloodied sword. A man standing over the twisted bodies of his men. A murderer.

Saka'ali.

"I—"

The Priestess drew me closer. The visage of that man shattered and rained down upon me. Then I saw myself on the hillside lying beside her as she slept in the cool air and warm sun. Her red hair gently flitted about in the breeze. I heard laughter and saw my daughter running along the hillside. She ran up to me and knelt before me and I looked into her eyes and in the reflection I saw myself, and I was smiling. I saw no sword, no armor, no blood on my hands as I reached out and embraced her, and held her close. I let her go, and saw that I am the one being embraced and my father stood before me and he was smiling as I had been, his face solemn and proud, and he nods to me. The man beneath the armor, the uncaged, the unbroken man, and his reddish hair and auburn beard turn black and I see myself staring back, smiling - unbroken.

I went to open my eyes, but they were already open. I shook the dream from my head, but it persisted. I stared into my reflection in the small pond and, startled, stepped back. I let go of the Priestess's arm.

"That man," I said. "He has no power against the Queen or her vile sorcery."

She lifted my hands on a pillow of air and looked into my eyes. A sparkle reigned in her gaze, and held me close.

"The magic has been with you all along, and your people, for all this time."

I snickered.

"Northerners, Priestess, do not use sorcery. It's considered stuff of myth and legend."

She let go of my hands and motioned to the pouch on my belt. I looked down, then unstrapped the pouch and opened it.

"They come from the domain of Unel Moya, the lotus eater, far to the West in the unborn mists."

I looked at her, again entranced by her gaze.

"I know not what you speak of, Priestess, nor have I heard of—"

"You must become a shadow to her."

I looked into the pouch. The purple petals were still hardy, but on the verge of withering.

"It's a flower. A flower that thrives in abundance in the Black River. That is all it is."

And then I remembered Lady Burnok, and her lotus, and the story she told. It's more than a flower. It is a symbol of our lands. It is engraved at the top of the entrance to our Great Hall, and at the entrance to the palace in Bin El Omen. More than a flower.

Be like Unel Moya...

I closed the bag and looked at her, and she was smiling.

"Be wary with the lotus."

"They are poison?"

"The effect can cause a dream state with many visions. Visions which will cloud your one true vision."

I remembered the dreams under the large oak where my father was killed. The oils from the flower must have seeped in through my hands, soaked in rain and sweat.

I turned to the pond, and stepped forward to see my reflection again. The same man, weathered and beaten, stood before me.

"I am lost. My decisions, my haste, my—"

"That man is you, Aurinko Soltari." Hearing my name come from her lips was jarring. "He knows what to do, because he knows *why* he needs to do it." My head hung, humbled once again by her words, her presence, her wisdom.

Her riddles.

"Why are you helping me?"

"I am the help you seek my warrior. My love. In here." She placed her hand above my chest, over my heart.

"I have forgotten..."

She reached up, and without touching my chin, raised my head and met my eyes.

"Yes," she said.

I drifted into her gaze and became lost. Her pale skin, her soft touch, her aroma, and the glistening jewelry all tormented me in ways unknown to me since... since... Her hair unbraided and fell to her shoulders and turned red. Her eyes changed from gold to blue. The tattoos and piercings all faded to an alabaster skin. And I smelled her. The scent of the tree flowers she wore in her hair graced my senses. She smiled.

"Solana," I said. Then gasped.

I dropped to my knees keeping my gaze fixed on her eyes, and bowed my head. "I remember." And tears overwhelmed me again.

"My wife. Your name is Solana."

She pulled me close to her, my head resting on her belly.

From her came her warmth, her embrace, her... love. The wind gently drifted past me, and swirled around me, rustling the trees, and escaping through the tops of the whispering pines. They shuddered one last word before all was calm, and I was alone.

"Solana."

Part Four

THE QUEEN OF SHADOWS

CHAPTER FORTY

The Queen

FROM THE CENTER OF the Great City, spirals and plumes of smoke rose into the darkened sky. The towers, great spires once topped with statues in memory of fallen heroes, stood as twisted black abominations keeping watch over the Northern Lands. The statues lay broken on the ground, in the street, and on top of bodies, still and dead. Black figures with long arms, severely clawed hands, and eyes like black onyx lurked the city streets. Black blades dragged behind them on blood-stained flagstones rang discordant and sinister. The once flawless beauty of the Great City, the hanging plants, the bold paints, were now gray and lifeless. The floral perfume and sweet, smoky smells were replaced with the stench of death and rot, and stood wearily as if the city would crumble to pieces in the slightest breeze.

A tall man prowled along the streets, past the kuori, past the broken things and the remnants of a battle waged what seemed ages ago. He wore a tan uniform accented with dark-tanned leather on the chest, arms, and legs. Behind him, a gray cloak flowed. His head was wrapped in tan cloth, covering his nose and mouth. His quick blue eyes peered out at the horrors on his path. A slim, straight sword hung at his side, and on his left breast, two short swipes of blue stood out. The hilt of a black dagger protruded from a sheath on his shoulder harness. He grunted as a kuori passed in front of him, dragging a broken black sword.

The kuori hissed.

He walked up the stairs of the Great Hall to the breezeway and the long corridor behind the columns.

Black figures writhed in the corners inside the domed Hall of Fallen Empires, and Queen Ta'Bedtian sat on the marble throne of the former young and sickly Lord of the Northern Lands. Her eyes were covered by a sash of dark green, and long strands of black and white hair hung from her like untamed ivy. A stray beam of gray, misty light cast upon her through the dome above. A door opened and revealed an unwelcome glow into the murky darkness. The tall man entered and removed his head and face wrappings, revealing tightly cut blonde hair and beard. He gagged, then recomposed himself. His blue eyes scanned the room. He shuddered and walked toward the throne, his footfalls casting no echo in the desolate chamber. He stepped into a small puddle of thick, black liquid and stopped. He peered at the liquid on the bottom of his boot and drew a tight, leathery sneer. Straightening, he continued to the dais and half-kneeled, keeping his knee slightly above the slime.

"Yazzir El Friz, you and your men are ready?"

Her voice was crisp, and direct, and fell dead within the chamber, succumbing to the black muck that covered the floor.

Yazzir stood.

"Yes my Queen," he said with a voice worn from sand and wind and age.

He stepped into the light from above, revealing a desert-strained face, half scarred from a burn which turned the left side of his mouth upward slightly into a permanent grimace. The queen rose, her tall thin rail of a body cloaked in a flowing gown of blue-ish white. Her hair fell around her shoulders. She stretched out her long, pale arms. The nails on her slender fingers glinted in the sunlight like silver spikes.

"My vision has changed Yazzir El Friz. There is a man who seeks to destroy me. His determination is strong and strengthens every day. He was to be brought here but has eluded me. He is... unpredictable." She stepped off the dais within an arm's reach of Yazzir El Friz. He instinctively moved to step back, stopped, and stood his ground. "This man will perish by your blade, master swordsman." She reached out and touched the scarred face. He winced. Her touch, like a brand pulled from a fire.

"Your will be done, my queen."

She dropped her hand to her side and cocked her head as if sniffing the air.

"My horde is nearing completion, my strength is returning," she said. "Yes, and soon I will unleash my wrath upon the wretched Southern Lands." She sneered, her teeth hidden in shadow. Yazzir turned away, unable to witness the apparition. "They will suffer the insufferable and burn under the fury of all my power as it falls upon them."

She turned and stepped onto the dais to the edge of the throne. Yazzir breathed a short-lived sigh of relief as a hiss came from the darkness beside the queen. This time, Yazzir El Friz stepped back as two R'Uma appeared from the gloom, the edge of their gray naked bodies awash in light, the rest in darkness, crouched and crawling.

"Succeed in your mission, Yazzir El Friz. The desires of both your Herra, and his son, depend on it."

Yazzir cleared his throat and bowed his head.

"Do not fail me."

He looked at the queen as she removed the blindfold, dropping it to the floor beside her. Her dark emerald green eyes were aglow in the gloom. She gazed into Yazzir El Friz's eyes, and the master swordsman felt the icy cold within him wrench his soul.

"You will find your mark West in Tinus Brigh," she said within his thoughts. A thin line grinned across her face. "I will be watching."

Yazzir El Friz shuddered, then bowed and turned. His boots tramped through the muck as he walked toward the light of the door.

"And Captain?" her voice hissed to him. He stopped. "He travels with one of your kind."

He glanced over his shoulder.

"A master swordsman. An El Friz."

Yazzir's blood burned through him, and he sneered.

"Yes, my queen." He quickened toward the door and through the long corridor to the smoke-filled light of the day.

Outside, he stopped at the top of the long marble stairs. He heaved out a deep sigh. He drew in air and choked on the acrid odor of the desolation. He pulled on his head wrappings and the cloth across his face. He looked out onto the city, crawling with musta kuori, and shivered. He hurried down the stairs to the west road, grateful to rid himself of the queen and her abominations with great distance.

CHAPTER FORTY-ONE

The Fall of Gal Abed

I LEFT THE CLEARING, hazy and unstable. My wife's name echoed in my thoughts as I returned to the camp.

Solana.

I stopped and took a sip from my wineskin. The sweet taste gave me pause and cleared my mind. Something changed in the air when I called out her name. Like a cool breeze, the kind that clears storm clouds and energizes the soul. I have suffered so long unable to remember her name, and that of my daughter, whose name still eludes me.

When I arrived at the council fire, Betir, Astonzi, and Fonchesca were waiting.

A short while later, Burnok and two others, soldiers of the Western Lands, walked toward us. I stood and went to him.

"Welcome back, brother." We clasped arms in greeting. His face was grim, tired, and his eyes hinted at fear. I motioned for him to sit.

"Please," he said. "I have been sitting on a horse all day. My arse needs a rest." The humor normally would show on his face, but some grave concern masked it. "These are two soldiers from Åkerfeldt's force. They have news from the Western Lands. But I'll be blunt and to the point. Gal Abed has fallen."

"What?" I said. Betir and the others stood.

Burnok nodded to the soldier on his right.

"Lord Westval announced his allegiance to the Queen of Shadows and has taken the fortress of Gal Abed from within," the soldier said.

I looked at Burnok. "And the Lady Burnok and her sister?"

"Safe. They escaped to the safety of the caverns under the city and sealed them off."

I heaved a sigh of relief.

"Forces under Westval's command now occupy the keep.," the soldier continued. "We believe they are part of a group who wish to see Westval become Lord of the Western Lands. Those not allied with him, we are told, were hung from the Bridge of Halos. They have shuttered the gates to the city."

"And your old friends," Burnok said, looking at Betir El Friz. "Rogues Army. They were disguised as merchants and traders and brought those kuori and other militants in by caravan. All allowed to pass under Westval's watch."

"The attack was swift," the soldier said. "Only Westval's forces were in Gal Abed."

"Because Åkerfeldt's were gone?" I said.

The soldier shook his head. "No. All guards, sentries, and security are part of Westval's force. Each Lord provides a force every three moons, relieving the one on duty."

"Understood. She must have promised Westval something."

Burnok looked at me from under his brushy brow.

"Westval is an opportunistic pig. All he needed was the idea and the support." He cleared his throat. "All that aside, Lord Åkerfeldt's soldiers will be here the day after tomorrow. They will need rest before the advance on Feren Ta." More waiting. He lifted his head. "The Western lands are no longer here to only support the Northern lands, Rini."

"I see."

"There is other news. Lord Åkerfeldt prepared to leave with a force nearing 2,500 soldiers, and equipment." He shifted his weight and crossed his arms. "We will see a little more than half of that. Åkerfeldt had a feeling he couldn't shake about Westval after their last counsel."

"You've spoken with Lord Åkerfeldt?"

"Aye. A portion of his force left to support Lord Keirnen, who has Gal Abed surrounded, and to seal the exit of Serpent's Pass, Westval's territory."

"1,000 soldiers," I said half-heartedly. "Why not send all to Gal Abed and reclaim the city."

"I asked the same question." Burnok looked at the soldier on his right. The man cleared his throat and rested a hand on the pommel of his sword.

"Lady Linnoitus ordered him to send the force here."

"This is our battle now too, brother. If killing the Queen of Shadows is the only way to stop this darkness, which has now spread to my home, then we will do what we must to ensure victory."

"Lord Keirnen's force, with the support of Åkerfeldt's, will prevent any additional allies from reaching Lord Westval. He cannot escape," the man said.

A chill went through me, and my thoughts turned to the Priestess. I wondered if she was still within the walls of Gal Abed, despite my recent vision.

Burnok took a drink from a water skin hanging across his body.

"So you see, brother, this is no longer just about the revenge of Rini Soltari."

The words hit me hard, for this man before me I no longer knew. The look of surprise on my face must have caught him off guard, for he rolled his lips, curling his beard together.

"I understand." I sat down at the fire. The weight of the news was a lot to bear. "I have been sitting idle for five days. With each passing day, she—"

"Is it always about you, brother?" Burnok pointed a thick finger across the fire at me. "This is bigger than just poor Rini Soltari now." Betir walked over to Burnok, but Burnok held up a hand, stopping him. "This is not your quest to bear alone anymore, brother."

I shot up, fists clenched. Burnok eased back and straightened himself, standing over me. He harrumphed, then re-crossed his arms.

"There it is," I said. Burnok raised an eyebrow. "The fear. The fear of losing your home, and your family." He shifted his weight and dropped his arms. "It hangs in your eyes, on your face, like a parasite."

A figure beyond Burnok caught my eye. Ghenesta was walking to the fire. Burnok turned around to see what I was looking at. I walked away, Betir watching me closely. I wandered back into the solitude the forest would give me.

I returned to the clearing.

Part of me hoped to see the Priestess in another vision again, her spirit, her presence. The sun was behind the trees, and the night songs of the forest would begin soon. A mist was forming atop the pond. I watched it swirl, float, and take a life of its own. I sat on the log and opened the leather pouch. I eyed the lotus petals. I wiped my hand on my pant leg and reached in, then pulled one out. I wiped off the other hand, then tore the petal in two. I placed the half-petal back into the pouch and closed it. I stared at the petal, then looked to the darkening sky.

I put the petal in my mouth, held it on my tongue, and chewed. The taste was sweet, like honey, then bitter, like spoiled wine. I spat out the petal and looked at the partially eaten pieces lying on the ground. They crawled around, looking for purchase on something, or trying to re-form themselves.

I blinked.

They were bits and pieces. Then all at once they rolled together and became whole again. The petal piece floated up in front of my face, and hung in the air, dancing, like a feather on a slight breeze, and beyond the petal in the coming darkness emerged a tall, thin woman in a white gown. I lurched back and fell onto the ground, my feet propped up by the log. I scrambled and stood, then drew my sword. The woman wore a large golden headdress. The headdress turned black as night and became her hair, and gold streaks came from a glyph on her forehead in the shape of 4 circles, each within the other. Her youthful face was long and narrow, her skin as white as the marble cut in Gal Abed. Her eyes were a piercing dark green-like...

... emeralds on fire.

She... so young. Too young. She...

I drew my other sword. I stepped back as she moved toward me. She stretched out her arms and stopped. Her body quivered like a reflection in a pond after tossing in a stone. Then her hair was fire, alight with rage. The fire burned down the length of her body consuming her and turning to ash as it went until it reached her feet and dissipated, the last remnants of ash floated into the air, vanishing.

I blinked, then shook my head. The nocturnal night songs of the forest were beginning. The mist from the pond was spreading and reaching higher. Soon the moans from mist shadows would come. I looked over the log and there lay the partially chewed pieces of the lotus petal. I sheathed my swords and wiped the sweat from my brow. I shivered as the chill mist reached my bones, and pushed my way past the shadows, stumbling back to the encampment.

Burnok was sitting at the fire alone. He looked up as I approached, saw it was me, then turned away. He tossed the stick he was using to poke the fire aside. A sat across from him. A few moments later, he turned to me.

"I am sorry brother," I said. His face froze for a moment, then relaxed.

"Sorry? That is not a thing you are likely to say." I sighed. He chuckled a bit. The words, the news, and the daggers we threw at each other still swarmed around us.

"I know your fear brother Burnok."

He held his head up.

"Fear?"

"Aye." I held his gaze. His body eased, and his eyes went to the fire. He slumped and nodded.

"I apologize, for not—"

"Visiting?" he said.

I took a deep breath.

"Aye."

His smile diminished and became more solemn. A breeze flurried around us, scattering the embers from our fire into the air and sending smoke into my eyes. I wiped them as tears helped to cleanse them.

"I also apologize for not visiting," Burnok said. "There's no excuse. You are my brother. I would have liked to have met your wife and daughter. I should have been there more."

"Solana," I said. He looked up at me. "That is my wife's name."

"It is a beautiful name." He caught me wiping tears from my eyes. "Brother, are you crying?" He came to me and placed a hand on my shoulder.

"Smoke, from the fire."

"Really, it's ok Rini. It is fine." I glared at him, eyes red from the smoke, a tear running down my face.

"Smoke, little brother. From the fire." I wiped the tear. He started to laugh, and I soon joined, his laughter contagious.

"Brother, yes. Little? I think not." Again he burst into hearty laughter.

The fire was dying, and a storm was moving in. Black clouds hung on the horizon, drifting, meandering toward us from the east.

Overnight, the dark clouds continued to move in, shrouding us in a deeper darkness, and the forest came alive with the mist shadows. The men dared not go near the forest edge. Fire appeared to quell the shadows, and we set tall torches around the perimeter.

The next day, we readied the force. Even though the food supply was low, everyone was eager to get to the coming battle. I ordered Fonchesca to organize parties to hunt for deer and rabbit. I stood near Sumu checking my gear and tack, preparing for the ride, when a sentry called out.

"Movement on the horizon! To the West!" I hurried to him, as did others. We knew what he saw. It was the call we waited for. Burnok and I crested the ridge where this sentry stood, and there in the distance was Åkerfeldt's force coming out of Soldier's Pass. Burnok's breathing hitched at the sight. I put my hand on his shoulder and shook it. He was smiling, as was I. Then his smile faded a bit, curious, as mine widened. The force appeared to be more than the number we expected. The long trail of men and horses wound out of the pass. We all stood and stared, not believing what we saw.

"I see more than 1,000 here brother Burnok," I said.

He nodded and grunted, then walked away. I followed and caught up to him at his horse. He stepped up and mounted the great beast.

"Talk to me."

He sighed. "If they bring more here, then I fear there is a grim reason, a reason not to be in Gal Abed."

"I understand." The two soldiers he brought with him the previous day rode to us.

"We ride to meet them." He said and nudged his horse, and the three rode out. I watched as they rounded a bend in the road and disappeared. Betir El Friz walked to me.

"He's worried about his home."

"I am familiar with the feeling," I said.

"Aye. He's worried about his family, and not having a home to go to." He held up a hand. "Hear my words." He placed his hand on the side of my arm and stared into my eyes with his cold steel glare. "He still has something to lose Rini." I gasped and shrugged off his hand. "I know those are harsh words, but it is truth."

He paused before continuing.

"He has lived his life in the Western Lands without worry of bloodshed. Without battle. This goes beyond worry. He is scared and, like you, ready to return to his home and fight."

"I hear your words Betir. But they only strengthen my resolve to put an end to this nightmare."

Later that day, Burnok, the two riders, Lord Åkerfeldt, and a small force of twenty rode into our encampment. Burnok and Åkerfeldt joined my cadre and me at the council fire.

"Lord Åkerfeldt," I bowed my head. "Thank you." I motioned for him and Burnok to sit. "Do you have news of Gal Abed?"

"Not much has changed, Commander," Åkerfeldt said. His manner was calm, stoic. His voice was soft, contradicting his countenance. "No new movement from Lord Westval. His force is locked in tight. We believe Lord Kiernen and his army will overtake Westval easily enough. We presume the soldiers of the Western Lands have little desire to ally with the queen, regardless of their allegiance to Westval."

"That is a bold assumption Lord Åkerfeldt. Fear is a great motivator." He chuckled and nodded.

"Aye Commander. But I think once they see Kiernen's force arrive, that fear may shift a little to our advantage."

I glanced at Burnok. He did not bear the fear he wore before their arrival.

"We were only expecting a force of 1,000 or less from what we were told, yet…"

"Yes, well. Before we could start the journey to Gal Abed, word came from Lady Linnoitus herself that said the defeat of the Queen of Shadows in the Northern Lands was of greater consequence and to continue as we were. I sent a smaller force back, not entirely trusting the messenger, to seal off Serpent's Pass and guard the river. I have it in good faith though regarding Kiernen's force. I am confident in his ability." He looked at Burnok. "I never did trust Westval." Burnok grinned.

"Nor I."

"We are camped on the plains about a half day's march from here. I would like to camp here with this portion of my men, messengers, cadre, and so forth. If, we are welcome?"

"More than welcome Lord Åkerfeldt." He smiled. "But take heed, our food supplies are dwindling and—"

"Fear not Commander, we brought plenty."

Another unexpected gift. "Thank you, Lord Åkerfeldt for your generosity."

"Last time we talked Commander, I remember you were not open to the idea of our help."

"Well. I have learned a little since then."

I called for wine and food, and we settled in to plan our advance. I was ready to put the pleasantries of diplomacy behind me and move on to action. I was more than prepared to leave this clearing, this camp, and ride into battle.

Chapter Forty-Two

Attack on Tinus Brigh

THE LIGHT FROM THE east cast a dark blue along the horizon as the sun crested. Soon the sunlight would bathe us with a welcome relief from the darkness. I ordered Fonchesca to send scouts to Tinus Brigh and Feren Ta two days ago, when Lord Åkerfeldt arrived, despite Betir's concern. They returned at dusk last night and reported the same as what we saw in S'Ruh. Musta kuori and a small detachment of Rogues Army in Tinus Brigh. The scouts from Feren Ta have not been seen or heard from since they left. I can only presume they abandoned the cause or were captured and killed.

As planned, we would attack the two villages simultaneously. My force now gathered outside of Tinus Brigh. Lord Åkerfeldt and Burnok would lead the force through Feren Ta.

I gave the signal, and we charged down the road into the village of Tinus Brigh. We were just over 300 strong for the initial attack, with myself, Betir El Friz, and Fonchesca leading an additional 300 soldiers to reinforce us. Tinus Brigh was a large village sprawled across an open plain surrounded by forest and foothills to the north, and more forest and hills to the south. Like S'Ruh, Tinus Brigh was gutted.

Fires glowed disdainfully atop the two mangled towers at the village gate, and the first group of husks advanced on the party.

The ground shook. Astonzi's party split from the rear to flank the village and attack from the north.

We rode past the gate towers and into the village. Musta Kuori came from all sides and were trampled under our horses or felled by our blades. We made good progress past them toward the village center. Shouts ahead announced the emergence of the Rogues Army into the fray just as the sun crested the horizon and cast its glow from the east upon us. A foul stench from the husk dead filled the morning air.

We had caught them unaware.

Betir and I advanced to the head of the party and took the Rogues Army soldiers head-on. They were at least one hundred strong.

Our swords met and sang. I unmounted one soldier, and he landed hard upon the earth and was trampled by his horse. I fended off an attack from my left, turned, and advanced on the swordsman. Sumu reared up on his hind legs and kicked out, sending the swordsman through the air and landing with a crack upon the earth. He was clutching his twisted arm, writhing in pain.

Betir El Friz dismounted and pulled soldiers from their horses as they rode past. Fending off their blade, he would turn and grab their sword arm, and with a yank, the rider would come free as the horse continued. He had three at the end of his blade, and they danced a dance of death in the streets of Tinus Brigh. I watched, mesmerized by his skill and grace, and was grateful to not be the one at the end of his blade.

The new day's sunlight glinted off their swords sending flashes of light in odd directions. The air filled with a cacophony of metal on metal. With a twist and a thrust, one soldier was run through. A pull, a turn, parry, and a slash, and another soldier dropped to the ground, clutching his throat, trying to stop the stream of blood gushing from it. He collapsed into the dust. The third soldier recognized the moves of the Rogues Army veteran and could see his last day was upon him. He attacked, blocked, turned, blocked, and swung. Betir El Friz's riposte met his blade, and he punched the Rogues Army swordsman in the face with the hilt of his sword, sending the man backward, blood streaming from his nose.

A whisper of a blade near me brought me back to my own fight, and I dodged a swing from my right as Sumu stepped to his left. I turned and blocked another blow with my sword. I leaped from my horse to face my attacker. He pitched forward with a haphazard swing, trying to adjust to the change, missing me. I swung with my short sword and slashed him across the gut. He jumped back just enough to prevent a deathly blow. He thrust, I blocked, and he swung again. A dark madness lived in his eyes. I blocked with both swords. I twisted his blade from mine, and I again swung with the short sword. This time I caught his free arm. He winced, then spun, attacked low, and I blocked, sliding his sword to the right. I caught him in the gut with the long sword as he fell on its point. He collapsed to the ground, gasping.

I knelt beside him. Blood trickled from the corner of his mouth. He turned and spit, covering the dusty road with his blood.

"Saka'Ali," he said, then raised his sword in a feeble attempt to run me through. I twisted his arm with my sword, breaking his sword from his grip. He grinned, and I twisted my sword up into his chest. His eyes glazed over and rolled into his head. I stood and pushed the man off my sword with my boot. He fell back and rolled listlessly into a pool of his own blood.

Betir was again in a heated battle with another soldier of the Rogues Army. This one was different. He stood taller than El Friz. He was dressed in the Rogues Army uniform, tan and white, with a head wrap of dark tan and a faded blue band holding the head covering in place. A veil hung from his collar. He was besting Betir's every move. The man advanced, and the swords clanged together and he spoke to him as they stood there, sword against sword.

"Betir El Friz," the man said with a slight smile. I stood and stepped toward Betir. He caught me from the corner of his eye and held up a hand. I stopped.

"Yazzir, El Friz," he said. "You're a little far from home, eh?" The man tilted his head slightly.

"You dare speak to me with the vile tongue of the Northern dogs?" Betir smiled.

"I am a northern dog," and he pushed Yazzir El Friz away.

"I always suspected something about you, Betir, but my quarrel is not with you."

"Is it not?" Betir said as he swung, and the swords clanged together, then slid apart.

"I am here for a man. That man," he said, pointing to me. "He must die. Do you defend the life of this Northern scum?"

Betir El Friz smiled again.

"I defend," Betir said, "my family."

Yazzir El Friz stepped back, then scowled.

"Then today you will die, for you are no longer a soldier of the Rogues Army, but a traitor." He spat on the ground.

"Yazzir, I have not been a soldier of the Rogues Army for some time," he laughed.

Yazzir El Friz put his sword in his left hand, then attacked, and Betir parried the blow easily. And another. They twirled, spun, clashed swords, each showing their might as a skilled swordsman. A master swordsman. An El Friz.

A growl came from behind me. I turned and was knocked to the ground by a beast of a man. He kicked me in the ribs, knocking the wind from me. I rolled to my side and stood and was kicked down again. The soldier laughed and said something, then kicked me again. He carried no sword. He was large and stocky. An odd addition to the Rogues Army. He grabbed my leg with his left hand and pulled me toward him. I kicked him in the gut with my free leg. He grimaced but held on. I gripped my short sword and swung, and he let out a maddening scream as I slashed across his wrist. He backed up, holding his stump of an arm to his chest while his hand remained clasped to my leg. I pushed it off with my sword and stood. He held his bloody stump with his other arm, which was also handless, and why he carried no sword. He growled and ran at me and onto my long sword as I raised it, piercing his throat. He gurgled out his last word and slid off my sword to the ground.

I turned just as Yazzir swung and caught Betir El Friz on the shoulder of his free arm. Yazzir smiled at the minor victory, which he probably hoped would put doubt in Betir's head. Yazzir stepped and swung again, low, and Betir jumped over the blade. His sword flashed in the sunlight, then came down on Yazzir El Friz. He parried just in time to prevent serious damage, but the sword cut deeply on his shoulder. The blood discolored his shirt as it drained. Yazzir El Friz grimaced. He stepped back and composed himself into a swordsman's stance, waiting for Betir to attack, but Betir stood his ground, sword down at his side.

"Quitting already, Yazzir?" Yazzir growled, then lunged, and Betir knocked his sword to the side. "You cannot best your master, Yazzir." He swung and Betir knocked the sword down again. "Why I honored you with the title of El Friz, I cannot understand." Yazzir turned and stepped forward with a lunge, and again, Betir knocked the sword playfully. "El Lapsi would be more appropriate."

Yazzir ran forward, eyes dark, face in a scowl, and swung down hard. Betir El Friz twisted his blade up, disarming Yazzir, and just as quick, he turned and had Yazzir in his clutches with his blade across the man's neck.

I stood and stared, dumbfounded. It was a finishing move my father taught me as a boy. A move he made me practice time and time again.

Yazzir's blade fell onto the dusty road of Tinus Brigh.

"You may have stopped me, Betir El Friz, but you cannot stop her. A'avé El Friz will have the Great City."

I walked to him and faced him. Sweat drained down his face. Betir's blade had made a thin red line across Yazzir's neck.

"The only thing the Rogues Army will see of the Great City," I said, "is the head of your Queen posted above our North Gate."

He grinned, then laughed.

"I know you... Saka'Ali." He turned to spit, forcing the sword deeper into his throat. He spat at me, but most dribbled from his bleeding lip. "Your land is dead but will rise anew under Herra Al Friz as promised by the... Queen of Shadows." He winced. "Even now... General A'avé rides... to claim her. They ride..." He grimaced as sweat rolled into his eyes, and he sneered. "They ride to claim their prize. You're... too late. And she... is too powerful."

"Only to the weak, Yazzir." Betir's blade tilted, sending a flash of bright light from the sun into my eyes, and I saw through the haze Yazzir El Friz drop to the ground clutching his throat and then fall silent next to his sword.

Betir El Friz turned to me. He looked down at the corpse of Yazzir El Friz and shook his head.

"He was a good soldier. Strong heart. Weak mind." He reached down and stripped the two blue swipes off the uniform and tossed them away. He walked to me and looked me in the eyes. "She knows who you are, and she's afraid."

A breeze swept through, pushing the foul stench of the dead and spilled blood through the village and the glare of the sun disappeared, then darkened altogether as a storm rolled in from the east.

Behind me, thunder clapped violently. Overhead, lightning streamed across the sky. One stream came from above and struck the top of a nearby tower, sending shards of fire over the sides.

She knew.

Rain began to fall.

"Take cover! Now," I screamed to them all. Memories of the blizzard plagued and fogged my mind. The word spread and all were now running for shelter. A hard rain soon drenched us. I grasped Sumu's reins. I pulled him off the street to an overhang, then lashed his reins to a post. Horses and men slipped in the mud and fell to the ground. Were we to have taken this village so easily? She was powerful and her sorcery stretched far.

We found cover in a nearby shop and watched from a window as the rain fell in droves. Betir El Friz turned to me and shook the water from his hair. A bit of fear in his eyes.

"This is unnatural."

"Aye. And now our force is split up and sheltered."

We were in a bakery, lost in the time before the Queen. The shelves were barren save for the food once for sale, now rotten and black. In the back of the shop, the things used to make the loaves and sweet breads sat idle, covered in dust and decay. The room was in tatters. The shop was empty, as lifeless as the black husks, and as soulless as the Queen of Shadows. The noise from the rain as it fell upon the roof of the shop was deafening.

And as quickly as it came, it subsided.

"Unnatural indeed." El Friz said. Another streak of lightning and a loud crack as it struck the other tower of Tinus Brigh, splitting it into shards of stone which rained down upon the village.

The thunder rolled beyond us and the rays of the sun sliced through the dark clouds, emitting its brilliance upon us.

The towers were burning. The village was free, and cleansed by the rain.

We emerged from the bakery. Soldiers appeared from a shop before us and from side streets. I hailed two of them.

"Find Captains Astonzi and Fonchesca and have them regroup their men, then report to me immediately in the village square!" The soldiers nodded and took to the muddy streets.

Time was short.

"Something isn't making sense," I said to El Friz.

"I sense it too." He sniffed the air and turned. "Behind us." To the side of the bakery was an alley leading to the back of the shops.

"There," I said. We entered the alley.

A horrible scream came from somewhere in the village beyond us, followed by shouting men. Then, as quickly as it started, it stopped. All that remained was the lone cry of someone injured or dying.

Betir El Friz stopped and turned to me. He shook his head.

We rounded the edge of the building and hovering over a partially devoured Rogues Army soldier was one of the Queen's daughters, her back to us. She stopped her feast, then raised her head and sniffed the air. She was naked, feral, her long black hair wrapped around her body. Betir and I moved closer to the edge of the building, out of sight.

He peered around the corner, then ducked back and muttered something.

There was a terrible hiss.

A breeze swirled through and the dank smell of death and rot wafted around us.

There was a horrible screech close to us, and the sound of a man screaming followed it. His scream cut short. We stepped out. The thing looked up and sniffed the air. Her teeth, long and sharp, black as night, dripped with blood. Her eyes were like two orbs of polished onyx. Her long fingernails were the color of dead bone. Her body was foul, like an animal uncared for, with skin like tanned leather. She turned and chomped down on the body, yanking and tearing an organ from its inside. She looked at us with a blood-soaked mouth and smiled, then relieved herself on her kill.

"Foul beast," Betir said.

Then he charged at her. The beast crouched and hissed. I stepped back, stunned by the sudden move. The thing launched her whole body at Betir. I charged after and took only two steps before the thing was dead. Its throat slashed, spilling its black blood on the rain-soaked ground. It lay there gurgling, trying to hiss, spasming, then ceased.

I walked up behind Betir and stared at the thing.

"Come. There will be more."

"Aye," he said, his eyes locked on the Queen's creation. "Aye."

We walked back to the main road and found our horses huddled under the overhang. The village lay in ruin. In the distance, a clatter of metal and shouts of men rose. Betir was already on his horse, heeling it into battle. I pulled myself into my saddle and followed.

Further into the village, soldiers and black husks were entangled. Betir El Friz rode through one group and, with only the skills an Eastern master swordsman possessed, sliced through four of the husks. He turned a corner and disappeared behind a building. I rode through the mass, hacking down the black things.

Before me, Captain Astonzi was in a fight with another swordsman. I saw a final parry and swing from Astonzi as his sword sliced across the swordsman's chest. The man fell to the ground, lifeless. Astonzi turned to me, and a dark cloud rolled past the sun, shrouding us in shadow. There was no recognition of me in his black eyes. My heart ached. I spurred Sumu and rode fast to Astonzi, and with one swing, loosed his head from his body. He crumpled and fell to the ground, his black blood spilling onto the muddy road. The shadow of the cloud passed and now the sun hung high in the sky, bathing us with its radiance. I stopped Sumu and paused, then swore to myself. I turned east, and rode back past Astonzi's body.

I rode into the central part of the village and saw a Western soldier facing a Kur'ya, caught in her gaze. Her black hair caressed her face, and a white gown flowed behind her like the wings of a bat. His sword lay on the ground behind him.

He walked closer, his gaze frozen, pulled into her world. She held her arms out as she drained his power from him, and she rose from the ground.

Her face turned a pale white. A face of a wraith. He dropped to his knees.

I pulled the veil over my eyes, and the horror disappeared behind a white haze. I heeled my horse faster and raised my long sword. She turned and saw her death flash in the sunlight, which burst from the clouds above. And she smiled. I swung and her smile remained on her face as her head hit the ground and rolled to the soldier's knees. Her body dropped in a miserable heap.

I reared my horse and went back to the soldier. He was sobbing horribly. A soldier unhinged by the horrors of the Northern darkness.

"Stand up," I ordered.

He stood, wobbled on his legs, then found his strength, looked around himself, and picked up his sword. He hung his head.

"Return to battle. This village is not yet won." He ran off down the road.

I stared at the gaping, smiling face of the wraith. I speared the head onto my sword, turned to the central square where a tall iron fence with barbed posts stood, and mounted her head on the tallest spike.

I climbed on Sumu and turned south, then halted, awestruck by what, or rather who, stood before me on the village street. On a small road leading south from the center of Tinus Brigh stood two children, a little older than my daughter. A boy and a girl. The worried look on their faces was overshadowed by fear. They were staring at the body of the Kur'Ya behind me. Her head now displayed high right above her.

I climbed from Sumu. He grunted and turned away as I approached the two children.

"Not to worry, little ones. She can't hurt you." They each took a step back. I was still holding my bloody sword. I wiped it on the body of a soldier near me, then sheathed it. I knelt on one knee. "I am a soldier, with the Northern Lands." The boy's face became solemn. "Do you, did you live here in Tinus Brigh?" The girl shook her head. "No? Where are you from?" The boy mumbled. "Sorry?"

He looked up at me. "Feren Ta."

"Are there more of you?" The girl nodded. I smirked. "Are you safe?" She shrugged. Behind them, in the far distance, I saw a figure move. I stood, and they startled and took another step back. A little further down the short road, a woman stepped out from behind a building. She was frantic, saw the kids, then ran toward us. She reached them, sobbing, then dropped to her knees and grasped them both closely. She wiped her tears on the back of the little girl's shirt, then looked at me. She gasped, then stood, and the fear washed away, and she smiled.

CHAPTER FORTY-THREE

The Cost of Feren Ta

W E HAD WON THE battle for Tinus Brigh, but as with any battle, it came at a heavy cost. We left no garrison behind to guard the village. I could not afford the troops. Captain Fonchesca's force joined us at the end as planned and helped secure the village. I told him about the death of Captain Astonzi, but left the details to my cruel memory. The woman on the street led Fonchesca and I to more refugees hiding in the forest south of the village. There, we found a large group of older men, a few soldiers, women, and children. Villagers from both Tinus Brigh and Feren Ta. Most of them were families of soldiers lost to the war we all faced. They camped near a cave in a forest clearing. When the soldiers saw me and Captain Fonchesca, tears streamed from their faces, and all but five of them joined us. I told them Tinus Brigh was secure and asked if they had any news of Feren Ta.

"It is too far south from here, Commander," a soldier said.

"Of course," I said. I had hoped for some word from Burnok and Aker-feldt.

I sent Captain Fonchesca ahead with 100 soldiers, including Ghenesta, to set camp where the road from Tinus Brigh merges with the Black Road, while the rest of us regrouped and resupplied what we could before we began the long march. We would reach the plains after nightfall.

The refugees broke their small camp and returned to Tinus Brigh for shelter and to rebuild, thankful to be away from the forest at night and the shadow mists.

Halfway to our destination, the stench of death blew in from the east.

It was just before dusk when we saw the first body hanging from a tree. Then another. And then more. I halted the march.

"This makes no sense," I said.

"Aye," Betir said.

"Soldiers, mostly. And not just Northern Army." A whisper came from the forest as a light mist began. "That one there," I pointed. "He is Rogues Army and..." The remains of the body hung from the tree by its wrists. The legs were torn from the torso by...

"Food? Or bait," Betir said. He spotted another half-torn body hanging from another tree. The smell came and went as the breeze shifted. The mist grew thicker in the forest.

"We must continue on our guard. The sooner we reach the open plains and relieve ourselves of this dire forest, the better."

We continued the march amid the mist and the mist shadows. The bodies appeared sporadically. Sometimes, only empty ropes hung from the trees, torn and frayed.

We lost one man to madness.

The moon rose above us as we exited the forest and marched toward the plains. Sounds of relief from the force echoed behind me, happy to leave the wretched forest behind us. I thought of the woman and her two small children and wondered how many more survived and lived in the forest or possibly forced into the open plains south of the Great City by the mist shadows. Or how many camped near the lakes of Laiho? Could the Northern Lands recover from this?

How many more...

I put the thought from my mind. I wouldn't fare well with such folly. I could not fight for what I did not know.

We reached the Black Road. In the distance, the torchlights of the encampment burned. The forest continued its chorus of moans and hisses as the shadows moved about, while on the plains, normal nocturnal chatter filled the night air.

I let Sumu roam to feed on the grasses of my homeland. I found Fonchesca near a large fire. He had a grim look on his face. He saw me, then his eyes turned toward the other side of the fire. There, my brother Tass Burnok sat on a fallen log, his face twisted in despair. I looked back at Fonchesca. He shook his head. There were no words for the horrors on the road here and no need to discuss it.

I walked to Burnok and sat next to him.

"We took Feren Ta," he said.

"I am relieved to see you, Tass. How fare you?" He turned to me and shook his head, then shrugged.

"You are battle-worn, brother," he said. "You have lived with bloodshed and death your whole life." A slight breeze blew and smoke from the fire drifted our way. He coughed, sat up straight and stared at the moon disappearing beyond the plains. "I am weak," he said.

"Weak?"

"Aye. I thought my rage for Gal Abed would help me. That fire within, you know?" I nodded vacantly, understanding, staring at the ground under my boots. "But when the battle started, I felt like I would buckle. I didn't. I fared well enough in the battle. Seeing black husks split apart by my axe, it was something so abnormal it didn't register... It was too unreal. But I turned and upon me was one of those, um, Var..."

"Var'Yo?"

"Aye. I knew him, who he used to be. And I paused. His eyes were black as slate, and... still, I paused. He raised his sword, and before I could hash it all out in my mind, I swung my axe. His sword and his head fell to the ground, then his body crumpled."

Betir El Friz wandered around from the other side of the campfire and stood and listened.

"And then this storm hit. A streak of lightning shot out of the sky and struck one of the gate towers, exploding it to shreds. The pieces rained down. I was with Åkerfeldt and I looked at him and he me, and we both knew this storm was unnatural."

"Aye. It was."

He picked up a rock from the ground and turned it over in his gloved hand a few times.

"Then the rain. The rain fell so hard that we charged for a stable I had seen earlier and found shelter. Many others joined us. Then the rain turned to ice, Rini. Ice falling from the sky. Little pellets at first, then as big as this rock." He held out the rock and tossed it into the fire, sending sparks up into the darkness. "The ice shattered roofs. Soldiers, hiding under tables and crouching like beaten children. I—"

He grumbled and bit his bottom lip, then took a long drink from what I presumed was wine.

"It was so loud. The racket... upon those metal roofs. It sent the horses into a frenzy. Lord Åkerfeldt's horse reared up. He lost his grip on the reins and was thrown into a nearby stable gate and upon a stack of, of... um..."

He coughed, trying to hold back his anguish.

"On... discarded nails, shoes, and other metals. The horse ran from the stable and into the storm and the falling ice shredded his hide. Streaks of blood ran like rain down his hindquarters as he disappeared into the sheets of rain from the storm. I turned to Lord Åkerfledt. He was still, and lifeless upon the heap, the wind knocked from his body."

He rubbed his hands together. They were trembling.

"I leaped from my horse and tethered it to a post and ran to him. He came to life in a gasp of air, then coughed and blood spewed from his mouth. His eyes widened, and he looked at me. He spoke but I could not hear his words over the storm, then his eyes became lifeless and he went limp. His back broken and pierced by a dozen long rusted nails."

Betir El Friz sat on the other side of Burnok and placed a hand on his shoulder. He let out a deep sigh and closed his eyes. His lips moved as if he prayed.

"I stood at the stable entrance and watched the storm. The ice had ceased, but the rain continued. Then it all stopped, as suddenly as it started." He hung his head and took a deep breath. "Overhead the thunder still roared and lightning streaked, claw-like, reaching out across the sky. I ran from the stable, slipping on the ice and mud on the road. I saw Lord Åkerfeldt's horse lying in the street beyond the stable. Its neck was broken, its body... in tatters, shredded from the ice."

He took a long pull from the wineskin, and set it down. He stared absently into the fire.

"More soldiers emerged from shelters. The streets were littered with the bodies of black husks, eastern soldiers, and some of our own, caught in the icefall or thrown from panicky horses whose bodies also lay in the streets. The eyes of the living were wild and struck with fear. Then black husks came charging out from everywhere. From side streets and rooftops, swinging those black blades. I cleaved heads with my axe and ran them through with my sword. More soldiers on horseback joined and skewered them on their lances. But... their deaths were noiseless. Not even a hiss, just..."

"Nothing."

"Aye. Vile and grim was the ambiance of that battle. Then, eastern swordsmen attacked but fell easily to the unfamiliar axes from the west for which they had no defense. I'm not sure they were trained soldiers, Rini."

He looked at me, questions stirred behind his eyes. I thought of the idiots sent in the first attack on the Great City. Pawns of the Queen, or Rogues Army, it mattered not.

He took another drink from his wineskin.

"Then it all stopped. No thunder. No screams. No pitch of battle. And a ray of sunlight burst through the clouds and a wild cheer went up from the lads, but was quickly silenced by a lone scream. Then another."

"That's alright brother. You do not have to continue."

Feren Ta was taken, also at a heavy cost. The anguish overcame him, and the tears flowed. There we sat until the rising dawn of a bright new day was upon us.

We were within two day's march of The Great City. I walked through the encampment and looked at the remnants of the force. We had fought all day in Tinus Brigh and Feren Ta and marched half the night. They were beaten down and tired. I returned to the fire.

"Where is Burnok?" I said.

"He excused himself to his tent," Betir said. He poked at the fire remnants with a stick.

"We must break camp and get within attack distance of The Great City," I said.

He chuckled, not removing his gaze from the fire. He tossed the stick into the fire.

"Today?" His tone wavered with disbelief. I stared into the dying fire.

"Aye. You heard the words of Yazzir El Friz. The Rogues Army marches upon the Great City."

"And you want to get to The Great City before they do."

"Aye. I know not how many they bring and—"

"Exactly." I frowned. Talking with Betir was like talking to my father. I felt as if I were a child around him. Always a lesson learned, or a scolding to be had.

"Betir, I do not care if it's 50 or 5,000. I do not want to lose the advantage of a planned attack because we are either outnumbered or stuck weary on the plains of the Great City fighting an enemy that —"

"Has no value in the overall fight?" He was nodding, staring at me. He exhaled and leaned back. "It is a good plan, Rini. Your men will follow you. I would recommend one thing." I sighed.

"And that is?"

"Send Fonchesca as you did before. Send his men. They are… well… somewhat rested. They can prepare a camp. Give your men time to—"

"Rest?"

"Yes."

"We leave at midday." I rose and walked toward the main encampment.

"Rini Soltari," Betir's voice boomed. I stopped, then turned. He walked toward me, his steel-gray eyes locked on mine. He stopped within a sword's length. "I do not dispute that you command this force. But you're forgetting something, Commander." He paused, and his eyebrows rose a touch. "Your men depend on their Commander to make sound and rational decisions. Their lives depend on it." My shoulders dropped, and I nodded. He placed a hand on my shoulder and squeezed. "You should rest, too."

I stood as a child stands, corrected, scolded. I knew I was right. But so was he.

"Aye."

I turned away, and his hand fell from me as I stepped toward my tent. Then I thought of something I meant to ask on the march from Tinus Brigh.

I turned around.

"Tell me something, Betir. Where did you learn that move you used on Yazzir El Friz?"

A slight smile appeared on his lips.

"Why do you ask?"

"My father taught me that very move and made me practice it every day. It has saved my skin more than once. He says it was known only to the family, and he was passing it down. He said it was taught to him by the greatest swordsman he knew. I assumed my grandfather taught both of you."

He laughed.

"No Rini." His smile was broad. "It is my move, and I taught it to your father."

He winked, and turned back to the camp.

Chapter Forty-Four

The Fall of the Southern Army

I FOUND FONCHESCA GROOMING his horse and checking his equipment.

"Captain Fonchesca," I said. He looked up and a faint smile appeared. "Lord Åkerfeldt is dead, and with the loss of Captain Astonzi, you will now command his men. The numbers for the Northern Army are grim, but make it happen. We break camp at midday to ride to the fields outside the Great City on the edge of Karvas Forest to secure the Black Road. Make sure all are prepared to leave." He bowed his head, and when he raised it, he was smiling. No longer faint, but prominent. He was a soldier reborn.

"Aye, Commander Soltari."

I walked through the main encampment. Soldiers and warriors from both lands camped together. The two forces united as one. Some were grim-faced, some shared stories of battle, new and old, some lay in fitful slumber. Some looked at me as I passed. Some bowed their head out of respect. None looked at me as if I were a madman. Those days lived only in the past.

I walked to Burnok's tent and entered. He was sitting in the middle next to his bedroll. He looked up and wiped his eyes and face. Then he stood.

"You caught me weak and unworthy," he said.

"Brother, you act like this is the first time I've seen you cry."

He smiled a bit, but the smile faded. He composed himself and then stood tall and crossed his arms.

"So, what unfortunate news do you have to share this time?"

I stood there, silent. Then said, "I'm moving the force at midday."

He looked at me, astonished.

"We're marching to the fields outside the Great City and camping on the edge of the Karvas Forest." He dropped his arms. Then blinked.

"You're serious."

"I am."

I shared the news of Yazzir El Friz and the advance of the Rogues Army.

"You are in charge of the Western forces now, are you not?"

He blinked again.

"I suppose I am." He rubbed his beard.

"Well, I can lead them if you like."

"No." He sat down with a groan as his enormous frame partially sat, and partially fell to the ground. He scratched the side of his face, then looked at me. "I will lead them. But I will follow you. If you leave at midday, so do we."

"Good. It is time to earn your place in the Western Lands, Tass." I pointed to him. "You can do this, brother." I walked out of the tent, then turned and peered back inside. "It's in your blood."

He looked at me, his eyes wide, and a small smile formed under the beard.

We sent the advance party as Betir recommended, then began our march to the plains outside the Great City at midday. Just before evening, as the sun lay above the treetops, we encountered two soldiers standing on the Black Road. They looked lost and disheveled. I halted the march.

"Ho there!" Burnok called out. The soldiers turned around and saw the force, then dropped to their knees.

Ghenesta rode up next to us.

"What manner of mystery is this?" he said. One soldier stood and then ran toward us. "He's Southern Army?" Ghenesta said.

"Please, help. Please, the storm, the—"

Then the soldier stopped and screamed. He pulled a dagger from his belt, and we instinctively backed our horses up. He held it out, pointing it at us. "You... This — I know you." He looked at Ghenesta, then he scowled. The other soldier collapsed on the road behind him, trembling, twitching. "Where were you, Commander?"

"Speak some sense. What are you doing here?" Ghenesta said.

The man looked around, and as he turned away from us, he revealed a bloody patch on the back of his neck. Blood oozed from his side. He turned to us, confused. He looked at me.

"Where—"

"You are in the Northern Lands, in the Karvas Forest," I said. "Why are you here? Where did you come from?"

"She — Queen of Shadows. Oh, no! Not—" His eyes went wide. He turned and ran back to his comrade, who was still twitching on the road. Then the twitching stopped, and the man lay still in death.

"They are too far gone," Betir said.

Ghenesta squirmed in his saddle. The man knelt beside his comrade, then cried, stood, and screamed.

"The mist!" he shouted at us. "The storm— death for all of you!" He screamed again then raised his dagger.

"Stand down sir!" Burnok yelled.

The man startled at Burnok's booming voice, frowned, and tilted his head, trying to make sense of anything. Then smiled, took the dagger, and in one swipe, slit his own throat.

Ghenesta gasped. We all gasped. Blood poured from the wound, and the man muttered something, but only blood came forth, and he fell face down onto the hard dirt of the Black Road. Betir looked away. Burnok stared in disbelief.

Ghenesta then spurred his horse forward and halted at the two dead men. He looked back at us, then snapped his reins and, in a full gallop, charged down the Black Road, disappearing beyond a bend in the distance.

Burnok lurched as if to give pursuit.

"No. There's nothing we can do for his madness," I said. I turned and whistled. Two soldiers ran up from behind us. "Clear that filth from the road. Move now!" They ran to the bodies and pulled them from the road.

I looked at Burnok and Betir.

"We will increase our speed to make camp before dusk."

We moved forward at a more spirited canter, and the column followed.

It was just after evening on the next day when we reached the edge of Karvas forest. The advance party had camp mostly prepared. I made my way to the command fire and dismounted. My boots hit the ground, and I paused, then removed a glove, reached down, and touched the grass of my home with my bare hand. The evening dew was setting in.

I remounted Sumu and rode to the top of a hill south of our camp. The sky had filled with a gray haze on our journey here, and now the haze covered the landscape like smoke from a fire. I looked eastward and caught my breath. Far in the distance, across the plain, stood the walls of the Great City. The city was a black ominous shape in the haze with pillars of smoke rising from it. Between it, and where I sat upon my horse, my old home. My land. The road, gray in the dusk, wound from it to the city. Trees obscured my home, but I knew nothing lay there except the ruin of my house.

A horseman approached. It was Fonchesca. Behind him rode two soldiers. Dread filled his face.

"Commander," he said.

"What is it?"

"There is something peculiar with the fields surrounding the city. I sent a small scout party to search the area and get what information they could.. They turned around soon after. They said the air around the city is wrought with death, and rot."

"Death?"

"Aye. I decided to wait until your arrival before scouting further."

I turned Sumu, and rode down the hill back to the camp. Fonchesca followed. I found Burnok and Betir El Friz. From the Black Road we rode a short way along the road to the Great City. The smell hit us at once. I nudged Sumu a little faster, and we galloped to the edge of the Karvas Forest, where it opened to the plains again. We were all holding cloth to our faces. One of Fonchesca's men was gagging, then vomited. He turned around and rode back to camp.

I veered off the road to the crest of a hill. My heart raced, my stomach knotted. The air choked us with the vile, repugnant odor of death. I rode along the edge of a ridge to a bluff overlooking the land. I paused and tried to catch my breath.

They lay strewn about the plain.

"Rini?" Burnok whispered.

Dead bodies of men and horses lay strewn about the fields surrounding the Great City. A standard pierced into the body of a dead horse bore the tattered rag of the flag of the Southern Lands.

"Commander, that... those are..." Fonchesca stammered. We stared at the fields of death. Betir broke the silence.

"The way the bodies are strewn about, it's like an explosion came from the city and blasted them outward." My stomach roiled.

"We must get closer."

We heeled our horses down the hill to the edge of the fields and the bodies nearest us. The visage only grew worse as the details of their death emerged in the hazy late evening. Entrails, heads, limbs twisted and shattered.

"It looks like they are, broken, as if they fell from a great height. Look, there," Burnok said. "The ground is ripped up and there is a great swathe cut through it. What could have done this?" Burnok said.

No one had an answer for him.

"Commander?" Fonchesca pointed to a body wearing the familiar tan and brown uniform I knew all too well. I shook my head trying to make sense of why the body of a Rogues Army soldier was amongst the others.

"He also looks crumpled, but he was run through with a sword as well," Burnok said.

"There's another," added Fonchesca.

"The greater question is why are the plains of the Great City strewn with the dead of the Southern Lands?" Betir said.

"The Goffs," I said. "They did this. They—"

I turned Sumu away and rode back up the hill. The others followed a moment later. I reached the road and stopped.

"The mindless bastards," Burnok said. "Why would they — what was the motive, Rini?"

"The Goffs have known about Ta'Bedtian and this vision since she was a child. This must be some vain attempt to do what they should have done ages ago."

"Or," Betir said, "they took advantage of the situation, Rini, and made for a land grab the same way they did when they overthrew the Eastern Empire."

"Their emperor is dead. This was Il'Gavar's doing."

"And the undoing of the Southern Lands," Betir said.

I stared at the horizon.

"It will be dark soon," I said. "We must return. There is nothing we can do for them."

"Rini," Burnok said. "What if they had been successful?"

The silence from the land spoke volumes. What if? There were no remnants to return to the south. The Empire of the New Dawn, Il'Gavar called it, was dead and rotting on the plains of the Northern Lands.

"Not one carrion bird on the field," Fonchesca said suddenly, snapping me from my trance.

The land around my once great city was a black void of death where no creature dared. No sane creature. Not in the sky. Not on the ground. I no longer recognized this place. I spat the foul taste in my mouth out to the ground.

"Do you hear that?" whispered Fonchesca.

"I hear it," Burnok said. "Is that..." Then I heard it. Our ears were not deceiving us.

"That is the sound of crying," I said. "A man... someone survived."

We fanned out, searching for the source of the sound. One of Fonchesca's Lieutenants called out.

"Over here."

We rode to the sound and found the man sitting against a tree. A soldier of the Southern Army, weeping. His head hung low, cradling himself. He did not acknowledge our presence. I looked at him. His uniform was sharp and clean. The uniform bore the silver threading of an officer. Next to him lay a scabbard, curved and snake-like. And lying on the other side of him, the body of a Southern soldier with a single bloody wound to the back.

"Ghenesta?" I said. I jumped from Sumu and went to him. I knelt beside him. "Ghenesta," I said in a terse voice.

He stopped, took a deep breath, then looked up at me. He wiped his face with a piece of blue cloth he was holding. He cleared his throat and tried to compose himself, to no avail. A tear fell from his face onto the snake-like scabbard next to him. He looked at it, then wiped it off with the cloth. I took him under his arm and helped him stand. He looked around, saw the body, gasped, then turned to me.

"Commander, um, Soltari." He cleared the muck from his throat. "I, uh..." His other hand was holding a small dagger coated with fresh blood. He looked at it as if trying to figure out where it came from and whose it was.

"Do you know where you are Ghenesta?" He turned to me, his eyes vacant.

"Yes, yes." He coughed up something to clear his throat. "Yes, of course."

He wiped the dagger with the blue cloth, then stowed it in a small sheath on his belt. He reached down, picked up his scabbard and sword, and clasped it to his side. He shoved the blue cloth into his belt, folded it over, and stood tall. Composed. An avatar for the army of the Southern Lands.

A shell of the last man standing.

"What happened here?"

Ghenesta wandered to the road where he could see the valley, and the bodies beyond. He looked down at the road and nodded, then turned to me.

"I'm not sure my story matters much now. I am, the sole survivor of the army of the Southern Lands, Commander." He bowed before me. "I am in your service."

"In his service?" Burnok said, then laughed. "You ought to be in shackles." Ghenesta turned to him. Not an ounce of anger on the broken visage.

"Shackles?" he said, confused by Burnok's words.

Ghenesta stood tall.

"I took no part in this. Nor did I have any knowledge of it." He turned to me. "It was —" I put my hand up, nodding.

"I know."

"And now the Southern Lands lie defenseless against the queen and her brood," Ghenesta said.

Burnok grumbled.

I mounted Sumu and reached out and he clasped my hand and climbed on behind me.

We rode to camp in silence. Only the sounds from our horses and the groans of their tack filled the void.

Chapter Forty-Five

Bodies

W E SPENT THE NEXT day moving the camp to the north side of the Black Road at the edge of Karvas Forest where we would launch our attack. We could not see the fields strewn with the Southern dea, but the smell of death still lingered like the gray clouds. The Great City hung on the far horizon, shrouded in fog from the Black River.

As day fell to evening, the forest, usually full of birdsong and the skitter of small creatures, fell deathly quiet. I sat alone in a fireless camp as the forest behind us fell dark, and a severe chill came through. Dried pine needles crunched under heavy boots approaching me. Burnok sat down.

"Brutal cold one tonight, Rini. And dark."

"Aye. It is still day, too dark for this period. The sun has yet to disappear beyond the trees." I shuddered from the chill. Soon, the voices and whispers from the forest would begin, chilling my bones more than the breeze.

"The supply wagons and the remainder of Lord Åkerfeldt's force will be here tomorrow."

"I am tired of waiting." Burnok turned to me, and I could sense his gaze and his bearded smile.

"Of course."

His leather armor and steel gauntlets creaked and moaned as he maneuvered himself into a more comfortable position.

"This reminds me of a trip we took with father, do you remember? He was cooking fish he pulled from the river that morning, and you had finally come out of the tent, all sleepy and disheveled, shaking from the cold. Something odd about how you acted that day. I still can't place it." Burnok was leaning against the log I sat upon. "Some words or something were said, then you started running into the forest. I ran you down."

"Hmph. I had no shoes, it wasn't hard."

He laughed. "So you remember?"

"Aye. It was the first time I was stabbed." His face went grim.

"Oh. Yes, well." He cleared his throat. "That was incidental and unfortunate."

"You grasped me and we fell to the ground. I fell on the dagger in my belt."

"I remember. Mother was like a calm fire tending to you."

"I didn't need her help."

He turned to me. "Sure."

I looked away and through the trees to where the Great City lay beyond the mist.

"It was cold, as it is now. The kind of cold that bites to the bone," I said.

There was a moan from my right, past Burnok, and he sat up rather suddenly. Then another, and a sigh.

"So they are here," he said.

A misty shadow passed by Burnok and he stood so fast he nearly tripped over the log we sat upon.

Fonchesca approached us, distraught and shaken.

"More of this. I'm not sure the men will make it through the night," he said.

"Would they feel better there, out in the open, then? Under the watchful eye of the Queen?"

"Commander, forgive me, but I think these shadows *are* the watchful eyes of the Queen."

I thought about this.

"Set torches on the perimeter and—"

"Rini," Burnok said. "Listen to the man. His concern is sound."

"And what of your men, brother Burnok?"

His face tightened as he pursed his lips under his great beard.

"I agree with your captain."

"Fonchesca," I said, still looking at my brother. "Gather some men. I have a mission for you. Tell the rest of the cadre to gather the force, and we will move camp once again to the open plain, there." I looked at him "I want sentries east and west along the Black Road to alert us of anyone coming. Nobody should be traveling this road unless they hail the Queen of Shadows."

"Aye, Commander."

I glared at Burnok. His beard did nothing to hide the smirk under it. Then he held up his hands, surrendering, and returned to the fire.

The sun set beyond the trees in the west and cast an eerie red glow across the clouds. We moved camp to the plain and could still hear the voices within the shadows, but it was bearable. No other note emanated from the trees beyond the moans and whispers.

Fonchesca and ten of his men stood before me.

"You and your men will go through the old eastern gate on my order. You will release the latch to the North Gate and report back here. Scouts are on their way to the North and West gates as we speak."

Fonchesca's face turned grim and his breathing became a bit more rapid.

"I know the events you witnessed during your escape haunt your memories. This is your redemption." He smiled, hesitantly, then held his head up.

Fonchesca and his soldiers left.

A hand fell upon my shoulder and startled me. Betir El Friz grinned.

"It has been so long since my eyes fell upon this city. It seems... dead."

"It is as long as she sits in the chambers of Lord Strome."

I walked back to where Burnok waited with some of the Western army.

"Fonchesca and his small force are ready to disengage the locking mechanism, and scout the inside from the North Gate."

"It is a good plan, Rini," he said. "We should be able to access the West Gate from the village rooftops."

"Aye. Countless times I warned Airik of that weakness, and his inaction may now be in our favor."

Hurried footfalls approached us. My hand reflexively went to the hilt of my father's sword. From the gloom emerged two men, soldiers of mine, wild-eyed. One was weeping. He dropped to his knees before me, sobbing violently.

"Commander," said the other, bent over, gasping for air. "Bodies."

"Bodies? Yes, we know of the bodies of the Southern Army."

"No... not Southern... army."

The first soldier screamed, then collapsed in a heap.

"Make sense. What do you mean, bodies?"

"Rini," Betir El Friz said, pointing.

Two more scouts wandered toward us as if lost in a haze. Betir went to one, grabbed him, and looked into his eyes. He turned to me and shook his head. He let the soldier go, who then took one step and fell to the ground. The other wandered past him and to me, then stopped when he saw me.

"Commander," he said, forcing himself to get the word out of his dry throat. Burnok grabbed a wineskin and handed it to him. He stared at it.

"What madness is this?" Burnok said in a low, grumbling whisper.

"I know not. Force some wine into his mouth."

He took the wineskin, pulled the man by his hair, tilted his head back, and poured wine into him. The man choked, but managed a swallow. Burnok released him, and some sense returned to the man's eyes. Then tears. Burnok took him by the shoulders and looked him in the eyes.

"You are safe. What happened? What did you see?" The man looked up at Burnok, pleading with him, then shook his head.

"I... so many."

"So many what?" I said. The soldier in my grasp became heavy and dropped to his knees.

"Bodies," the soldier at my feet said. "Bodies. Piled at the gates. Hundreds. Women. Children. Men." He looked up at me, tears streaming from his eyes. "Even animal. Bodies, hanging..."

The other man screamed, and Burnok shook him out of it.

"The hanging bodies..." he wailed, then covered his face.

"What? What is it? Make sense," I said.

The soldier at my feet gained a moment of clarity, then the tears stopped. "They... moved."

Then his eyes glazed over with madness, and he fell onto his companion. Fear lurked behind Burnok's eyes.

The soldier he held onto spoke. This time with clarity. The wine taking its hold.

"Bodies piled at the gates as high as the ramparts. And the smell..." He gagged at the memory. I understood, recounting my grim memory of the night of the first attack. "Bodies hang from the gates and walls. Dead, withered. Some... alive, twitching, moving. Moaning. Some Northern soldiers. Some, Southern."

"Where are the others?" I said.

He looked up at me with vacant eyes.

"Coming. Found someone," he said, then he collapsed. Burnok let him drop to the ground.

An intense chill shot through me. Burnok and Betir El Friz stared at the ground. Disbelief hung in the air like the whispering shadows in the mist. Dread washed over me.

"Those missing I sent to the Western Gate," I said, falling into a bit of hopelessness.

"Maybe they saw something different," said Burnok. I shook my head.

"No." I pointed to the soldier at his feet. "He was at the western gate," Burnok grunted, then something in the distance caught his eye.

"More approach. Three of them," Betir said.

We walked to the edge of the encampment. Two soldiers were half dragging a man across the field. He was bound and dressed in a light garb. I recognized it immediately.

"Rogues Army," Betir El Friz said.

The two soldiers stood the man up. He was bleeding from the edge of his mouth.

"Commander, we found this dog hiding in the village."

The man looked at me, then grinned and said something in the Eastern tongue. Betir El Friz stepped forward and smacked the man hard across the face with the back of his hand. The reaver shook it off, then, with clearer eyes, saw Betir, and they opened wide as if an apparition stood before him. He bowed, then gasped, jabbering something in his language.

Betir responded.

"What is he saying?" I said.

"He can tell you. This one speaks the language just fine."

"You know him?"

"Aye. I know him." He turned his attention to the man. "Speak, you. Tell us what you know."

"I, uh, no traitor," he said. His manner of speech reminded me of the way Igvar spoke. The accent was heavy.

"You have no army left to deceive K'Orpi El Friz. They are all dead. Including Yazzir. So speak now."

K'Orpi El Friz cleared his throat. "Most of my force, the ones who stayed, were killed when south army came. Killed by her sorcery. They say they were Army of the New Dawn."

"Sorcery?" Burnok said.

"Aye. Clouds came down from sky, hard and fast, like giant finger... She killed all. And it caught my force." He paused and caught his breath. "May I have some water, or wine?" Betir handed the man the wineskin the other soldier used and tilted it to the man's lips.

"Many thanks." The man coughed. "So violent a storm. Wind, rain, came in large drops and then became ice raining from sky. Ice the size of fists. I could only hear scream of ice hitting everything. I shelter, like coward. When storm leave, bodies cover fields, men, and steed. Broken. I was only one who survive."

"We have seen the fields."

"Yes. Of course. Our master, Yazzir El Friz, he only one allowed in city. He counsel with Queen, then gather force and left for uh, what is name?"

"Tinus Brigh," I said.

"Aye." He looked at me. "To kill you, Saka'Ali." He grinned slightly.

"Mind your tongue," Betir said.

"How did Yazzir El Friz enter the city?" I said.

"Rooftops."

"Go on."

"There is no more to say."

"What do you know of A'avé El Friz?" Betir said. The man looked up, frightened.

"You know of the Ghost?"

"Aye. Yazzir was kind enough to tell me before I slit his throat and left him in the streets of Tinus Brigh." The man's eyes narrowed.

"You, General? You killed, Yazzir El Friz?" Betir didn't have to say anything. The man saw it in his eyes as the truth, then gasped. "So is true. They are all dead." He dropped to his knees and wept. Then, as quickly as he started, he rose and looked at Betir.

He began a string of words in his language. Panic and anxiety beset him. Betir put his palm up, and the man quieted.

"What did he say?"

"He wishes to fight alongside us."

"Fight with us? Why?"

"He wishes to avenge his brother, who was with Yazzir El Friz. He says Yazzir, deceived his brother into joining this fight."

"Deceived? Deceived how?" The man looked at me.

"Uh, yes. How to say, my brother not smart. He have no skill. He here only to carry things, serve Yazzir El Friz."

I turned to Betir.

"We encountered similar Rogues Army during the initial attack. One of our prisoners was a halfwit, a man so devoid of thought he did not know what he was doing. He only knew what to say, but did not know what he was saying."

"Yes, yes. That is like my brother. Please, I will take up sword with you. I am El Friz. I can help."

Betir raised his hand, then drew his thin saber. I stepped back.

"Do you K'Orpi El Friz declare yourself now a soldier of the Northern Army?"

"Yes, yes." The man smiled gratefully. I looked at Betir, not knowing what he was doing, or why he was doing this.

"And do you K'Orpi El Friz renounce the reaver band of the Rogues Army and your General A'avé El Friz?" The man shifted, excited.

"Yes, yes, I do. Thank you, thank you. My sword is your sword."

"A glorious death, K'Orpi, is not yours to have."

K'Orpi eyes widened and he mumbled something in his language, fast as if beckoning—

Betir El Friz's saber whistled across the man's throat. Blood leaked from the wound. K'Orpi reached for his neck but was hindered by his bonds. Betir stared into his eyes, watching the life drain out of him. Betir released him and K'Orpi fell backward to the ground, and in a moment, was dead.

I stood there, dumbfounded.

"As you say... this is our battle to fight," Betir said. "He would have betrayed us as swiftly as he did his General. He always was a coward and a rat, which is most likely why Yazzir left him to wither in the West village."

Betir turned to the soldiers who had delivered the man.

"Drag him to a tree and tie him up facing east so when, or if, General A'avé El Friz comes for that which was promised him, he'll see with his own eyes, that only death awaits him."

Betir reached down and ripped the blue stripes from the man's uniform, stripping him of his master swordsman status.

"Take his sword and drive it through his mouth and into the tree. He is a traitor and has betrayed the title of El Friz."

The two soldiers looked unsurely at each other, then turned to me. I nodded.

Betir wiped his saber on the dead man's clothing, sheathed it, and walked away. Burnok looked at me and let out a long, deep sigh.

The two soldiers grabbed the man.

"Wait," I said. I reached down to K'Orpi's side and pulled a dagger, black as shadow, from his belt. I held it in my hand. I nodded to the soldiers, and they dragged the body to the road.

Burnok's gaze was upon me.

"I fear brother Tass, I would have done the same." I turned the dagger around in my hand. "Come, the time is now."

CHAPTER FORTY-SIX

Breath of Yoomala

FOG CREPT IN FROM the Black River and surrounded the city. Burnok, Betir, and I watched from a hillside. We could see the bodies piled in front of the gates.

"Can we not push through the gates? Certainly, with the weight of the bodies, they should open," Burnok said.

"The gates open outward with special latches on the inside to prevent such a thing."

Burnok grunted.

"Well then, we have something in the Western Lands we call the Breath of Yoomala."

"I have heard of it," said Betir El Friz.

"It is an oil we can put on the end of arrows and light them. It burns hot and cannot be extinguished with water, should those nasty things," he nodded to the Kuori perched on the ramparts, "have any sense to do so."

I considered this for a moment.

"Burn the bodies?" I said.

"Aye."

I glared at the bodies piled up, then thought of my wife and daughter, and the burning of my house to cleanse them and return their bodies to the soil.

"Fine. We strike immediately with your fire. The gates of the Great City will burn as one great funeral pyre."

Burnok grasped my shoulder, shook me, then left.

"I will send Fonchesca and his force in to disable the locks on the North Gate." I breathed out a heavy sigh. My breath lingered in the chill air. "And so it begins."

A short time later, archers were poised within range of the gates. The night was still, dead, thick with mist and shadow. No air moved. I stood with Burnok and Betir, looking at the quiet city. Still life. Not even the Kuori on the walls moved. Movement came unannounced when the soldiers returned from the gates, their mission a horrifying one. An officer with the group saluted me, indicating oil now covered the bodies of the dead at both gates.

I looked at the moonless sky. Black. Black like the darkness hanging over the lands. A shiver went through me as I looked down the row of archers. The strange oil glistened on the ends of their wrapped arrows.

"Light the arrows," I said.

An officer from the Western Lands relayed the order. A soldier came forward and opened a small tinderbox. He pulled a matchstick from it with a small flame lingering on the end. He touched it to the first arrow, which lit fast and burned low. That archer then touched the fire to the next arrow, and on down the line, one by one, nocked arrows glowed with intent. The darkness around us was quickly dispelled by the fires. The heat from such a small fire was oddly intense. Twenty archers now readied themselves to let loose the Breath of Yoomala. We had announced our presence with a light in the darkness.

The kuori moved. Alert now.

"Fire!"

The arrows streamed across the night sky and found their mark in the decaying dead at the North Gate. A moment later, the bodies exploded into a fury of fire and shook the ground under our feet. Some of us reflexively took a step back and shielded our eyes.

A kuori tumbled from the wall and fell into the flames. Its body writhed and cracked from the heat, then it stopped, melting in the inferno. Its companions scrambled along the wall. The bodies hanging from the ramparts squirmed from the heat and caught afire, as did the ropes. The bodies fell into the fire shortly after.

Another explosion, this one distant, and we watched the inferno rise from afar at the Western Gates.

Burnok chuckled. "Now that is, a fire," he muttered.

"We have knocked on the gates of the Great City," Betir said.

"Aye. At long last," I said.

We watched, mesmerized by the glow of the fires. They burned with a sickening rage and fury of an unquenchable thirst as it consumed the dead. Women, children, soldiers, and city merchants. Citizens of the Great City. And I knew there were no more survivors here. My wife and child were gone in flame. Her family, too, I assumed were also gone. And the life, if one could call it that, which existed now within the walls, was an all-consuming black shadow that spread across my homeland. Its evil sorcery now lived in our great forests, and walked in our villages. The death and destruction from this force has spread long and wide, and has gone on far too long.

"We attack at dawn," I said, rather abruptly. The words escaped from my mouth as the thought formed.

"Dawn?" said Burnok. "Rini, those fires will rage all night and long past dawn."

"I don't think so, brother. They are burning too hot, and the dry corpses won't feed that flame for long before it is quenched. The gates, too, should be burned sufficiently, or weakened. No, we attack at dawn."

"I will let the men know," Burnok said and walked off toward camp.

"I know you are eager to take back this city and redeem yourself, Rini," Betir said. "But I am troubled with your haste." He stared at me from beneath his hood with cold gray eyes.

"I cannot watch my city lay in ruin for another day, Betir. You may be able too, for it has been long since you've seen her." I looked back at the darkened city and the raging fires. "All I see is ruin and decay. A filth upon my city that needs to be cleansed. I need to know if..."

"It's too late to save them. Any of them." He clasped his hands in front. "Rini, they are passed. Your wife and daughter... you cannot save them by—"

"What know you of family? Did you return for your father's funeral? Or your mothers? Were you there when I buried my father, your brother? Or his wife, my mother? You know nothing of family. Such things are mysterious and foreign to your soul."

He hid his face in complete shadow inside the hood of his cloak.

"Aye. You are right. My sword is my family. I know not what you have gone through, are going through. I did not see my brother murdered. I was not present, not even for my mother, whom I loved deeply. I know only emptiness, Rini. A void where family should be is filled with my selfish ideology." He looked up and his steel-gray eyes peered at me again from within his hood. "My life was set by my own hasty choices."

He let the words sit in the chill air.

I sighed. I had struck his heart with my words, and he countered with his own.

"I—"

"What I do know, nephew, is tactics. As do you. Revenge, redemption, desire, these emotions cannot define or make your decisions on the field of battle. Your haste will cost more lives." He pulled his hood back and stared into my eyes, into the cold blackness of the abyss. My own dark shell. "Your haste... has already cost lives, and not just of your men. Or have you forgotten?" He stood, towering over me, then turned away.

"I have not forgotten, nor shall I ever. The memory of them is why I will not watch the Great City for another day while this Queen of Shadows rallies some new dark force, nor will I give this General A'avé another day to get closer to the Great City." There was movement in the distance, just over his shoulder.

"If we attack at dawn," he said, then raised his head high. "Then we do not stop until we are victorious, or die victoriously."

"No truer words have been spoken. Someone comes," I said.

I turned and whistled and motioned four soldiers from the nearby ranks to follow. We approached the figure moving toward us.

"It's one of Fonchesca's men," Betir said.

"Commander...," the soldier said, then collapsed to his knees, catching his breath.

"Where is Fonchesca?" I said.

"Inside... city." He took a deep breath and let it out, then wept. "Dead, Commander."

"What? Make sense. Dead how?" The soldier was bleeding from a wound on his arm.

"I killed him."

"You..."

"Aye. I killed Captain Fonchesca." The man's tears fell harder, stronger. Betir kneeled beside the soldier.

"Son. Why did you kill Fonchesca? What happened?"

The soldier pulled up his waterskin and put it to his lips, gulping a fair amount, then caught his breath.

"We went through the East tunnel. Nothing changed since our escape, but we could not disengage the mechanism. We arrived there just after some sort of explosion. The mechanism was broken, jammed. We found our way through the tunnels and up into the false shop."

He took a deep breath and cleared his throat. His eyes were still wide with fear, or torment.

"We saw the inside of our Great City and its death and destruction and became sullen and defeated. Somewhere, a rage built up in Fonchesca and he charged out of the shop. He tried to take out the gate forces in all the chaos around the fire. We followed."

His tears flowed again.

"We became overwhelmed by Kuori and some of those, those shadow soldiers. We fought well, but then I saw Fonchesca struck down from behind. It was quick. The kuori moved like none other I have seen. I made to leave, but there were so many. I worked my way back to the shop, and there before me was Captain Fonchesca... but... he had eyes of black and a snarl on his face only known to the dead." He looked up at me. "I moved fast and loosed his head. He fell, and I made it out of the east gate. I am the only one alive, even though some of our force still... walks."

He looked at his arm.

"I am bleeding."

"Aye," Betir said.

"I remember being injured in the melee, but I do not believe it to be from a black blade." He looked up at me again. "Please forgive me, Commander. I ran like a coward. I—" The man made a choking sound, fell sideways, and passed out.

I motioned to the two soldiers. "Bring him back to camp."

The two soldiers walked past me.

"Fonchesca fought bravely, he—"

"He acted out of emotion, and now he is dead," Betir said, and again, his words hung in the chill air.

There was a scream behind us and a scuffle.

I turned and saw Fonchesca's soldier, sword drawn, slash through one soldier and run the other through the heart. I drew my sword, but Betir already had his drawn and was moving toward the fight. With one brutal strike, Betir removed the head of Fonchesca's man. Black blood shot from the body like a fountain, and the body and head fell to the ground with a barely audible noise.

Betir stood over the body, then looked at me and sheathed his sword.

"The time for talk is over Betir El Friz. We attack at dawn."

Chapter Forty-Seven

Reclaiming the Great City

D AWN CAME FROM BEHIND the shadows of the night. The darkness held on until its dying breath and the black of the night gave way to the early light behind the broken gray clouds.

Not a bird chirped. Nor any forest animal moved. The air and land was lifeless, gray, and dead.

As the sun crested the eastern horizon, the charge upon the Great City would begin. The city I once knew in a dream no longer shimmered. It stood, shrouded in gloom, wrapped in firelight, exhaling a dark cloud of virulent filth. It moved like heavy breathing and burned like the forges of a blacksmith. The four towers on each corner of the Great Hall of Fallen Empires stood black and pestilent. Our city square was now overshadowed by tall spires of spiked monsters, each with its black head aglow in raging flames. The Great Hall sat transformed into some blackish-green hollow belly of evil.

The new domain of Ta'Bedtian, Queen of Shadows.

A picture of the musta kuori formed in my mind, the brood rambling through the streets of the city, moving like maggots on a carcass, and dragging their large black blades behind them - the scraping sound like metal on a grindstone - shrill and bone wrenching. And the Var'Yo - the living turned to shadows by those black blades of the kuori, waiting in the gloom.

Plumes of smoke rose from the city in black stalks.

The horns sounded from Burnok's force, signaling they were ready to strike from the west, and awoke me from my contemplation. We acknowledged their call with a hail from my force. We readied to storm the North

Gate. The bodies were burned to ash and bone, and the gate dismantled and weakened.

We would be the lightning strike at dawn.

Today the vile chaos in the Great City will burn, and the Queen will burn with it, and the city reborn from the ashes. The scorched fields will bloom with flowers of fire to mark our land, our place, as the birds take flight and nestle in our silent forest once again.

Soon.

And the sun parted the darkness with its dawn.

Soon.

We formed a long line on the hills overlooking the Great City. The Kuori lined the ramparts. And then we all saw the disturbing venue. Hanging from the North Gate in front of the doors were bodies of Northern Soldiers.

And they moved, twitching, squirming.

"Commander," Ghenesta said. "Are—"

"We charge on. There's nothing can be done for them except to set them free." He looked at me. "They are Var'Yo now."

I knew them all...

The North Gate was black from the Breath of Yoomala, but the path was not clear. We would manage.

We would have to manage.

I looked to Betir El Friz on my left.

I drew a chestful of morning air, then exhaled. I ordered a young lieutenant from the west for the row of archers to strike arrows. He echoed my command and the archers complied.

I called on a soldier of the north. I ordered him to take his team through the Eastern tunnel to disable the mechanism, get the gates open, and engage any forces there. He turned and left with thirty soldiers. They disappeared beyond the treeline, then appeared moments later before disappearing around the walls of the city.

I gave the command to the lieutenant to fire, which he echoed, and from behind the ranks, several hundred arrows took flight into the gray matter above. Moments later, we saw the impact. Kuori fell from the rooftops and ramparts. Some arrows went into the city, some fell short. I gave the command again, and a second volley of arrows flew. More kuori fell from the walls. One fell forward onto the ground outside the wall and rolled into the black muck in the moat surrounding the city.

I gave the final command to strike arrows, stood in my stirrups, then raised my father's short sword into the air. The sun crested the horizon as the gray shadow became a light gray and rose high, revealing more of the new hideous designs of the towers of the Great Hall. Spires, twisted and broken, flames burning atop them where statues and symbols of our land once stood.

Without ceremony, holding my sword high and with the sound of leather reins tightening and swords unsheathing, I swung my sword down. The horn sounded, another responded from the west, and arrows flew. The quiet sky of the dawn exploded with a thunderous roar as the screams and shouts of soldiers and horses descended upon the Great City of the Northern Lands. Sumu ran wide-eyed and straight. The arrows landed ahead of us, and more kuori fell. And like a grand illusion, the gates parted only slightly, enough for a column of horsemen or soldiers to pass through.

I rode through the gates and past the hanging bodies of Fonchesca's men. I pulled Sumu to the left and halted him. The soldiers had pushed the kuori away from the gates. I hacked down a husk. More horsemen entered and engaged.

"Get those gates open!"

I slashed at another kuori, and Sumu kicked down another, cracking the skull open, revealing naught but an empty shell. We continued to push the kuori back. The gates then parted wide, and without a hitch, the stream of horseman and soldiers swarmed in. A group climbed the ramparts and cut the hanging bodies free.

The soldiers on foot moved down the side streets and climbed the ramparts while we pressed forward. The musta kuori swung their black blades aimlessly, hitting soldiers caught in the throng. One went down, dead, then rose moments later. We did all we could to prepare the soldiers for this, and after taking Feren Ta and Tinus Brigh, they saw all they needed to achieve victory.

Betir El Friz charged past me, turned down a city street to the west, and disappeared. I blocked an attack from a kuori, then hacked it down. An influx of kuori overwhelmed us and more soldiers fell. I pressed on with Sumu and the other horsemen, cutting a swathe through the mass of black husks. Their advance slowed. In the distance stood the first of the city squares. I ordered the horsemen to spread out and block the advance of the kuori, but no more kuori came at us. They retreated to the city square. Behind us, the battle raged, soldier against kuori, soldier against soldier. Battle-hardened soldiers weeped, forced to strike down their comrades or die. The streets flowed with the red blood of warriors, and the black blood of the musta kuolema. The husks lay like broken shells, shattered on the streets, like the insects we find on trees before the turn of winter.

Empty.

Lifeless.

More soldiers and horsemen came through the gates. Soon, we would win the battle for the gate. Our advance continued to the first city square, and in the far distance, the Great Hall loomed in the gray haze.

A memorial statue of the first Lord of the Northern Lands stood tall in the center of the square. The fountain around it ceased to flow, now filled with black muck and remnants of bodies of city folk, decomposed, and partially eaten or dissolved, as if the muck itself were feasting on the dead. The smell was wretched and foul, like the rotting flesh of a diseased wound.

A soldier near me retched into the street. Another followed. The stench was debilitating, and it was moments later I bent over Sumu and heaved into the street. I wiped the spatter from my lips, then pulled my face covering over my mouth and nose, hoping the thin fabric would abate the smell. Sumu was becoming unmanageable in the foul stench.

A stench that reminded me of...

"Be wary of Queen's daughters," I shouted, but nobody heard as the side streets leading into the square filled with kuori and Var'Yo. I looked around at the horsemen and soldiers coming in from the rear. This would be a battle hard fought, physically and mentally.

Something moved near me in the fountain. A figure was rising from the black mire. Another soldier also watched the thing rise and was hit, unguarded, by a black blade. His body fell face forward in the liquid and hissed as the muck dissolved the flesh and bone. The remnants slid from the side and fell to the street.

The muck drained off the rising figure, and there stood a kuori. It moved from the fountain, and joined the fray, clawing its way through the melee. Another figure rose. It turned to me, then pulled a blade from the pool, the liquid draining off, slow like black honey. It hissed and came at me, and a moment later, its head was tumbling onto the street. The rest of it disappeared in the mire to be born again.

Then the charge came from behind, and the fight began anew. We pushed into the kuori with our horses kicking. They fell easily when hit. Avoiding the black blades became more difficult, especially from the top of my horse. I drew my long sword and leaped into the fray. The streets were slick with blood. I stepped up to the side of the dead fountain. Soldiers and kuori and horses void of riders filled the city square. The horses were panicking and kicking and bucking. The kuori didn't attack them. I parried a blow, then hacked a husk in two. A swing came from my left from a shadow, a Westerner, that I blocked, then ran my short sword through his throat. I twisted the blade, opening the hole wide. The black blood flowed, and he fell over the side of the fountain wall into the muck, and the muck came alive. I watched again in horror as the muck dissolved flesh and bone, and the remnants of his corpse slid from the wall and to the street.

I loosed the head of another kuori, narrowly missing its swing. The sounds of battle came from sword against black blade, warriors shouting or crying out, the hissing of Var'yo, and the cracks from Kuori as the husks fell upon the stone. No screams came from them when they died. That was more unsettling now than before. Near a side street, I watched a kuori swing at a soldier, miss, and thrust its cursed blade into a black horse. The horse reared up and kicked out, sending the kuori flying through the fight. It stammered, then fell, catching several soldiers and a husk underneath its weight.

A loud commotion came from the west. Behind the mass of kuori on the side street, a force of soldiers and horsemen appeared, led by Betir El Friz. The tide was turning, and we would win this battle, then push on to the Great Hall.

I fended off three more attacks and nearly lost my footing on the side of the fountain. I avoided one attack and was scarcely missed by another, when the black horse, its eyes wide and black as night, raged through the streets, trampling all in its path. It turned toward the North Gate and disappeared from my sight just as a blow hit me from my left, knocking me from the edge of the fountain onto the bloody street.

Chapter Forty-Eight

The Kur'Ya Advance

A SOLDIER FELL NEAR me as I lay on the ground, his chest sliced open. He was gasping for breath. I rolled over and pushed myself up from the blood-soaked streets. Red and black blood converged in puddles of life and death. Both kuori and Var'Yo swarmed around me. I did not see who struck me, or with what.

My stomach churned, and my left shoulder burned.

A kuori came at me, blade raised high above its head and I slashed with my short sword across its neck. I screamed in pain. My arm burned and throbbed from the maneuver. I looked at the wound. Blood soaked through the cloth and leather of my uniform. The cut was clean and superficial.

A Var'Yo swung at me. I raised my sword to block and slipped in the blood on the slick stones of the street. His sword came crashing down by my head and hit the street hard. The reverberation caused him to drop the sword. I knocked his legs out from underneath him and he fell sidelong in front of me. I slit his throat, and the black blood poured forth. One of my veteran soldiers.

I crawled away to dry stone and stood. The kuori had thinned; the horsemen had abated the advance from one side street, and the path to the north gate was clear. The force fought the remaining Var'Yo and kuori. Men no longer shed tears striking down their brothers in arms. Their commitment to get through this alive overshadowed any emotion. A price they would have to pay later.

I looked to the south, at the Great Hall. Morning light bathed the blackened building. Sumu stood near a side street away from the battle. I hacked my way to him and caught Betir El Friz out of the corner of my eye. He had also dismounted. The kuori and Var'Yo were no match for his skills. He made quick work of them all. He saw me running to my horse, then backed up to his. I slashed through four more kuori before reaching Sumu. He looked unscathed but was shaking. I stroked his side and neck, and he nickered and bobbed his head. I pulled myself up into the saddle and grimaced from the soreness in my muscles and bones.

From the city square and the Great Hall, was a long straight road scattered with living and dead kuori. Some horsemen had already fought through. Betir rode to me. I was grateful for his actions.

"With the forces combined, we'll make quick work of this," he said. I looked at him on his horse. The glare of the sun behind him. I hid my eyes, and his silhouette turned to me. The last time I was in this square, I was on Outo. Now, the square, and the Great Hall, were barely recognizable.

"We can not finish the battle on horse," I said, nodding to the Great Hall.

The sun darkened, and we looked up. Clouds rolled in from every direction. Dark clouds.

"If we make the final battle," Betir said. He looked at me. I touched the pouch on my side.

"We will make it." I sheathed my long sword and turned Sumu toward the Great Hall.

We regrouped and rode past the fountain and down the long, wide cobbled street leading to the Great Hall. The street, once a path of beauty lined with decorative archways along storied dwellings of stone, now mainly sat in ruin. Green plants with red and orange flowers once hung over the sides of the small decorative bridges between the arched pathways. Stone staircases with ornate iron rails accented the buildings. The lifeblood which once flowed through the Great City had ebbed and died. Bodies of the kuori and Var'Yo now lined the road, and black blood flowed between the flagstones. The remnants of the plants hung dry and lifeless, and the stone and iron staircases were charred black, crumbled, and dead.

Broken.

We followed the road to the center where our once great Tower of the Fallen stood high and erect above the city but now lay in twisted ruins. A group of dead Northern soldiers met us there. I thought I recognized some faces, but it was a lifetime ago. I could not be sure. They attacked and were met with the swing of our sharp blades across their throats, and they fell, for the last time. They had little fight in them.

"These soldiers fought when the Queen invaded,"I said. "They are not from our party."

We rode around the ruins of the tower. Its fountains were also filled with black muck and partially consumed bodies. The stench reverberated through the force, and the streets echoed with men retching and choking.

A small army of musta kuori rose ahead of us, coming from the side streets. We stopped. Shouts came from the rear as more kuori came. I ordered men down the streets to push them back.

I turned my horse in a circle and eyed the enemy surrounding us. I looked over to Betir El Friz and nodded.

I spurred forward and swung my blades putting metal to bone. The rest of the force followed me. A group of soldiers turned and spurred through the small band behind us and down the side streets. I reared Sumu up. He kicked a few, knocking their heads back with a snap. Again I heeled him forward, now behind my men, and sliced down the small force of kuori.

These kuori wore black tangled leather and wielded black misshapen swords compared to the sharpened clubs they carried before. They attacked from all sides, but they had no skill to fight. No honor in it. No purpose.

"Fan out!" I yelled.

The men split and fought hard. A few were unmounted and fought the kuori hand to hand. And slowly, as before, a small force of Var'Yo rose. More and more of them now.

I dismounted and sent Sumu on to the Great Hall. I began slicing my way through the husks. They were strong, but I fought hard and they fell before me. They knew no fear.

"Commander!" The yell came from behind me.

I crouched my body and came up hard, planting my sword through a large kuori. Its huge red eyes bulged, and it coughed a stream of blood, black as night, and collapsed to the ground. This kuori was different. Much different. I had no time to consider this newfound hell.

I freed my sword and swung to my right, impaling an older man. He was tall and strong. His eyes, a mass of black, as he attacked and missed. I knew this man. I pierced his throat with my short sword, freeing him from the musta kuolema. His last breath echoed from the gaping blood-filled hole, and he fell, his black eyes staring at me.

A crack of steel on metal by my ear made me duck and there stood Betir, having stopped a blow to my head by another of the large, red-eyed kuori. I swiped across the kuori's gut as Betir sliced across the head. The kuori crumbled in a rush of black blood. I stood wide-eyed and stared at Betir.

The sound of a charge of horsemen echoed from beyond the ruins of the Tower of the Fallen.

"Ho, Soltari!" Commander Ghenesta appeared with a small mounted force of Western soldiers. They hacked their way into the melee and cut down the forces like a quick harvest, deterring the flood from one side. The kuori gave up the fight and retreated. Some galloped up the stairs and into the Great Hall.

The sun disappeared, and thunder rolled. The streets around us were suddenly quiet. Blood flowed from my right arm, and my face was marked twice in the chaos.

I sat down and wrapped the wound on my arm to conceal the blood. I tired.

I finished the wrapping. I could not raise my arm. I looked to Betir, and he shook his head.

"I will reach the queen before I turn," I said, "and end this dark world of sorcery." At that moment lightning streaked across the sky and thunder cried out. "We must get to the Great Hall, now!" Ghenesta held out his arm. I grasped it and climbed upon his horse. He heeled it and we rode to the stairs of the Great Hall. "Where is my brother?" I said.

"I have not seen him since we entered the Western gate." My heart stopped, and I prepared myself for the inevitable.

I stood on the stairs of the Great Hall once again. The force lined up next to me and behind me. All riders dismounted except Ghenesta. The clouds rolled in even blacker than before, and all eyes went to the sky. It was like all time stopped and a darkness came and shrouded everyone like an unwanted cloak. Then everything went silent.

Dead.

Lifeless.

My energy drained, or—

"Veils!" I yelled and pulled the veil over my eyes.

The command carried through the ranks, and the soldiers followed. Heavy footsteps came from behind me, then a grunt. Burnok stood there, axe battered and bloodied.

"You live," I said. He looked at me as if there was any doubt otherwise, and the gloom of the shadow lifted. "We need the archers. Where are they?" I said.

"On the ramparts, at the gates," Burnok said. "In case your friends from the east—"

"Look!" Someone yelled.

A woman stepped out from behind the columns of the Great Hall. She wore a black silk cloak that flowed behind her like a bat's wings. Her body was bathed in black leather armor, and her hair was as black as the eyes of the Var'Yo. Her skin as pale as the dead. A black armor gauntlet lined with gold trim sheathed her right arm. She smiled, then looked at me.

"Pri'Eten," I said to myself. The regret of sparing her demise came on suddenly and was overwhelming. Or it was regret for murdering the three Rogues Army soldiers.

Behind her, nine more Kur'Ya stepped out, similarly garbed in black with cloaks of silk and one arm sheathed in armor. Even through the veil, I could sense a slight tug at my core.

"Hide your eyes," I said. "Get those veils on! Before this day is through, we will post the head of their Queen above the northern gate!"

A fearsome cheer rose from the ranks. The troops now rallied for more blood. The Kur'Ya smiled as if their victory was already at hand.

Envisioned, by the Queen of Shadows.

The force chanted, ready for battle. One soldier broke away from the front and drifted toward Pri'Eten. He wore no veil. He walked halfway up the stairs. Pri'Eten reached out with her armored hand and twisted it. The man contorted and dropped dead there on the steps.

The chanting stopped. Thunder roiled above. Then all was quiet as the stench of rotten flesh and death came from the Great Hall.

And the hissing echoed through the city, and warriors who battled hard, slain foes, monsters, and their risen brothers, now shuddered.

Chapter Forty-Nine

The Queen's Daughters

S HRIEKS AND HISSES CAME from atop the stairs. Burnok turned. Eight R'Uma emerged from behind the massive columns, crawling on all fours like preying beasts. The dark mane of hair wrapped their bodies, shadowed their faces, and their vile teeth. They crouched next to the Kur'Ya like trained animals, poised, ready, dangerous. Their foul stench wafted down the steps like a black fog. Several soldiers coughed, gagged, and some vomited.

Thunder crackled, then boomed above us as two fingers of lightning reached down and struck the festering black towers of the Great Hall, and crackling sparks rained down on us.

"We should attack in force, Commander," Ghenesta said. "Once they descend the stairs, charge them with the horsemen."

Another soldier stumbled from the ranks and walked up the stairs, lost in the gaze of Pri'Eten. He stopped, then dropped. Lifeless. Pri'Eten reached out her gauntleted arm at the dead soldier, as she hovered in the air.

"Good plan," Burnok whispered to me.

"Give the command, Soltari," Ghenesta blathered. I was not compelled to respond.

Lightning once again caressed the towers flanking the Great Hall. The tops crumbled and stones fell to the ground below.

My left arm, which I suspected felt the bite of a black blade, now throbbed and ached.

"Now Commander!" Ghenesta yelled.

Charging up the stairs on horseback was ludicrous.

"We—"

Ghenesta raised his curved sword into the air, stood in his stirrups, and opened his mouth to say something when a claw of lightning shot down from the sky in a great thunderous roar and struck the raised sword of Commander Ghenesta. The lightning flowed down the snake-like blade and through his body as he shrieked in silence, his whole being in a spasm of chaos. His body split apart inside with raging madness, and his eyes shot from his skull. The lightning traveled through him and to his horse. He slid from his shrieking steed, his body quivering, his flesh smoldering, and his face drenched in burnt, black blood, followed by his sword. The curved snake of a blade hung motionless in the air for a moment, then fell and stuck through the lifeless body of Commander Ghenesta. His horse collapsed, its hindquarters paralyzed and broken. A soldier mercifully ended the horse's torment, and everything quieted to a dark hush. The smell of burnt flesh covered the horrific scene.

A shriek of joyous laughter came from within the Great Hall, and I shuddered. The laughter became a chorus of maddening songs, celebrating this minor victory. Then I realized I only imagined the laughter, half expecting it. But there was only silence from within the hall. And those at the top of the stairs only stared, a slight baleful grin on their faces, while the R'Uma squirmed, eager to be let loose upon us.

I looked back at the daughters of the queen, the Kur'ya, and Pri'Eten, then to Burnok, and for the first time, I caught what genuine fear looked like on his face. He was staring at Ghenesta and the swiftness of his demise. His eyes darted to me, and he gathered himself mentally. His brow furrowed, and his eyes raged.

"Come, brother, now is the time," I said.

Lightning flashed and thunder roared, and a light, misty rain fell from the dark clouds. A grating sound came from the hall, the sound of metal dragging on stone. The sound was deafening.

I yelled the command to charge, and the force moved forward. The queen's daughters hissed. They launched themselves from the top of the stairs and, with one hop midway, into the force. At the same moment, from behind the Kur'Ya, a throng of musta kuori flooded from the Great Hall. The stronger, larger, red-eyed beasts wielding large black swords. Some stopped and let out a grinding hiss, then leaped into the fight.

The last battle for the Northern Lands was in full swing.

I hacked and swung, while my disabled arm hung at my side. I dodged the bodies of the dead and the black blades of the kuori. Above the storm of the battle, the hisses of the R'Uma echoed nearby, with the revolting sound of men's throats being ripped out, and the gurgling of their last bloody breath not far behind it. The stairs soon clogged with hundreds of bodies and large husks kept pouring out from the great hall, their red eyes glowing and sinister. All the Kur'Ya were now levitating, catching a gaze here and there, and in a quick and silent death, soldiers succumbed to their power and fell dead. I noted one Kur'Ya waver after drawing energy from her victim.

A streak of blue lightning shot from one Kur'Ya through three soldiers on the stairs, the remnants of the bolt becoming a black sword of light, a blade of shadow, its edges blue shimmering death.

Betir El Friz was near me, and the crack of husk bodies behind me told me Burnok's axe was in full swing.

"Betir! They are weakened. When they draw their sword, they can no longer use their powers!"

"Aye!" he said before disappearing into the battle.

Pri'Eten stood watching me, waiting to catch my gaze.

The stairs soon transformed into a mountain of corpses in the day's dead light. Not long after, the Var'Yo rose from the dead and joined the fight.

"Brother! Look!" Burnok cried.

He pointed behind us. A small army comprised of Northern and Western soldiers advanced from the road to the North Gate. An army of dead. He turned and gaped, his stare petrified.

"All may be lost, brother! Those men were guarding the Northern gates."

Another bolt of lightning drew my attention back to the top of the stairs. More blades of black light had emerged from the Kur'Ya's gauntleted arms. All but Pri'Eten advanced into the crowd of soldiers, swinging their blades, which cut through flesh with ease. Clean were the cuts. Black and burned were the wounds.

I was getting weary. My arm was tired, and my sword was heavy in my grasp. My strength waned as I fought through the haze behind the veil. Pri'Eten continued to stare down at me, no longer smiling. One of the western soldiers broke her gaze as he passed in front of me and I felt the slight draw on my strength lift briefly. She did not have the control to drain my energy or lock her gaze upon me.

I pulled one of my men in front of me.

"Climb here and I shall give you a high place of honor among all Northerners!"

With her gaze now broken, my energy renewed. I followed the man up the stairs as he hacked away at the husks.

We were near the top when he stopped, as did I. The bloody point of a black sword through his body was moments from piercing my right eye. The sword disappeared back through the body and blood gushed from his wound.

I swung over the top of him and removed the head of a husk. The soldier dropped and rolled down the pile of corpses, lifeless. Then stirred. Soon, he would stand and fight again.

Soldiers from the Western Lands were upon the R'Uma now. I saw two raise their axes to come down on the head of one daughter, as another crouched, then leaped in a fury and latched to a soldier's neck with her deadly teeth. The body of the western soldier, entwined with the wretched beast, tumbled back down and onto a sword protruding from the mass of corpses. Not even a whisper of a scream broke through the solitude of war.

I paused, taking in what I had seen.

Burnok used his axe to block the attack of a R'Uma, and she impaled herself on the pointed shaft. He put his boot on her shoulder and freed his axe as another leaped at him. He dodged, and she went tumbling past him and met the swing of an axe from one of his men, removing her head as easily as he would split a log for fire.

The deadly Kuori still washed past us, a never-ending flood from the hive. We had killed all but two of the R'Uma. At the bottom of the stairs, they moved amongst the dead, drenched in the blood of their victims. One rose and stared into the rain, her mouth filled with gore, her eyes a glazed pale white. She looked away and leaped to the throat of another soldier. She had launched more than halfway across the stairs with a deadly grace and ease, as if on the wings of a large bird.

A soldier from the western lands turned from the fray, swung, and her body fell from the victim, her head still attached to the throat. The mass of black hair soon disappeared under the bodies.

"Burnok!" I yelled. "We need to ebb this flow of kuori! Get your men to form a line up here with their axes!"

He turned toward the stairs, put his hands to his mouth and made a call. A band of Westerners climbed the mountain of bodies, using the back side of their axes as picks as they did.

I reached the top by the first column and put my back to it. The flow of kuori was dying. Soon, the last remnants of the queen's army would flood past me.

When the last one passed, I stepped out. Pri'Eten stood before me, her black sword of light emanating from her gauntleted hand. She smiled. I swung my short sword at her head, and she blocked. She swung in a wide swath, and I stopped her untrained riposte. We stood, the two blades locked. She penetrated the veil with her gaze, though it was far weaker than before. The tug at my energy was only a distant reverberation. Her energy now spent on summoning that black sword of light. I twirled her blade around in a circle and pulled down. She fell forward, and I took her in my grip, sword at her throat, using the move I saw Betir use on Yazzir El Friz. The move my father taught me incessantly. Her eyes were wide with fear.

"This time, there is no mercy, sister of shadow," I said and ran the length of my blade slowly across her throat. Her sword of light dimmed, and flickered, then extinguished, and I let her go. She fell clutching her throat as her life bled out.

Thunder rumbled.

The rain stopped.

And a chill wind blew across the chaos below me.

Chapter Fifty

Demoni Kuori

I WATCHED THE BATTLE move back to the streets. Burnok stood on the stairs amid the dead, commanding his men. A leader born from battle. The Kur'Ya were gone; the R'Uma were all dead. The force from the North Gate was being pushed back. I looked for Betir El Friz, but could not find him.

I walked behind the tall columns and into the dark corridor leading to the hall of my Lord. I removed the veil. The white marble floor was slick with rain, a rain-stained red and black. I walked into the hallway and sat on a dry patch on the floor. I leaned against the wall to get my bearings and prepare for my encounter with Ta'Bedtian. The braziers were dead. The hallway appeared like a ruinous maw waiting to swallow me whole. The stench of death filled the dank and lifeless emptiness. My wet uniform and armor grated against my skin. My arm throbbed uselessly beside me.

I took in a long breath and unlashed the pouch from my belt. I opened it and reached in, pulling out one of the lotus leaves. The purple and white leaf was drying, dying.

Soltari...

The sinister voice echoed in the hallway and inside my head. I shook it free.

I put the leaf in my mouth. The taste was bitter. The sweetness of it was gone. I forced myself to chew, but the bitterness became too great, and my mouth lost feeling. I gagged.

The dark hallway flickered, then flashed, and a rumble echoed off the stone walls. I blinked, waiting for the inevitable dreams, the horrors and visions the lotus would fill my head with. Instead, I sat in the dark hallway.

It flickered with quick flashes of lightning outside. The leaves had lost their potency.

I slumped against the wall.

A greenish haze appeared at the end of the hallway near the entrance to the chambers of the dead Lord Airik. The haze wavered as a shadow moved within it and into the black of the hallway, disappearing. A clicking noise came toward me. I was heavy, tired, now an unmovable stone. I had no strength to move, or scream, as the clicking sound came closer. A shadow bobbed slowly with the rhythm of clicks. I tried to lift my good arm but couldn't. The clicking stopped in front of me, and there, in the black, I caught a reflection, a glint, like black glass moving, face to face.

There was no sound of breathing, only a slight grating of bone on bone as it moved, inspecting me. And in the glass reflection of the eyes, I saw a man glowing in red and orange. The face of a man, the face of a dead man, dying man, withered, like leaves of a lotus. Then the glass disappeared, bone grated on bone, and the strange clicking noise returned and moved away down the hall. I looked into the green haze, and again saw a shadow move within it. I coughed and spasmed and a foul stench, a recognizable stench, drifted to me.

The hallway flashed momentarily, but the shadow consumed the light whole. The green haze flourished. I struggled to lift my body from the floor. When I turned, my arms stretched out before me and disappeared into the darkness and I fell into the black of the abyss. I landed gently, slowly, flat on a cold marble floor. Floating above me was a porcelain figure in a greenish haze wearing a long flowing white gown, sent adrift by a breeze from the winds of limbo. Behind her a kuori flew on great black wings, its face featureless and made from... black glass.

"I sense you..." the porcelain figure said.

She wore a great gold and brass headdress that covered her eyes and rested on her head like a half-risen sun, spikes stretching out and up. The top was like a wayward compass rose on an old map.

The greenish haze fell further away above us, replaced with an orange glow from fires below us. She removed the headdress, and long black hair fell from under the mask and from behind her. She raised the headdress and it melted away in gold swirls and flitted out of existence.

She hovered over me, then was on me. She moaned, lost in a trance. When she spoke, her mouth did not move.

I have you.

A voice like a whisper, an incantation, a dream. Her dark green eyes were enhanced with thin gold glyphs. Her nose was set straight and narrow, her lips pursed and tight. The sides tilted up into a sinister grin, and she snarled, revealing two rows of sharp black teeth. She rested on me and laughed, then sat up straight, the whole of her body sitting on top of me like lovers do.

She looked up and swayed back and forth. I struggled but could not move, the weight of my body still too heavy, numb, broken. A scream echoed from somewhere as the orange glow became brighter and the green haze disappeared.

Falling, further, distant, eternal.

Her long fingers clawed into my chest, then slid slowly up to my shoulders and then my neck. She leaned down, and her hair caressed my face, swallowing me into her shadow. Her face close to mine, her lips so near, and all at once I involuntarily retched up the remains of the lotus between us and she screamed as the flow burned her skin and her body dissolved and in the orange glow black creatures flew and one caught me and swept me away up into the black and I woke with a start sitting in the hallway of the Great Hall.

Near me lie a puddle of vomit.

I gasped and spit the bitterness from my mouth and stood, leaning on the wall for support, trying to catch my breath.

I shook my head to clear the strange magic, but the shimmering phantasm lingered.

I walked the length of the corridor into the haze and to the chambers. The foul visions hung in my thoughts like a shimmering mirage at the edge of the desert.

Intoxicated.

From the opening came a soft weeping. I stepped back. The weeping was barely a murmur coming from the chambers, but it was present. And real. I wiped my brow, my thoughts confused, rambling.

I stepped through the high-arched doorway. Across from me, upon my Lord's dais, and on the throne of marble, sat Ta'Bedtian, Queen of Shadows.

She wore a white gown and decorative armor plates along the arms, covered in a writhing gold filigree. Atop her head sat a headdress, like the one in my vision, with long points on each side and top, and smaller points between those. In one hand she limply held a long, ornate scepter from which rose a small fire of orange and purple at the crest.

Weeping.

She was... weeping.

The smell was wretched. The smell of rot. The smell of R'Uma. Two of them lay at the Queen's feet like trained pets. One rose to its haunches, and hissed, sniffing the air around it.

Movement came from one of the decorative pools filled with black muck. From the pool, a figure wriggled, thrashed about, and rose slowly, born from the black mire. The tall musta kuori stood, and the slime drained off its body. It crouched and hissed air between its ghastly teeth and in the darkness of the hall, its eyes were aglow, red, and sinister. It turned and lumbered into the black recesses of the hall.

The weeping stopped, and the Queen pulled her staff straight, then stood.

She was tall and slender and... beautiful. She swayed back and forth, her head turning left and right as if listening for something.

I shuddered.

I stepped forward and the Queen's arm shot out in my direction. A wave of cold, shivering wind blew across me. I stepped back and turned away briefly.

I sense you... I know you...

Outside, thunder rumbled. The shimmer of the room faded. I reached into the pouch and pulled another small piece of a lotus leaf. I placed it in my mouth and stepped into shadow. The R'Uma laid down like a dozing dog. The Queen stopped swaying and tilted her head. Lightning flashed and lit the crystal and glass dome in the ceiling. There were breaks in the clouds and bits of sunlight occasionally drifted through.

Then she raised the staff with a fury, and a crack came from high above. I leaped with a start, and black shards rained down from the darkness above. Large chunks of a foreign material crashed to the floor. I pressed further into the shadows.

With the shards dropped an enormous figure, landing on two feet in the middle of the hall. A strange new kuori rose on two legs, standing tall, like a man, its height incredible. It stood a whole three or four heads taller than me. I stepped back, but I was against the wall. I put my hand on the hilt of my sword as the ominous creature raised its face to me.

Black.

Glass.

A sadistic laugh came from the dais.

The creature stepped toward me. Each step made a clicking sound on the marble floor like the tapping of metal on stone, and each joint grinded like bone on bone. Then it stopped in front of me. And my reflection in its glass face showed a man torn by two worlds. Reality and unreality. Sanity, and insanity. Life, and death. The man in the reflection was not scared, even though fear showed on his face.

It reached out with an unnaturally twisted long arm and grabbed me by my wound, placing its clawed hand around the cut. I winced and held back the searing scream. My strength drained away and my entire arm raged and I cried out inside, the pain unbearable. I drew my short sword from its scabbard, slowly, painfully. My arm burned in the creature's grasp and my knees buckled and I hung there in its grip, weakened. My head swam.

More laughter from somewhere mingled with the gloom.

My free arm dangled from my body, the sword clutched in its weakened grasp. The strength to raise it disappeared into the black void.

Its black glass eyes held mine with its gaze.

"No..."

All at once I caught my breath, and my sword came up and through the creature's gullet. A gasp echoed from across the chamber. It let go of me and dropped to its knees. I yanked my sword free and knelt there, panting, trying to regain my breath, as the giant creature grasped its gurgling throat, staring at me from beyond the glass. My arm throbbed. I looked at the massive kuori. Its featureless face glared back.

My heart raced.

The black blood of the creature covered the front of its body, glistening. Then, the gurgling stopped. A laugh echoed somewhere in the room. A woman's laugh. The creature removed its clawed hands from its throat. The blood flow had stopped. I watched in horror as it stepped up with one leg, then the other, and towered over me. I fell back against the wall. I propped myself up on my sword.

The thing then crouched, and from its back, it spread two massive leathery wings. It jumped, and I flinched from its sudden movement. Its broad wings flapped, the thunder of their beating echoed around the chamber, and died in the muck on the floor. It flew in a wide circle, then flew up and clamped its clawed feet onto a perch on the ceiling and hung, like a large grotesque bat, then folded its wings around it.

"Impressive isn't it?"

The female voice rang out. I jumped even though the voice was soft and crisp, like a new dawn. And without emotion.

"I call them demoni kuori. They are the most remarkable creation ever conceived."

I slid deeper into the shadow of the room.

Hopeless.

Helpless.

Unsure of which was dream, or reality, in the shimmering haze.

"I know you are in here with me, Soltari. I sense it even though I cannot see you. You cannot win this battle." I cringed at the sound of my name coming from her. "You may have eluded those before me, but this you cannot escape."

The shimmer of the mirage remained under the influence of the lotus. She set the staff into the holder on the floor and raised her arms. The braziers on all the walls lit and the room's green haze dissipated into an orangish misery.

Thin layers of webbing covered the walls, and a white robe of silk cloaked the throne. Attached along the roof were shells, like... cocoons... wrapped in black silk, hanging from the high ceiling of the Great Hall. Hundreds of the black spawns of the Queen.

"Now you see, your realm is but a spot in history on which the fire of chaos has been set aflame. And will soon forget."

Empty threats, I thought.

"Empty?" she said. She laughed. "You are powerless here, Commander."

She lifted off the helm. Her long black and white hair fell around her, past her shoulders. Even at this distance, her eyes flickered in the torchlight like emeralds on fire. Her face was narrow and angry. Her eyes set high on her face, giving it an unnatural length, yet still beguiling.

I looked away and pulled the veil across my eyes, and the covering over my mouth. I was a shadow. She looked around the room.

"You have many secrets and I have seen them all. So much heartache."

I stepped to one side, watching her. She moved like a vision, an apparition, reminding me of the way the Priestess moved by the small pond.

"You are all that remains of your land, Commander. You and your barbaric ways."

Then, in one swift and graceful sinister move, she floated above the marble floor. Hovering in an ominous stance, like death takes before consuming a soul. And she continued to rise higher, and higher, up to the dome. She stretched out her arms, and her gown billowed out and changed into thin, veined, silky wings.

I gasped.

I shook my head and blinked, expecting another oncoming vision from the lotus, but the bizarre scene remained. The braziers died around the chamber, and the sinister greenish haze filled the room again.

Her span of wings grew gray and white and bluish, shadowing her features from the greenish light of the hall. She let out a shriek of laughter, and her R'Uma stood and hissed.

"Welcome to the dawning of a new empire, Commander. The Empire of Shadow!"

CHAPTER FIFTY-ONE

The Queen of Shadows

H ER VOICE ECHOED THROUGHOUT the hall.

Her thin wings opened and closed like those of a demon moth. There was movement within the cocoon nearest her. The spawn was breaking its shell. Soon, hundreds of the Queen's spawn would be upon me and the rest of the land. An army from the air for which we had no defense.

The green haze that filled the stone hall glowed with a more ominous, darker green haze. The sound of hardened shells cracking permeated the chamber as the creatures moved.

I became frozen, and part of me found some pleasure knowing I would soon join my wife and daughter in the realm after this one. A tear slowly meandered from within, rolled down my grime-stained cheek, and fell onto the marble floor with a crash of lightning. Thunder rolled outside.

Then thunder rolled inside as the crack of a hundred cocoons un-leashed a cacophony of noise. I pushed flat against the wall as thousands of fragments of giant cocoon husks fell to the floor and smashed, sending shards in all directions. The mucus-like slime filled the room with a fetid, sickening odor.

One by one, then many by many, giant winged kuori dropped to the floor and slowly stood to their great height. The Queen landed upon her dais. She reached out and moved her gold braided arm in whimsical motions, drawing symbols of fire in the air like the priestess had done in her caravan. Her vile creations crouched, then launched themselves into the air, flying around the dome in a circle. The flap of their great wings created a vortex of wind and stirred the foul, putrescent stench of the great hall. The muck on the floor vibrated and moved with each beat of their wings. And then with one final swoosh of her arm, they crashed through the crystal and glass dome, sending fragments and shards to the floor, shattering in an explosion of fury. The demoni kuori took flight through the hole in the sky. One by one, they swirled in the hellish green haze and the once Great Hall birthed the demons out into the day, out into the storm, and out into battle. The Queen watched her brood ascend into the void with the satisfaction of a mother.

Grim and vile were her creations.

All was quiet. The stillness deafening as the chaos echoed in my mind, replaced by a rumble of thunder outside and the wind across the open dome. The muck ceased to churn. All sound ceased. The chamber lay still and dead. Not even a whisper of wind. The Queen lowered her arms.

I stood and stepped forward, and my boot crushed a piece of glass in the silence.

She turned to me, then cocked her head to one side.

"You live in shadow, warrior. Interesting. I thought the Northern vermin did not partake in, or believe in sorcery."

The shimmer of the haze was fading. My vision cleared even behind the veil. I reached into my pouch and drew out the last lotus leaf, the others having dried and turned to dust. I turned it over and over with my fingertips. I tore it in half, put one half in my pouch, then pulled my face covering down. The air was cool on my sweaty skin. I put the half in my mouth and let it rest on my tongue. The leaf was bittersweet, and the room became hazy. I chewed the leaf and swallowed, waiting for the inevitable hallucinations. I pulled the face covering up before the stench penetrated my senses too much and I vomited the chewed leaf into the black muck.

The Queen stepped from the dais and stood in the middle of the hall under the shattered crystal and glass dome. The R'Uma stood and I could see glints of light near them as the chains restraining them fell to the floor. One hissed while the other surveyed the room.

"All is lost for you, warrior," she said to the room. "Soon, your army will be my army, and there will be no stopping my forces."

She looked around the room. Her green eyes gleamed.

"Tell me," she said as she stretched out her arms. "What makes you so remarkable?"

I went to speak, and only a wisp of air came from me. My tongue was numb from the leaf. She grinned.

"You cannot even speak, or dare not to, much less wield a sword or," she laughed, "rule a land." Rule a land? The words floated, unmoving.

Her eyes glowed in the depths of the darkness. Her long fingers extended from her white hands. She turned to me and waved her arm in the air. Golden glyphs of fire appeared, and her gaze swallowed me into her darkness. The glyphs hung in the air. She turned away and drew more glyphs. They hung in the air. Symbols of fire in the darkness. She drew glyphs of fire all around her.

"The last thing you see now warrior of the dead north." She swiped the runes away. "The last thing you will recognize." And drew new ones. "Is the wisp of air from your last breath." She swiped those away and turned back to me. "Everything lives in shadow," she whispered. She drew new glyphs in the air. "Until a single strand of light is cast..." A sensation of being pulled from my position came over me. The Queen gave a slight chuckle.

"Found you."

Visions poured through my head. Memories, one by one by one, flashed through my conscious mind. My father. My wife. My mother? My childhood. The sickly Lord and the fields of the Northern Lands strewn with dead horses, blood, war, death, over and over and over, pulling at me, drawing me out, tormenting me as a sword thrust through me, another from behind and a scream, a man screaming in dire pain, and shrieks of loss and love and anger and anguish exploded from every sense. I fell to my knees and cried out, and a woman was laughing, then sobbing, then I was standing... outside the Great Hall... watching a battle... men screamed... called out... a flurry of black things on wing... black steel.... black metal... black...

"As you can see, your friends are all dying and those that are left will soon be engulfed in a cataclysm of death only I could imagine for them. I will see my mission through to the end."

A flash and Gal Abed was on fire... crumbling, falling from the cliff-side. Thick black smoke filled the air. Bodies burned, crawling and screaming for help. The white Keep of the city transformed into the Great Hall, and pillars of black smoke filled the sky. Pools of black muck dissolved the bodies of the living as they screamed and thrashed about, watching their limbs disappear.

The cataclysmic visions ended. I can see her. In the middle of the hall. Wavering, stumbling. The haze stronger. She dropped to a knee. I stood.

I coughed and cleared the bittersweet taste from my throat.

"What is this quest, Queen of Shadows?"

She looked up and around the room. She struggled to stand, then dropped again.

"So. So you speak," she said, panting, breathless. She shook her head.

She smiled, then recomposed herself, stood, and stumbled. She drew herself up straight, unmoving.

"To see the destruction of the City of the Southern Moon and the Goffs hanging by their necks within the Dome of Men as I bring it and the Gallery of Visions down around them. To ensure a coven like the Sisters of the Whispering Dawn never exists again in my lands, their temple burned to ash, and to destroy all who approved of the horrors within it. You have already seen what I have done to those who came to vanquish me. I will not stop until my black army reaches the City of Kerenimor and the Emperor lies headless at my bare feet and the temple in which he sits is burned to ash to be carried away by the gales from the sea."

She scowled, then turned away.

"The destruction of my city, my homeland... has no place in your vengeance for the Goffs. Why did my family have to die?"

"Surely, warrior Soltari, you don't have to ask that question of a southern clairvoyant. But to put your restless soul at ease, it's all part of the grand vision." She laughed, then became sinister, and in a mocking voice said: "I needed fresh flesh and blood, and the oh-so-noble warriors of the northern lands were such an easy target."

"Easy?"

She looked toward me, then stepped forward, and staggered as she did. She stopped and regained her composure.

"Aye, swordsman. Your people, once mighty warriors, now complacent, and in your shallow minds, you thought you could not be defeated in any battle. Years of war taught you nothing, for with the simple wave of my hand, I wiped out your force in the north. You know nothing of the powers of sorcery." She stood unsteadily. "Ah yes... Or maybe you do... Lotus eater." She laughed.

"Flesh and blood? For what treacherous end?"

"To build my army. The army that will see your end and an end to the Southern Lands."

"Go ahead then sorceress Queen of Shadows, conjure up another one of your storms, do your will, for before you can finish, your head will lie at my feet and your reign of terror will be at an end. I am weary of this foul sorcery, weary of war and battle, weary of this life. There is nothing more you can take from me."

The Queen scoffed, then laughed and stepped toward me, swayed a bit, then continued. She stood barefoot on broken glass in the black muck. She sensed me through the shadow of the lotus.

"You cannot. You have not the power to conjure another storm, do you?"

She sneered and looked right where I stood. She stepped forward, and stopped, looking for balance, her arms out. Her thoughts and perception confused by the effect of the lotus as she probed my thoughts, looking for something, anything.

"For one so barbaric from a history steeped in bloodshed, there is intelligence about you," she said. "This land once belonged to an abominable empire, an empire the southern people, destroyed. Now a new empire is coming."

She no longer wavered. Her strength returned. My energy was being torn from my soul. I stepped from the shadow without consideration of my actions. Without control of my actions. I held the short sword in my hand. The shimmer of the lotus was still present, but somehow, she was no longer affected by it.

"One thing you should know about your precious sisters and their temple," I said. She turned to me. Saw me. Motioned to me. "The emperor had them burned and razed the temple."

She stopped... and pondered this. Briefly. Then she grinned and continued to me. She wavered as she walked in slow, seductive, ominous movements, leaving footprints of blood as the broken shards of glass cut her feet.

"Il'Gavar told you this?" She laughed. "Il'Gavar lied to you, warrior." Her eyes went dark and her face narrowed. "I killed the sisters. All of them. Then I set free the Kur'Ya." She spat on the floor. Questions rolled through my foggy mind. Why would Il'Gavar make up the story? What purpose did it serve? If, he was the one lying.

"As long as the emperor and the Goffs live, I will not waver in my commitment to see their destruction."

I stepped forward and my knee, weakened by my weight, buckled. I dropped to the floor, to the muck, unable to stand, or lift my sword.

"Your emperor... is dead," I muttered. "With... everything gone... what purpose... do you serve?" She stopped, and the tug on my energy stopped. "All you have done, all the.... death... in vain."

Her eyes were now on fire, her face a prism of rage.

"Did Il'Gavar tell you what they do to the mothers and fathers of those who birth emerald-eyed daughters?" For a moment, her face calmed and saddened, then snarled. "They tell them they have served the lands well and will be rewarded, then they imprison them, with the other mothers and fathers, along with any children they may have had, and breed them like slaves hoping to birth more emerald-eyed daughters." Her eyes were in flames, enraged. "And if the mother should fail or grow too weary... or too old to bear a child..." she snarled, and spittle escaped her seething lips. She stood straight. Her face became expressionless. "I'll spare you what happens to a child birthed in the pit without the trait."

She stopped in deep thought, lost in a memory or vision, then held her head high and smirked.

"Warrior, you are a pawn in the myths of the Southern Lands. No longer shall you interfere with the inevitability of all that is to be."

Her long white fingers wrapped into clenched fists and all at once my soul was yanked from my body, from my being, and dragged through the muck, and into the fire. I fell withering, writhing on the floor, like one of her spawns. I vomited through my face covering, then pulled it down with weakened arms and spit out the bile and lotus remnants.

Needles covered my body, pain all over. My skin screamed and burned. My lifeblood... spilled over.

Chapter Fifty-Two

Broken

Voices screamed out of the black.

You can not win this fight...

......You are alone......

...There is no one to help you here...

I coughed and retched. Some strength tingled through my body and out to my legs and arms. I rolled my hands and knees. Remnants of lotus leaves and bile fell from my mouth to the blackened floor.

My left arm stung, but I could move it slightly. My right hand tingled as pins and needles caressed it, but I could feel the whole of my sword arm.

She laughed a bitter rendition of laughter.

"Brave warrior, where is your determination to die?"

I coughed and gagged again and opened my eyes. She leaned down and her lips rustled near my ear, her breath hot and moist, seductive.

"Before you is the last thing you will see warrior of the dead north. Your own bile, and the cheap tricks of a weak mind."

Her words changed to a sinister smile.

"The last breath you take, and everything you had, have, or will have, belongs to me."

I fell over onto my back. The green haze of the room was swallowed by the black as my vision slowly died. I could not breathe. The shattered dome above was a broken circle with sharp, deadly edges. It glowed a dark blue and black against the specter of the green haze.

"I will take much pleasure from you, hero Soltari."

She leaned back down and bit my earlobe. The wet, sultry heat from her breath upon my neck as she kissed it beguiled me.

"You have failed. You cannot defeat me. I have seen it. I have seen myself standing victorious above the bodies of the faithless Goffs. Their blood, their lifeless flesh a threnody of a dark, forgotten way. It is you who is deceived. It is you and your people who must die and put an end to the world's pain. It will be your sacrifice to those you say you love."

My body shook and jerked as it starved for air. My sword arm twitched hard, sword in hand, and I fell into the black, empty, space of death as the Queen of Shadows hovered over me, face to face. Her long hair caressed my cheeks. Her glassy, dark emerald eyes locked on mine. Her smile became a menacing row of sharp teeth.

"I will sit on the emperor's throne. I will become the Empress of the Darkness."

My vision brightened as a ray of sun burst through the smashed dome and died as I sat on a hillside next to my wife and my daughter. They lay there, covered in blood, their eyes missing, crows bounding nearby. I pick up my daughter's limp body. She dissolved into dust and I stood on the rusty earth of the foothills, sword in hand, the broken edge of it through Lt. Estarenza's throat as he screamed out my name and called me a murderer and I screamed and all was dark as two green emeralds appeared, then her malevolent face above me, laughing.

Tears streamed from the sides of my eyes.

"There is a darkness that lives inside you. A darkness with great power. We are not so different, you and I."

She laughed and it was sinister and full of contempt and the laugh echoed through the broken chambers and into the ether.

I sobbed at my weakness, now with the end at hand. I tightened my hold on my father's short sword. The vision of my father's death slammed into my mind and the Queen broke out in a half-witted laugh.

"Your father?"

"You... You killed him." I cried out for my father, helpless.

"I remember the vision of him. All the sisters shared it. But I didn't kill him. I was but a young girl when we had the vision."

"Your vision..." I gasped. "Wrong..." I coughed, my whole body shook.

"Our visions were never wrong, soldier of nothing. That is why you are here." She laughed. "Don't you see? They knew the vision was of the great Taivas Soltari, envoy and swordsman."

I sputtered something incoherent, then: "Not... my father..."

"Your father was murdered by Rogues Army, hired by Prime Goff Il'Gavar himself."

"No..."

She leaned in.

"They did not know that the queen in the vision was me then, no." She laughed. "But I did. And soon, so did he. Il'Gavar planned a way to use me. He wanted me to rise to power, Soltari, don't you see? By eliminating your father, he thought he eliminated the one thing that would stop me. He wanted the empire returned, the Northern lands cleansed, and all that came with it."

She leaned back, then stood. I rolled to my side, coughing. Sharp spasms tore through my gut. I rolled to my hands and knees and stared at the tip of the sword inlaid into the floor, stained with the black mire.

"Why..."

My strength drained, and my head swam. I grasped my sword tighter, the only tangible thing keeping me from the abyss.

"Why? Simple. Arrogance. To reclaim the empire. The Southern Lands are nothing more than a weak people with an army covered with decorative swords and shiny helmets. They held no chance in battle against you, the land of warriors. They knew the sorceress in the vision would be the undoing of the Northern Lands, and then they could sweep in and reclaim it for themselves. But..." she jeered. "We know how that went, don't we?"

Rini...

Her whisper came from nowhere.

"Solana..."

Sweat dripped from my face, then a drop of blood.

Blood.

"My love. I am so sorry I failed you."

Another drop of blood fell to the marble mosaic and echoed through the hall. It mixed with the sweat, the black scum, and other filth.

Blood.

A dream of my daughter fluttered into my mind. I kept my grip on my sword, grounding myself in this reality.

The Queen stood over me. I tried to crawl away, but with no strength, I hunched over, shaking uncontrollably. The hiss of the two R'Uma was closer. I raised one leg underneath me, kneeling on one knee now.

"Oh, great warrior stop groveling at my feet. Why do you weep so? Is it for... love?"

Laughter.

All is lost.

"I have seen your end, Commander. And it is violent and bloody. Come, my sweet darlings, fresh flesh for you to sink your teeth into." The R'Uma appeared behind her, crawling on all fours to her side like obedient dogs, snarling and hissing at me. The weight of the Queen's hold on me getting stronger.

"Solana..."

I pushed the other visions aside. She stood before me, coated in blood, hands outstretched. I shook the image loose and focused on a bright day on the hillside with her by my side. A sunny day. But the vision disappeared as the Queen ripped it from me. Her pull on my mind still weakened by the effect of the lotus.

"Your death will not be honorable. You are all that remains of your kind, and your death, while hideous, will be swift and forgettable. My lovelies here prefer the warm meat of the living."

My daughter stood before me. Her red hair flowed in a breeze. Her blue eyes held my gaze and pulled me in.

She yelled.

"Daddy!"

Then tilted her head. I wept. A tear fell into the muck on the floor of the Great Hall and burned the foul black matter. Wisps of smoke rose from it as the tear sizzled and made a clear spot in the black. My daughter looked up at me.

"Will you be coming home now, Daddy?"

"Not just yet, my angel. Soon my darling... soon..." I coughed. "My little..."

My daughter spoke to me. A word.

She said... her name. And I heard it.

The illusion faded and the Queen of Shadows stood before me, flanked by her two hideous and foul creatures.

My daughter's name surged through my body, and all the visions cleared from my mind except that of her face, her blazing eyes energizing me.

I said her name now, and more energy surged through me. I rose and stood before the Queen of Shadows. She mumbled something incoherent, something foreign, and her sinister eyes showed fear and despair. She repeated the strange word and stepped back. She screamed this word as all hope left her.

I said my daughter's name again, and my muscles tightened, and my eyes flickered. The Queen opened her frightened mouth to say something, but was silenced by my father's sword as I ran it through the bottom of her jaw and out the back of her skull.

Silence.

All the noise inside my head, vanished. All the torment disappeared.

One last sick gasp and she spasmed. And all my rage, all my hatred, and all the fear welled up through my sword arm and I became a wraith screaming a name I had long forgotten in the frozen north as I slowly twisted my blade in her head and a burst of intense energy flowed through my body and I cried out as it filled my soul.

This empty husk of mine raged with energy.

And my daughter's name echoed through the hall!

The Queen's deep emerald eyes flickered, then faded. Gasping, hideous screams emanated from the fetid daughters and I watched in abhorrent horror as their skulls split and the life exited their bodies. They collapsed and writhed in the muck. One tore at its flesh until it was dead in a large pool of blood. The other rolled into a pool of black muck and was consumed by the abhorrent liquid.

The Queen fell backward, and landed in the muck on the remains of her foul creature. Her body quivered and convulsed, and blood trickled from her wide eyes, nose, ears, and mouth. Then her chest exploded and a stream of black shadows escaped in a fountain of blood, rising high above in a swirl of the darkest of blacks, and her whole body convulsed, then went limp as the shadows dissipated like embers thrown from a fire after tossing on a new log.

I stood over her and stared at the masquerade of death, of shadow, and saw her now as she once was...

She was beautiful. Her long flowing hair crept around her golden face with a southern grace. Her eyes stared back at me, dark green, like emeralds on fire. Her lips were pursed in a delicate blue swirl. Her half-naked body was clothed in a pale gossamer skin. Her gown flowed around her like a thin pool of elegance, like a sapphire in the morning light. She did not move, yet her form stroked the winds of space like clouds caressing the sky with a tender touch.

Her fingers splayed out, long and slender. She was a dream. She was a ghost who sought you out in the night and made love to your soul. She was the night. And she was the shadow. Her lips did not move, and she did not speak. When she did speak, her words danced from her throat and moved through the air gracefully as a dying autumn leaf. Her last word. A single, dying word, incoherent and silent.

The sound of the word hung in the dark air around me. A drop of liquid fell, and the sound echoed through the hall. Her dead eyes stared at me. Another drip. Then, a breeze. A gentle breeze blew through me, moved my ragged hair, touched my eyes, and dried the slow march of tears.

A drop.

A drop of blood dripped from the end of my sword into a small pool of crimson liquid below. My eyes fixed on hers. Gemstones set into a bewitching masterpiece of flesh and bone.

Another drop.

Her gaze fixed on the bringer of death. The volatile dawn of a red undertow flowing from her body overcame her clouded gown. It flowed and spread like a disease violating the white tide that embraced her body. She was so wondrous to look upon.

A drop.

I stared at the Queen, at her allure, then thought of the one most beautiful to me, the one who strengthened me, with her red hair billowing in the breeze, her pale face, and crimson smile. I let go of my sword and it clanged to the marble floor, reverberating through the great chamber of sorrow, the great hall of death and shadow and sorrow.

I dropped to my knees and stared into the blue eyes of the vision in my head, her arms outstretched to me. She came to me and I embraced her, my daughter. Tears flowed, and in my vision she spoke and said her name again, a name forgotten, a name which escaped me in time, lost in the depths of sorrow and madness.

And vengeance.

And I heard it.

I spoke it.

"Oona."

My little one disappeared from my arms the way light does when a cloud passes overhead. I rested my hands on my knees and sobbed in the shadows of the hall.

It was done.

I stood and stepped away from the violent scene. As I turned, a radiant light cast through the shattered dome, and before me stood my wife and daughter. They reached out and touched my face. I held out my arms to embrace them, but they were only light.

"Rini," Solana said, and smiled. My daughter's eyes glinted in spectral light.

"Are you home now, Daddy?" She said. Tears flowed from my eyes like a waterfall. I dropped to my knees.

"Aye, my little one. I am home now."

I squeezed my eyes shut to push out the tears, to clear them, and when I opened them, Solana and Oona were gone.

"No..." I whispered. My head fell into my hands and the anguish of their absence grabbed at my heart.

"Rini," a deep voice said. I looked up. Standing in the light was my father. I tilted my head. He nodded to me, and then a tiny smile appeared on his face as he shimmered away into the light.

I cleared my throat, then picked up my sword from the floor and sheathed it. I turned to leave, and there, standing in the doorway, was a figure, a dark figure, silhouetted by the light coming in from the hallway.

And in the silhouette, a sword hung from the left hand.

"I'kuinen," he said. I wiped the remnants of tears from my eyes and stared at the shadow in the doorway.

"What?" My voice was a vacant whisper.

"The word she said, before you killed her. I'kuinen."

"I don't know—"

"She blessed you. For all eternity. That was her dying word. A blessing."
He turned to leave, then stopped and said over his shoulder. "It's a Roama
word." The figure walked away from the door.

I'kuinen.

A whisper came on the wind and flew away.

Chapter Fifty-Three
A Shadow Emerges

I STEPPED INTO THE sunlit corridor from the chambers, leaving the vileness behind me. Betir El Friz stood there, leaning against the wall under a dead brazier. He had his arms crossed. He saw me, then turned away and grimaced.

"So, you did it after all," he said under his breath, not looking at me. Blood trailed behind me from the severed neck of the Queen. "Vengeance is a foul thing."

"I have a promise to keep." He turned to me, then looked into the face of the dead Queen. He huffed at it.

"Grim. But, beautiful. Would it surprise you to know I've seen this face before?" I walked past him.

"Doubtful."

He followed me in silence. We reached the end of the corridor and stepped into the open air behind the columns and to the top of the stairs. I gasped at the destruction before me. Burnok was sitting there, his blood-stained axe draped across his legs. He heard us and looked up, then immediately turned away.

"By the Gods," he said. He stood and walked to us. "Dreadful thing, isn't it?"

I wasn't sure if his comment was about what I held in my hand, or the destruction. I looked at the mounds of bodies. Remnants of musta kuori lay scattered everywhere. A rather large one with wings caught my eye.

"Those," Burnok laughed. "Those were..."

"She called them demoni kuori." He turned to me.

"Fitting name. Foul. When they came bursting from the top of the Great Hall, I surely thought all was lost and you were dead. Then in the heat of the battle, those putrid things, and the other black ones just stopped, writhed, and then with a cracking noise I'll never forget in all my days, fell to the ground, in pieces. The large ones came crashing down from the sky. The, uh, the... dead..."

"Var'Yo?"

"Aye. They just stopped moving and stood there. Like statues. Then they shuddered and a strange, eerie noise like wind blowing through a tight canyon came from them and it seemed... never-ending." He wiped his brow with the back of his hand. He was cut several times, and blood caked his arm. "Then it stopped as if someone snapped their fingers, and they just collapsed into a heap." He looked at me. "But that's not the strange part, brother."

I couldn't help but grin at his fantastic story.

"When that wind sound, noise, whatever it was, stopped. Then a small jewel-sized point of light floated from each of them. Then the lights disappeared like..."

"Embers from a fire."

His eyes widened. "Aye!"

I walked past him to the edge of the stairs and sat. My body ached, and my energy was lost.

"One of them," Burnok continued to Betir, "stood, staring into the distance. A Western soldier. I looked into his eyes. He was dead, or well, dead in a foul way, and I could see this faint glimmer of light, like a soul screaming to get out. I shuddered and stepped back and that's when he began that screaming sound. I turned, and by the Gods, I ran."

He stepped into the sunlight and cast a long shadow over me.

It was over. The battle was won. And yet... Something was still missing. Betir El Friz sat down next to me.

"Rini, do you hear me?" Burnok said.

"Yes," I said, keeping my gaze on the stairs. Burnok grunted and walked out of the sunlight.

"Looks like your wound is no longer a worry, eh?" Betir said.

I rubbed the spot where my arm throbbed. He placed his hand on the pommel of his sword. I squinted to see him. The effect of the lotus was still present, but wearing off.

I looked about the Great City, the ruined city square, the miserable death and destruction, the black shells of the Queen's dead, and the crimson blood of soldiers. A short distance from me lay bodies of those she called her daughters, threatening and wretched, even in the peace of death. I saw the broken shapes of twisted wings and black masses that fell from the sky.

The Queen's final abomination.

Rows of soldiers made their way through the aftermath of the battle, around the black husks, the winged monstrosities, and past the fallen soldiers.

I took a deep breath. Facing me was the sum of our raid on the Great City. I stood and drew my father's bloody sword. The soldiers there turned to me. I raised the sword high, then raised the head of the Queen of Shadows. Cheers erupted from the remnants of the Northern armies, and spread throughout the city.

Burnok looked at me questioningly. Upon her face was the peace of death. No scowl. No evilness. No viciousness. No insanity. No demon. No. Burnok saw that upon my face, and turned away, disgusted and ashamed.

The swords, axes, and fists of the soldiers reached into the air and cheered this victorious day. Burnok spit on the ground next to me. His smile was now a glower of suspicion and crookedness.

"Brother, I see darkness upon you," he said.

"We are victorious, Tass Burnok. The light of day has broken through the clouds. There is no more darkness here." I lowered my sword and the head of the Queen. "Why do you not celebrate our victory? Look around you. The Queen is dead, her armies vanquished."

"Aye, it is over brother," Burnok said. "It is done."

He walked down the steps to the soldiers, and they ran up to him, all cheering, for they knew the end was here.

"The darkness still lives," Betir said suddenly, then stood and faced me. "Killing her did not end it."

He looked into my eyes, and I sneered, then saw myself in the reflection. I stepped back and sheathed my sword.

"Thank you." He smiled, then placed his hand on the back of my neck. "Without your guidance, I would certainly have perished."

"You will get no argument from me, dear nephew." He pulled me to him and embraced me, then let me go.

The sound of thunder rolled through the city from the north, but not from the sky. The thunder grew louder, then stopped.

"Commander," a voice called from the throng of soldiers. Betir stepped aside. There was movement beyond the North gate, outside the city. Horsemen, hundreds if not a thousand.

"Your old friends have arrived, Betir," I said and walked down the stairs.

A soldier brought Sumu to me and I hitched the head of the Queen to the saddle. The others mounted, and Betir, myself, and Burnok rode past all the ire and destruction to the North Gate and through it. As we went, I pulled twenty horsemen from the crowd, and they followed us out onto the plain.

Across the hillside stretched a line of horsemen. Their yellow banners streamed in the wind.

"Careful with this one. When he speaks, he speaks with forked tongue," Betir El Friz said.

A horseman carrying the standard of the Northern Lands and another carrying the standard of the Western Lands joined us. Another horseman came from outside the city, a Westerner. He carried the tattered standard of the Southern Lands. I nodded my approval, but only in the name of Commander Ghenesta, for he, a lone soldier, fought alongside me in battle. The banners lapped in the wind as the sun crested the sky and made its way to the West. We stopped and kept a fair distance from the Rogues Army. The line birthed four horsemen, flanked by two more with banners, and they rode to a distance halfway between us.

"They should not be trusted, especially under the guise of counsel." Betir frowned, truly puzzled.

We rode forth. Behind us, the remnants of the joined armies formed.

The four horsemen of the Rogues Army wore tan leather armor and cloaks to shade them from the sun. Cloth covered their faces. An older man in the center removed his hood and face covering. He had darkened leathery skin from his years in the eastern waste, and his yellow and olive eyes showed the sign of many battles. He wore a leather harness with intricate designs etched into it, attached to a leather belt from which hung a long rapier, and next to it the hilt of a dagger, black as shadow.

"Well. This is an unexpected blessing," he said, clearly, as if our everyday speech was as familiar to him as it was to me. "General Betir El Friz, as I live and breathe."

Betir smirked. "A'avé. Does your father know where you are?" A'avé's face angered.

His gaze turned to me, and there was a glimpse of recognition of me from him.

"I am A'avé El Friz, General of the Rogues Army," he said. "You are the Soltari of the North, yes? The one they call, 'Saka'Ali'." He grinned. His eyes flitted between me and Betir El Friz. Then he laughed. "I see it now, Betir. I knew there was something... piggish... about you. You are a northerner!" He laughed, then spat. "Which makes thee a traitor."

"Only to the North, A'avé."

A'avé grunted.

"State your purpose here, A'avé El Friz," I said.

His grin faded. "I am here to claim that which was promised us. Or to fight young Soltari of the North, by the will of our Herra Aa'vikon Ha'amu Al Friz." He followed the statement with a few words in the eastern language, probably praising his Herra, his father. "It matters not to me."

"As allies of the Queen of Shadows?"

He bowed his head. "The same."

I unhitched the head from my saddle and tossed it on the ground before him. "Her reign is over."

He grimaced, then a moment later he grinned.

"No Saka'Ali, her reign spreads across all the lands and cannot be stopped. We will avenge our Queen and—"

"Vengeance has no end, A'avé," Betir said. "You of all people should know this."

A'avé's buckskin shuffled a bit, and he reined it in. He looked up at the sky. More sunlight broke through the blackened clouds. He looked at his soldiers on the right and left of him.

"Our time is nigh, traitor Betir. It is time the East took back that which was taken from them."

"Then your quarrel, General, is with the Southern lands," I said, and rested my hand upon the hilt of my father's sword, beckoning it for strength and wisdom.

He scoffed and laughed.

"Southern, Northern, even the West. All of this land was once ours. We are the native people."

The two horsemen next to him raised their fists into the air and a cheer rose from his army.

"Hah," grunted Burnok, then turned away.

"Forced into the desert, forced from our homes, forced from the land, which gave us strength and all we needed. Ha! Fair trade, bartering. We are conquerors, Northerner, and you make us shopkeepers. We were rulers, and you set us upon the road. We were—"

"Weak," Betir El Friz said. "You were weak." A'avé scowled. "But now your people are strong. You are warriors, you are tradesmen, you are also… peaceful. I have wandered the Eastern lands for ages, A'avé El Friz. I have seen the people. I have journeyed with them. Lived among them. I have even dined with Herra Jalali. Have you? Has your father?" A'avé looked away. "They do not wish for war. Or for land. They do not ask for redemption for failures of the former emperors, the trespasses of our ancestors, or even yours."

"I did not come all this way to banter like lovers. We were promised the Great City, and the city we shall have."

"At what cost?" I said. "And once you claim the Great City, then what?"

Betir turned to me to hide a slight grin from A'avé.

A'avé El Friz looked across the four of us.

"Ah, I see it now. Northern, Southern, and Western, allied against the Eastern nation."

"Allied against the southern Sorceress Ta'Bedtian, A'avé El Friz, and her allies. As you should have been." I said. "Leave in peace. The Northern Lands have no quarrel with the Eastern Lands, proper."

"Eastern folk will never ally with the invaders of the north."

"Your faction of the Rogues Army stands alone, General. Even amongst your own kind," I said.

A'avé El Friz looked at the men on each side of him and received no support. The wind changed and blew in from the West.

Betir El Friz nudged his horse forward to A'avé. I heard him speak but knew not what he said as he spoke in the Eastern tongue. A'avé frowned and responded animatedly. Betir responded in kind, and then an odd and unexpected thing happened. They clasped arms and bowed. A'avé looked at me, tipped his head, then turned his steed. He stopped and turned back to me.

"Commander, we are men of flame and steel. Battlefields beckon us. Without the art of war, we are lost." He glanced at Betir El Friz, then back at me. "Understand that… Lord Soltari."

I squirmed in my saddle, then said, "We all have our battles we fight A'avé El Friz. Not all battles can be won by sword."

Burnok chuckled.

"That's my line," he said under his breath.

A'avé turned and rode back to his force, followed by the others. Betir faced me. He was grinning, satisfied with either himself, his accomplishment, or both. Betrayal is not an emotion I wore well, and it showed.

"Easy nephew. Nothing nefarious is going on. His love for his Queen outweighs any respect he holds for me, for you, his Herra, or possibly his father. But, she is dead and you are now perceived as the new Lord of the Northern Lands, Aurinko Soltari."

He bowed his head.

"Lord?"

He looked at me and grinned. "Aye. Through the blessing from the Queen of Shadows."

"Blessing?"

"Her dying word."

I did not wish to be Lord of anything. I glared at him. My fingers tightened on the leather reins, and my gloves groaned under the stress. I turned my horse and rode back to the ruins of the Great City.

Alone.

CHAPTER FIFTY-FOUR

I'kuinen

I RODE UNDERNEATH THE North Gate, now adorned with four heads. On one side, the head of a musta kuori, and one of a demoni kuori. On the other side, the head of a R'Uma, and the head of a Kur'Ya. Pri'Eten's. All hung by soldiers of the Northern Army without direction. And in the center, I hung the head of the Queen of Shadows.

Promise fulfilled.

I took no pride in the graphic display. Anyone could see the city in ruin, or walk through the Great Hall and see the death and destruction within. Soon, word would reach the rest of the lands. A'avé and his men would carry the news back to the Rogues Army, those of the Black Dagger faction, and his father. Burnok would send word to the west. And the Southern Lands would learn their fate. In time, the flesh would rot from the faces of the queen and her brood and they would fall to the ground to be crushed under the hooves of a horse or cart. Discarded like refuse.

What would never leave would be the memory of it all. The abyss, the destruction, the anguish. And the memory of where my home sat burned to the ground as a massive funeral pyre for my wife and daughter. There, I will plant a garden, and build a memorial.

I rode to the steps of the Great Hall. Burnok had returned and was commanding his soldiers, regrouping. He saw me approach. He smiled, then a grim look fell dawn on his face.

"I saw your display. It was... troubling." He glanced at the North Gate, then at his boots.

"Thank you, brother, for... for everything. Being there. I—"

Burnok chuckled. "Rather uncharacteristic of you." He smiled and tipped his head. "But you are welcome."

I looked around and noted a few Western soldiers, unscathed by battle. "You have word from Gal Abed?"

"Aye. Lord Westval is dead. Lord Keirnen's forces took over. That is all I know for certain but can presume once whatever black hell she unleashed died with her, as it did here." He pointed at the soldiers. "They were part of a small force sent to help. They are from Lord Keirnen's land." He turned to me. "While the concept is understandable, unlike you, we will not be posting Westval's head at our gate. Instead, he, and any men who knowingly followed him in this endeavor, will be unceremoniously hung from the bridge of Halos, or simply nudge over—"

"And his lands?"

Burnok folded his lips in, curling his beard.

"Undetermined. His and Lord Åkerfeldt's both."

I looked at a dead kuori lying on the street.

"Unelma."

"Unelma?"

"Aye. That is my daughter's name."

"You remembered it?"

"Aye, just before... She gave me the strength to..." I sighed. "Unelma was our light brother. She was our everything. So wild and carefree. Her hair was red like fire, like her mother's. We called her Oona. She wanted to see you and to travel to the west. So excited she was that night..." He placed a hand on my shoulder and gripped it hard, shaking me slightly.

"You have done all you said you were going to do. They would be honored, and proud of you."

"Commander?" A soldier was running down the steps from the Great Hall. "Commander." He stopped and bowed his head.

"What is it?" The soldier looked up.

"Survivors sir. In the passages under the Great Hall."

"Lord Airik?" The soldier frowned and shook his head.

"How many?"

"We're not sure, but if I had to guess, 400 or more?" I gasped, as did Burnok.

"So many. I thought the city dead."

I knew why she kept survivors. I knew what their purpose was.

"Excellent news," I said.

He bowed his head and ran back up the stairs. Burnok's face was expressionless. Then he gasped.

"Rini, look!" He pointed toward the North Gate. On the road to the city, coming from the west, a long line of caravans rolled. My heart leaped for one caravan stood out amongst the others. Its eloquent and unmistakable design shimmered in the distance. The carts were loaded with wares from the Western lands.

"By the Gods Rini. There are so many."

Words escaped me, and my body filled with a torrent of emotions. I wavered, and Burnok caught me and eased me to the ground. I sat on the top steps and watched as salvation crossed the open plains of the Northern Lands.

I stood alone at the ruins of my home. Nothing remained. The passage of time and the winds of storms had scattered the ash across the land. Sumu wandered the open field where my wife, daughter, and I spent our time basking in the warmth of the sun. The plains and forested hills of the Northern Lands stretched out, shadowed by the oncoming night, and dark clouds from a storm that had passed and poured cleansing rain upon us and the Great City.

A natural storm.

Now, dusk was upon me. and I found peace and solace in the quiet, and the fresh, cool air. Battle no longer suited me, and I felt like a stranger in this place. I no longer recognized my homeland. All I had known was burned, in ruin, and dead. Turned to ash and memory.

I'kuinen

She spoke the word as a calming wind blew around me.

"Priestess."

A beam of passing sunlight broke through the clouds and shined upon me. Its warmth on my face caressed and soothed my rampant emotions. I closed my eyes.

"I remembered her name."

Oona, the wind said.

In my mind, my daughter ran up to me and embraced me. I no longer wore the uniform of a warrior but the soft clothes of a common man. A father. The man I saw in the pond. A breeze brushed my cheek and hummed.

Solana.

I had longed for and now wore the clothes of a husband. She appeared with my daughter, Oona. Their eyes glinted in the sunlight. Solana held my leather armor, black and soiled with blood, and grime, and foul muck. They were folded just as the day I pulled them from the chest before leaving for battle. I took the clothing from her, and we three walked to a small pyre. I placed the armor on top then opened the leather pouch and poured the dried remains of the lotuses out onto the pile. The amulet fell out. I ran my finger across it, then laid the pouch on top, the page from her journal still inside.

I picked up my father's sword and Oona frowned. I smiled. I held it high into the air. The sun gleamed upon it. I said a quick devotion to my father, turned the sword upside down, and grasped the hilt with both hands.

"Daddy?" Oona said.

Her small face beamed up at me, questioningly. I thrust the sword through the pouch, the leathers, the wood of the pyre, and into the ground. It buried itself and I felt my flesh break free and from me spilled the pain and anguish, the sorrow and madness, the death... and the darkness.

The sun was warm against my face, filling me with peace and happiness. The darkness in the northern sky cleared, and the fire of the sunset burst from the west and glinted off the clasp hanging from a chain around my neck. The clasp I wore for so long, the clasp I earned by the blood of my family. The weight of which I would carry as a grim reminder of who I once was for my remaining days.

The fading sunlight gave way to the bluish-black of the oncoming night. A night I no longer feared.

I set flame to the small pyre. It caught and soon roared, and the fire consumed all that was my burden.

I was free.

Afterword

This book has been in the works for a long time. It was first birthed as a short story at the end of the last century. I used that 1300-word story as the foundation for my first experience participating in National Novel Writing Month in 2004. 50,000 words streamed out of my head, creating a good chunk of material. Very little of it is found in this book, ironically. But there it was. And, there it sat for years until just before the pandemic when something out of the blue whacked me upside my thick skull and said, "Hey, remember? You wanted to be a writer!" Oh yeah... I pulled this ball of mud off the shelf and got to work.

This book, *Darkness of the Northern Sky*, is my debut novel and first published full-length work apart from a piece in an anthology or two. A lot of passion went into this as I figured out my path and the path of the character(s). My hope is you enjoy the book for its story and content. If so, leave a great review!

Of course, I'm not the only one who helped create this story. I've had a lot of support from family, friends, beta readers, ARC readers, and an editor or two. And then there are authors like Michael Moorcock, Douglas Adams, H.P. Lovecraft, and so many others who don't know it, but have influenced my writing. And the music... my God, the music that helped write this tale. From Rush to Opeth to Uriah Heep and Hawkmoon, Blue Stone to Mythos to Kitaro. Finnish folk music, and Black Metal. It's quite the eclectic mix. But it's all here swaddling the words.

This may be my first published full-length work, but the dream does not stop here... Look for Book 2 (and ultimately 3) of Soltari's next adventure, and much more!

From the Author

THANK YOU FOR READING ***Darkness of the Northern Sky***. If you enjoyed this book, please take a moment to hop online and write a brief review. You can find quick links on the book website, **darknessofth enorthernsky.com**. Your feedback is important to me and will help other readers, naturally, decide whether to read the book too.

If you'd like to get notifications of new releases and special offers on upcoming books, see the next section "Free eBook!" for more information on how to do that.

Again, regardless, I do appreciate your time in reading this book. It's been a long time coming, and it will be hard to put the final stamp on it and call it "done".

There will be more from Commander Soltari in the future. As we say here in flyover country USA, "he ain't done yet".

Free eBook!

More Information

For more information on upcoming releases and other fun free stuff any of our websites:

Book Website
http://www.darknessofthenorthernsky.com

***

Publisher Website
http://www.speedlimitanarchy.com

***

Harper's Fall
A fictional town created by A.E. Engle where many of his stories take place.
Think Arkham or Derry.
http://www.harpersfall.com

About the Author

A.E. Engle is an award-winning poet, author of *Darkness of the Northern Sky*, editor of two locally produced anthologies, and publisher. He lives in the central U.S. (commonly called flyover country). He is a husband, father to six (yes, six), and a grandfather. A long-time metalhead and lover of sword and sorcery fantasy, sci-fi, and more, Mr. Engle began writing in the mid-80s when Elric, AD&D, Rush, Iron Maiden, and Judas Priest were at their peak.

Mr. Engle writes across a spectrum of genres and has drafts of short stories, novellas, and novels spanning horror, noir, sci-fi, general, and of course, fantasy.

He is a veteran of the U.S. Air Force and state Army National Guard where he was trusted to turn screws on multi-million dollar aircraft. He is also the author of *Abilene*, a short story about a military veteran, PTSD, and suicide. He is working on an 8-part series of sci-fi short stories, an anthology of short stories, and continuing Soltari's adventure in two upcoming novels.

www.ingramcontent.com/pod-product-compliance
Lightning Source LLC
Chambersburg PA
CBHW031844310726
48972CB00005B/1399